PRAISE FOR *TRUTH BE TOLD*

'I couldn't turn the pages fast
enough . . . a terrific debut'
Jenny Blackhurst, author of *Before I Let You In*

'A classic whodunnit gets a very clever
modern treatment that left this reader's
heart racing right up to the last page'
Liz Nugent, author of *Lying in Wait*

'An astute debut . . . turning our
obsession with true crime inside out'
Stylist

'Josie's dark past becomes fodder for the podcast
du jour – if that doesn't hook you, the twist will'
Cosmopolitan

'A delightful writer who has
produced a taut thriller'
Chicago Tribune

'I was completely hooked from the very first
page . . . If you like twisty psychological
thrillers, this is your book'
J. T. Ellison, co-author of *The Devil's Triangle*

'Beautifully and sympathetically written'
Kate Moretti, author of *The Vanishing Year*

'Reminiscent of the hit podcast *Serial*, this debut
is an exciting read about what happens when
the past continues to haunt the present'
Dallas News

D1396150

529 941 09 3

TRUTH BE TOLD

Kathleen Barber was raised in Galesburg,
Illinois. She graduated from the University of Illinois and
Northwestern University School of Law, and previously
practised bankruptcy law at large firms in Chicago and
New York. *Truth Be Told*, which was previously published
as *Are You Sleeping*, is her debut novel. When she's not
writing, Kathleen enjoys travelling the world
with her husband.

TRUTH BE TOLD

KATHLEEN BARBER

PAN BOOKS

First published as *Are You Sleeping* 2017 by Galley Books
an imprint of Simon & Schuster, Inc.

First published in the UK 2017 by Macmillan

First published in the UK in paperback 2017 by Macmillan

This edition published 2019 by Pan Books
an imprint of Pan Macmillan
The Smithson, 6 Briset Street, London ECIM 5NR
Associated companies throughout the world
www.panmacmillan.com

ISBN 978-1-5290-4207-8

1 3 5 7 9 8 6 4 2

A CIP catalogue record for this book is available from the British Library.

Designed and typeset by Andrew Barker Information Design
Printed and bound by CPI Group (UK) Ltd, Croydon, CRO 4YY

Visit **www.panmacmillan.com** to read more about all our books
and to buy them. You will also find features, author interviews and
news of any author events, and you can sign up for e-newsletters
so that you're always first to hear about our new releases.

for Mom

Charles "Chuck" Buhrman had no enemies. A mild-mannered professor of American history at a small midwestern liberal arts college, Chuck was respected by his colleagues and well liked by his students. Each year, students in the History Department at Elm Park College held an informal vote to determine their favorite professor, and each year, Chuck Buhrman was crowned the winner. By all accounts, he was similarly well regarded in the community of Elm Park, Illinois, where he made his home. People recalled his participation in thankless volunteer projects like organizing the annual town Halloween parade, selling raffle tickets to support the civic arts center, and manning the cash register at the library rummage sale. Even his family life seemed picturesque: a young, beautiful wife and a set of adoring, well-behaved daughters.

Chuck Buhrman was living the American Dream. But then, on October 19, 2002, this popular and congenial man met an untimely end—shot at point-blank range in the back of the head in his own kitchen.

Warren Cave, the seventeen-year-old next-door neighbor, was arrested and charged with the murder. He was convicted and is currently serving a life sentence.

Chuck Buhrman's murder was a shocking, senseless crime, but at least justice has been served, right?

Right?

I

But what if Warren Cave *didn't* do it? What if he's spending his life in prison for a murder he did not commit?

My name is Poppy Parnell, and this is *Reconsidered: The Chuck Buhrman Murder*. I'm going to spend the next several weeks investigating these questions and others that may arise. My goal? To take a hard, unflinching look at the scant evidence that might have convicted an innocent man, and to perhaps uncover the truth—or put to rest any lingering doubts—about what really happened that fateful night in October 2002. I hope you'll join me for the ride.

chapter 1

Nothing good happens after midnight. At least that's what Aunt A used to tell us whenever we begged for later curfews. We would scoff and roll our eyes and dramatically pronounce she was ruining our social lives, but over time I came to see the wisdom in her words. Trouble is the only thing that occurs between midnight and sunrise.

So when my phone rang at three o'clock that morning, my first thought was, *Something bad has happened.*

I instinctively reached for Caleb, but my hand grasped only cool sheets. Momentary panic fluttered in my throat, but then I remembered Caleb was three weeks into a trip overseeing aid workers in the Democratic Republic of the Congo. Still half asleep, I dimly worked out it was eight o'clock in the morning there. Caleb must have forgotten about the time difference or miscalculated it. Frankly, neither mistake seemed like him, but I knew how draining these trips were on him.

The phone rang again and I snatched it up with a hurried greeting, eagerly anticipating Caleb's familiar Kiwi accent, the soft rumble of his voice saying, "Jo, love."

But there was nothing. I sighed in frustration. Caleb's calls from abroad were always marked with exasperating delays, echoes, and strange clicks, but they had been particularly difficult on this trip.

"Hello?" I tried again. "Caleb? . . . I think we have a bad connection."

But even as the words left my mouth, I noted the lack of static. The connection was crisp. So crisp, in fact, that I could hear the sound of someone breathing. And . . . something else. What was that? I strained to listen and thought I heard someone humming, the tune familiar but unplaceable. A warning tingle danced up my spine.

"Caleb," I said again, even though I was no longer convinced my boyfriend was on the other end of the line. "I'm going to hang up. If you can hear me, call me back. I miss you."

I lowered the phone, and in the second before I pushed the disconnect button, I heard a hauntingly familiar feminine voice quietly say, "I miss you, too."

I dropped the phone, my hand shaking and my heart thundering against my rib cage. *It was just a bad connection,* I told myself. Those had been my own words echoed back at me. There had been no "too." It was three in the morning, after all. It hadn't been her. It *couldn't* have been. It had been nearly ten years; she wouldn't call me now, not like this.

Something bad has happened.

I grabbed the phone and checked my call log, but there were no clues, just a vague *UNKNOWN CALLER.*

Something bad has happened, I thought again before sternly ordering myself to stop. It was only Caleb, only a bad transcontinental connection, nothing that hadn't happened before.

But it still took me two doses of NyQuil before I could fall back asleep.

* * *

It was almost eleven by the time I woke, and in the light of day, the mysterious early-morning phone call seemed like nothing more than a bad dream. I fired off a quick, confident email to Caleb (*Sorry we had such a bad connection last night. Call again soon. xoxo*) and laced up my running shoes. I paused in the doorway of the Cobble Hill brownstone to chat about the weather with the elderly woman who lived on the first floor, and then took off toward the Brooklyn Heights Promenade.

When Caleb and I moved from Auckland to New York two years ago, I had imagined that glamour would infuse even the most mundane aspects of our lives. I had expected to be taking in cutting-edge art on my walk to the train, browsing heirloom tomatoes alongside Maggie Gyllenhaal at the Brooklyn farmers market, and admiring the expansive view of the Statue of Liberty as I jogged across the Brooklyn Bridge. In reality, the most street art I saw was chalk-drawn hopscotch boards and the occasional spray-painted tag on a trash can. I never purchased heirloom tomatoes at the farmers market because their cost was laughably astronomical, and the only celebrity I ever rubbed elbows with was a Real Housewife (who, I should note, took vocal offense to the price of those same tomatoes). As for jogging across the Brooklyn Bridge, it remained a good idea in theory but a terrible one in practice. The bridge was consistently clogged with camera-touting tourists, bicycles, and strollers. I found I much preferred the calm of the Promenade, with its wide path, notable lack of tourists, and similarly impressive view.

I arrived home sweaty and invigorated with just enough

time to shower and fix a sandwich before I had to leave for my afternoon shift at the bookstore. Growing up, I had imagined myself wearing a suit and heels to work every day (the exact outfit fluctuated with my mood, but often resembled those of Christina Applegate's character in *Don't Tell Mom the Babysitter's Dead*). I would have been shocked to discover my nearly thirty-year-old self wore jeans and Chuck Taylors to work; teenaged me would no doubt have considered it a failure. But while I might not be on the path I had once envisioned, I was largely content working in the bookstore. Early on in our tenure in New York, I had used a temp agency to find some administrative positions, but they'd made me want to tear out my hair, and then I discovered that the bookstore down the street was hiring. I started with a few hours a week, supplementing the income with a part-time gig as a barista, but over the last couple of years, I had increased my hours until it was a full-time position. I loved every minute I spent in the bookstore, loved being surrounded by stories and helping patrons select titles. When things were slow, I read the biographies of American presidents and told myself that someday I would finally put the history degree I had earned online to use.

That afternoon I was working with Clara, whose gorgeous Ethiopian features and impressive collection of literary-themed T-shirts I envied. Vivacious and warm, Clara was the closest thing I had to a friend in New York. Sometimes we took a yoga class or a run together; sometimes she invited me to see some friend or another in an off-off-off-Broadway play or at a poetry reading. Earlier in the summer, Caleb and I teamed up with Clara and her now ex-girlfriend for

Tuesday-night trivia at a bar on Court Street, and those nights had been the highlight of my week.

The ex-girlfriend had begun calling Clara again, and, as we shelved a new shipment of books, Clara asked my help in decoding their latest conversation. As we debated whether "see you around" meant "let's make plans" or "maybe we'll run into each other," the door chimed with the arrival of customers, and we both looked up.

I don't believe in signs. I don't put stock in destiny, I don't worry if a black cat crosses my path, and I've only had my tarot read for laughs. But if there ever was a time to believe in omens, it was that afternoon, the echo of the strange voice on the phone tugging at my memory, when a woman stepped into the bookstore with a pair of twin daughters. My vision tilted and my knees went weak; I had to clutch a nearby table to avoid collapsing.

"Hi," the woman said. "I'm looking for Nancy Drew books. Do you carry them?"

I nodded mutely, unable to tear my eyes away from the twins. It wasn't that they looked like us, not at all. They were blond with freckled cheeks and big dark eyes—near polar opposites of our ink-colored hair and blue eyes. Beyond that, the girls were clearly at odds, sulking and exchanging the occasional blow behind their mother's back. Lanie and I never fought like that. Not until we were older, that is. But there was something about them, an emotional charge they carried that robbed me of my senses.

"Sure," Clara said, stepping around me to their assistance. "Let me show you."

7

I excused myself to the bathroom to avoid staring at the girls. I pulled my phone from my pocket and checked the call log again. *UNKNOWN CALLER*. What if it hadn't been Caleb? Could it have been Lanie? It had been almost a decade since I had spoken to my sister; something *had* to be wrong if she was calling me.

By the time I emerged from the bathroom, the twins and their mother were gone.

"I know, right?" Clara said sympathetically. "Twins always give me the creeps, too. Probably residual trauma from watching *The Shining* at the tender age of eight."

"*The Shining*?" I repeated, still shaken. I had read the book, but couldn't recall any twins.

"You're kidding me. You've never seen *The Shining*? My older brothers watched it all the time. They used to chase me around the house shouting, 'Redrum! Redrum!' " Clara smiled and shook her head affectionately. "Those assholes."

"I'm an only child," I said. "No siblings to force me to watch scary movies."

"Well, you're really missing out. What are you doing tonight? Unless it's something awesome, we're absolutely having movie night at my place."

I readily agreed, for some reason not wanting to be alone that night more than I'd ever admit, and the movie served as an effective distraction. That is, until I checked my email and saw Caleb had responded: *Sorry, love, didn't call last night. Internet signal has been too weak to make a call for days now. Things are going well here, work-wise. We're on schedule, should be home in another week or so. Will update soon. Would kill a man for a salad. Miss you bunches. Love you.*

8

Caleb's email chilled me more than the creepy happenings at the Overlook Hotel. If it hadn't been him on the phone, I was certain it was Lanie. A barrage of memories crowded my mind: Lanie spinning like a top under a night sky, sparklers held in each extended arm; Lanie slamming the bedroom door in my face, her eyes bloodshot and her mouth a grim line; Lanie pushing aside the covers on my twin bed and climbing in beside me, her breath warm on my cheek as she whispered, "Josie, are you sleeping?", never waiting for an answer before beginning to softly tell secrets in the dark.

"Josie-Posie, I have to tell you something," she had said on one such occasion, the timbre of her voice teeming with conspiratorial excitement. "But you have to promise me it stays between us. Anything said here in this bedroom stays between us, always."

"Always," I agreed, hooking my ring finger around hers in our secret sign. "I promise."

Lanie's secret had been that she had kissed the eighteen-year-old leader of our tennis day camp behind the municipal building that afternoon, a shocking revelation given that we were thirteen that summer and that she had somehow managed to charm the good-looking boy away from his duties. I had been scandalized, hissing something about our parents not being happy about that.

"They don't have to know," she said sternly. "Remember, between us. Always."

Always. Her voice was so clear in my mind. It had to have been Lanie. Would she call again?

And if she did, would I be ready to answer?

* * *

The following afternoon, I was off from work and took the train to the Union Square Farmers Market. Once there, however, I was disenchanted by the crowds and the picked-over kale and pears, and I ended up doing my shopping at (the only marginally less crowded) Whole Foods. Sitting on the R train, balancing a couple of bags filled with frozen veggie burgers and overpriced but beautiful produce on my lap, I overheard someone say:

"Dude, have you heard about this Chuck Buhrman murder thing?"

Blood roared in my ears, and my vision went blurry. It had been more than a decade since I had heard my father's name, and hearing it casually tumble out of the mouth of a skinny teenager with a lip piercing made my stomach turn.

"Is that the podcast everyone is going on about?" the girl's friend asked. "I don't do podcasts."

"This is different," the first girl insisted. "Trust me. It's a fucking trip. This guy got convicted for murder, right? But the evidence was all, what do you call it, *circumstantial*. The biggest thing they had was the guy's daughter who claimed she saw it. But here's the thing: first she said she didn't see anything at all. So we know she's a liar. But what's she lying about? You've got to listen to it, man, it's addictive as fuck."

As the train slid to a stop at Court Street, the girl was still enthusiastically endorsing the podcast. I felt so blindsided that I doubted I could stand, let alone climb the subway stairs and, laden with groceries, walk the final stretch to our apartment. My knees buckled as I rose, but I managed to propel myself through the crowded underground hallways and up aboveground. In my dazed state, I used the wrong exit, emerging on the far side of Borough Hall, and walked two blocks in the opposite direction of home before I came to my senses. Reorienting myself, I managed to place one foot in front of the other enough times to reach home.

I slid my key in the lock and hesitated. I had spent the weeks since Caleb left hating the resulting stillness of our apartment. I missed his mild chaos. I found myself resenting the way everything remained exactly where I left it. Caleb's running shoes, trailing across the living room floor with shoe-laces stretched out like tiny arms, hadn't tripped me in weeks. I was no longer finding half-drunk mugs of coffee in the bathroom, dog-eared books stuck between the couch cushions, or the clock radio softly playing classic rock to an empty bedroom. I could feel his absence in the lack of these minor domestic annoyances, and they tugged at my heart each time I entered our home.

But, with my hand shaking as it held the key in the lock and my father's name ricocheting around my brain, I welcomed the solitude of our apartment. I needed to be alone.

Dropping the groceries in the entryway, leaving the veggie burgers to slowly defrost on the ground, I rushed to my laptop. I typed my father's name into a search engine with trembling fingers. Bile climbed up my throat when I saw the number of hits. There were pages upon pages filled with a startling parade of news articles, opinion pieces, and blog posts—all dated within the last two weeks. I clicked the first link, and there it was: the podcast.

Reconsidered: The Chuck Buhrman Murder was splashed

in bold red letters across a fuzzy black-and-white picture of my father. It was the headshot he had used for work, the one where he looked less like an actual college professor and more like a caricature of one, with his tweed jacket, crooked eyeglasses, and thick black beard. The faint twinkle in his eyes threatened to undo me.

Daddy.

I slammed the computer shut and buried it beneath a pile of magazines. When all I could see was Kim Kardashian staring up at me from the cover of a glossy tabloid I had shamefully bought waiting for the train one day—more evidence of how everything fell apart without Caleb around—I was once again able to breathe normally.

My cousin Ellen didn't answer her phone when I called, and I left her a voicemail demanding that she tell me what she knew about the podcast. After twenty minutes of sitting on the couch willing my phone to ring, I gave up and began searching for tasks to distract myself: I put away the groceries, I wiped up the puddle the veggie burgers had left in the entryway, I ran a bath but then drained it before climbing inside, I started painting my toenails but abandoned the project after only three nails had been polished a gloomy dark purple.

Red wine was the only thing that helped. Only after sucking down a juice glass full of the stuff was I calm enough to revisit the podcast's website. I refilled my glass and pushed the magazines aside. Gingerly, I opened the computer.

The website was still there, still advertising a podcast that promised to "reconsider" my father's murder. I frowned, confused. There was nothing to reconsider. Warren Cave murdered my father. He was found guilty and he received his punishment. How could this Poppy Parnell, this woman whose name made her sound more like a yarn-haired children's toy than an investigative journalist, spin an entire series out of this? Taunting myself, I hovered my cursor over the *Download Now* button for the first of the two available episodes. Did I dare to click the link? I chewed my lip as I wavered, took another gulp of wine to steel myself, and clicked.

Ellen called just as Episode 1 finished downloading. Gripped by morbid fascination, I nearly declined the call in order to listen to the podcast, but I shook it off and answered the phone.

"Ellen?"

"Do not listen to that podcast."

I exhaled a breath I didn't know I was holding. "Is it bad?"

"It's trash. Sensationalized trash. That pseudo-journalist is turning your family's tragedy into a commodity, and it's disgusting. I have Peter looking into whether we can sue her for defamation or slander or whatever it's called. He's the lawyer; he'll figure it out."

"Do you really think he can do that? Put a stop to it?"

"Peter can do anything he puts his mind to."

"Like marrying a woman half his age?"

"Not really the time for jokes, Josie," Ellen said, but I could hear a hint of laughter in her voice.

"I know. It's just nerves. Please thank your esteemed husband for his help."

"I'll let you know more as soon as I do. How are you handling it?"

"Well, for starters, I wish I hadn't found out by overhearing a teenager on the train. Why didn't you tell me?"

"Because I was hoping I wouldn't have to. I'd hoped it would all just blow over, but apparently America has an appetite for that brand of opportunistic, sensationalist reimagining of the truth."

"I can't believe this is happening. What am I supposed to do?"

"Nothing," Ellen said firmly. "Peter's on top of this. And I'm still not convinced this won't burn out on its own. How much 'reconsidering' can she really do of an open-and-shut case?"

Even though Ellen emphatically warned me not to listen to the podcast, I remained tempted, the same way one was tempted to pick at a scab or tug at a torn cuticle until it bled. I knew nothing good could come from listening, but I wanted—no, I *needed*—to know what this Poppy Parnell person was saying. How could she possibly justify "reconsidering" my father's murder? And how could that be the premise for an entire series? I could effectively summarize the case in one sentence: Warren Cave killed Chuck Buhrman. End of story.

I topped off my wine and wished Caleb were home. I ached for the calming sensation of his big, warm hands on my shoulders, and his soothing voice assuring me that everything was going to be all right. I needed him to fix tea and turn on that odd reality show about toothless men making illegal whiskey. If Caleb were home, I would have been comforted and protected; I would not have been gulping wine alone in the dark, electric with terror.

And yet part of me was relieved by Caleb's absence. The very idea of having to tell him about the podcast, and thereby being forced to admit all the lies I had told, filled me with liquid dread. I desperately hoped Ellen was right, and that the podcast would fizzle out on its own before Caleb returned from Africa.

I didn't listen to the podcast, but I could not stop myself from obsessively Googling Poppy Parnell all night. She was in her early thirties, not more than two or three years older than myself. She was midwestern, like me, and held a BA in journalism from Northwestern. I also saw she had once run a popular crime website, and had a long list of bylines in publications like the *Atlantic* and the *New Yorker*. When I had exhausted that, I switched to an image search. Poppy Parnell was a thin strawberry blonde with angular features and wide, almost startled eyes—not conventionally attractive enough for television, but too pretty for radio. In most photographs, she wore too-large suit jackets and leaned forward, her mouth open and one hand raised, mid-gesture. Poppy looked like the kind of girl I would have been friends with a lifetime ago.

Scowling at Poppy Parnell's smiling face, I poured the rest of the wine into my glass. I reached out to slam the computer shut, but something stopped me. The podcast was still open in another tab.

Daddy.

Cursing Poppy Parnell and myself, I pressed *Play*.

Excerpt from transcript of *Reconsidered: The Chuck Buhrman Murder*, Episode 1: "An Introduction to the Chuck Buhrman Murder," September 7, 2015

I didn't know what to expect when I first met Warren Cave. By the time we were formally introduced, I'd spent several long afternoons with his mother, Melanie, a classically beautiful woman of enviable style and impeccable poise. Melanie's son is one of her favorite topics, and she speaks highly of him, extolling his warmth and generosity, his skill with computers, and above all, his faith.

In addition to—and in contrast with—Melanie's glowing characterization of her son, I had done my homework on Warren Cave. I scoured the police notes, trial transcripts, and articles profiling him.

Like most people who have even a passing familiarity with the case, the image I had of Warren Cave was that of a skinny kid with stooped shoulders and acne, his hair stringy and dyed black. Photographs depicted him perpetually clad in all black and never making eye contact with the camera. Warren Cave was the kind of teenager most of us would cross the street to avoid.

I had difficulty reconciling that image with the young man his mother had so favorably described. Had her maternal love blinded her to her son's true nature? Or was the hardened image of his youth nothing more than posturing? Did the truth lie, as it so often does, somewhere in the middle?

When I first met Warren Cave in the Stateville Correctional Center, the maximum-security prison near Joliet, Illinois,

where he's been living for the last thirteen years, I didn't recognize him. He has embraced weight training and replaced his
skinny frame with hulking muscles. As he explained to me, his
weight-training regimen is more for necessity than pleasure.
In prison, he says, one cannot afford to be weak. This is a lesson Warren learned the hard way: his face is marred by a scar
stretching across his left cheek, a harsh reminder of an attack
by a fellow inmate one year into his sentence.

Warren, who keeps his hair close-cut and natural ash-blond
now, still avoids eye contact. His expression is usually guarded, but he smiles warmly when I mention his mother. Melanie
drives two hours every Sunday to visit her son, and he says
that she is his best—and only—friend. Aside from his mother
and Reverend Terry Glover, the minister at First Presbyterian
Church in Elm Park, Warren has no other visitors. Andrew
Cave, Warren's father, left the family shortly after Warren's
arrest and died from prostate cancer eight years ago. None of
Warren's friends from his youth have kept in touch.

I don't waste any time getting to the important questions.

POPPY: If you didn't kill Chuck Buhrman, why would his
      daughter say she saw you do it?

WARREN: That's a question I've asked myself every day for the
      last thirteen years. And you know what I've come up
      with? Diddly-squat. The Lord works in mysterious ways.

POPPY: Are you saying she made it up?

WARREN: Well, *I* didn't kill Chuck Buhrman, so, yeah, kind of.
      But I guess I can kind of see how she might've gotten
      confused. Back then, I had strayed really far from the

path. I was using a lot of drugs and listening to music with satanic themes. The beast had its claws in me, and I have to wonder if she saw that somehow. It must've confused her. She was just a kid.

POPPY: You were just a kid yourself then.

WARREN: I was old enough to know better.

POPPY: Had you spent much time with her or the family before Chuck was killed?

WARREN: No. We moved to Elm Park in 2000, so we'd only been living there for two years by the time Mr. Buhrman died. I wasn't exactly the block-party-attending type, if you know what I mean. I mostly kept to myself. I don't think I ever spoke to Mrs. Buhrman. Sometimes I'd spot her in the garden, but other than that she basically never left the house. She was kind of weird, you know. She joined a cult, right? I did talk to Mr. Buhrman once, though. One afternoon my mom was having trouble with the lawn mower. My father was traveling for work, and I was too much of a jerk then to help her out so Mr. Buhrman came over to give her a hand. He and I ended up talking about the Doors for a while. He seemed pretty cool.

POPPY: Did you know your mother was having an affair with Chuck Buhrman?

Maybe it was the abruptness of the question or maybe it was the strength of his religious beliefs which condemn adultery, but Warren visibly tensed when I asked this.

WARREN: My mother is not an adulteress.

POPPY: So you had never witnessed anything that made you wonder whether your mother was sleeping with Mr. Buhrman?

WARREN: Don't come here and insult my mother.

POPPY: I didn't mean to offend you. I'm only trying to get to the truth. I understand that, at that point in time, your father was frequently away on business and your parents were having marital problems.

WARREN: Can we move on?

Warren was rigid and almost noncommunicative for the remainder of our meeting. His strong reaction left me with a bad feeling. *Had* Warren known that something was going on between his mother and Chuck Buhrman? There's no question that Chuck was having an affair with Melanie—she herself admitted to as much on the witness stand, her husband left her over it—but it's unclear whether the affair was common knowledge at that time.

This is an important point. The affair is, after all, the motive the State ascribed to Warren. The State argued that Warren, already a troubled teen, was so upset about his mother taking up with the neighbor and destroying what was left of his parents' already strained marriage that he killed the object of her affection. But an impartial reading of the trial testimony shows that the State was unable to prove that Warren had known about the affair, and it had difficulty producing witnesses who could testify to widespread knowledge of it.

In the end, the State's failure to prove motive didn't matter because there was an alleged eyewitness. But a question continues to nag at me—and not just for the reason that you might think. Did Warren know about the affair? And if Melanie's family knew about the affair, what about Chuck's? What exactly did his wife and children know?

Excerpt from transcript of *Reconsidered: The Chuck Buhrman Murder*, Episode 2: "The State's Evidence—Or Lack Thereof," September 14, 2015

The most troubling thing about Warren Cave's sentence is that the evidence used to convict him was so scant. He'll spend the rest of his life behind bars based on nothing more than a few fingerprints and a hefty dose of character assassination.

The linchpin of the State's case was Lanie Buhrman's eyewitness testimony. Without it, the remaining "evidence"—and I'm using quotation marks around that word—could rightly have been dismissed as circumstantial, or would likely not have been enough to convince a jury beyond a reasonable doubt.

I get it, of course: Lanie was a conventionally attractive, articulate girl, and she was clearly devastated by her father's death. Contemporaneous accounts describe her as breaking down on the stand and looking generally heartbroken. She tugged at the jury's collective heartstrings, and they wanted to believe her.

On the other hand, eyewitness testimony, while eliciting an emotional response in the jury, is notoriously unreliable. Many factors can impact the accuracy of such statements. Consider, for example, that the story Lanie told on the witness stand—that she had gone downstairs for a glass of water and happened upon her father's murder—was not the story she told at first. Initially both Buhrman twins claimed to have been asleep before being awoken by the sound of a gun firing.

Former detective Derek McGunnigal was one of the first

people on the scene, and he described his interaction with Lanie Buhrman to me.

McGUNNIGAL: First order of business was talking to the girls. Let me tell you, it wasn't easy. They were really shaken up. We had a hell of a time just getting them to open their bedroom door for us. It took a good fifteen minutes of coaxing before they let us in, and then they clasped hands and refused to separate. Official procedure requires interviewing witnesses independently, but I could tell there was no way they would talk without each other. They barely spoke as it was, telling me they had been asleep and hadn't seen or heard anything until the gun went off.

   Shortly after I finished with the girls, officers returned with Erin Buhrman, who had been spending the night with a friend who was recovering from oral surgery. I didn't want the poor lady to have to watch us process the murder scene, so I brought her upstairs to the master bedroom. Her daughters heard her arrive and made such a fuss that I let them in with their mother against my better judgment. It wasn't by the book, but I didn't have the heart to make them leave.

   I shouldn't have let them remain in the room, but Erin wasn't offering us much other than tears so it didn't seem like it was hurting anything. I was trying to get her to remember as much as she could—had she seen anyone suspicious around the neighborhood over the last couple of days, was anything missing, that kind of thing—and she was getting more and more worked up.

Just when I really thought the lady was going to break down on me, Lanie said, "I saw it."

Everyone in the room just froze. Since this was the first I'd heard about it, I was immediately suspicious. You wouldn't believe how many folks insert themselves into a police investigation just for the drama of it. That goes double for teenaged girls—I'm not being sexist or anything, that's just my honest-to-Pete observation. I didn't want to scare her off, but I wanted to be certain she wasn't just jerking me around, so I asked her to describe exactly what she'd seen. And that was when she named Warren Cave as her father's murderer.

POPPY: I've read that a witness's first utterance is usually the most truthful one. What made you believe Lanie's second statement?

McGUNNIGAL: To be clear, I'm not the one who made that call. I can tell you that my boss thought the girls had been too scared to open up until their mother was there. They had been homeschooled, you know, and hadn't had much experience with authority figures. He thought having their mother there made them feel safe enough to talk.

POPPY: But you disagree?

McGUNNIGAL: That's not what I'm saying. I'm just saying that Lanie Buhrman didn't seem any calmer with her mother in the room. If anything, she seemed more agitated. But, well, there's a reason why my boss still runs the force and I'm working in loss prevention these days.

POPPY: Were you fired for disagreeing with your boss about Lanie Buhrman?

McGUNNIGAL: I'm not here to talk about myself. All I'm saying is that, in my opinion, she didn't seem that much more comfortable with her mother in the room. But who knows what that means—her mom was kind of spooky, you know? Even before she joined that cult. Anyway, the fact is that Lanie Buhrman described the murder scene exactly, right down to the place that the shooter must have been standing. There's no way she could have gotten all that right if she'd been upstairs the whole time. Her first statement had to be a lie.

So anyway, I sent a pair of officers next door to the Cave house. Melanie Cave was on her front porch—she had been watching the whole investigation from there— and she wouldn't let the officers inside, arguing that Warren was asleep and couldn't tell them anything. When they told her they were there to arrest her son, she became notably distressed.

POPPY: Do you believe Melanie Cave purposefully lied about Warren's whereabouts?

McGUNNIGAL: No, I think she truly believed her son was upstairs. Now, on the other hand, she was purposefully evasive about the whereabouts of her husband. She kept saying that he was "out," and refusing to elaborate. At the time, we thought something might have been fishy there, but we later learned it was only a marital spat.

Besides, if Melanie knew Warren wasn't upstairs,

I don't think she would have let in the officers without a warrant. But she eventually did and directed them to his bedroom. As you know, he wasn't there. The officers switched into high alert, assuming Warren to be armed and dangerous, and quickly searched the rest of the house. We were starting a neighborhood search when Warren rode his bicycle up the driveway, soaking wet. He immediately took a confrontational attitude with the officers, refusing to tell them where he'd been and calling them pigs and worse. He was arrested under suspicion in the death of Chuck Buhrman, and charged with resisting arrest.

Warren readily admits that he behaved badly that night, and he knows that he did himself no favors by sparring with police officers. I asked Warren what was going through his head.

POPPY: Many people have found your behavior the night Chuck Buhrman died to be suspicious. Can you tell me what you were thinking?

WARREN: I get why people think I acted guilty. I'm certainly not proud of my behavior that night. But you have to remember that I was a seventeen-year-old anarchist who hated the police on principle. Also, I had spent most of that night robo-tripping in the cemetery.

POPPY: Robo-tripping?

WARREN: Yeah. You know, when you drink a bunch of cough syrup to get high?

POPPY: That's a thing?

WARREN: Yeah. But it's dumb. Don't do it.

POPPY: I won't. So, on the night Chuck Buhrman was murdered, you have no alibi because you were drinking cough syrup alone in a cemetery?

WARREN: Yeah.

POPPY: Why a cemetery?

WARREN: I dunno. It seems really disrespectful now, but back then it was something I liked to do. See, an overdose of cough syrup makes you hallucinate. And there's nothing trippier than hallucinating in a cemetery. At least, that's what I thought back then.

   You don't know how many times I've wished I was doing something else that night. I should've just stayed home, but even if I had been out doing something dumb, I should have been doing it somewhere where someone else would see me. But you never think about that kind of stuff—needing an alibi, I mean—before you're arrested.

POPPY: But you *did* see someone else that night, right?

WARREN: Well, yeah. Not in the cemetery. I was alone there. But on my way home I cut through Lincoln Park, and as I rode past that part with the picnic tables, someone threw a beer can at me. I wasn't sure if I was hallucinating or not, so I stopped. And then I realized some kids were sitting on one of the picnic tables, and they were definitely throwing beer cans at me. When one of them threw a glass bottle, I lost it and charged them. I don't really remember what happened, but some of these guys dragged me down to the lake—it's just a couple of feet from the picnic tables, you know—and pushed me under. They were holding me down, and I really thought I was going to die. I must have passed out for a minute or two, because the next thing I knew I was laying on my side next to the water and they were gone.

POPPY: And you have no idea who they were?

WARREN: No. And I've done everything I can to find them. I thought they looked about my age, so my attorney brought me yearbooks from Elm Park and nearby towns. But it was dark and I was high that night, and I just couldn't be certain. I thought I might have recognized a couple of guys, but nothing ever came of it.

This was the first I'd heard of Warren potentially identifying some alibi witnesses, and I spoke with Claire Armstrong, Warren's then attorney, about this.

ARMSTRONG: It would've been a huge help if Warren could have identified the individuals who threw him in the lake. If we could have convinced them to testify, we could've placed Warren at least a mile away from the crime scene. Unfortunately, he was never certain about who he'd seen. He indicated that some faces looked familiar, but those individuals denied involvement. Complicating matters, they were "good kids"—you know, student council, sports, straight-As. A jury would never believe Warren over them, and without their co-operation, they were useless. Besides, Warren himself wasn't even sure that it had been them. I ran a couple of ads in the local paper, imploring anyone who knew anything to come forward, but I didn't get any leads.

I would have thought Warren being drenched with lake water would lend credence to his story and suggest he was innocent, but the opposite proved true. Police theorized Warren intentionally entered the lake in order to destroy evidence, like gunpowder residue and any other trace bits of evidence that might have connected him to the Buhrman house. Even assuming that's true, wouldn't blood be the larger problem? Could lake water really clean up blood so effectively? I pressed former detective McGunnigal for answers.

POPPY: What about the blood? How could Warren Cave shoot Chuck Buhrman in the back of the head at point-blank range and not get at least sprayed with blood? Lake water wouldn't wash that from his shirt, so how did you explain finding not a spot of blood on his clothing?

McGUNNIGAL: The theory has always been that Warren Cave wore something over his clothing. Outerwear of some sort, or perhaps even plastic. We believe this outer layer ended up at the bottom of the lake—along with the gun.

That's right, not only is there no smoking gun in the Buhrman case, there's no gun at all. No murder weapon was recovered from the scene, nor have the police been able to locate it in the intervening thirteen years. Warren Cave's bedroom was searched the night of the murder, and the rest of the Cave house was searched the following day. The cemetery and the park were also searched, and the lake was dragged, all without success.

POPPY: If you dragged the lake and didn't find the gun, why do you think it's down there?

McGUNNIGAL: Dragging a lake is an imperfect procedure, especially for a smaller object like a gun. I wasn't surprised we didn't find it.

POPPY: It didn't concern you that you never found the murder weapon?

McGUNNIGAL: We didn't need it to make a case. We had his fingerprints at the crime scene, and the Buhrman girl *saw* him do it.

Oh yes, the fingerprints. If Lanie's testimony was what put Warren in a jail cell, the discovery of his fingerprints in the Buhrman home—and the way he lied about it—was what padlocked him inside. Warren initially insisted that he had never been inside the Buhrman home. Later, after his attorney had been hired and he had been presented with the indisputable fact that his fingerprints placed him inside the house, Warren changed his story.

WARREN: I broke in. It was a Wednesday afternoon, just a few days before Mr. Buhrman died. I'd skipped school and was hanging around in my bedroom when I noticed Mrs. Buhrman leaving the house with the twins. She never really went out because, you know, she was kind of not right in the head. I'd heard my mom talking on the phone about how crazy she was, and I figured that meant she probably had some pretty good drugs over there. So when I saw her leave, I just went. Got the key out of the hiding spot—they used one of those fake rocks, like everyone else—and went inside. She had some Xanax, so I took that and some cash.

Admitting to burglarizing the victim's home is not an admirable defense, but I believe it's an honest one. The State's interpretation of the fingerprint evidence has always failed to fully account for the fact that Warren's fingerprints were not just in the kitchen—they were on *both floors of the house*, including the upstairs bathroom and master bedroom. If the fingerprints were left in commission of the murder, what was Warren doing upstairs? How did he even get up there? I've been in the Buhrmans' former home, and take it from me, it's not a home with a lot of hallways and dark corners. More importantly, there's only one staircase. While it's theoretically possible Warren could have snuck upstairs undetected and back down again without alerting Chuck Buhrman to his presence, it's unlikely. At the end of the day, Warren's problem might have been that he was *too good* a thief: no one noticed the house had been burglarized, and no one believed him after the fact.

With all this discussion of where Warren's fingerprints *were*, I think it's only appropriate to mention where they *weren't*: on the bullet embedded in the wall.

The State was untroubled by this. Warren wore gloves, they suggested—in my opinion, an unlikely scenario given that his fingerprints were found in many other places—or someone else loaded the gun. *Wait a second, Poppy*, you say. *Someone else? Did Warren Cave have an accomplice?* While it's certainly a theory that Warren might've had an accomplice, the State's implication has always been more shocking: the State believes that Chuck Buhrman loaded his own gun.

Here's the thing: Chuck owned a .38 caliber handgun, and that gun is still missing to this day. Erin told police her husband had purchased the gun for her parents after a break-in on their farm and the gun was only registered in Chuck's name through a bureaucratic error. She stated she was unsure what happened to the gun after her parents' deaths in 2000, but she claimed to have never seen the gun in her home.

I'm not sure what—if anything—this diversion about a weapon that may or may not have belonged to Chuck means to the larger narrative. To those who are convinced that Warren Cave is guilty, it's a handy explanation for how he got his minor hands on a gun: he stole it from his intended victim, of course. They assume the gun had been passed back to Chuck after Erin's parents' deaths—or that the gun had never actually changed hands in the first place—and that Warren exploited that. But how likely is that scenario, really? Likely enough, it seems, for a jury.

In the end, the physical evidence was shaky and circumstantial, and the foundation of the State's case against Warren Cave was the testimony of the victim's fifteen-year-old daughter, who had changed her story twice in the first thirty minutes that she spoke with police. Was she just traumatized, as the State maintained at trial? Or was she telling a calculated lie?

For Melanie and Warren Cave, it doesn't matter.

MELANIE: All we want is the truth. Lanie, if you're listening,

I want you to know that we forgive you. I give you my word that neither my son nor I will pursue any charges or seek civil penalties against you. We just want you to tell the truth. We just want Warren to be free.

chapter 2

It was nearly five in the morning by the time I finished listening to the second episode, and I didn't think I would be able to sleep even if I wanted to. My head felt full of static, and beneath that was an insistent drumbeat of discontent. *If the fingerprints were left in commission of the murder, what was Warren doing upstairs?*

Had Warren been upstairs that night? Could he have been standing in the hallway, just yards away from where I slept, gun in hand? I shivered. For that to be true, he must have been exceptionally quiet to avoid detection by not only my father but also my sister, who had been awake.

But if he hadn't left the fingerprints that night, he must have left them another time. Warren was right about how infrequently my mother left the house then; I could easily recall the afternoon he described. We had gone to the mall to pick out a gift for Aunt A's birthday. I had a vague memory of Mom digging through drawers that night, muttering to herself. I asked what she was doing, and she mumbled something about losing her mind and misplacing things, or was it vice versa? Our mother was often absentminded about her belongings; I didn't place any significance on it at the time. But what if she was looking for the medication or cash that Warren stole? And if he left the fingerprints on the second level days before the murder, did it stand to reason that he left the fingerprints downstairs then, too?

Stop it, I ordered myself. It didn't matter when the finger-prints were left. Maybe he left more the night he killed my father, or maybe that night he decided to wear gloves. It was just a diversion, a distraction from the real evidence: Lanie *saw* him pull the trigger.

Once I was aware of *Reconsidered*, I saw it everywhere. Anyone wearing headphones became a potential (or, depending on the level of my anxiety at that moment, probable) listener; anyone uttering anything that sounded even vaguely like Buhrman gave me pause. On line at Trader Joe's, I thought I heard someone say *Reconsidered* and tensed. But a fearful glance over my shoulder revealed the speaker's companion shaking her head vehemently and saying, "Stop telling me to reconsider. Your roommate's a barbarian and I'm not setting him up with Denise."

Deep down, I knew the extent of my paranoia was unwarranted, but I was unable to shake the persistent sensation that people were staring at me. I stopped leaving my apartment for any reason other than to go to work. I ordered all my meals in, and when I ran out of toilet paper, I ordered that in, too, because in the modern era you could order in anything. I stopped sleeping. I sat up all night, reading everything I could find about Poppy Parnell and her podcast.

Sometimes I wondered what would happen when Caleb returned from Africa and heard about *Reconsidered*. Sometimes I was terrified he had already heard about it, that he had put the pieces together and understood that I had lied about my past, and that he was never coming back to me. We had talked only once since I first heard about the podcast, and that call had been an unsatisfying five-minute conversation in which our words echoed back at us and the delay was so severe it was almost comical. Certainly not the right moment to mention that there was a hot new podcast reexamining your father's murder.

But thinking about Caleb made my heart hurt even more violently than thinking about my father, and so I pushed those concerns from my mind. I would cross that bridge when I came to it. For the time being, there was the podcast to think about.

By Friday afternoon, I had managed only a few hours of intermittent sleep over the last two days, and the demarcation between asleep and awake had blurred until the only state of consciousness I could muster was a lethargic near-trance. I was attempting to shelve a new shipment of books at work, but my brain was so sluggish that I stared at a copy of *One Hundred Years of Solitude* for a full five minutes, unsure how to alphabetize Gabriel García Márquez.

Clara watched my pitiful progress for a minute before gently taking the book from my hands and saying, "You okay, Jo? Don't take this the wrong way, but you're looking kind of rough."

"I haven't really been sleeping," I admitted, blinking.

"Do you want to, like, run to Starbucks or something? I can cover for you, no problem. Some coffee might do you good."

"Thank you," I managed, my throat closing. "But I'm going to be all right."

* * *

Whether I was actually going to be all right remained to be seen. The podcast was frighteningly pervasive, even infiltrating the aisles of the bookstore, a space usually reserved for arguing whether commercial success equated literary achievement and debating whether Hemingway was a misogynist or a misanthrope. If these lit snobs were bickering about something they heard on the internet rather than playing chicken with arcane literary references, I felt doomed.

On my walk home, my body vibrated with lack of sleep and itchy panic. I kept my head down, certain that everyone I passed had been listening to Poppy's drivel and now knew everything about my painful past. Years ago I had changed my name legally, officially leaving Josephine Buhrman behind, but that was a mere technicality that would provide little comfort once podcast fans began running image searches. Now that their interest had been piqued by my father's face on the *Reconsidered* website, how long would it be until they sought out images of all of us? What if they had started already? Had I been naïve to convince myself that a podcast was nothing more than modern radio, just words floating through the air? It existed on the internet, alongside Google images, just waiting for groups of dedicated web sleuths.

I stopped at the wine store but abandoned the bottle I had intended to purchase when a girl joined the queue behind me and immediately began tapping away on her phone. The suspicion she might know who I was overwhelmed me, and even though I knew I was acting crazy, I rushed out of the store. Back on the street, I spotted the painted window of a previously unnoticed hair salon and ducked inside.

"I need a haircut," I said, my voice sounding too loud in my own ears. The young receptionist looked at me uneasily. I was aware I should lower my voice, try to soften my frazzled edges, but that seemed beyond my capabilities and I doubled down instead, leaning forward and adding, "Immediately."

"All right," she said slowly, her voice as careful as if I were waving a gun in her face. "Let me see if anyone is available."

She rose cautiously from her desk and walked to the back of the salon, glancing over her shoulder at me twice, clearly distrustful. She held a whispered conference with the three black-clad stylists gathered in the back of the salon before one of them, a whippet-thin platinum blonde, shrugged and stepped forward, her armful of thin bangles clanking together.

"I'm Axl," she said. "I can take you."

"Cut it off," I commanded, sitting down at her station. "Cut it all off."

I had a sudden, jarring flashback to an afternoon almost ten years ago, a damp, drizzling late-May afternoon that found me sitting in a chair in a discount hair salon in London. *Cut it off*, I had said in what I had hoped passed for a brave voice. *Just cut it off.* That stylist had taken one look at my red, puffy eyes and the days-old makeup crusting my face and shook her head. *I don't think you're in the right mind-set to be making any drastic decisions about this beautiful hair, pet,* she'd said. *How about I give you a nice trim instead? Freshen you up?* Lacking the energy to disagree with her, I had nodded meekly and walked out looking like a more well-groomed version of the same person I had been when I had entered. Weeks later, there had been a similar experience in

Paris, with a cigarette-scented woman holding my hair in her hands like it was a sentient animal and bemoaning the idea that I would heartlessly destroy it. Wash, rinse, and repeat in Amsterdam and Barcelona. I finally convinced someone in Rome to give me a bob, but by the time I met Caleb in Africa four years, fifteen countries, and more short-term, paid-under-the-table food service jobs than I could count later, I had stopped thinking about my sister whenever I saw my own face and had let my hair grow out. It had been long ever since. I was out of practice for negotiating a haircut, and I steeled myself for disagreement.

But Axl just lifted her shoulders in an indifferent shrug. "Whatever you say."

"And dye it," I directed, emboldened. "Like yours."

Her magenta-colored lips twisted up into an amused smirk. "You're the boss."

I regretted my decision almost immediately. The peroxide stung on contact and gradually warmed until it felt as though my scalp were covered in a carpet of fire ants. Tears streamed from my eyes and I wanted to beg Axl to take mercy on me, but I clenched my teeth and suffered through the pain. My previous attempts to erase Josephine Buhrman had lacked conviction; I needed to chemically scrub at her vestige until nothing remained.

After the peroxide had been rinsed from my hair and my locks had been lopped into an unsubtle pixie cut, Axl spun me around in the chair to face the mirror. "What do you think?"

The change was startling, almost dissociative. My hair, or what was left of it, had not gone quite as platinum as I'd hoped, settling instead into a light butter-yellow. Without the distraction of hair around my face, my eyes looked enormous and the dark, bruise-like circles under them were suddenly that much more apparent. My eyebrows, still ink-black, were a pair of aggressive crescents above my eyes. I looked unhinged. I felt unhinged.

"The eyebrows," I managed.

Axl nodded, and soon peroxide was burning my eyebrows and I was worrying about chemically induced blindness. But the momentary terror was worth it: when she presented me with the mirror again, I looked eminently more reasonable. I studied my reflection and noted with satisfaction that I looked nothing like Josephine Buhrman.

Even though Axl wasn't a very skilled colorist, I tipped her 80 percent and then walked out onto the street, unshackled from the concern that people were staring at me. Or at least knowing that any stares were likely due to my extreme hairstyle and not because I looked like a member of the Elm Park Buhrmans, that cursed family. Whether my spontaneous makeover was a direct result of paranoia or the reasoned adoption of a disguise, I didn't care. All that mattered was that I was finally able to stop thinking about the podcast for at least a few minutes—finally able to feel once again like the person I had worked so hard to become.

Poppy Parnell ✓
@poppy_parnell

#Reconsidered is the no. 1 download on @iTunes right now! Thanks for the support! #ChuckBuhrman

5m

chapter 3

When Caleb returned from the DRC on Monday night, he was shaggy and skinny, just like he had been when I first met him.

"Honey, I'm home," he called as he pushed open the door, the joke trailing off into a ragged cough. My heart squeezed. I could hear the weeks of antimalarials, mild food poisoning, and eighteen-hour workdays in his hoarse voice. I wanted to usher him straight to bed, tuck him into the sheets I had freshly laundered for his homecoming, my instinctive desire to tend to him so strong I forgot I had been awake all night obsessing over the podcast and sick knowing it was only a matter of time before Caleb learned about it.

"Just tell him," Ellen had said, sounding irritated about my repeated post-midnight phone calls the past several days. "It's not like you can keep it a secret at this point."

"I thought Peter was going to sue her. Get her trash off the internet. What happened to that?"

"Apparently it's more complicated than I thought. Anyway, even if it weren't, too many people know about it now. Did you know it was spoofed on *SNL* last weekend? There's no way Caleb *won't* hear about it. You're going to have to tell him."

"But how?"

"Josie, you're a grown-up. I'm sure you can figure it out. Maybe now's the time to come clean anyway."

I knew Ellen had a point, but the idea of owning up to my lies filled me with dread. When I first met Caleb, I had told him my parents had passed away. It was a careless, throw-away line I had been using as I backpacked and hitchhiked my way across Europe, Southeast Asia, Europe again, and then finally Africa. Those relationships had seemed disposable; there was no need to ruin the mood with stories of my murdered father, my insane mother, and my despised sister. But Caleb had turned out to be the furthest thing from disposable, and then the lie fed upon itself and grew, and I had never known how to tell him the truth.

The evening of Caleb's homecoming I was caught up in a vigorous debate with myself over whether I should confess—and, if so, *how*—but once I heard him walk in, all the arguments I had made and the anguish I'd felt over making them faded away. I needed to be in his arms. The shadows of the past could wait.

Caleb was dropping his dirt-stained duffel bag in the entryway as I rounded the corner, my heart thundering giddily.

"Hey, babe."

He looked up at me, his gray eyes weary and ringed, and his smile froze on his face. "Fucking hell, Jo. What happened to your hair?"

I startled, realizing that I had spent so much time thinking of how to break the news to Caleb ("I have something to tell you" sounded too ominous, too much like I had been having an affair, but "So, have you heard about this podcast?" didn't carry enough gravity) that I had completely forgotten about my drastic makeover three days prior.

"Oh," I said with a forced laugh. "I saw this hairstyle on someone else and decided to give it a try. You know me, impulsive."

He blinked. "It's . . . jarring."

"Exactly the look I was going for," I said, my voice thinning to an unnatural pitch.

Caleb was too exhausted to do anything other than take my words at face value. He told me that I was still beautiful, kissed me on my head, and then proceeded to sleep for the next thirteen hours.

I had not always hated my sister. For the first fifteen years of our lives, she had been an inextricable part of myself; I existed only as one half of a matched set. I had once truly believed I would cease to be if I were separated from her.

That was back when she still cared about me, though, before she traded my respect and love for booze, drugs, and low-grade anarchy. Back then, she had been daring rather than rebellious, just a pigtailed girl with scabbed knees and a sense of adventure. She led me on countless escapades, up into the loft of our grandparents' barn and down by their pond; she showed me the hole in the wall behind the sink in our small backyard playhouse where she hid her illicit treasures, the candy pilfered from the cabinet, broken costume jewelry stolen from Ellen, and tawdry novels lifted from our mother's bedside table. (It was the last of these items that led our mother to ransack our bedroom and playhouse until she discovered Lanie's hiding spot. Books and jewelry were returned; candy was confiscated.)

But for every act of mischief, for every night of sleep Lanie ruined by telling me stories of men with hooks for hands and hitchhiking ghosts, my sister was also the first one to come to help me, to comfort me when I was sad. We had once so delighted in our twinship that we felt sorry for our mother, who had a sister, my Aunt A, but not a twin, and our cousin Ellen, who had no siblings at all. We thought we were special; we thought our bond was invincible.

But then Dad was killed and Mom abandoned us and Lanie went completely off the rails. I tried to hold on to her, but Lanie didn't want to be saved. She made *that* perfectly clear.

It had been ten years since I last saw my twin sister. There had been a time, early on in our separation, when she was all I could think about—I saw her everywhere: pouring drinks in a rowdy pub in central London, contemplating *Winged Victory* in the Louvre, lighting a cigarette on a darkened Roman street. And every time I closed my eyes there she was, hollow-cheeked and borderline feral. She stalked my subconscious and materialized whenever my mind wandered for even a fraction of a second.

But as time and distance wore on, my memory of her faded. Occasionally, I woke up in the middle of the night sweating, convinced that something was wrong with her, and I would spend the rest of the night sitting by the phone, waiting to hear that something had happened, but then morning would come and life would return to normal.

Since that strange three a.m. phone call and the subsequent discovery of the podcast, the shadowy figure of my sister had once more been lurking on the periphery of my thoughts. I had largely avoided succumbing, but with my sister's usual impeccably cruel timing, thoughts of her were impossible to shake the night Caleb returned home. With his familiar lanky form finally slumbering beside me once again, I tried to sleep, but images of my sister at her worst (smudged eyeliner, vacant eyes, bloody nose) flickered rapidly across the inside of my eyelids.

Sleep was out of the question, no matter how desperately I wanted it. I rose quietly, then microwaved a cup of tea, grabbed an afghan, and curled up on the couch, planning to watch episodes of *The X-Files* on Netflix. Programming about aliens and human-sized worms prowling the sewer system was the ultimate in escapism and rarely failed to calm me when I was anxious. Despite this, I froze at least once every twenty minutes, certain I heard my phone ringing. My connection to my sister had been dulled over the years—first by drugs, then by distance—but my body insisted Lanie was calling out for me. I hadn't decided if I would answer.

By the time the sun broke over the tops of the downtown Brooklyn high-rises, there had been no call that Lanie was dead, maimed, or otherwise, and I decided I had been mistaken. It seemed Lanie and I weren't connected after all; maybe we never had been.

"Morning, love," Caleb mumbled, padding out of the bedroom and rubbing a hand over his sleepy face and through his loose brown curls. "How long have you been up?"

"A while," I admitted, handing him the slice of buttered toast I had prepared for myself and dropping another into the toaster.

He made short work of it and grinned. "I've missed your cooking, babe."

"Stop it," I said, hitting him playfully in the stomach. "Like I'm supposed to believe you were dining on gourmet fare in the DRC. I know how you aid workers do it. It's all gruel, beer, and snack cakes."

Caleb caught my hand and tugged me toward him. I licked my lips and stepped closer, tucking my fingers into the waistband of his pajama pants, looser than they had been when he left. When my fingertips hit his mildly feverish skin, something inside me softened. Everything was going to be okay. The podcast no longer mattered; the past and the lies I had constructed on top of it no longer mattered. All that mattered existed within the circuit of our hearts and flesh.

Caleb lowered his face to mine, our lips connecting. I barely noticed his teeth had not been brushed in more than twenty-four hours. Caleb was home, and everything was safe and warm again.

My cell phone sounded shrilly from the bedroom, crumbling the cocoon that had been forming around us. My stomach dropped. *Lanie.*

"Leave it," Caleb murmured, grabbing at me as I pulled away.

But the mounting dread was too strong to ignore, and I nearly choked on my racing heart as I hurried to answer the call.

"Josie, sweetheart, I'm sorry," Ellen said, the unnatural softness in her demeanor sending prickles down my spine.

"What?" I asked, more an impotent puff of air than a word.

"There's no easy way to tell you this. She's dead. I'm so sorry."

I touched my breastbone, my fingertips pushing into my skin. I could still feel my sister pulsing beneath my chest; she didn't feel dead. "Are you sure?"

"Yeah, honey, I'm sure. I haven't seen . . . her, if that's what you're asking. But Mom got a call from someone with the Life Force Collective this morning."

I paused, Ellen's words permeating my consciousness slowly. The call had come from the Life Force Collective. Lanie wasn't dead.

My mother was.

"Oh. All right."

The flatness of my own words surprised me. I had imagined this moment more times than I could count, and I had always expected that I would cry, that I would scream, that I would be inconsolable, flattened by the lost chances. I expected a sense of emptiness, of despair, but as it turned out, I felt nothing.

Ellen inhaled sharply. "Well. Yes."

I nodded, a gesture Ellen could not see. Pulling the bedroom door shut, I asked, "How did it happen?"

"She . . . Oh, hon, she hung herself."

A shiver ran through my bones as I pictured my mother's thin body swinging in the air, her neck at an unnatural angle. A sob threatened to escape my throat, and I was strangely pleased that I had to choke it back. Perhaps I wasn't so cold after all.

47

"Where should I send the flowers? To the funeral home or to your mom's house?"

"Skip the flowers and just hand-deliver *yourself* to Mom's house."

"Ellen, I'm not going home."

"Josie, you *have* to come home. You're her daughter."

"The daughter she abandoned more than a decade ago! I don't *have* to do anything."

"She was still your mother."

"She's dead. It doesn't matter if I'm there or not. She's going to be just as dead if I'm there as she is if I'm here."

"I'm going to pretend you didn't just say that. You know very well funerals are not for the dead. They're for the living the dead have left behind. We need you here. *My mother* needs you here. If you think things have been bad with that podcast—not that you ever *once* bothered to call Mom to see how she was handling things—they're about to get a whole lot worse. That bitch Parnell is going to be beating down my mother's door, and you *will* be there to help deflect her."

"Ellen, you know I told Caleb both my parents were dead," I said, dropping my voice and glancing toward the bedroom door.

"And you honestly think that's a secret you can keep? Even now? *Especially* now?" She paused for my response, but I had none. She sniffed. "Fine. Tell him that *my* mother died. Problem solved. Just come home."

"I can't. I'm sorry."

"Goddammit, Josie—"

"I'm sorry," I repeated, disconnecting the call.

My cousin generally insisted on having the last word, so my finger was poised to decline the call that immediately followed. The phone rang again, and once more I hit the red button to ignore it. After the third attempt, I powered the phone down completely. Ellen could call all she wanted, but I wasn't going back to Elm Park.

Caleb, holding the half-eaten remains of my second piece of toast, pushed open the door and peered inside. "Jo? Is everything okay?"

I opened my mouth to say *Yes* but a strangled sob slipped out instead. Caleb took me in his arms, rubbing my back in gentle circles and asking me what happened.

"Aunt A died. I have to go home."

The words left my mouth without warning, but hearing them aloud, I knew Ellen was right: I had to go home. I owed it to the memory of my mother, and more importantly, I owed it to Aunt A, who had taken care of me when my mother wouldn't. Aunt A had given so much of herself to be a rock for my sister and me, and I couldn't let her go through this without support.

"Oh, no," Caleb murmured, wrapping an arm around me and holding me close. I burrowed into his thin chest, squeezing my eyes shut and stifling wails as images of my mother flooded my mind. I saw nothing but happy memories from a long time past: my young, beautiful mother with her hands in my hair, weaving the thick black strands identical to her own into a braid; my mother smelling of chamomile tea as she leaned over to kiss me good night, her long hair tickling my face; my mother wearing that apron with ruffles at the

49

shoulders, putting a dab of vanilla under my and Lanie's noses while baking cookies.

"I'm so sorry, love," he said softly. "I know your aunt was like a mother to you."

I stiffened at the reminder of my lies. Unaware, Caleb continued whispering comforting words in my ear. I didn't deserve having this wonderful man console me when I had lied to him about my tragedy—the immediate one and the many others that made up my life—and I pushed him away.

I yanked my suitcase from underneath the bed and flung open the closet. Shaking off Caleb's attempts to help, I seized every article of black clothing within reach and threw them haphazardly into the suitcase. It didn't matter what I wore. I wasn't going home to impress anyone. I hoped I wouldn't even see anyone, especially—

I cringed, wondering if she was still in Elm Park, if *he* was. Ellen, a committed gossip, certainly knew, but she knew better than to breathe either of their names to me. I had made it abundantly clear that I wanted both of them erased from my life.

"Yes, thank you," I heard Caleb say clearly in the hallway. "I need to book travel from JFK to Chicago O'Hare, please . . . Today, if at all possible . . . Yes, I know I can do this online, but I need the bereavement fare."

Caleb's nurturing spirit was what had first attracted me to him. We had met in Zanzibar, where he was working with underprivileged schoolchildren. I had been bumming around the idyllic island, ignoring not only the local Muslim sensibilities by drinking too much and wearing too little but also the very same children Caleb was trying to help. We had crossed paths in the night market when one of his students had approached me to practice her English. Caleb's patience and kindness captivated me immediately; what he saw in me, I never understood.

I peered around the corner to see him in our small hallway. He stood there in only his pajama bottoms, the phone hooked under his stubbled chin, a pencil in one hand and our grocery list, flipped over to make room for flight information, in the other. He was nodding and jotting notes even though his eyes were half closed and crusted over with sleep. In that moment, I would have given anything to stay with him, in this comfortable, happy life we'd constructed for ourselves, for just a bit longer. Just a few more afternoons spent drinking coffee beside him on the couch, tag-teaming the *New York Times* crossword puzzle; racing him to Prospect Park, dodging baby carriages and dogs the whole way; cooking curries together in the small kitchen, bumping elbows as we chopped onions and measured out spices; all the little things that made life worth living.

"Yes, I need two tickets. The first passenger is Jo Borden. B-o-r-d-e-n. The second passenger is Caleb Perlman. P-e-r-l-m-a-n."

"No!" I objected suddenly. "Just one! Just me. Just one."

Caleb politely informed the airline representative he would call back and then turned to me with a befuddled expression. "What are you talking about? Don't you want me to come to the funeral with you?"

Of course I wanted Caleb to come with me. More than that, I *needed* him to come with me. There were very few people in my life on whom I thought I could rely, and Caleb was far and away the most solid of this small group. He kept me grounded, steady, and largely sane. If anyone could protect me from being drawn into the madness that was my family, it would be him.

But, of course, it was my family that was the problem. I could still remember the sticky, moonless night that Caleb and I spent perched on a retaining wall overlooking the Indian Ocean, smoking cigarettes and talking until dawn. The whole thing had felt so cinematic that when he asked about my family, I not only trotted out my rehearsed lie about dead parents but I embellished it by killing them off in a car accident, borrowing details like the country road and the drunk driver from the deaths of my mother's parents. He had looked appropriately sorry for asking, and I had nodded bravely and offered a half-truth about being raised by my aunt. I thought it a lie I would live with for a week at most, but I remained enmeshed in it five years later.

"Caleb, honey, I want you to come. I do." My voice quivered with emotion on that *I do*; I needed him to understand how much I really needed him. "But I can't drag you to Illinois. You just got home. You need to rest, and I'm sure you have a ton of work waiting for you in the office."

"None of that matters. *You* matter. I want to take care of you."

"I can take care of myself."

Caleb sighed, his face softening. "I know, babe. It's one of the things I love most about you."

My aching heart warmed. Sometimes I worried Caleb had a savior complex, and that he mistook a desire to save me for love. I was buoyed to hear him cite one of my more redeemable qualities as a basis for his love, and I could not help but press for more. "Really?"

Caleb smiled and smoothed back my ruined hair. "Really. You're a very capable woman, Jo. You traveled the world on your own for years. I don't know anyone else who could have done that, and I know a lot of travelers. Most people get burned out or can't figure out a way to make money, but you kept yourself going for five years. I admire that kind of independence."

"Thank you," I said, squeezing back a fresh round of tears. "But, Caleb, really, this is something I can handle on my own."

Caleb scratched his chin with the eraser end of the pencil. "How about this: you go to Illinois alone today, and see how you're feeling. I'll come whenever you need me. Just say the word, and I'll be there. Okay?"

I nodded in feigned agreement, fully intending to be back on the East Coast before Caleb got near a plane. Then I kissed him, trembling with the thought this might be one of the last times our lips met. Holding his face in my hands, I stared into his soft gray eyes, wondering if he could ever understand. If I came clean, if I got out ahead of things, could there be a chance to salvage our relationship? The truth sat on the tip of my tongue, but before I could open my mouth and release it, I swallowed it again.

Erin Ann Blake Buhrman, 49, passed away on September 20, 2015. The daughter of Patrick and Abigail Blake, Erin was born in Elm Park, Illinois, on February 8, 1966. On August 2, 1986, Erin married Charles "Chuck" Buhrman. Erin was preceded in death by her husband, her parents, and her brother, Dennis. She is survived by her daughters, Josephine and Madeline, and her sister, Amelia. A visitation will be held on Wednesday, September 23, at 2:00 p.m. at Wilhelm Funeral Home in Elm Park. A short funeral service and burial will take place on Friday, September 25, at 11:00 a.m. at Elm Park Cemetery. In lieu of flowers, the family suggests donations be made to the National Center for Suicide Prevention.

chapter 4

Two hours later, I called Ellen from Gate 25 at JFK, a stack of celebrity gossip magazines on my lap and a Red Eye from Starbucks in my hand.

"Tell me you're coming home," she said in lieu of *hello*.

"My flight boards in twenty minutes."

"Thank God. I have my mother on the other line, and she's been crying for the last thirty minutes. I need reinforcements. When do you get in?"

"Just after two. Are you going to pick me up, or should I rent a car?"

"I'll pick you up. Have a safe flight."

"Wait, Ellen." I took a deep breath, mentally preparing myself to ask my next question. "What about Lanie?"

"Josie, I have to go."

"Don't avoid the question. Will Lanie be there?"

"Josie, my mother is in tears on the other line. I have to go. I'll see you soon."

Ellen disconnected the call without another word.

My flight was delayed by more than two hours, during which time I jumped at least seven times thinking I had overheard my father's name. Only once did that turn out to be the case. Agitated by the delay and my increasingly unmanageable paranoia, I tried to distract myself with Facebook.

It was a ruse that worked for only a moment. Mentions of the podcast lurked among the usual barrage of cheerful announcements (engagements, babies, culinary successes) like snakes in the grass. One link in particular caught my eye: *Why Exactly Poppy Parnell Is Investigating That Chuck Buhrman Murder: An Interview with the* Reconsidered *Host.*

Yes, I thought. *Why exactly* is *Poppy Parnell investigating this murder?* Even though I knew I would regret it, I clicked through.

Why Exactly Poppy Parnell Is Investigating That Chuck Buhrman Murder: An Interview with the *Reconsidered* Host
by Eric Ashworth

Everyone is listening to *Reconsidered: The Chuck Buhrman Murder*, right? If you're not, stop whatever you're doing and go download it. Right now. I'll wait.

Everyone with me now? Good.

The serial podcast, hosted by blogger-cum-journalist Poppy Parnell and funded by the communications giant Werner Entertainment Company, promises to reconsider the 2002 murder of midwestern professor Chuck Buhrman in weekly, hour-long installments. The twist is that these podcasts haven't been prerecorded, or even outlined. Parnell is investigating the case *right now* and is generating the podcasts in real time. A true-crime junkie's wet dream, this format allows listeners to be intimately involved in the investigation. Parnell even welcomes armchair detectives to tweet leads and theories to her.

Even more intriguing than the revolutionary format is the

subject matter. The case doesn't fit the mold for this type of investigative journalism. The murder of Chuck Buhrman is not a cold case. It's not even unsolved.

That's right: the local police maintain that they got their guy. Within hours of the murder, a suspect—Warren Cave, the then seventeen-year-old neighbor—was arrested. Eyewitness testimony helped convict him, and he was sentenced to life in prison.

It sounds like an open-and-shut case with not much to reconsider. In the first few minutes of the podcast, Parnell invites us to question whether Cave actually pulled the trigger. But why should we?

Some elementary Googling turned up a small niche of online conspiracy theorists that have been espousing Cave's innocence since the early '00s. But you can find support for just about anything on the internet, and these are largely the kind of people who create websites in neon green fonts on black backgrounds and casually mention that 9-11 was an inside job. How—and why—did Parnell choose this case? And how did she get Werner Entertainment to back her?

Even though she's neck-deep in her investigation, Poppy Parnell, the brains (and beauty) behind *Reconsidered*, graciously granted me an interview so I could ask her just that.

Q: First, Poppy, let me get this out of the way: I'm completely obsessed with *Reconsidered*. I've listened to each episode at least three times and I've been taking notes. I think I speak for most of us when I say that I had never heard of the Buhrman case until your podcast began. How did you get interested in it?

A: My mother, actually. She met Melanie Cave at a gardening conference in Iowa last year, where they bonded over their shared love of heritage roses and hatred of aphids. When Melanie heard about my old blog and that I'm an investigative journalist, she asked my mother for my contact information. And here we are.

Q: Ah, yes. Your roots as a humble blogger. Tell us about it. It was a true-crime blog, right?

A: Yes, that's right. From 2008 through 2013, I ran a blog called *From the Unsolved Archives* where I catalogued unsolved murders and kidnappings. It's no secret that websites run by true-crime enthusiasts can get mired down with conspiracy theories, and I worked really hard to keep my blog firmly out of tin-foil-hat territory. I kept things strictly to the facts—while refusing to blindly adhere to the conventional interpretation of those facts. I'm really proud of the work I did there, and of course the blog laid the groundwork for my transition into an investigative reporter.

Q: Let's get back to the Buhrman murder. You want us to believe that Warren is innocent. But there was an eyewitness!

A: Let me set the record straight: I take no position on Warren's guilt or innocence. I assume I will eventually—but there's a whole lot of investigating I have to do before I reach that point. For now, I just want my listeners to question the dominant narrative. The alleged eyewitness is an excellent example. Lanie Buhrman notably changed her story at least once on the night of the murder, so why should we believe her?

Q: You think she's lying?

A: Maybe. Maybe not. Maybe she was, as Melanie puts it, "confused."

Q: Don't all mothers of accused murderers think their children are innocent? I mean, Jeffrey Dahmer's mother probably thought he was innocent, too.

A: I only have a passing familiarity with Dahmer's case, so I can't really speak to that. In general, though, I'd agree: most mothers probably believe—or at least *want* to believe—that their sons are incapable of gunning down the neighbors. When Melanie first contacted me, I'd assumed it was a case of maternal delusion. It wasn't long, however, before I got the sense that she was onto something. There's more to this case than meets the eye.

Q: Like what? Give us some examples.

A: Listen to the podcast! I don't hold anything back.

Q: All right, that's fair. How did this project turn into the podcast?

A: In the past, I've worked for Werner Entertainment Company as a consultant on some of their crime programs. I was having lunch with someone I met in that capacity, and I happened to mention my research. I had always envisioned the final product as an article, but my friend got really excited about it, and, before I knew it, the podcast was born.

And aren't we all glad to have it? The next installment of *Reconsidered* will be available for download tomorrow. Until then, I'll be stalking Parnell's Twitter account for additional clues. Leave your conspiracy theories in the comments, where they belong.

The article was dated yesterday, meaning that a new episode was now available for download. Seemingly of their own volition, my fingers navigated to the *Reconsidered* website and clicked the *Download Now* button before I came to my senses. I regretted listening to the first two episodes; I hated the seeds of doubt that she had planted in my mind. *Warren Cave is guilty*, I reminded myself sternly. *Do not listen to that podcast.*

Instead, I clicked back to the article and began skimming the comments before deciding that was an even worse idea. Emboldened by anonymity, the commenters had disgusting, hateful things to say about my mother, about my sister, things that far exceeded anything I had ever thought about them, and my anger toward both was legitimate and intense.

Setting my phone to airplane mode, I told myself that I had been right not to involve Caleb in this mess. He could never understand my complicated family. How could he? The stark difference between Caleb's family and mine had been obvious from the moment I met them, when Caleb and I had traveled to the South Island for Christmas. They were admirable people, all of them: his mother was a pediatrician, his father a carpenter, both earnest and dedicated to their jobs. His older sister Molly, a sleek, whip-smart barrister, had an amiable husband and two adorable, apple-cheeked children.

I had been nervous about meeting Caleb's family, especially on a religious holiday. I had long ago given up on organized religion, as my father being murdered and my mother joining a cult led me to believe there was no grand design and certainly no benevolent God. In contrast, the Perlmans took the birth of Jesus Christ quite seriously. It surprised me to see Caleb, a man who I had never known to attend church and who I had often heard rail against Christian ministries in Africa, go through the stand-sit-kneel motions of a Catholic mass, the prayers and responses tumbling from his mouth without hesitation. I worried my lack of faith embarrassed him, but neither he nor his family seemed bothered by my apathetic brand of atheism.

It wasn't until evening, after the third bottle of wine had been opened and Molly had beaten us all at rummy four times, that I began to loosen up, and fast on the heels of that relaxation came a pang of sadness. I would never have an adult relationship with my parents. My father had been taken from me when I was still a teenager; my mother had abandoned us and made it abundantly clear that she did not want to be found. For the remainder of the holiday, anything that Mrs. Perlman did that reminded me vaguely of my own mother—baking cookies, reciting a poem, laughing a certain way—sent me into an internal tailspin.

On the trip home to Auckland, I almost confessed. I was one breath away from telling Caleb everything, from the sudden, violent death of my father to the painful fading of my mother, even the heartache that Lanie had caused. But then I had recalled the warm hugs Caleb exchanged with his family, the clear love they shared, and I kept my mouth shut. He would never understand.

When we were finally permitted aboard the airplane, I found myself seated between a man who had already staked his claim to the shared armrest and a cheerful young woman with a drooling infant on her lap. I squeezed into my seat and immediately commenced battle for a portion of the armrest, which the man ceded with a grunt. As I buckled my seat belt, the woman handed me an index card with a miniature organza sack of jelly beans stapled to it.

Hello! the card greeted me in pink bubble letters. *My name is Rosie and this is my first time on an airplane! I am very excited about flying, but I might get scared or uncomfortable and I might cry. I don't mean to disturb your flight! I hope you like these jelly beans!*

"Thanks," I mumbled, forcing my tired, overstressed face into the approximation of a smile. "Jelly beans. Yum."

"If you don't like those flavors, I have other options," the woman said, opening her purse to reveal a collection of similar note cards.

"These are great, thanks."

"This is her first time on a plane," she continued. "Our ultimate destination is California. I purposefully took a layover in Chicago. Do you think that was stupid?"

"I don't know," I said, hoping she wasn't going to talk the whole flight. I was emotionally and physically exhausted, and I wanted nothing more than to close my eyes for the next two hours.

"I couldn't decide whether it would be better for Rosie to have one really long direct flight or two medium-length flights with a layover. Here's hoping I made the right decision!" She smiled brightly. "We're on our way to San Francisco to visit my sister. Have you ever been?"

San Francisco. I was suddenly wide awake, my spine tingling as I said, "Yes."

"What did you think? My sister is always trying to get us to move out there, but I keep telling her, it's nice, but it's no New York."

"It's no New York," I agreed, flashes from my brief time in San Francisco swimming into my vision.

"Where—?" she started to ask.

"My mother is dead," I said abruptly.

"Oh," she said, pulling little Rosie to her chest, as though I were infectious. "I'm sorry."

"No," I said, my cheeks flushing in horrified embarrassment. "*I'm* sorry. I'm tired and a little mixed up right now."

She nodded tightly and turned to chat with the person across the aisle. With my anxiety now at an all-time high, I attempted to order three miniature bottles of vodka from the flight attendant. He informed me, rather unkindly, that I could only purchase two at a time, and so I chugged them as quickly as possible and ordered the third, much to the alarm of Rosie's mother.

Then I closed my eyes and waited for the alcohol to take hold. *San Francisco*, my heart thundered. Caleb and I had spent three blissful weeks together in Zanzibar before his contract had ended and he had flown home to New Zealand. His departure ignited something of an existential crisis in me. Being with him had made me feel like a better person, and I was suddenly disenchanted with the aimless wandering that had become my life. When the ragtag group of European hippies I had traveled with to Africa began pooling resources to venture down to Lake Malawi, I let them go without me.

I didn't want to travel, and I didn't want to go home. Mired in indecision, I did nothing and spent my days wandering alone through the gloomy alleys. But when I saw on Facebook that Lilly, a friendly girl and fellow American I had met in a hostel in Chiang Mai two years prior and then spent a month traveling around Thailand with, was now living in San Francisco, I knew what I had to do. I sent Lilly a message and spent the last of my money on a ticket to California without waiting for her response.

I felt sick with anticipation when I arrived in San Francisco. The Life Force Collective's compound was somewhere in Northern California; I was closer to my mother than I had been in years. Still, I had no idea how to go about finding her. Every dark-haired woman I passed on the sidewalk drew a second glance from me, even though I had no reason to suspect my mother was in the city. I spent night after sleepless night on Lilly's couch, scouring the internet for evidence of my mother or the cult that had consumed her.

And then one afternoon, as I wiped tables in the coffee shop where I'd picked up some work to fund my stay, I saw a guy my age reading a thin paperback called *The Dark Side of Sunshine: The True Story of the Life Force Collective*.

"What is that?" I demanded, my voice hollow.

He shrugged. "Some book about a cult I've never heard of. It was on the quarter rack at the used bookstore down the block, so I thought why not?"

"I'll give you five dollars for it," I said, my pulse galloping.

For the remainder of my shift, the slim book burned a hole in my back pocket. I could hardly wait to get back to Lilly's and dive in. My internet searches had only turned up pages of vendetta, propaganda, and insanity; a physical book promised something more solid. I read it cover to cover in a single sitting. It was nothing I hadn't heard before about the Life Force Collective (it was founded by former child star Rhetta Quinn, its commune was located somewhere in Northern California, its members believed in free love and living off the land), but it was presented in such an authoritative manner that I felt my first flicker of hope.

When I finished the book sometime around four in the morning, I sent the author a message through his website: *My mother is in the LFC. Can you help me find her?*

Two hours later he responded: *I can't promise anything, but I can put you in contact with them.*

The next week, I borrowed Lilly's car and met Sister Amamus at a Dairy Queen north of the city. I had expected someone willowy and ethereal, someone like my mother, but Sister Amamus was of hardier stock, with wide shoulders and the large hands of a ballplayer. She waited for me outside, standing barefoot in a parking space, colorful scarves fluttering around her and long earrings tinkling like wind chimes.

"Uh, I think you should probably put some shoes on," I said to her.

She waved me off and padded into the store, gauzy layers rippling around her. She ordered a large Snickers Blizzard, and looked at me expectantly. I handed the clerk my credit card.

I waited as she spooned ice cream, but impatience got the better of me and I leaned forward, my words tumbling over each other as I asked, "Do you know my mother?"

She took another bite before looking at me frankly. "Sister Anahata wishes you well. But she does not want to see you."

I sat back, stunned. I could only hope she was confusing my mother with someone else. "Is that the name my mom is using? Erin Buhrman?" I wished I'd brought a picture of my mother with me, but I didn't have any of her—or any of my family. Instead, I tried to describe my mother. "She kind of looks like me. A little shorter, I think. But black hair. Lots of it. Blue eyes. She, uh, she likes baking. And lemon tea and daffodils. She . . . she can be kind of a hermit."

Amamus smiled indulgently, her mouth full of candied ice cream. "I know Sister Anahata."

"So you're saying that Sister Anahata is Erin Buhrman."

"I don't know anyone by that name."

Frustration grew, and I curled my hands into fists. I hadn't come all this way to dance my way through some half-rate "Who's on First?" routine. "Cut the bullshit. If you know something about my mother, I need you to tell me."

Amamus sighed and seemingly took pity on me. "Your mother came to us to start a new life. Please respect that."

"Then why even meet with me?" I asked desperately.

"To assure you that your mother is happy and healthy. You don't need to worry about her."

"But how am I supposed to trust you? Can you prove to me that you even know her?"

"Don't contact us again," Amamus said, standing up. "Be well."

She picked up her Blizzard and walked out the door without looking back.

From *Slate*, published September 22, 2015

Chuck Buhrman's Widow
Takes Own Life—Podcast to Blame?

by Jasmine O'Neill

Almost everyone in America knows who Erin Blake Buhrman is.

Such notoriety is something Mrs. Buhrman went to great lengths to avoid. But in 2002, Mrs. Buhrman, described as a gentle woman and devoted mother, was thrust into an unwelcome spotlight by the murder of her husband, Chuck Buhrman. (Refresh your memory of the case here.)

In the wake of her husband's death, Mrs. Buhrman endured a very public examination of her husband's private life. His affair with Melanie Cave, the married next-door neighbor and mother of Warren, became front-page news. While local media claimed the details of Buhrman's affair with Melanie Cave went to establishing motive and were therefore relevant, some argued that the salacious details were printed for sensational effect.

The sudden death of her husband, the public destruction of her marriage, and the trial, during which she spent nearly three hours on the stand, all chipped steadily away at Mrs. Buhrman's already delicate emotional state until she left her Illinois hometown for a Northern California commune run by the Life Force Collective, or the LFC. (Want to learn more about the LFC? Read our primer on celebrity-led cults here.)

LFC members generally renounce contact with non-cult members, and Mrs. Buhrman—or Sister Anahata, as she came to be known—was no different. She abandoned her sixteen-year-old twin daughters to the care of her sister, Amelia Kelly, a middle school teacher in Elm Park.

A source inside the LFC, speaking on the condition of anonymity, told me Mrs. Buhrman was happy with her life on the commune. "Sister Anahata exuded nothing but love and contentment. She was an example to us all."

But all that was shattered earlier this month when a podcast entitled *Reconsidered: The Chuck Buhrman Murder* burst onto the web. The podcast claims to be reviewing the case from an impartial, third-party perspective, but some argue it is the same sensationalist faux news that caused Mrs. Buhrman such anguish after her husband's death.

Poppy Parnell, the host of the podcast, is a self-proclaimed "investigative journalist" and former webmistress of a true-crime blog. The now-shuttered blog was frequently criticized for inciting witch hunts and smearing the reputations of innocent parties. Records show that Ms. Parnell and her blog were sued twice for defamation; both times these suits were settled out of court.

One might wonder how a blogger like Ms. Parnell was able to land such a high-profile platform, but that inquiry ends with who has been providing the funding for and producing *Reconsidered*: Werner Entertainment Company, emphasis on the word entertainment. These are the same folks that brought you *The True Life Diaries of a Meth Addict* and *Pedophilia: The Inside Story*. Werner Entertainment has been roundly criticized for taking serious topics and reducing them to spectacles.

But its origins and motives aside, everyone can agree that *Reconsidered* has been a huge success. The program has over ten million downloads to date. Thousands of threads, posts, articles, and webpages have sprung up to discuss the case. All of this has been great news for Ms. Parnell and Werner Entertainment.

It was less great news for Mrs. Buhrman. According to my LFC source, shortly after *Reconsidered* began airing, reporters and curiosity-seekers began appearing on LFC property. This alone was surprising: the LFC guards the location of its commune quite closely. Potential LFC members must meet a representative in San Francisco and undergo a screening process before being permitted to make the journey to the Northern California commune. That these individuals found the location speaks to an extremely high level of devotion to the project, nearing on obsession. This influx of outsiders disrupted the flow of life on the commune, and, my source tells me, destroyed the sanctity of certain important events.

My source recalled one specific event—an "aging" ceremony, which celebrates the arrival of a teenaged girl to womanhood—that was disrupted by a group of eight or ten teenagers. These self-described *Reconsidered* fans snuck into the ceremony disguised in ritual robes they had stolen from the laundry, and attempted to record the ceremony on their smartphones. When they were exposed, they reacted violently, striking LFC members and making specific threats against Mrs. Buhrman.

According to my source, the incident at the aging ceremony was a low point for Mrs. Buhrman. "Ever since the resurgence in interest in the death of her husband, Sister Anahata had been acting depressed. She began spending all her time alone in one of the solitary huts—places where our sisters and brothers can go if they need to meditate to seek clarity, or if they are suffering from a contagious disease—and refused to take part in mealtimes. She was wasting away."

Then yesterday morning, Mrs. Buhrman was found hanging from a tree. As far as my source is aware, she left no suicide note and had not mentioned her plans to anyone.

Her death has hit the LFC community hard. "Sister Anahata felt that sadness and tragedy had followed her throughout the conventional world," my source said. "That's why she came to us at the Life Force Collective: to break the cycle of despair and begin living life in the light as she was intended. She'd worked hard to leave her past behind and was living a life of joy. When an influx of darkness from the outside world began dragging her down, we should have noticed. We should've been more attuned to our sister's well-being. But we were too absorbed in the struggle to maintain our way of life in the face of recent scrutiny. We were distracted, and we let her down. Her blood is on our hands."

The LFC is taking responsibility for Erin Buhrman's death. But how much of that responsibility should be shouldered by Poppy Parnell and her bosses at Werner Entertainment? Or those of us who have greedily gobbled up each new podcast? Or clicked excitedly over to Reddit to swap theories? Or spent time Googling the players in this real-life drama? Maybe this fevered consumption of a nearly thirteen-year-old tragedy was too much for her. Maybe we all have a little bit of blood on our hands.

chapter 5

I arrived at O'Hare travel-weary and with a headache. It had been ten years since I had last stood in its buzzing halls, heart-broken and desperate. On that occasion, I had left early in the morning, before Aunt A or Ellen was awake, crying inter-mittently the entire drive. By the time I reached the airport, I had no tears left. I had a pulsing headache from sobbing, my throat was sore, and my eyes were swollen and aching. Clutching a boarding pass for a one-way ticket to London purchased with the credit card Aunt A had given me for emer-gencies, and the passport I had obtained for a spring break trip to Mexico that had never come to fruition, I dialed Aunt A's number.

She answered the phone sleepily, and I felt a pang of guilt.

"Aunt A," I said, the words coming out cracked.

"Josie?" she asked, her voice quickly sharpening. "Are you all right?"

"No," I choked, a fresh sob working its way up through my chest. "I'm not."

"Are you hurt? Where are you? Tell me what's wrong."

"You can ask my sister what's wrong," I spit, more venom-ously than I had intended. "I'm not going to talk about it. I just want you to know I'm not coming home."

"Calm down. What did Lanie do?"

Hearing her name threatened to send me into a new set

of hysterics, but I swallowed it as best as I could. "I'm not—I can't. I'm sorry. But I want you to know how much I love you and how much I'm going to miss you. I'll write when I can—"

"*Josephine Michelle,*" Aunt A interrupted, her voice vibrating with emotion, "you do *not* abandon me like the rest of this family."

"I have to go, Aunt A," I whispered. "The car is in the long-term lot at O'Hare, okay? I'm sorry."

The worst part was that I wasn't sorry, not really. Not enough, at least. Aunt A was the kindest woman I'd ever known, with a patience and capacity for forgiveness that astounded me, and I should have at least felt guilty about hurting her. But I was so consumed by pain I was unable to consider anyone else's feelings.

And so I powered down my cell, cutting off Aunt A's protests, and then withdrew the largest allowable cash advance on the credit card, purchased an overpriced thriller at the airport bookstore, and waited to begin my new life.

I had not told Ellen about the flight delay, and part of me hoped she wouldn't be at the airport. I could turn around and be back in Brooklyn before the day was over. Or I could hole up in a hotel room for a few days, avoiding my needy family and well-intentioned Caleb and every person who thought my father's death was entertainment. Or I could just stretch out on the airport floor and sleep.

But Ellen was waiting at baggage claim, her golden hair held back by a pair of enormous black sunglasses, her spray-tanned hands on the hips of her black shift dress. She looked as though she'd stopped eating again, her skinny arms and narrow hips an almost comical juxtaposition to the breasts Peter had bought her for her last birthday. Despite everything, I couldn't help but smile when I saw Ellen. She remained exactly as expected: collagen-filled lips pursed, wearing a familiar expression of disdain as she surveyed the unwashed masses. I snuck up behind her and threw my arms around her.

With a satisfying shriek, Ellen squirmed away and whirled around. Her righteous anger morphed into alarm when she saw me.

"Good God, Josie, what have you done to yourself?"

"It's just hair," I said, touching it self-consciously.

"And thank heavens for that. I'll make an appointment for you with Mom's stylist. Don't worry."

I wasn't actually worried—I had come to appreciate how the slightly frazzled pixie cut mirrored my slightly frazzled mental state—but I nodded my acquiescence anyway. I knew from years of experience there was no point in arguing with Ellen—about anything, really, but especially about hair.

I retrieved my luggage from the carousel and followed Ellen to her car. She issued a lighthearted barb about the condition of my suitcase as I heaved it into the trunk, and then slammed the trunk shut and pulled me into a tight hug.

"I'm so glad you're here," she said, clasping me against her bony frame and nearly suffocating me with Chanel No. 5. Just as suddenly as she'd embraced me, she pushed me away. "I've missed you, you bitch. God. I can't believe how long it's been."

"I've missed you, too, Ellen," I said, smiling. "It's really good to see you. Even under the circumstances."

Her eyes softened. "I'm sorry about your mom, hon."

"Yeah." I nodded. "Thanks."

"Do you want to talk about it?"

"No," I said, climbing into the car. "I just want to think about something else for a bit. Tell me about you. Tell me about work."

Ellen obliged, happy as always to have an audience. She regaled me with news about her interior design business, her stepdaughters, and a trip to Venice she and Peter were planning. I welcomed the near-constant stream of chatter until a sign for Elm Park forced me back to reality.

"Ellen," I said suddenly, interrupting her monologue about the travails of learning Italian. "Is Lanie going to be there?"

Ellen pulled her sunglasses down. "Did I tell you that Isabelle wants to move in with her boyfriend? I know she's twenty and can do whatever she wants, but I think it's a mistake. I keep telling her, 'I know I'm only your stepmother, but he's not going to buy the cow when he gets the milk for free.'"

"I live with my boyfriend."

"Oh, right," Ellen said, putting a hand over her mouth in an exaggerated show of faux embarrassment. "No offense, of course, darling."

I knew I was playing right into her hand, but I couldn't help but respond. "Plus, you're only—what?—eight years older than her? Does she actually listen to you?"

"Why shouldn't she? I'm young and I'm beautiful and I'm

married to a rich man. I must be doing something right." Ellen glanced over at me. "I'm also kidding, Josie. It's okay to laugh."

The idea of Ellen making a self-deprecating joke was more amusing to me than the so-called joke itself, and I finally did laugh.

"You're not kidding and we both know it. Now, tell me: is Lanie going to be there?"

Ellen sighed. "Of course. Your sister might be a screwup, but she's not going to miss her own mother's funeral. What did you expect?"

I shrugged and slumped down in the bucket seat. "I guess a part of me thought she might be dead."

"Don't be so dramatic," Ellen ordered, stretching a hand out to squeeze my shoulder. "Just try not to think about her, okay, honey? This week is going to be hard enough without worrying about your sister."

I nodded my agreement, but inwardly my heart lurched—because when it came to Lanie, there was *always* something to worry about.

Seven miles north of Elm Park, after we had departed from the interstate and were traveling on a county route, we passed a familiar gravel road winding between a pair of desiccated cornfields. Part of me wanted to beg Ellen to turn down that road, follow its rutted path to the farmhouse that stood—or at least used to stand—at its terminus. The impulse was ridiculous, of course. There was nothing for us there anymore. Grammy and Pops had been gone for fifteen years, and the farm's new owners had probably ripped down the house and started factory farming on its footprint.

"The family farmer is a dying breed," Pops had told me once, lighting a pipe as we sat on the farmhouse porch together. I was ten years old and did not know what he meant, but I wanted to be taken seriously—more seriously than my sister and cousin, who were engaged in a squabble over some watercolors out back—and so I had nodded sagely. It wasn't until years later, after he was gone, that I understood. When Mom and Aunt A sold the farm, it was to a corporation, not another farming family. There was no soft-spoken man with a midwestern drawl and overalls, no friendly woman baking fresh apple pies and tending the chickens. Just cold, impersonal business.

It was hard to reconcile the farm being nothing more than a line on some corporate balance sheet. We had spent nearly every weekend on the farm, and I had pleasant, sepia-tinted memories of chasing chickens and playing hide-and-go-seek in the barn. In particular, the memory of our Fourth of July gathering in 2000 was etched on my heart. It was the last time we were all there: Grammy and Pops would be killed by a drunk driver less than one month later, and, three months after that, Uncle Jason would leave Aunt A. The Cave family had already moved into the house next door to ours. It was the beginning of the end.

But we didn't know what was coming for us, and so we celebrated. Uncle Jason had driven to Indiana and stocked up on fireworks, which made Mom and Aunt A cluck their tongues in disapproval and Pops's and Daddy's eyes light up with mischief. While we awaited nightfall, the adults prepared a feast. Pops supervised while Daddy and Uncle Jason grilled hamburgers and chicken breasts, drinking beers and telling bawdy jokes in muted tones. Mom set out an impressive array of salads: green, pasta, potato. Aunt A drank too much wine and ruined most of the deviled eggs she tried to prepare, leading us in a slurred rendition of "America the Beautiful" all the while. Grammy made three pies for dessert, including my father's favorite, pecan, even though she teased him it was a winter pie.

Snacking on sloppy deviled eggs, Lanie, Ellen, and I crept down to the pond. Our mothers' younger brother had drowned in the pond as a child, and we were forbidden to play there unsupervised—but that summer, twelve years old and practically grown up, we no longer felt obligated to obey such rules. We constructed makeshift fishing poles from sticks, dental floss, and safety pins, and used stale Cheetos and stolen bits of raw hamburger meat as bait, neither of which proved enticing to the fish we were certain were in the water.

A frog captured Lanie's attention, and she leaned forward, trying to coax it toward her cupped hands. But she misjudged the stability of the muddy bank and tumbled in head over heels. The water wasn't deeper than a foot or two, but she fell with a spectacular splash and emerged soaking wet and covered in algae. Ellen wrinkled her nose in disgust, and that was all the encouragement Lanie needed. She took off, chasing Ellen toward the farmhouse, slimy hands outstretched like a zombie. I ran on Lanie's heels, yelping with excitement. Lanie caught up with Ellen just as they reached the adults and smeared a handful of green algae across Ellen's face and through her golden hair. There was a quiet second, the calm before the storm, and then Ellen started to scream. Our mother had been horrified by Lanie's behavior, but Daddy and Aunt A laughed until they cried and even Grammy looked as though she was struggling not to chortle as she led Ellen and Lanie around the back of the house to hose off.

Later that night, as the sun dropped behind the horizon, we roasted marshmallows over a bonfire as Uncle Jason set up the fireworks. Lanie made a double-decker s'more for Ellen, who—this was years before she would become obsessed with calories—ate it with relish. The incident with the algae was forgotten. We were a family, and there was nothing that could come between us. Or so we thought.

Cold beads of sweat sprang up along my hairline when the WELCOME TO ELM PARK sign came into view, marking the spot where the cornfields gave way to the town's uninspired grid of paved streets and square lawns. Elm Park had once been a bustling town bursting with potential, but like so many small midwestern towns before it, its prospects had faded. By the time I left, the first of the factories was already gone, relocated to a country with cheaper labor; in the ensuing years, the other factories had followed, as did most of the big-box stores and both of the movie theaters. Ellen narrated all this as we drew closer to the city limits, her tone such that I expected little more than a ghost town, just boarded-up buildings and deteriorating homes.

But Elm Park looked just as I had remembered. The

welcome sign was the same weathered oval with faded green letters and paint peeling from the carved elm tree leaves decorating the border. Just beyond the sign I could see the dark, hulking hospital, and on the other side of the street, the 7-Eleven with a handful of loitering teenagers sipping Slurpees in front of it. I had the feeling that if I were close enough to see their faces, I'd recognize them.

Intellectually, I knew that wasn't true. Anyone young enough to be skulking about convenience stores would be too young for me to have known when I lived in Elm Park. But as Ellen and I drove farther into town, the uneasy sensation that the entire place had been undisturbed by time only intensified. The most noticeable changes I spotted were that the elementary school had a newer, shinier jungle gym and that a couple unfamiliar restaurants dotted the edge of campus. As Ellen drove past Ray's Bistro, a memory hit me so hard that I dug my fingers into the seat's upholstery to avoid crying out.

In the weeks before Ellen and I left for college, Aunt A had grown increasingly emotional about our departure. She had been following us around for weeks with watery eyes, offering to drive us to the mall or the swimming pool, despite both of us having driver's licenses (and having stopped hanging out at the mall years ago). I almost felt guilty about leaving, but I knew Aunt A didn't want us to stay in Elm Park forever.

Like Lanie seemed poised to do. We had once loved touring Elm Park College's campus with our father and imagining our own matriculation there (the dorm room we would share, the majors we would choose, the picnics we would have on the quad), but things had changed. I planned to attend the University of Illinois, which had an undergraduate enrollment of 32,000 people—10,000 more than the population of Elm Park—while Lanie rejected the idea of college altogether. She'd graduated from high school by the skin of her teeth and had refused to apply to college, despite Aunt A's pleading. We had no idea what she planned to do. She hadn't been living with us for months, and it had been weeks since I had seen her. The most recent sighting was brief, when I had caught her in the kitchen "borrowing" some money from Aunt A's purse.

Somehow, though, Aunt A had extracted a promise from Lanie to attend a going-away dinner at Ray's. Aunt A had dressed up for the occasion, wearing a silky tunic that disguised her slightly round figure and setting her long, glossy brown hair in rollers, and Ellen and I had followed her lead, both in sundresses with full skirts and lipstick. Our reservation time came and went without Lanie materializing. The three of us picked idly at the bread basket while Aunt A repeatedly sent the waiter away with assurances that our fourth would "just be a couple more minutes."

It wasn't long before neither Ellen nor our waiter could conceal their irritation, and Aunt A finally conceded defeat. As if on cue, just as our waiter disappeared into the kitchen with our drink and appetizer orders, my sister breezed through the door. In a room full of people dressed in their Sunday best, Lanie wore a white T-shirt with a ripped neckline, denim cutoffs, and mud-caked Dr. Martens boots. Her makeup was smeared, eyeliner collecting under her eyes in exaggerated shadows. Her septum piercing looked tarnished, like it possibly had blood on it. She didn't look like she had showered in days. And she was clearly high.

"I'm here," she announced loudly, drawing the attention of everyone in the room.

"Lanie," Aunt A hissed, gesturing to the empty seat beside her. "Sit down."

Lanie smirked and dropped into the seat.

"So nice of you to join us," Ellen said sarcastically.

Aunt A shot her a warning look and turned to Lanie. "We just ordered drinks and appetizers. Do you know what you want? I'll call the waiter over."

Lanie waved a hand in my direction without meeting my eyes. "I'll have whatever she's having."

Aunt A flagged down the waiter, who had emerged from the kitchen to stare distrustfully at us, and ordered a Diet Coke and a garden salad for Lanie.

"So what have you all been talking about?" Lanie asked, leaning back in her chair, her glazed red eyes jumping from Aunt A to Ellen and back, again not landing on me.

"You," Ellen said.

I kicked my cousin under the table. She glowered at me.

"Actually, we've been discussing how exciting it is that Ellen and Josie are leaving for college tomorrow," Aunt A said brightly.

"Yeah, it's fucking fantastic," Lanie sneered.

"Hey," I said sharply. "What's your problem?"

Ellen snorted, and Aunt A shot me a look that was equal parts disappointed and sympathetic. Lanie sat up, bobbing her neck like a snake ready to strike, and opened her mouth just as the waiter arrived with our drinks and salads.

"I don't want this," Lanie said as he tried to present her with a plate.

He hesitated, glancing at Aunt A for direction.

"I don't want this," Lanie repeated, her voice rising in volume. "Get it out of my fucking face."

"Of course, ma'am," the waiter said through gritted teeth, pulling the salad away.

"It's delicious," I said, taking a bite of my identical salad.

"You *would* think that," Lanie said. She looked around at all of us before standing up and throwing her napkin down on her seat. "I have to pee."

We chewed in silence for fifteen minutes until Aunt A went to check on her. Even before Aunt A returned to the table, I knew that Lanie was gone.

Discussion thread on www.reddit.com/r/ reconsideredpodcast, posted September 20, 2015

⬆ **Why should we believe her? (self.reconsideredpodcast)**
⬇

submitted 12 hours ago by notmyrealname

I haven't been able to stop thinking about episode 2 since it aired. It blows my mind that Warren was convicted on such ~little~ physical evidence. It really got me thinking: why should we believe Lanie? Everyone just took her at her word, but why? Especially after she lied the first time?

⬆ spuffyshipper 150 points 12 hours ago
⬇
I've been wondering the same thing. Didn't anyone question her at the time?

⬆ armchairdetective38 89 points 12 hours ago
⬇
She was the star witness for the prosecution and she was cross-examined by the defense team.

⬆ spuffyshipper 74 points 11 hours ago
⬇
But the defense team only accused her of being "confused," not of actually lying, right?

⬆ urugly 10 points 11 hours ago
⬇
what did you expect them to do? she was a pretty white girl and he was a big scary metal freak

⬆ armchairdetective38 89 points 11 hours ago
⬇
She was only 15 years old (16 by time of trial) and traumatized. The defense team wouldn't have wanted to push her too hard for fear of alienating the jury.

miranda_309 90 points 11 hours ago

This exactly.

Source: I am a public defender.

elmparkuser1 165 points 12 hours ago

IMHO, Lanie Buhrman is not a credible source. I grew up in Elm Park, and I was a freshman the year the twins were juniors. They had only been in public school for half a year at that point—they were homeschooled first, remember—and Lanie already had a really bad reputation. She ran around with a really rough crowd and was always in trouble. I walked in on her getting high in the girls bathroom one time at like 9 AM. I wouldn't trust her farther than I could throw her.

chapter 6

Aunt A lived in one of the older sections of town, her neighborhood populated by rambling Victorians in various states of disrepair. Some, like Aunt A's, had been renovated and maintained, while others had fallen into neglect and were blighted by peeling paint, decaying trim, and sloping roofs. Although Aunt A often referred to her home as a money pit, she took pride in its upkeep. It had been purchased during a more hopeful time in Aunt A's life when she thought she might fill all four bedrooms with a large family, and when she envisioned herself and her ex-husband spending long weekends together on restoration projects.

As a child, I had been captivated by the house's showy exterior, with its wraparound porch, turret, and widow's walk, so different from our own modest Dutch Colonial. It didn't take long after moving in for me to become disenchanted. Old homes might be glamorous from the outside, but inside they are drafty and haunted by constant, eerie creakings of indeterminate origin.

Unfolding myself from the passenger seat, I was almost flattened by a sweeping sense of déjà vu. Suddenly, I was fifteen again, standing in this same driveway, one hand clutching my sister's, the other wrapped around the handles of a suitcase. The mounting dread I had felt that afternoon returned, oozing darkly through my body. That had been the moment I realized everything was forever changed: my father was dead and my mother had retreated deep inside herself, further than ever before. The most frightening part was that this time it seemed permanent.

Aunt A stood on the porch holding her cat, Bubbles, in her arms, just as she had that long-ago afternoon. Her face even wore the same bittersweet smile. It pained me to see how much older my aunt looked. Aunt A's thick chestnut-colored hair was streaked with gray and pinned up in a loose bun that aged her ten years. Her familiar face was lined with distinct creases, and every part of her seemed more subject to gravity.

A lump formed in my throat.

"I'm sorry," I said without meaning to.

Aunt A smiled, her eyes glistening with tears, and she descended from the porch to enfold me in a warm, feline-scented embrace. "I know, darling. I know."

The lump dissolved into hot, salty tears that crowded my tear ducts, but I refused to allow them to fall. I had no right to cry. I was the perpetrator here; I had left Aunt A, just like her husband and her sister.

But the tears refused to be denied, and I pushed myself away from Aunt A before she could see them.

"Excuse me," I mumbled. "I need to use the restroom."

As the front door swung shut behind me, I heard Aunt A say to Ellen, "That poor girl."

Aunt A's kindness squeezed my heart and made me feel even worse. I should never have abandoned her.

* * *

I dried my tears in the downstairs bathroom, and then could not stop myself from scanning for evidence of my sister. I had forbidden Aunt A or Ellen to mention Lanie, and I had heard nothing of her since I had left Illinois all those years ago. Ellen once sent an email with the subject heading *News About Lanie* and I had deleted it without opening it, shaking with rage. I then sent Ellen a missive reminding her exactly why I had no interest in speaking with or about Lanie ever again, to which Ellen simply replied "Understood." Aunt A used to try to get me interested in Lanie's life, but, after the first dozen times I shut her down completely for even breathing my sister's name, she stopped making further attempts. I knew they both thought the total ban on anything related to my sister was extreme, but cutting her out completely was the only way I knew how to survive.

Now, though, back in the house where we had once both lived, I couldn't help but wonder what she had been up to all these years. I found nothing other than a photograph half hidden behind the sheet music on the upright piano. Lanie was wearing a wedding dress, a white tulle confection that did not suit her, and standing between Aunt A and Ellen, both of whom were dressed in black. No one looked happy. Lanie's face was puffy, and her eyes were avoiding the camera. Aunt A was clenching her jaw the way she did when she felt resolute, and Ellen wore the resentful expression of a hostage. The picture might have been humorous if it hadn't been my family. No one told me Lanie had gotten married. I wondered who her husband was, if it had lasted. I wondered if she was happy.

I slid the picture behind the sheet music again, flipped over so the image didn't face out into the room.

"Josie."

I turned to find Peter, Ellen's husband, standing in the doorway. He was a good-looking man in his mid-fifties, twice as old as Ellen, tall and broad with an expansive midsection, and had the booming voice to match.

"Peter, hi."

"It's been a long time," Peter said, pulling me into an awkward half-hug where he clasped one of my hands and also patted me on the back.

I extracted myself from the embrace and nodded in agreement. It had been three years since Ellen and Peter honeymooned in Fiji, a veritable hop-skip-and-jump from New Zealand, where Caleb and I had been living at the time. The newlyweds had swanned into Auckland, Ellen unnaturally tan, and had treated us to a champagne-filled dinner at a restaurant way out of our price range. After we kissed them goodbye, Caleb had squinted at me, a little drunk and a little dazed, and asked, "*This* is your family?"

Peter was a little rounder than he had been then, and his hair was striped with silver, but his affable smile was the same. "How're you holding up?"

"I've been better."

"Well, you look good."

"Shush, Peter, she does not," Ellen said, stepping into the room. "I know you're just being polite, but honestly. You're not to give her any encouragement about that hair."

"Don't listen to her," Peter said, winking at me. "Ellen

just wants to be sure that she's the only blonde in the room."

Ellen laughed and swatted her husband away. Their playfulness surprised me; I'd always taken a rather cynical view of their marriage. Ellen claimed vaguely to have met Peter through mutual acquaintances, but she had once drunkenly confided to me they met online. I could only imagine their respective profiles, and assumed that Ellen had selected Peter for his money and power and that he had chosen her for her youth and beauty. If Ellen remembered that too much wine had loosened the truth about their origin story, she pretended that she did not. The one time I mentioned it, I practically heard her eyes narrowing over the phone. "I have no idea what you're talking about," she had said coolly, and promptly changed the subject.

"Now," she said, grabbing my shoulders and studying me, "we really do need to do something about that. I called Mom's stylist, but she's booked up until Friday. Your mother's visitation is tomorrow, and we cannot have you looking like an escaped mental patient. Wait here, I'll run to Target and pick up a box of hair dye."

"But—" I started.

"No buts," Ellen commanded, holding up her hand and snapping her fingers shut to mime a closing mouth. "I'm in charge here."

Ellen was a natural choice for a leader: opinionated, confident, and in possession of an enviable head of glossy blond hair. At fifteen, I had so eagerly welcomed Ellen's guidance that I practically genuflected at her feet. Back then, the anxiety over switching from homeschooling to public school had me breaking out in hives and having dreams in which entire football fields of teenagers queued up to take turns laughing at me. Without Ellen to dictate my wardrobe or provide a map for navigating the school's social minefield, I would have crumbled. Ellen's lessons on wielding curling irons and mascara wands distracted me from the devastating loss of my father and the painful unraveling of my mother, and for that I was grateful.

On my first day of classes, I put on the outfit Ellen had picked out for me, curled my hair the way she had shown me, and painted my face as she had dictated. When I stepped back to look at myself in the mirror, I was pleased. I looked cheerful and pleasant, not at all like someone with a dark past.

Ellen smiled approvingly as I entered the kitchen.

"Don't you look lovely," Aunt A said, looking up from her cup of coffee.

As I grinned and pirouetted, my mother floated in for her morning glass of orange juice. Her hand on the refrigerator door, she paused and frowned at me.

"What do you think, Mom?" I asked tentatively, fluffing my hair for her benefit.

"The boys will love you," she said hollowly. "Be careful."

Then she slammed the refrigerator shut and retreated up the steps with the juice container in one hand, a dirty glass in the other.

"She's just tired," Aunt A said quietly, laying a hand on my shoulder. "She didn't mean—"

I shook her off. "I'm fine."

"Where's your sister?" Ellen demanded, pouring herself a bowl of cereal.

Aunt A checked her watch and yelled up the back staircase. "Hurry up, Lanie! Don't want to be late on your first day!"

It was another ten minutes before Lanie finally slunk down to the kitchen. Ellen paused with a spoonful of Special K on its way to her mouth.

"What the hell?"

"Language, Ellen," Aunt A scolded.

I swiveled in my chair and followed Ellen's gaze. Lanie was barefaced and plainly unshowered, her thick dark hair knotted and hanging in her face. She was wearing a black thermal undershirt that I recognized as our mother's, the same beat-up Levis that she had been wearing for at least the last year—the ones that had the beginnings of a hole in one knee and an ink stain on the pocket—and a pair of ratty cross-trainers.

Without a word, Lanie headed for the box of granola bars on the counter.

"Hey," Ellen said, standing up. "What happened to the outfit I picked out for you?"

Lanie shrugged, unwrapping a granola bar. "I changed my mind."

"You can't wear that," Ellen said, crossing her arms over her chest.

"Says who," Lanie demanded, jutting her chin out. Her eyes glittered with an unfamiliar relish of challenge, an eagerness for a fight.

"That's not what we agreed on," Ellen insisted.

"Leave her alone," Aunt A commanded. "Your cousin can dress herself however she sees fit. She doesn't need your approval."

"I'm just trying to help, Mom. She's going to make a bad impression on the first day."

"Your opinion has been noted. I'm sure Lanie will take it into consideration, but the decision is hers." Aunt A paused and turned to Lanie. "Although, dear, you might want to brush your hair."

Lanie smirked through a mouthful of granola bar.

She didn't brush her hair that day, or for a week thereafter. Only when it was so greasy and gnarled that the school counselor called home to check up on her did she consent to wash it. Her clothing never improved. Despite Ellen's repeated attempts to cajole (and some days force) her into clean pants and sweaters, Lanie continued to dress herself as though she were a vagrant and developed the habit of rimming her eyes thickly in black liner.

But it was more than just her appearance. Ellen, in her quest to aid our transition to public school, had compiled a list of unsavory characters best avoided. The list took up two pages of college-ruled notebook paper, front and back, and warned us away from, among others, terminal nerds, band geeks, the entire girls' volleyball team, and kids who listened to My Chemical Romance. Topping that list was anyone in the Strong family, and it was Ryder Strong who Lanie immediately gravitated toward. A skinny girl with a mean little mouth, scabby arms, and overprocessed kinky blond hair, Ryder was infamous for coming to class in seventh grade with a flask full of Jack Daniel's and stabbing one of her many cousins with an X-Acto knife during a school assembly that past fall. In no time, Lanie was running around on Ryder's sneakered heels, smoking Marlboros in the girls' bathroom, and cheering as guys with stick-and-poke tattoos nearly killed themselves with skateboards and half-pipes.

It wasn't much longer before Aunt A began to get phone calls from the school saying that Lanie had skipped class, and then Lanie started coming home smelling like sweet smoke, and then she started not coming home at all.

After Ellen had returned my hair and eyebrows to a shade closer to their natural hue, she proclaimed herself exhausted and retired with Peter to her old bedroom. I snickered at the thought of Peter's large, distinguished form sleeping under Ellen's pink plaid comforter underneath her old Britney Spears and *NSYNC posters.

But me? I dreaded the thought of going up to my and Lanie's old bedroom almost as much as I dreaded being alone with my thoughts, so I was grateful when Aunt A opened a bottle of red wine. We poured it into coffee mugs, shamelessly filling them to the brim, and sat on the couch together, Bubbles stretching his soft, ancient body across our combined laps.

"She did a good job," Aunt A said, nodding toward my hair.

"What, you didn't like the blond, either?" I asked, trying to make a joke even as my voice cracked.

Aunt A reached over and squeezed my hand. "Are you all

right, sweetheart? It's okay if you're not. This family has had a rough go of it."

I bit my lip and shook my head. "I don't know how any of us could be all right. Mom's dead, and we can't even properly grieve her because of that stupid podcast."

"That *podcast*," Aunt A spit, her words wobbling with venom. "Honestly. What trash. How dare that woman call herself a journalist. Journalists cover real news. They don't spend their time interfering in decade-old closed cases. It's disgusting."

"It is. I feel sick every time I overhear some stranger talking about who *really* killed Chuck Buhrman." I swallowed the question that began to rise: *But what if it wasn't Warren Cave?* I hated Poppy Parnell for making me doubt the only closure we'd ever had.

"You know who we have to thank for all this, don't you? Melanie Cave. As if that woman hasn't done enough. Carrying on with your father, raising the monster who killed him, and now refusing to let him rest in peace. She paints herself as a victim, but she's the real linchpin in all of this."

I remembered how fascinated I had been with glamorous Melanie Cave when she, her husband, and her son had first moved next door. With her perfectly coiffed ash-blond hair and enticing apricot-colored lipstick, she had seemed the polar opposite of my own mother with her loose, inky hair and bare feet. My interest would later feel like betrayal when I learned I wasn't the only Buhrman fascinated with the contrast between Melanie Cave and Erin Buhrman.

"Have you listened to it?"

Aunt A nodded with a grimace. "The first two episodes. Have you?"

"Same. I downloaded the third episode at the airport, but I haven't listened to it yet."

"Don't," Aunt A said, shuddering. "I'm not listening anymore. I wish I hadn't started. The only reason I did was because everyone was talking about it, from the folks on TV to the other teachers at school. Even the students, and they're no more than thirteen years old. I thought I owed it to your mother to know what they were saying about her. Well, that and I wanted to understand why there were so many people camped out in my front yard."

I twisted around to look out the picture window. I saw no evidence of campers, just a row of pedestrian trash cans lined up on the curb, awaiting garbage pickup.

"They're gone now. Apparently, they have *some* human decency and have made themselves scarce since your mother's death. But before that, there'd be ten or twelve of them out there at any given time. They were mostly young people with iPhones and handheld video recorders. I couldn't even step outside to pick up the mail without them shouting for a quote for their YouTube channels or blogs or whatchamacallits, or asking about the whereabouts of you girls."

I flinched, hating the idea of Aunt A facing down aggressive fans on her own. "I'm sorry you had to deal with that. I had no idea it was so bad. They never found me in New York."

"I suppose that's one benefit of living in that concrete jungle. There are enough people there that you can be anonymous when you want to be."

I nodded silently. The city's sheer crush of humanity did make it easy for a person to blend in, but I suspected Poppy Parnell and her fans hadn't been able to find me—assuming they had tried—because I had legally changed my name from Buhrman to Borden. Aunt A knew about the name change but seemed uncomfortable with it, sending all holiday and birthday cards addressed only to "Josephine."

"I've called the police several times already," she continued. "They're usually able to dispel the campers for the night, but they just come back . . . and bring their friends. And the police claim they can't do anything about that so-called journalist unless I get a restraining order, which seems like making a mountain out of . . . well, out of a smaller mountain." Aunt A shook her head wearily. "Maybe I should. I know your sister's thoughts about it. She said that Parnell woman has been going through her trash. Her *trash*. If I catch that woman anywhere near the trash cans, I won't be able to set that court date fast enough."

"Lanie . . . lives in town?" I asked, piecing together her words.

Aunt A smiled gently and took my hand. "She does. You should call her, Josie. Let her know that you're here. You two have a lot of catching up to do."

I pulled my hand away. "There's nothing I want less than to catch up with my sister."

Our old bedroom was just as we had left it: the walls covered in blue-and-white-striped wallpaper; the twin beds spread with matching blue-and-white quilts; a long-forgotten stuffed bear propped against the pillows on my bed. The hulking computer still sat atop the white desk, the corkboard behind it still dotted with faded snapshots and ten-year-old invitations to high school graduation parties. Dusty pink bottles of Bath & Body Works body sprays and Victoria's Secret perfume still lined up on the dresser, and there was an Ashlee Simpson album still inside the CD player/alarm clock.

I picked up a small model of the Washington Monument from the desk, rubbing my thumb over its jagged tip, broken when Lanie, angry that I had told Aunt A she skipped school, had flung it at me. It had once been a tangible reminder of happier times, a memento from a family vacation to Washington, DC, taken the summer before everything had been completely destroyed. It was our father at his best: eager to share his extensive knowledge of American history, almost giddy during the tour of the White House's East Wing. Even our mother, though she disliked crowds and had been in a rather bleak mood at that point, seemed to enjoy herself. We took in the cherry blossoms and the monuments as a family, and then my father and I headed for the National Museum of American History, while my mother and sister went to the National Gallery of Art, chattering excitedly about the impressionist works they would see.

I set down the souvenir and crossed to the family photos Aunt A had assembled for us, framed snapshots clustered on the walls. My fingertips brushed the dusty frames, skirting the images within that seemed from another lifetime: Lanie and me as grumpy infants in our mother's arms, her eyes tired but her smile wide and genuine; Lanie and me at five years old, looking on with giddy grins as our father carved a jack-o'-lantern with a wicked-looking kitchen knife; Lanie and me flanking Ellen as the three of us perched on a bale of hay, Pops holding bunny ears up to Lanie's head, Grammy laughing and only half in the shot. I stared at my sister's childish, innocent face and fought the urge to rip all the frames from the wall.

Instead, I sank down onto the bed, pulling the stuffed bear into my arms. Lanie and I had received matching bears as Christmas gifts when we were five. I had named mine Brother John after the oversleeping friar in the nursery rhyme. We had learned the song from our father, who would sing it to us each night. Because our father otherwise never sang—he always said he couldn't carry a tune even if it had handles—the song took on an almost mythic quality. Brushing matted fur out of the bear's beaded eyes, I began to sing quietly.

"Are you sleeping, are you sleeping? Brother John, Brother John. Morning bells are ringing, morning bells are ringing. Ding dang dong, ding dang dong."

Without knowing why, I shivered. Why had the familiar tune unsettled me?

I squeezed the bear to my chest and wished desperately that my arms were around Caleb instead of this little sack of fake fur and beans. Poor Caleb, alone in our apartment and still weary from jet lag. He was probably too tired to make himself dinner and had ordered in pad thai. I struggled to remember if there were even any groceries in the refrigerator. I wanted to be home, taking care of him.

I texted him to say that I had arrived in Elm Park and that I loved him, but I was almost immediately overwhelmed by a flurry of responses inquiring about the morales of Ellen and myself and when I wanted him to come. Any answers would have been lies, and I couldn't bring my fingers to form them. Instead, I closed my Messages app and promised myself I would send him a note in the morning, a ploy that would permit me to ignore the questions and simply apologize for failing to respond. I could claim I turned my phone off so I could get some sleep, or better yet, that my phone had died and I had forgotten the charger at home.

And then someday, maybe I would finally stop lying to the man I loved.

In the meantime, I flouted Aunt A's warning to not listen to any more of the podcast, plugged in my earbuds, and hit *Play*.

Excerpt from transcript of *Reconsidered: The Chuck Buhrman Murder*, Episode 3: "The (Un)Usual Suspects," September 21, 2015

One of the questions I'm asked most often is: "Poppy, if Warren Cave didn't kill Chuck Buhrman, *who did*?"

I don't really have an answer. To be perfectly clear, I'm not even certain that Warren Cave *didn't* kill Chuck Buhrman. He seems sincere to me, but gut feelings aren't the same thing as evidence. He might have shot Chuck Buhrman, he might not have. All I'm doing is considering all the possibilities.

Let's explore some of the alternate suspects.

One of the most obvious is Andrew Cave, Warren's father and Melanie's cuckolded husband. Countless people have told me that Andrew discovered his wife's affair on the same day Chuck was killed, giving him a possible motive. He also owned a registered handgun, giving him access to a weapon—although ballistics testing later determined this was not the murder weapon. Furthermore, on the day in question—allegedly after leaving his wife—Andrew Cave drove upstate to his hometown in the Chicago suburbs. A dozen people saw him in a local sports bar that night, and he got into a fistfight that landed him in the emergency room.

As long as we're considering spouses, you might say, what about Erin Buhrman? Like Andrew Cave, Erin had an alibi for the night her husband was killed. She was staying with a friend who was recovering from oral surgery, and the friend's neighbors confirmed Erin's car was parked in front of the house all night. Unlike Andrew Cave, Erin did not know about the affair between Chuck and Melanie until after Chuck's death. She testified that she first learned about it from the newspaper. Moreover, she was clearly crushed by the death of her husband, so distraught that she ended up joining a cult. Again, I understand that gut feelings are not evidence, but it seems unlikely that she could've been cold-blooded enough to commit the murder.

While Chuck was generally well liked by both colleagues and students, there were a couple of professional skirmishes that engendered ill will. In the spring of 2002, Chuck caught a student cheating during a final exam and reported her to the administration. She was expelled, and left several angry voicemails on Chuck's office line. Could the student have been so angry over this that she came back months later and killed him? It seems like an outlandish theory, but my initial examination into this student has turned up a sealed criminal record. I'm still digging, and I'll keep you updated when I learn more.

In another academic dustup, the year before Chuck was killed a fellow history professor was up for tenure. Chuck opposed granting it on the basis that this professor had published a paper espousing a controversial position that Chuck felt would reflect poorly on the school. Other members of the Elm Park College History Department, none of whom would consent to being quoted on the record, told me that things became heated. The other professor did not receive tenure and immediately thereafter left the school. I understand he now teaches at a community college in Iowa. Is that the kind of grudge that's serious enough to kill? I don't know.

Here's what else we're not sure of: Chuck's former colleagues also mentioned some rumors that Chuck had been carrying on with students and possibly other professors, but no one had anything to substantiate these claims. No one could even produce a name. If he was indeed carrying on multiple affairs, he was being discreet. Could one of Chuck's paramours have been behind his murder? After all, they say hell hath no fury like a lover scorned . . .

chapter 7

I switched off the podcast, but not before memories of my father's murder began running on an insistent, horrifying loop through my head. That day had started so well: It was a beautiful Saturday in late fall, the sun shining and the air crisp. Our mother went out to help her friend, and, as she had been going through an unusually dark period even by her standards, I was joyful, believing this outing to be a harbinger of good things to come. Our father was cheerful, and Lanie and I spent most of the day outdoors with him, raking leaves and playing tennis at the park. We ordered in pizza for a special treat, and then Lanie and I turned in early, worn out from the day's activities.

"Today was really fun," I said to Lanie as I snuggled underneath my covers.

"Yeah," Lanie said, sounding distracted. "Do you hear that? Is Dad on the phone?"

"I think it's just the TV. Why?"

Lanie was silent for so long that I almost dropped off to sleep, but then she said, "Josie? Can I tell you something?"

"Of course."

She lowered her voice to a whisper. "I read Mom's journal."

"What?" I said sharply, sitting up and sending my sister a glare that she couldn't see in the dark. "Lanie, that's *private*. She's going to be really mad."

"Do you know *why* it's private?" Lanie said, her voice sharpening a bit. "She's been keeping things from us. She wrote that—"

"I don't want to hear it," I insisted. Our mother had always been very clear that her journals were strictly off-limits, for no one's eyes but her own.

"Fine," she hissed, clicking on a flashlight.

"Lanie," I protested. "Come on. If you want to read, go read downstairs or something. I'm really tired."

"No, I want to read in bed. Just close your eyes."

I sighed loudly to signal my displeasure and rolled onto my side as Lanie reached under her mattress and grabbed a tattered paperback copy of *Interview with the Vampire*. She had bought the scandalous book for a quarter at the library book sale, sneaking it underneath approved copies of *The Odyssey* and *Little Women*. I knew she kept *The Vampire Lestat* and Stephen King's *It* in her hiding place behind the sink in the playhouse, and I briefly considered using that knowledge as leverage to get her to turn off the light, but I was too tired to argue.

Sometime later, I awoke with a start, images of bursting fireworks in my head. Disoriented, unsure how long I had been asleep or what had awoken me, I sat up and looked at Lanie's bed. It was empty. Downstairs, the back door slammed. Fear pricked through my veins, and, scarcely daring to breathe, I listened intently for other noises. The house was eerily silent.

Suddenly, footsteps pounded up the stairs. I clenched my blankets to my chest, nearly blacking out from terror. Was someone in the house?

The bedroom door banged open, and a scream tore through my throat before I realized it was just my sister.

Lanie, face ashen and eyes wild, gestured frantically for me to be quiet as she raced to the window. Pressing her forehead against the glass, she squinted into our dark backyard. A small moan escaped her lips and she muttered something that sounded like "first the girl."

"What did you say?" I squeaked out.

She whirled to face me, dark braids swinging as if electrified. The expression on her face—cornflower eyes dark, pale cheeks hollowed by shadows, jaw bulging with clenched teeth—stopped my heart.

"Lanie, you're scaring me," I said when she didn't immediately say anything. "What's going on? Should we get Dad?"

"Dad's dead," she said hoarsely.

I gaped at her. *Dead?* Even as my stomach dropped, inappropriate laughter burbled up in my throat. Our father—our strong, vital father, the man who had earlier run us ragged on the tennis court—couldn't be *dead*. The very idea was absurd. *"What?"*

"He's dead," she repeated, her voice wavering.

"No," I said, climbing out of bed. "No, that's not true. We'll just go downstairs and—"

"Don't!" she shrieked, lunging at me and catching me by the arm. Her fingernails bit into my skin, causing drops of blood to rise to the surface. I barely felt it—I was too preoccupied with my sister's naked terror. My sister was the most fearless person I knew, and she was scared out of her mind.

"You can't go down there," she said, squeezing my arm more tightly.

Numbly, I nodded.

"Now help me," she commanded, beginning to drag the plastic milk crates we used for storage over to the door. Books and sports equipment spilled from them as she stacked them in front of the exit. "Come on. Help me. *Please*. Before . . ."

I shivered at the ominous *before* and began grabbing blindly at objects to add to the barricade. "Before what? Is someone else in the house?"

Lanie shuddered and mumbled something indistinct.

"Tell me," I insisted desperately, catching at her arm. "What happened? Is Dad really . . . ? And why are you so sweaty?"

"Let go of me!" she whispered, shoving me away roughly. I tripped over a loose book and smacked my head on the bedframe, igniting a flurry of stars in my vision. I cried out in pain, and clutched a hand to my head.

"Shut up," she hissed wildly. *"Shut up!"*

I held my hands over my mouth to hold in any inadvertent squeaks. "Is someone else in the house?"

Lanie grabbed me by my arm and pulled me into the closet, pulling the door shut behind us. We huddled together on the floor in the pitch-darkness, straining to hear anything out of the ordinary, but any noise was drowned out by our thundering hearts and ragged breath.

"Someone's in the house," I whispered, no longer a question. "Lanie, we have to call the police."

"No," she whispered fiercely. "We can't."

"But—"

"No," she insisted, squeezing my hand so hard I thought my bones would break.

"Why not? What happened?"

"Dad," she said haltingly. "I should . . . I shouldn't . . . I have to tell you."

"Tell me what? What happened?"

"Downstairs. Dad. I shouldn't . . ." she trailed off. "It's my fault."

"Lanie?" I whispered, my stomach plummeting.

"God, Josie," she whimpered. "We're all fucked."

Fitful sleep finally came around five in the morning, only for me to awaken suddenly an hour later, panicked about the people I would see at the visitation. I was well aware of the gossip my family had once inspired; I could only imagine the podcast and my mother's death had revitalized old rumors and whipped them into a fever pitch. I pulled the covers over my head as a defense against the impending morning, and must have fallen asleep again because the next thing I knew it was noon and Ellen was tugging the covers off me.

"Get up!" she commanded, clapping her hands together sharply. "The family viewing starts in thirty minutes."

Startled, I sat up in bed. "I swear I set my alarm."

"Well, you either didn't or you turned it off. No time for a formal inquisition. Just get up and get in the shower."

I swung my feet over the side of the bed obediently and paused as a wave of nausea swept over me. "Ugh," I said, clutching my head. "I think I'm sick."

"Do you see this black hair dye under my nails?" Ellen said, holding up a hand. "I look like some sort of tragic emo kid. I didn't ruin a perfectly good gel manicure for nothing. Get up."

"I'm getting up," I insisted. "I'm just . . . ugh."

"Listen," Ellen said, sitting down on the bed, her voice softening. "I get it. This sucks. In so many ways. But we've got to go to this visitation."

My chest tightened and my eyes stung with tears, and with a start, I realized this wasn't sickness: this was grief.

"I can't imagine my mother wanting us to gather in some stodgy funeral home to remember her," I sniffled. "I'm sure she'd rather we be outside, spreading sunshine or whatever."

"I know, honey," Ellen said, wrapping an arm around my shoulders and pulling me close. "But funerary rituals aren't for the dead. They're for the living. They're for my mom."

With a pang, I remembered the aching sadness in Aunt A's eyes. I had come all the way to Elm Park; there was no sense in skipping the visitation. "You're right."

"Of course I am," she said, pushing me away playfully. "Now go get in the shower. You stink."

I emerged freshly scrubbed and smelling decidedly better to find that Aunt A and Ellen had already gone to the funeral home. They had left behind Peter and his daughters, who had arrived from Chicago that morning. Sophie, a girl in her late teens with carroty hair so vibrant it couldn't be natural, was ironing an unfamiliar black dress for me.

"That's not mine," I said dully.

She smiled brightly. "Ellen thought you might want to wear this instead."

I nodded, ready to surrender responsibility for my appearance to my cousin. It was of little surprise to me that Isabelle, the older sister, the one who wanted to live with her boyfriend, was ready to apply my makeup.

"Wait," I said as she picked up a mascara wand. "Let's skip the mascara. I'll just end up crying and it'll run."

"Sorry," Isabelle said, smiling apologetically. "But Ellen instructed me to insist that you wear mascara. She said, and I quote, people will expect material evidence of grief."

"She thought of everything, huh?"

"She always does," Peter said, handing me a tumbler of whiskey.

It was his contribution I appreciated most. I downed the drink in two gulps, the bitter, oaky flavor settling on my tongue and tasting like dread.

On the way to the visitation, Peter fiddled with the radio at a stoplight and for a few seconds a Dire Straits song filled the car. A sudden memory of my mother dancing along to the same song shook me, and I realized I had made a mistake. I had spent the past night obsessing over my father's death, when I should have been thinking about my mother's. After all, if the statistics posted on the Reconsidered webpage were to be believed, over five million people were currently focused on my father's death. Someone had to remember my mother.

More than that, though, someone had to remember her the way she deserved. Poppy Parnell's fans knew my mother only as a passive victim; they thought of her as a jilted woman, a heartbroken widow, a woman destroyed by her own demons. They didn't know that my mother was smart, or that, even after she dropped out of college to have Lanie and me, she never stopped studying. It had been our mother's idea to homeschool us, an idea that our father initially fought, arguing Mom would be in over her head. But she had taken the responsibility seriously, sending away for textbooks and workbooks and developing lesson plans. Even toward the end, when her black moods were arriving more frequently and lasting longer, she remained adamant about teaching us. She was dedicated to sharing her knowledge with her daughters.

Similarly, the fans didn't know that my mother had a beautiful singing voice, or that she liked to paint, or that she once nursed a bird with a broken wing back to health. They didn't know that my mother had invented new endings to fairy tales to protect Lanie and me when we were children: in her versions, the Big Bad Wolf shoved Grandma in a closet rather than devouring her, and the trolls that lived under the bridges were only misunderstood.

I knew that my mother had some struggles, and that she always had. Sometimes she treated all of us strangely, refusing to speak to our father and behaving as though Lanie and I were much younger than we actually were. And there were times when she wouldn't come out of her room for days, and sometimes she refused to wear anything other than a thin floral nightgown. But those things didn't define my mother. She was kind and sweet and we'd loved her.

Just as certainly as I loved her, though, I hated her. She

had left us deliberately twice: once for California, and once when she departed this plane of existence. I would have to bid farewell to a body that my mother no longer inhabited.

I'd have to utter the goodbye that she had left unsaid.

Peter offered me his arm as we exited the car twenty minutes later, and I took it even though I didn't really think I needed the support. The funeral home did not look threatening. It was just a one-story brick building with a small concrete porch and ornamental portico. If not for the location—squeezed between #1 Nails and Merle's Pizza House—and the tidy sign advertising WILHELM FUNERAL HOME in a plain font, it could have been someone's residence. The foyer, which smelled strongly of floral air freshener, was more ostentatious than the exterior of the funeral home, with gold-and-cream-striped wallpaper and thick navy carpeting with a red-and-cream floral pattern. Across the room, a huge floral arrangement stood before an enormous, gilt-trimmed mirror. I caught a glimpse of my reflection and was surprised to find I looked remarkably calm. I was less surprised to see that Ellen was right about the hair. Of course.

On our left was an open doorway, a brass plaque bearing my mother's name beside the doorframe. ERIN A. (BLAKE) BUHRMAN was printed in small, dignified letters—something so unlike what my ethereal mother would have chosen for herself that I nearly laughed out loud. I swallowed the inappropriate laughter and my body shook with the effort. Peter, thinking I was holding back tears, put a comforting hand on my shoulder.

I was still on the verge of laughter as I stepped through the doorway, but then something shiny caught my eye and I realized it was the edge of the coffin—my mother's coffin, which contained my mother's body—gleaming from the front of the room. The laughter died in my throat, hardening into a painful lump. I couldn't go any farther. Other mourners (or, as the case likely was, rubberneckers—tragedy draws horrible people like flies to honey) were beginning to arrive, and I was distinctly aware that I needed to complete the most gruesome part, the part where I confronted my mother's lifeless form. But I couldn't move.

"It's okay," Ellen whispered, materializing at my side. "You can do this."

"I can't," I said, panic rising in my throat like warm lightning.

"You can," she assured me, her voice smooth and confident as ever. "Come on. I'm right here."

Clutching Ellen's hand like it was the only scrap of driftwood in a dark and punishing ocean, I took a few halting steps forward. My eyes darted desperately in every direction but toward the casket: to Aunt A, deep in conversation with Reverend Glover, who had grown thin and papery since I had seen him last; to Isabelle and Sophie, whose eyes were glued to their respective iPhones; to a small cluster of round women in dark dresses gathered by the far wall. And then I was standing in front of the polished casket with my heart in my throat. I forced myself to look down, my head turning before my eyes followed.

Her face was at once the face I remembered from my

childhood and yet something else entirely. The features were visually similar, but could have been molded from plastic. Her once-magnificent hair was cropped short and peppered with white strands. Spots formed in my peripheral vision.

I broke away from Ellen and lurched for the exit. Ellen took a step to follow me, but I waved her off.

"I'm fine," I lied, my tongue thick. The body in front of me was not my mother.

It could not be my mother.

I weaved my way through the crowd of bodies in the entryway, keeping my gaze on the ground to avoid accidental eye contact until I reached the women's restroom. I stumbled inside and leaned over one of the sinks, grasping the cool porcelain. With the tactile sensation of the sink to ground me, I took several deep, ragged breaths.

Each time I thought I might have succeeded in composing myself, that it might be safe to leave the bathroom, the irrational thought *That wasn't my mother* bubbled up from deep within and I was hyperventilating all over again. I had not been prepared for the disorienting sensation of seeing my mother's corpse, or the pain and regret that it had inspired. Hurt and devastation surged through me, making it hard for me to breathe.

Behind me, one of the toilets flushed. I straightened my spine and checked my reflection, wiping at my running mascara with my fingers.

My eyes were still on the mirror when she emerged from the stall. Our eyes locked, widened. We both gasped.

"Josie," my sister said, her voice shaking. "You look great."

"So do you," I intoned automatically.

But she really did. Lanie looked better than I had expected her to, better than me. She had put on weight, but only enough so that she no longer looked emaciated. She had a short pixie cut—a better cut than the hack job I had done to my own hair—and her makeup was soft, understated, and surprisingly tasteful. As I took her in, cataloguing her well-tailored clothing and her pale-pink lipstick, I noticed she was leaning first on one kitten-heeled foot and then the other, picking at the skin alongside her manicured nails. The corner of her mouth was twitching, and her eyes darted back and forth from me to the door. If she didn't look so well, I would've assumed she was strung out.

Lanie glanced at the door again. "Did you just get here?"

"Yeah, a few minutes ago."

"When did you get to town?"

"Yesterday afternoon."

"Were you going to call me?"

"I didn't know you lived here," I said, ignoring her real question.

Lanie narrowed her eyes slightly. "You didn't?"

I held up a hand to stop her further inquiry. "Lanie, can we not do this right now?"

Lanie's face softened and she reached out as though she was going to touch my shoulder, but she seemed to catch herself and brought her arm back to her side. "Okay. Have you . . . seen the body?"

I tried to speak but choked instead. "Briefly."

I tasted salt and realized that tears were streaming down my face. I was furious at my body for betraying me, for falling apart in front of my sister. *She* was the one who couldn't control herself, who couldn't keep it together. *I* was the composed sister, the one who could manage her emotions. Or, at least, that was how it was supposed to be.

"I haven't seen her yet," Lanie said quietly, wiping away my tears with her soft thumbs. "I'm scared."

"It's awful," I warned. "But I'll go with you. If you want."

"Please," she said, taking my hand. Even though we hadn't seen each other in years, and we hadn't been friends in an eternity, her palm against mine felt right. We exited the restroom hand in hand, all the bad blood between us forgotten for the moment.

It was a moment that lasted only until the door closed behind us and we spotted the one person who could splinter us again.

Adam appeared virtually unchanged. He looked a little older and considerably more tired, but he still had the same golden hair, those same cola-brown eyes, that same lanky build. He still looked like Adam, and that fact alone was enough to fling an icy stake through my heart. I unconsciously dropped my sister's hand.

Adam's eyes widened and he exhaled my name: "Josie."

My heart rate quickened as immediately as if someone had flipped a switch, and before I could even sort out what that meant or chastise myself for it, I saw her.

No more than seven or eight years old, she stood at Adam's side, looking down at her handheld tablet. I didn't need to see her face to know who she was; that cloud of black hair was unmistakable.

As if she felt my gaze on her, she flickered her saucer-like, pale-blue eyes up at me. Delicate dark brows knit in confusion, and she turned to Adam.

"Dad," she whispered loudly, "why does that lady look like Mom?"

The corners of my vision darkened, and my knees went weak. I backed away from them, unable to tear my eyes off the child, who was returning my stare with one of her own. Lanie reached for my arm, but I brushed her off. As I pivoted and plunged back into the crowd, I could hear Lanie and Adam both calling my name, a traitorous chorus.

It didn't make any sense. None of it made any sense. I gave myself a hard pinch on the inside of my elbow, and then I did it again, gritting my teeth as I squeezed the tender skin with all my force. It had to be a dream. No other explanation was plausible. My mother could not be dead, not before I had the chance to tell her I was sorry. I was sorry I wasn't a better daughter, I was sorry I didn't protect Dad, I was sorry I didn't know how to help her when she needed us. She could not be dead, and my father's horrific death could not be the subject of a pop culture phenomenon sweeping the nation, and my sister could not have made a child with the first man I had ever loved.

From Twitter, posted September 23, 2015

sasha w
@alxfan13

hey @poppy_parnell i'm at erin buhrman's visitation & josie is here lookin rough af #reconsidered

20m

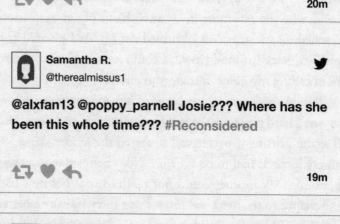

Samantha R.
@therealmissus1

@alxfan13 @poppy_parnell Josie??? Where has she been this whole time??? #Reconsidered

19m

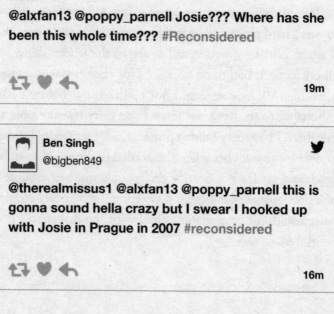

Ben Singh
@bigben849

@therealmissus1 @alxfan13 @poppy_parnell this is gonna sound hella crazy but I swear I hooked up with Josie in Prague in 2007 #reconsidered

16m

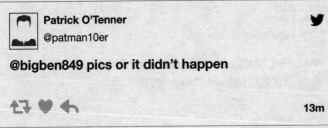

Patrick O'Tenner
@patman10er

@bigben849 pics or it didn't happen

13m

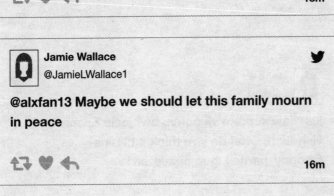

Jamie Wallace
@JamieLWallace1

@alxfan13 Maybe we should let this family mourn in peace

16m

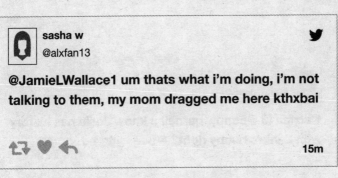

sasha w
@alxfan13

@JamieLWallace1 um thats what i'm doing, i'm not talking to them, my mom dragged me here kthxbai

15m

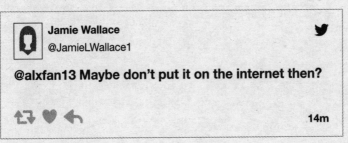

Jamie Wallace
@JamieLWallace1

@alxfan13 Maybe don't put it on the internet then?

14m

119

mm
@midwesternmamma

@JamieLWallace1 MAYBE YOU SHUT UP
#JUSTICEFORWARRENCAVE

3m

---

sasha w
@alxfan13

just saw super awk convo btw josie & lanie at visitation, what do you think it means @poppy_parnell #reconsidered

10m

T.T.
@tiny_dancer45

@alxfan13 @poppy_parnell u know Josie has history with Lanie's hubby right? #reconsidered

8m

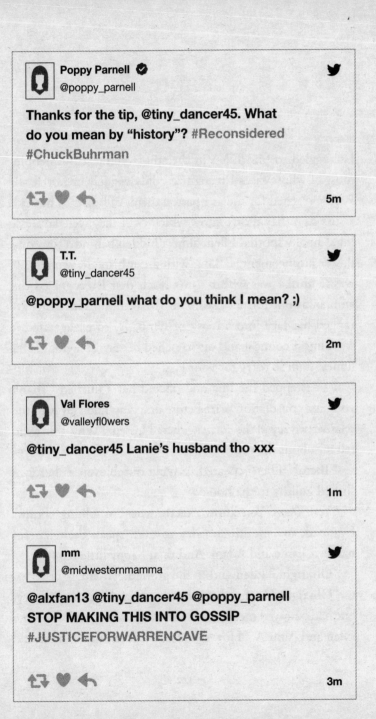

Poppy Parnell ✔
@poppy_parnell

Thanks for the tip, @tiny_dancer45. What do you mean by "history"? #Reconsidered #ChuckBuhrman

⟲ ♥ ↩   5m

T.T.
@tiny_dancer45

@poppy_parnell what do you think I mean? ;)

⟲ ♥ ↩   2m

Val Flores
@valleyfl0wers

@tiny_dancer45 Lanie's husband tho xxx

⟲ ♥ ↩   1m

mm
@midwesternmamma

@alxfan13 @tiny_dancer45 @poppy_parnell STOP MAKING THIS INTO GOSSIP #JUSTICEFORWARRENCAVE

⟲ ♥ ↩   3m

chapter 8

I struggled to find Ellen in the still-swelling sea of people, most of whose faces I recognized only vaguely or not at all. People reached for me as I passed them, calling me "honey," a sure sign they didn't know which twin they were addressing. I finally spotted Ellen, almost hidden behind a towering flower arrangement, talking with a tan brunette woman. It wasn't until I was within arm's reach that I recognized the woman as our former classmate Trina Thompson. Trina arranged her face into a mask of sympathy so exaggerated it was almost comical and outstretched her arms, saying, "Oh, honey, I am so sorry for your loss."

I sidestepped the hug and offered her a hurried "Thank you" as a consolation prize before dragging Ellen away to the relative privacy of the corner, where I hissed, "Why didn't you tell me about them?"

"Them?" Ellen repeated, playing dumb even as her eyes shifted guiltily to the floor.

"Yes. *Them.* You know exactly who I'm talking about." I gulped, my mouth too dry to even speak their hateful names. "Lanie and Adam. And their happy little family."

"Oh, right," Ellen said to the ground. "Them."

"Oh, right," I echoed. My heart squeezed with hurt. Everyone had betrayed me: first my sister and Adam, and now even Ellen and Aunt A. "How could you not tell me? How could you let me walk into this without being prepared? Today, of all days?"

"Because you didn't want to know, remember? I *tried* to tell you. On more than one occasion. I dropped all kinds of hints, too. But you didn't want to hear it."

Ellen was right. My righteous anger abandoned me, and all that remained was bewilderment.

"How did this happen? Adam barely tolerated Lanie. And after everything she's done . . . How can Adam love her?"

"It's not about love," Ellen said, as though that made anything better. "They only got married because of the baby."

"It's not 1950," I protested. "That logic doesn't hold."

"Hey, don't look at me. I don't get them, either. But you dodged a bullet with Adam. I heard he spent most of their first year of marriage hooking up with Trina over there."

Nothing surprised me anymore. If Adam was going to marry my sister, why shouldn't he also have an affair with Trina Thompson?

"She ruined him," I murmured, more to myself than Ellen.

Ellen frowned. "Trina did? That seems a little extreme."

"No, Lanie did. Lanie completely ruined him. The Adam Ives I knew would never have cheated on his wife."

Ellen's expression flickered. I cut her off before she even opened her mouth.

"I know what you're thinking, and all I have to say is this: there's one common denominator there, and it's my sister."

Any pain I experienced at discovering Lanie and Adam's relationship paled in comparison to what came next: standing in a receiving line with what remained of my family, making awkward small talk with people I barely knew, all while trying to ignore the fact that my mother's body lay just out of my peripheral vision.

Ellen, acting as a human buffer, placed herself between Lanie and me in the receiving line. On my left side, Aunt A graciously accepted condolences, while on my right, Ellen's practiced, honeyed voice greeted nearly every mourner by name. Neither of their voices, nor even my own, mechanically thanking people for coming, was enough to drown out the sound of my sister's voice as she repeatedly introduced herself: "I'm Lanie Ives, daughter of the deceased." The extreme proximity to my sister after so much time apart was unsettling, and hearing her repeat her married name was even more so. Out of the corner of my eye, I watched her smile demurely. She at once was and was not the sister I'd left behind, and I wasn't certain which was worse.

As I shook the liver-spotted hand of an elderly man who described himself as a friend of my late grandparents, I glimpsed Lanie's old friend Ryder Strong step into the room. Time had been unkind to Ryder: her face was dry and creased, her hair brittle, and she had thinned down to practically nothing, leaving her a collection of bony limbs sticking out of baggy clothing.

Ignoring the receiving line, she walked directly to Lanie, flustering the short, soft woman from Aunt A's knitting circle who had been speaking to her. My sister shrank minutely from Ryder, her eyes wide and anxious. Adam tensed at her side and put a hand on Lanie's shoulder.

"Sorry about your mom," Ryder said abruptly.

"Thank you," Lanie said quietly.

Small eyes narrowed, Ryder stared at her for a beat longer, then turned to leave.

"Wait," Lanie said, grabbing Ryder's arm. Ryder spun around, surprised, and I saw Lanie's fingers tighten around her arm. "Thanks for coming. It means a lot."

Ryder opened her mouth to say something, but then just nodded and left.

I wondered what had happened between them. It had once been impossible to separate Lanie from Ryder. In fact, during our senior year, after a fight with Aunt A over her dismal grades and poor attendance record, Lanie moved into the apartment Ryder shared with her older sister Dani, Dani's heavily tattooed boyfriend, and a one-eyed cat called Sid Vicious. I nearly worried myself into an ulcer over Lanie's departure, sure that without any parental supervision, Lanie would stop going to school entirely and might very well cause permanent harm to herself.

Once, I had driven over there, planning to insist my sister come home. Parked in front of the building, a cheaply constructed complex in a run-down neighborhood, I rehearsed the case I'd make to my sister. *Just until you finish high school. Mom would have wanted us to stay together.*

As I summoned the bravado to go inside, two figures stepped outside. Both were wearing dark hoodies, but I could plainly see Ryder's hair sticking out from one, and I could recognize my sister's slouching stride anywhere. My hand was on the door handle when I saw Lanie wave to someone, and a bulky guy with a scraggly beard approached the girls. He said something to Lanie and held out his hand; she reached out to meet him and, as they held hands, Lanie's eyes darted around guiltily. Then he punched Ryder lightly on the shoulder, said something with a smile, and walked away quickly, head down.

I was in shock. That was a drug deal. As Lanie and Ryder slunk back toward the apartment, hands shoved deep inside pockets, I leapt from the car.

"Lanie!"

They both turned, startled. Lanie's eyes narrowed like a cat's. "Get the fuck out of here, Josie."

Ryder cackled, and together they ducked into the fluorescent-lit hallway. I gave chase, but the vestibule door had locked behind her. There was nothing for me to do but leave, just like my sister wanted.

I stole a glance at a mourner's watch; only one hour left of the visitation. I could survive one more hour. I had to. I pasted on a smile of grim resolve and resumed my game of trying to remember every detail about each person shaking my hand. Tom Grant, who had lived across the street from us on Cyan Court and had helped Daddy and Pops build the playhouse in our backyard; Jared Waters, who had dated Ellen senior year in high school; Richard Deville, the head of the Elm Park College History Department, my father's old boss. I wondered if Mr. Deville had been among the anonymous sources Poppy Parnell had consulted; I wondered if he felt guilty about his participation. When he stopped in front of me, though, I just shook his cool hand and thanked him for coming.

"How are you holding up, honey?" Aunt A asked, rubbing comforting circles on my back.

"Hanging in there. How about you?"

Aunt A smiled wearily. "I'm okay. I'm overwhelmed by the number of people who have come to pay their respects to your mother."

"They're ghouls, Mom," Ellen said, leaning over me. "They know that Aunt Erin is that cult woman from that podcast, and they just want a piece of the action."

Aunt A clucked gently. "Not all of them. Not my colleagues from work, or the women from book club or knitting club. Or the gym. Or how about your old high school friends and their parents?"

Ellen rolled her eyes. "Those last ones are definitely ghouls."

As Aunt A shushed Ellen, Adam's parents joined the queue. They looked almost exactly as I remembered them: Mr. Ives with his bold ties and million-dollar smile and Mrs. Ives with her beautiful posture and ageless skin. Their gaze flickered briefly over me and landed on my sister, their faces wearing matching expressions of sympathy. I had nothing to say to Adam's parents, and I ducked out of line to once more seek solace in the women's restroom. Aunt A's expression was sad as she watched me hurry away, but not surprised.

Stepping into the hall, my eyes landed on a lean figure in a dark suit, the back of a head topped with soft brown hair, and my heart seized. *Caleb.* I took a step toward him, my hand outstretched. In the second before I touched him, he turned, and I realized the man was a stranger.

"Lanie," he said, "I'm sorry for your loss."

Thrown off balance by my mistake, I backed away, grasping inside my purse for my phone. I needed Caleb; I needed to hear his familiar voice telling me that everything was going to be okay. Just as my fingers closed around my phone, I collided with someone. I turned, apologizing profusely, but the words died in my mouth when I recognized Poppy Parnell.

The corners of her mouth tugged into a sly smile as she looked me up and down. "Josie Buhrman?"

"No," I said, attempting to step past her.

She subtly shifted her body to block my passage and shook her head, her eyes twinkling as though we were playing a game. "No, I'm certain it's you." She rearranged her expression into a professional smile and extended a hand. "My name is Poppy Parnell. I'm an investigative journalist, and I'm—"

"I know who you are."

A self-satisfied expression flashed across her face; she quickly flattened it into one of sympathy. "I thought you might. First, allow me to say that I am extremely sorry for your loss."

I laughed bitterly. "You aren't sorry in the least. This is great for your ratings."

"This might surprise you, Josie, but I don't subscribe to the theory that all publicity is good publicity. I take no joy in your mother's passing."

"I'm not having this conversation with you," I said, gesturing back to the viewing room. "Not while . . ."

Infuriatingly, she nodded in agreement. "This isn't the time or place to discuss business. I would've contacted you another way, but you're a hard woman to find. Can we set up some time tomorrow to talk?"

"I have nothing to say to you," I said, turning away from her.

A thin arm shot out and latched on to my bicep. "Please."

"Let go of me," I said, my voice as stern as possible.

"Josie," she said, as though we were friends and I was hurting her feelings.

"Kindly remove your opportunistic hands from my cousin," Ellen said, stepping into the hallway.

Poppy dropped my arm, pivoting at the sound of Ellen's voice. "You must be Ellen Kelly."

"Ellen Carter," Ellen corrected, crossing her arms over her chest.

"Right," Poppy said, pulling a notebook from her shoulder bag and making a note. "I'm Poppy Parnell. I have a podcast called *Reconsidered*. Maybe you've heard of it?" Poppy looked expectantly at Ellen, but Ellen just stared at her with a thoroughly uninterested expression on her face.

Taking advantage of the momentary distraction and sure my cousin could handle herself against Poppy, I disappeared into the crowd.

After we had shaken the last hand and accepted the last hug, only family remained in the viewing room. Peter stepped out to confirm arrangements for the cremation and funeral on Aunt A's behalf, and his daughters slouched in back, their fingers skittering across their phones. Aunt A bid a quiet goodbye to my sister and her family, and Ellen and I sank into straight-backed chairs, completely exhausted. I stared numbly ahead, marveling that the visitation had left me so emotionally depleted I no longer found the sight of the coffin unnerving.

"How are you doing?" Ellen asked, rubbing my knee. She paused and frowned. "I think you missed a spot shaving."

I swatted her hand away. "Thanks, Ellen. I'm okay, I think."

Out of the corner of my eye, I saw Lanie and her family exit the room. My heart twisted a bit to notice she hadn't even glanced in my direction before leaving, but how upset could I really be? I wouldn't have returned a smile even if it was offered.

"At least that's over," Aunt A said, collapsing into a chair beside Ellen. "It feels obscene to finally be in the same room as your mother again, and for it to be like this."

Fresh tears stabbed my eyes, evidence that I wasn't as spent as I thought. I wiped them away, turning my head as I did so, and glimpsed a figure hovering in the doorway. I gasped involuntarily.

"Of all the nerve," Aunt A hissed.

Melanie Cave wore a maroon dress, dark enough to almost resemble black but far too red for propriety's sake. She had faded considerably in the last ten years. Once trim with youthful, unlined skin, she had grown paunchy in her midsection and her face sagged. She was still poised, still elegant, but she was no longer the siren she had once been.

The three of us sat frozen like proverbial deer in headlights as Melanie made her way across the empty room, the twenty feet from the door to our chairs seeming to take an eternity.

She came to a stop directly in front of Aunt A and leaned down to reach for her hands, her neckline gaping to flash an expanse of sun-spotted cleavage.

"Amelia," she said, her voice raspier than it sounded on the podcast. "I'm—"

"Get out," Aunt A growled, her eyes flashing steel.

Melanie's painted lips parted, ready to say more, but then her gaze landed on me. Drawing herself erect, she said coolly, "It's been a long time."

I was conflicted. In some ways, Aunt A was right: Melanie Cave was the one responsible for our misery. She was the one who had been having an affair with our father, the one who had done such an abysmal job of raising her child that he resorted to murder, the one who had contacted Poppy Parnell and turned our tragedy into a pop culture commodity. I wanted to spit in her face, insist that *it hasn't been long enough*. But part of me knew that Melanie Cave was a victim in this, too, either an unhappy woman whose son did the unthinkable, or if Poppy Parnell was right, a woman whose son was unjustly jailed for life. It wasn't necessarily her fault that she wanted to free him. She was his mother, after all.

But *my* mother was lying in a coffin in the front of the room, and someone had to be responsible.

"You shouldn't be here, Mrs. Cave," Ellen said.

Ignoring Ellen, Melanie held my eyes unflinchingly. "It's time to tell the truth."

I blinked, startled.

"Mrs. Cave," Ellen repeated firmly. "Don't make me have you removed."

"Shut your mouth," Melanie spit with sudden savageness, whirling on Ellen. "My son is wasting away in prison while *this bitch*"—she emphasized her words by throwing a pointed finger at me—"runs around without a care in the world."

I began to protest, to tell Melanie that she had it all wrong, but she wasn't done.

"All I'm asking," she continued, her volume rising, "is that she tell the truth! She needs to *stop lying* and admit that she didn't see my son that night. *She didn't see anything.*" Melanie snapped her attention back to me, her finger once more wavering in my face. *"You didn't see anything."*

"All right," Ellen said, rising. "That's enough. Keep your witchy fingers with their half-rate manicures to yourself."

"He's spent *twelve years* in prison," she continued. "The best years of his life! And still you circle the wagons and refuse to talk." Melanie leaned down to me, her face close enough that I could see a vein throbbing in her temple, could smell the cloying floral of her skin cream. "Your father was at least an honorable man, which is more than I can say for the rest of you."

I was too shocked at the mention of my father to say anything.

"I was a better match for him than your crazy mother, and he knew it. Is that why you lied about seeing Warren? To take away my son and punish me? You cold, vindictive *bitch*."

Finally, I found my voice and hissed, "I'm not Lanie, you dried-up old hag."

Melanie narrowed her mascara-laden eyes at me distrustfully. "Then you tell 'your sister' that I want to talk to her."

"Stop," Aunt A interrupted loudly. "I won't let you harass my nieces. You've done too much harm already."

"*I've* done too much harm?" Melanie scoffed. She backed out of the room, pointing a finger at me. "I'm watching you, Lanie. You know what you need to do. Tell the truth."

"'I'm watching you'?" Ellen repeated mockingly as the door shut behind Melanie. "Was that supposed to be a threat? Does she think we're *afraid* of her?"

I laughed along with Ellen, but a chill ran down my spine.

Aunt A's friends were waiting for us on the front porch, bearing trays of cheese and crackers and bottles of wine. Aunt A, whose upper lip had been admirably stiff all day, dissolved into tears when she saw this, and her friends swarmed around her, making sympathetic noises and enfolding her in their arms. I waited until Aunt A came up for air, and then told her I was headed upstairs to rest. I shut the door to my old bedroom and pulled the curtains, blocking out the fading daylight. In the darkness, I stretched out on the bed and checked my phone. Over the course of the day, I had accumulated four missed calls from Caleb and six unread text messages.

Caleb's voice was warm and sticky when he answered the phone, and I dearly wished I were home with him, spooned underneath his arms, listening to his musty breathing.

"Oh, babe, I'm sorry. Were you asleep?"

"I shouldn't have been. Just this bloody jet lag. You'd think I'd learn to conquer it one of these days. But I'll be all right. How about you, love? How are you doing?"

"I've been better," I admitted, my throat catching. "Today was the visitation. It was . . . hard."

I ached to say more, to obey Melanie Cave's (albeit misdirected) edict to tell the truth. I wanted to explain the painful twisting of my organs I had felt when I saw my mother's body, the nearly inconceivable heartache I experienced when I realized any pipe dreams I had nurtured about reconnecting with my mother were gone, the particular exquisite agony of discovering my twin sister had married and had a child with the first man I had ever loved, and the crushing guilt I felt about abandoning Aunt A. But when I opened my mouth, nothing came out. There was a minefield of lies between us, and the only safe thing to do was to say nothing at all.

"God, Jo, I can't imagine how you must be feeling. I'm so sorry. How is Ellen holding up?"

"You know. As expected. This is hard on everyone."

"I wish I was there. I *should* be there."

"Honey, no," I said sharply, hearing the wheels starting to turn in his head. Without seeing him, I knew Caleb was sitting up in bed, reaching for his laptop, about to start pricing flights to Illinois. "You can't even stay awake right now. What good are you going to be here?"

"I could take a caffeine pill. I should be there. You need me."

It's time to tell the truth, my mind screamed.

But my mouth, unable to find words for the truth, continued to lie. "I need to be here for Ellen. This is harder on her than it is on me, and I really need to focus on her. I wouldn't be able to give her my full attention if you were here."

"That's awfully noble, but don't you think I might be helpful?"

"Please just trust me on this. This is something I need to handle alone."

"If you say so," he said, sounding unconvinced. "But I'm thinking about you."

"Thank you. I appreciate it. All right, look, I should probably get going. A bunch of Aunt A's friends are downstairs, and I think there are wineglasses to refill."

I froze, terrified I would be caught in an untruth, but Caleb must have assumed that Aunt A's friends were there to mourn her, not get her drunk, and he just made a sympathetic noise.

"Of course, of course. You do what you need to do. I love you."

"I love you, too."

Excerpt from transcript of *Reconsidered: The Chuck Buhrman Murder*, **Episode 3: "The (Un)Usual Suspects," September 21, 2015**

And then there's Melanie Cave. She's been a favorite suspect of armchair detectives right from the beginning. In broad strokes, their theory is this: On October 19, 2002, Melanie's husband, Andrew, learned she was having an affair and told her he wanted to end the marriage. She tried repeatedly to contact her lover, but he rebuffed all advances. She grew angrier and angrier until late that night, she walked next door and shot him.

To corroborate this theory, they point to Andrew Cave's statements that he had left town that day because he learned about the affair. According to these statements, the argument between them was intense. I sought confirmation on this fact from Warren, but, as he does whenever I mention marital discord between his parents, he clammed up.

They also point to the voicemails. On the day in question, Melanie called Chuck no less than twelve times. On half of those occasions, she left voicemails. The first five voicemails are Melanie simply asking Chuck to call her, notable only because the last three were all left within one fifteen-minute span.

But the sixth . . . well, listen to it yourself.

MELANIE, ON VOICEMAIL: You arrogant son of a bitch. Call me back. Call me back *immediately.* This is all your fault, and you *will* answer for it.

"You will answer for it" sounds like a threat, especially

knowing that Chuck Buhrman died not long after those words were uttered. In addition, many point to Melanie's tone of voice, describing it as "chilling." I have to admit, I was startled the first time I heard the voicemail. It sounded nothing like the pleasant woman I've gotten to know over these last months.

POPPY: Melanie, tell me what's going on in that last voicemail. You have to admit, you don't sound particularly friendly.

MELANIE: That's no surprise! I wasn't feeling friendly; I was very upset. Andrew had confronted me about the relationship with Chuck, and I told him the truth. I thought my marriage was over. I needed to talk to someone, and Chuck was the only one who would understand. I just wanted to talk. If I knew that would be the last time he heard my voice . . . well, I would've said something different.

Not everyone buys Melanie's explanation. In fact, one of her former classmates, Patsy Bloomfield, is so convinced of Melanie's guilt she self-published a book about the case called *The She-Devil Next Door.* I purchased an electronic copy from Patsy's website, where she also shares pictures of her grandchildren and sells throw pillows with cross-stitched adages like "The early bird catches the worm," and as soon as I read it, I knew I needed to talk to Patsy. She agreed to sit down with me for an interview.

POPPY: In your book, you state Melanie was responsible for Chuck Buhrman's murder. How did you come to that conclusion?

PATSY: I consider myself a little prescient. When I heard
Melanie's next-door neighbor had been murdered,
I instantly knew Melanie had been involved with him.
And she had! I also had a very strong feeling that she
was in some way responsible for his death.

POPPY: I understand you are an Elm Park native as well. Did
you know Melanie Cave?

PATSY: I've known Melanie since we were both in diapers. We
grew up on the same street, and were in the same class
every year since kindergarten. The first slumber party I
ever attended was at Melanie's house. She was Melanie
Richards back then, you know, and this was long before
she grew breasts and learned to shake her behind to get
what she wanted. I remember her mother made us ice
cream sundaes with whipped cream and maraschino
cherries on them. I thought I'd died and gone to hog
heaven. Her mother was always such a nice woman.

POPPY: Can we go back to something you just said? "Shake her
behind to get what she wanted"? What did you mean by
that?

PATSY: Just what it sounds like. Melanie has always been too
pretty for her own good. She learned early on she could
use her looks to get anything she wanted.

POPPY: Is that one of the "personality defects" that you reference in your book?

PATSY: Women like her—women who use their looks to get
what they want—never learn to take other people's

feelings into account. To Melanie, all that matters is male attention. Let me tell you about our senior prom. Melanie went through four dates before the dance even took place, and then she couldn't stop herself from dancing with the date of just about every girl in the room. She was prom queen, you know, so she thought it was her God-given right.

POPPY: Did she dance with your date?

PATSY: She did more than that. But that's my point: Melanie has always just taken what she wanted, especially where men are concerned.

POPPY: It seems like a long leap from date-stealing to murder, don't you think?

PATSY: Every killer has to start somewhere. My point is that Melanie has never cared about anyone but herself. She never believed that consequences applied to her, and I have no trouble believing she lashed out when she didn't get exactly what she wanted for the first time in her charmed life.

POPPY: Your book doesn't address Lanie Buhrman's testi-mony. If Melanie shot Chuck, why would Lanie say she saw Warren do it?

PATSY: Maybe she did. Maybe Melanie convinced her son to do her dirty work, and he was the one to pull the trigger. Then again, I've been listening to your podcast. Lanie Buhrman is hardly trustworthy.

chapter 9

It was past midnight when I disconnected the earbuds from my phone. *Melanie Cave.* My stomach turned when I remembered how close I had been to her that afternoon, close enough to see the powder collecting in the lines around her eyes and smell peppermint on her breath. She had looked me directly in the eye and demanded the truth, but had she been honest herself? It seemed a bold move to bring on an investigative reporter if she was guilty, but then again, maybe it was a brilliant bluff. It made more sense than any of the other alternate suspects Poppy had floated, or that I had heard suggested back then—it even made more sense than Warren Cave. Melanie had motive—she had wanted our father, and he had (seemingly) used her. Could *"You didn't see anything"* have been a threat rather than a plea?

Wide-awake, I began searching the internet for reactions to the episode, desperate to know what other people thought about Melanie Cave. One post on Reddit in particular caught my eye.

⬆ **I think I saw Melanie Cave the night of Chuck**
⬇ **Buhrman's murder (self.reconsideredpodcast)**
submitted 1 day ago by conspiracytheroress
I grew up on Cyan Court. In 2002, I was only seven, but I have this distinct memory of seeing a woman running through

the trees the night Chuck Buhrman was killed. When I told
my parents, they said that I must have been dreaming, but
I'm sure of what I saw. I didn't see a face or anything, but the
more I think about it, the more I'm sure it must have been
Melanie Cave, running to hide the murder weapon. I wish
I still lived in Elm Park. I'd go looking for it.

armchairdetective38 197 points 1 day ago
How much of this memory came about after listening to episode 3? We know what time Melanie Cave
called 911. She couldn't have been running through the
neighborhood.

conspiracytheroress 54 points 1 day ago
But we're just assuming that she called 911 immediately.
Maybe hiding the weapon didn't take long, and then she
ran home and called 911. How much do we really know
about the timeline?

notmyrealname 158 points 1 day ago
You should call Poppy Parnell.

realitycheck99 200 points 1 day ago
You should call the police.

armchairdetective38 87 points 1 day ago
IF what you say is true.

deathbydefamation 91 points 1 day ago
so what's your theory? that melanie cave killed chuck
buhrman? or that she hid the gun for warren? don't forget,
lanie buhrman SAW warren cave

I caught my breath. I could see how Lanie might have mistaken Melanie for her son. She might have camouflaged herself in his heavy metal T-shirts and black clothing, or maybe Lanie had only seen someone running into the Cave house and *thought* it was Warren. My stomach soured as I seriously considered for the first time that there might be some validity to Poppy Parnell's theory.

Suddenly, I remembered one afternoon the spring before our father died. It was one of our mother's good days: we had just finished a lesson on biology that had involved planting seedlings in cups. Our mother had spilled soil all over herself, and she had gone upstairs to clean up while Lanie and I wiped down the worktable. There had been a knock on the door, and I, eager as always to avoid housekeeping, hurried to answer it. I found Melanie Cave on our porch, her usually careful hair mussed and her eyes red from crying.

"Is your mother here?" she asked.

"She's not available," I said. "Can I help you with something?"

Melanie opened her coral-tinted mouth, and then shut it. Her green eyes watered.

"Mrs. Cave?" I asked. "Are you all right?"

"What are you doing here?" Lanie's voice came from behind, suddenly cold.

Melanie hesitated, and then said, "Peaches got away." It took me a moment to understand she was talking about their cat. She gestured with her hands, indicating something the approximate size and shape of a football. "She's about this big, white with tan spots. Have you seen her?"

I shook my head. "I haven't. Do you want us to help you look?"

"We can't," Lanie said staunchly.

"But her cat—"

"Come on, Josie," Lanie insisted. "We promised Mom that we'd have the kitchen cleaned by the time she got out of the shower."

"You're good girls," Melanie said, smiling sadly.

I shivered now, remembering that interaction. It was so obvious, in hindsight. Melanie had come over to confront my mother about the affair. Had Lanie been able to intuit that Melanie was going to harm our mother?

I shook my head to clear that train of thought and, reeling myself back in, I went to go get a cup of tea. From the hallway, I could see the kitchen light was still on. I assumed it had been overlooked in the semi-drunken cleaning attempt made by Aunt A's friends, but I found Aunt A sitting at the kitchen table. Her shoulders were slumped; one hand was wrapped around a half-drunk mug of Sleepytime Tea, and the other around a box of tissues. Used tissues were mounded in front of her, and her eyes were red and leaking.

"Aunt A?"

"Josie, honey," she said, looking up and wiping at her eyes with the back of her hand. "Please, come in. I was just . . . thinking about your mom."

I hesitated. My mind was still spinning with thoughts of Melanie Cave, and I wasn't sure I was emotionally prepared to return to mourning my mother. But Aunt A looked so small and miserable I didn't know how to refuse, and so I took a seat beside her, haltingly patting her soft, warm back, affecting my best imitation of feminine comfort. After years of solo travel followed by cohabitation with a man whose moods could easily be controlled by food and sex, my skills at consoling other women were tepid at best. Still, Aunt A leaned into my touch, her sniffles lessening.

"I miss her so much," Aunt A said quietly. "And I've been sitting here trying to work out if I missed her more when she first left, or if I miss her more now that she's dead. Isn't that strange? I have no idea why that matters to me."

"I've been wondering something similar," I confessed. "I thought I gave up on her years ago, so why am I so sad?"

"Grief is a funny thing," she said with a sad, lopsided smile.

"Have you figured out which it is? Do you miss her more now or then?"

"I'm beginning to think they're incomparable. I miss her *differently* now than I used to. Now I have sadness and regret, when back then it was mostly anger."

My eyes flickered downward. I had never recognized anger in Aunt A. "Were you angry with her because she left you to take care of us?"

"Oh, honey, no," Aunt A said, pulling my hand down from her back and clasping it in hers. "Of course not. I love you and your sister as though you were my own, and I have never been angry about raising you. *Never.* We had some challenges, but I never considered it anything less than a privilege to take care of you girls."

My heart twisted; tears turned my vision blurry. "You can't believe that."

"I do," she said fiercely, squeezing my hand so that it almost hurt. "My anger had nothing to do with you girls. I was furious with your mother because she abandoned *all* of us. Just took off like a thief in the night, without so much as a note. And right after that scene with your sister . . . I didn't know what to think. I was sick with worry. I thought . . . well, I thought that she'd decided she couldn't live without your father and had killed herself. And then, once I knew where she was, I was so, so angry that she thought those strangers could make her happier than I could. Than *we* could." Aunt A choked back a sob that shook her entire body. "I wasted so much time on anger. I thought . . . I thought that there was still time. I thought she would come home someday."

"I think we all thought that, at least a little," I whispered. I certainly had, right up until the afternoon I spent in the Dairy Queen with Sister Amamus. I never told Aunt A about that encounter—I never told anyone, not even Lilly, whose car I had borrowed—and I knew tonight wasn't the right time to mention it. It painted a more callous picture of my mother than I liked to remember. But I couldn't help but wonder if Aunt A had ever attempted to contact her sister, if she had any more success than I had. "Did you ever look for her?"

"No. Maybe I should have. I just . . . I thought . . . I didn't. And now I have so many regrets. Not only for myself, but also for you girls. Your mother was such a special, compassionate woman. I wish you could have known her better." Aunt A looked up at me with heartbreaking earnestness. "Tell me, how do you remember your mother?"

One look into Aunt A's anguished eyes told me all I needed to know about what she wanted to hear, and I began telling her about warm memories of my mother: family vacations, surprises she made for Lanie and me, baking together. I left out the less happy memories, the ones where our mother shut down, refused to come out of the room, wouldn't speak to us for days. Even so, I couldn't help but wonder aloud, "I know she was hurting, but we *needed* her. How could she leave us?"

A fat tear slid down Aunt A's cheek. "I don't know, honey. She refused to talk to me about the night your father died, and she refused to see anyone about it. I think she felt guilty for not being home, and I think that guilt was like a cancer in her. She had always blamed herself for our brother Dennis's death, and she blamed herself in a way for our parents' deaths. I think your father's death on top of that was just too much for her."

"But that doesn't make any sense. I can understand why she might have felt responsible for Uncle Dennis, and I can sort of see why she might have felt guilty about not being home the night Dad died, but Grammy and Pops were killed by a drunk driver. There's no way that was her fault."

"You're right, of course. But your mother had planned to have dinner with our parents that night, and she canceled. They decided to go to the movies instead and were killed on the way home. She always thought that if she hadn't canceled on them, they never would have been in that intersection."

"She shouldn't have blamed herself for that."

"Your mother was an exceptionally sensitive creature. It was one of the most beautiful things about her, but I think it made life more painful for her." Another tear rolled down Aunt A's cheek. "That poor, sweet woman. I loved her so much."

"I loved her, too," I murmured.

I swallowed hard. "Aunt A, what about Melanie Cave? I know Mom said she didn't know about her, but do you think that she suspected?"

Aunt A stiffened. "That woman. Your poor mother. She had no idea." Aunt A laughed bitterly. "After Jason left me, I saw infidelity everywhere. I told your mother to worry about Melanie Cave, but she didn't listen."

I took a deep breath. "In the most recent episode of *Reconsidered*, Poppy suggests that Melanie Cave killed Daddy."

Aunt A set her mouth in a straight line. "Her son killed your father."

"But—"

"Melanie is a vile woman, but your sister *saw* Warren pull the trigger."

I swallowed the bitterness that rose in my throat.

"Josie, honey, listen to me," Aunt A said, squeezing my hand with renewed vigor. "I'm going to offer you some unsolicited and probably unwelcome advice. *Forgive your sister.* She's made a lot of mistakes in her life, and I know that she's hurt you in ways you'll never be able to forget. But forgive her. She's the only sister you've got, and a sister is a truly special gift."

I yanked my hand away and pushed my chair back from the table. "Lanie is not a gift. She's a curse."

From Facebook, posted September 21, 2015

Patsy Bloomfield, Author
Today at 9:15am
Check out the most recent episode of <u>Reconsidered Podcast</u> to hear me discuss the Chuck Buhrman murder with host Poppy Parnell! And then head over to <u>www.patsybloomfield.</u> <u>blogworld.com</u> to purchase a copy of THE SHE-DEVIL NEXT DOOR!

> **Rosie Howe** Great!
> Today at 9:20am
>
> **Lenny Miazga** I just ordered a copy! Can't wait to read it!
> Today at 1:13pm
>
> **Celia Dileo** Beautiful work, Patsy! God bless.
> Today at 3:34pm
>
> **Dallas McClung** Are you worried about libel suits?
> Today at 6:17pm
>
> > **Patsy Bloomfield, Author** Libel is defined as a FALSE STATEMENT. Nothing I wrote in the book or said on the podcast was false.
> > Today at 6:20pm
>
> **Sean Fields** You should be ashamed of yourself.
> Today at 9:12pm
>
> **Desiree Herren** WOW! I can't believe Melanie Cave isn't locked up yet!
> Today at 9:47pm

chapter 10

I was standing in the kitchen picking at a cold lasagna someone had left on the porch, unable to decide whether I was hungry or just tired, when I heard the front door open.

"Hello?" my sister's voice called from the foyer.

I froze, a forkful of lasagna halfway to my mouth. I quietly returned the fork to the dish and glanced at the back staircase, debating whether I should stand perfectly still in the hope that she wouldn't hear me or dart up the stairs in an attempt to outrun her. I had no interest in speaking with her.

Before I could make a decision, Lanie stepped into the kitchen. It still shocked me to see my sister looking so clean and composed. For ten years, I had remembered her as I had last seen her: stumbling down the front stairs of Benny Weston's house, dressed in ripped jeans and a pink sweater that had once been mine, hair tousled and eyeliner smeared, a vacant smirk on her face.

But now, with cheeks flushed a healthy pink and a light-blue cashmere sweater that highlighted the color of her eyes, she smiled tentatively at me and said, "Hi."

I opened my mouth to return the greeting, but my eyes were distracted by the princess-cut diamonds sparkling obscenely in her earlobes.

"Are those Mom's earrings?"

Lanie's hands flew to her ears, fingertips grazing the jewelry's sharp edges. "It's not like she's using them."

"That's not the point. They're not yours."

Lanie nodded, a little too readily, and started to pull the earrings off. "Do you want them?"

"Stop. Don't. It's just strange to see them on you."

The diamond earrings were a gift from our father for our mother's thirty-fifth birthday. Our mother rarely wore jewelry or dressed up, but the earrings quickly became part of her routine. To her, they were more than glittering rocks; they were tangible evidence of love in the dark days after her parents' death. I associated their appearance with baked goods and field trips; I never saw her wear them after our father was killed. I used to wonder what had happened to them.

"Aunt A told me I could borrow them for the wedding. I didn't see the harm in keeping them. She was my mother, after all."

"She was *our* mother."

"I know," Lanie said, tilting her head slightly. She frowned a bit. "Did she have any pearl earrings?"

"Thinking of swiping those, too?"

She shook her head. "Josie, can we talk?"

Aunt A's entreaties to forgive my sister bounced around inside my skull, but the sight of her wearing our mother's earrings, earrings that had been pillaged to celebrate her marriage to a man she had stolen from me, made my throat clench and my heart cold and intolerant. I shook my head. "No."

"Please," she insisted. "I know it must have been a surprise to see me with Adam yesterday."

"*No,*" I said more forcefully. "I do not want to talk about Adam."

"But—"

"You want to talk?" I cut her off. "Fine. Let's talk about Dad. Let's talk about who killed him."

Lanie's mouth dropped open. "Are you kidding me? You've been listening to that podcast? It's all lies, Josie. You know that." She paused to glare at me. "You *do* know that, right?"

Did I know that? What I knew, better than anybody, was that Lanie was capable of incredible deceit. But still . . . I had a hard time believing that she would purposefully lie and send an innocent man to prison.

"I can't believe this," she hissed, eyes narrowing. "You think I lied."

"Not lied," I said quickly. "But . . . is it possible you were mistaken?"

"*No,*" Lanie said, adding emphasis by snatching up the chair in front of her and slamming it down hard. My body tensed from muscle memory, ready to dodge any objects she might choose to hurl. "I can't believe you'd ask me that. You're my *sister.*"

"Have you listened to the podcast? She makes a pretty good case against Melanie Cave. Her husband had left her *that day*, Lanie. And that voicemail . . ."

"I don't care! I don't care if Melanie Cave wrote a confession and signed it in blood. I *saw* Warren do it." She stamped the chair against the floor again. "I *saw* him."

"But are you sure?" I pressed. "It was dark. Maybe . . . Is

it possible you saw *Melanie* running back to the Cave house but just *thought* it was Warren?"

"Say that's the truth," Lanie said, her eyes smoldering with barely repressed fury. "Say Melanie killed our father, and I mistook her for Warren. How could I ever admit that now?"

My heart leapt in my throat, nearly choking me. "What are you saying?"

"That you're wasting your time."

"But the *truth*, Lanie," I began.

"We know the truth!" she screamed suddenly, grabbing the casserole dish from the table and heaving it at me. I jumped out of the way, and lasagna splattered across the floor. Veins bulging in her neck, Lanie screamed, "It was Warren Cave! I *saw* him!"

We stood frozen, staring at each other, panting and wide-eyed.

"What's going on?" Ellen asked, sweeping into the kitchen via the back staircase. She looked from me to my sister to the lasagna on the floor. "Oh."

Lanie pivoted on her heel, preparing to make an exit.

"Hold it right there," Ellen commanded. She pointed to the lasagna on the floor. "Clean that up."

"Fuck off, Ellen," Lanie snapped, stalking out the door.

"What happened?" Ellen asked me.

I shook my head.

Ellen nodded and smiled her insouciant grin. "Fine. If you won't talk, the least you can do is eat with me. Let's get lunch."

* * *

As Ellen backed her car out of Aunt A's driveway, a silver Lexus parked across the street pulled away from the curb. From its driver's-side window, I thought I caught a glimpse of ash-blond hair, a thin face hidden behind enormous sunglasses.

"Wait," I said so suddenly that Ellen slammed on the brakes. "Was that Melanie Cave?"

"Where?" Ellen asked, looking around.

I pointed in the direction of the Lexus, but it was already turning the corner. My stomach felt jumpy and my extended hand felt tingly. What was Melanie Cave doing watching our house?

"New plan," I said, my voice shaking. "We're skipping lunch and getting drinks instead."

"Now you're speaking my language." Ellen smiled, pulling onto the street.

Ellen took me to Last Call, Elm Park's most reputable watering hole. As a resident of New York City, where space was at a premium and bar patrons were willing to pay upward of $20 for so-called artisan cocktails, I was astounded by both the spaciousness (there was a large bar, booths along the walls, and at least fifteen tables, not to mention a jukebox, *Big Buck Hunter*, and a vintage *Pac-Man* game) and the low cost of its drinks (my Jack and Diet cost me a paltry $2.50 and Ellen's white wine hardly broke the bank at $3.00).

"So," Ellen said, taking a sip of wine. "Are you going to tell me what happened?"

I winced. There seemed something disloyal about confessing that I had wondered about Lanie's honesty, and even though I knew Lanie had done nothing to earn my loyalty, I couldn't bring myself to say anything to Ellen. "Can we talk about something else?"

"Sure," Ellen nodded. "You won't believe what Trina—"

"She was wearing Mom's earrings," I broke in suddenly, unable to keep my feelings bottled up, no matter how much I wanted to. "Like they were hers. Like she was entitled to them."

Ellen's face softened. "Mom has more of your mom's jewelry. I'm sure she can find something special for you."

"That's not the point. Lanie shouldn't have her earrings, *especially* her earrings. Don't you remember when Lanie got her ears pierced?"

Ellen shook her head blankly.

"We were ten years old. You had just gotten yours done for your birthday, and we were so jealous. We begged and pleaded, but Mom wouldn't relent. She said we weren't allowed to pierce our ears until we were thirteen. I locked myself in the bathroom in protest, and, while Mom and Dad were unscrewing the door handle to get me out, Lanie lifted money from Mom's purse, rode her bike to the mall, and convinced a stranger to pretend to be her guardian. She came back all smug with these perfect little cubic zirconia studs. Mom was *furious*. She really flipped out, and went to physically remove them from her ears. Dad finally talked her down. They told me I could pierce mine then, too, but I didn't." I fingered my earlobe, which hadn't been pierced until I went off to college. "I wanted to be the good one."

"You *are* the good one. You always have been."

"It didn't matter, though, did it? She left us both." I gulped at my drink, attempting to drown the sudden memory of my mother wearing a crown of woven dandelions, mixing a biology lesson with one about backyard gardening. "I always thought she'd come back. I know that sounds crazy, but I did. I always thought someday she'd find what she was looking for, and then she'd . . . just come home. But now she's dead . . . And the worst part is that she *chose* to die. She *chose* to leave us all over again. It just seems so unnecessarily selfish."

"Oh, sweetheart."

"I'm so angry, Ellen," I said, tears stinging my eyes. "I'm so angry at her."

"If you're angry at anyone, you should be angry at Poppy Parnell. It can't be a coincidence your mother killed herself after her podcast gained popularity."

"Well, I'm angry at her, too. For what she did to my mother, and for what she's doing with that podcast, making me all confused about what happened to Dad."

Ellen looked up sharply. "What do you mean, making you confused?"

I shook my head, refusing to elaborate. "She's manipulating the story, telling half-truths."

"Speaking of," Ellen said, sipping her wine carefully. "What did you tell the boyfriend?"

"Nice segue," I said sardonically. "I did just what you suggested. I told him that your mother had died."

Ellen made a face. "I was just *talking*, hon. I hadn't really thought it through. Someday you and Caleb will want to get married—"

156

"Maybe. Not everyone needs a piece of paper to legitimize their relationship."

Ellen rolled her eyes. "Allow me to rephrase: if, in the future, you and your Kiwi honey decide that the aforementioned 'piece of paper' is useful in achieving legal immigration status, you two might want to get married. And what then? Are you going to keep my mother from him forever? That will break her heart."

I dropped my head on the bar, my forehead bouncing against the liquor-slicked wood. "Ellen, I don't know. I'm doing my best, all right?"

"Sit up. I'm just trying to help."

I righted myself with a sigh. "I need to tell Caleb the truth. I know that. But I've made such a mess of everything. He'll never forgive me."

"He will," Ellen said, placing a comforting hand on my shoulder. "He loves you."

"He loves the lie I told him about myself."

"He loves you," she insisted. "Remember when Peter and I visited you two in New Zealand? The way he looked at you, Josie . . . that man is smitten."

I grimaced. "Let's see for how much longer."

"You and your negativity. On the way to pick you up the other day, I listened to this podcast—not *that* podcast, obviously, an inspirational one, and—" Ellen cut herself off to glance down at her phone buzzing its way across the scratched bar. Peter's face filled the screen, and she frowned, waiting the call out without answering. "I told him I was going to be with you and not to bother me. He must've forgotten. Where was I? Right—"

Her phone interrupted us with a sharp buzz, heralding the arrival of a text message. Together, we glanced down to see Peter beckoning Ellen back to the hotel for some undefined parenting emergency with more exclamation marks than I would have thought suitable for a man of his station.

"What kind of parenting emergency can Peter possibly need you for? You're basically the same age as his daughters. Do they really obey you?"

"Whether or not they obey me is irrelevant. They respect my opinion. I'm much cooler than Peter. Anyway, I'm sure it has something to do with Isabelle and that boyfriend of hers. That loser has been a constant source of distress." Ellen slid off her barstool and looked at me expectantly. "I am sorry, though. Come on, we can try again later tonight. I'll buy."

I shook my head and wrapped my hands around my drink. "I'm not ready to go home yet. I might just stay here for a little while longer."

Ellen pulled a face. "Don't be that woman drinking alone in a bar, Josie. That's just sad."

"I won't stay long," I promised. "I'll just finish this drink, and then I'll walk home. It'll be good for me."

Ellen hesitated but her phone buzzed again, and she frowned and kissed me goodbye. I was left sitting alone at the bar, something I hadn't done in years. It used to be a standard part of any given evening, back when I was in my early twenties and still wandering. Sipping liquid courage, I would flirt with the bartender, half hoping someone would approach me, half terrified someone would.

Someone always did. I would occasionally attract other

single female travelers, desperate for an ally, but mostly I got young men, usually fellow Americans who had mistaken my dark hair for something more exotic than Illinoisan. They would strike up a conversation, usually *Where are you from*, the traveler's version of *What's your sign*, and if I liked him or if his midwestern twang made me feel nostalgic, I might follow him back to his hostel to meet his friends or listen to a CD of his mediocre garage band. In time, these guys began to seem interchangeable, and there was a comforting familiarity to my interactions with them.

But there was nothing comforting about sitting alone at the bar in Elm Park. At least half of the other patrons were looking at me—some openly staring, some sneaking what they thought were stealthy glances over mugs of beer. I could almost hear them whispering to each other. *That's Josie Buhrman. You remember, her father was murdered and her mother was crazy? And her sister? That hell-raiser? And there's that podcast, you know the one. Just look at her. What did she do, cut that hair with a hacksaw? What a mess. Guess it runs in the family.*

My cheeks flaming with embarrassment, I ducked my head and glared into my drink. I hated that my short hair allowed those vultures a clear view of my reddening neck. I had lowered my head nearly down onto the bar when I felt the uneasy sensation of all eyes lifting off me at once. I braved glancing up to see what had captured their collective interest.

Adam.

Last Call's dim lighting softened and blurred the lines of his face, and for a second he looked eighteen again. My heart instinctually and traitorously clutched, but then the neon light of a beer sign reflected off his wedding band and brought me back to reality. He glanced around the bar, and our eyes locked. The spot on my left hip, where I had drunkenly had his name poorly tattooed by a Flemish-speaking tattoo "artist" in the back room of a bar in Brussels—and later covered with an elaborate floral design by a more reputable, actual artist in Athens—burned. Reflexively, I placed my hand on my hip, as though Adam could see through the clothing and the expensive cover-up job and read his name on my body. He didn't deserve to know I had once been so heartsick over him. I was no longer that girl, and he was no longer the boy I had once loved.

I met Adam Ives on my first day at Elm Park High School. I had been both immensely excited and blindingly terrified about transferring to public school. Nearly everything I knew about public school I had learned from television; Ellen had filled in the gaps with her own dogma. Aunt A had chastised Ellen for putting "conformist ideas about beauty and classist notions of popularity" into our heads, but the damage (as it was) had already been done. I knew other students were people to fear, and to impress, even though I didn't understand why or how they would humiliate me.

"Break a leg." Ellen smiled, depositing me in the doorway of my first class.

"Wait," I hissed, clutching her as she turned to leave. "What do I do now? Just go in and find a seat? Do I need to tell the teacher I'm here?"

"Just sit in one of the empty seats. Try to avoid the ones

in the front row or the very back. And," she added, surveying the classroom with her sharp hazel eyes, "don't sit next to that guy in the blue shirt."

"Why not?"

Ellen shrugged. "Because he's a douche bag. Just avoid him, okay?"

"What's a douche bag?"

Ellen stifled a giggle. "And keep your mouth shut."

As I nodded my agreement, Adam brushed past us on his way into the same classroom.

"Hey, Ives," Ellen said, grabbing him by the arm. "This is my cousin Josie. She's new here. Look after her, all right?"

Adam's caramel-colored eyes sparkled as he smiled at me, and a liquid warmth oozed through my body. Later, I would attribute the sensation to love at first sight; later still, I would dismiss it as hormones. Adam embodied the same easy confidence as Ellen, a self-possession that I coveted. As he steered me into a seat beside him, he reviewed my schedule and discovered we had three classes together; he then proceeded to walk me to each of these classes, as well as my others.

"You don't have to do this," I told him. "This school isn't that big. I can find my own way."

"Come on," he said with a mock groan. "Can't you just let a guy be chivalrous?"

"That's an eighteen-point word," I said, impressed.

Adam's cheeks flushed endearingly. "I play a lot of Scrabble. My dad says it will help me on the SAT."

"I was homeschooled," I told him. "Sometimes, Scrabble was our vocabulary lesson."

That afternoon, after the final bell had rung, I was putting my books in my locker and trying to remember where Ellen had said to meet when Adam sauntered up. He leaned against the locker beside mine and grinned, all nonchalance and shiny white teeth.

"Looks like you survived your first day."

"I did." I smiled. "And you know what? I think I'm getting the hang of this school thing."

"Awesome. So, listen, Josie, some of us are going to the movies on Friday. Think you might want to come? Should be cool."

Not trusting myself to speak without squealing, I nodded.

"Or," he added with a teasing laugh, "we could stay in and play Scrabble."

I burst out laughing. "Tempting. But let's go to the movies."

Later, on the car ride home, I said, "I think Adam Ives asked me out on a date."

Ellen shrugged. "You could do worse."

"That sounds fun, Josie," Aunt A said, flashing me a smile in the rearview mirror.

I looked to Lanie for her reaction, but she was glaring out the window, her mouth set in a determined scowl.

"Hey," Adam said, dropping onto the barstool Ellen had vacated.

The casualness of his greeting infuriated me, and I snapped, "Are you kidding me? Just 'hey'? Like nothing has changed?"

Adam closed his eyes and shook his head. "Josie, everything has changed."

"No kidding."

Adam sighed and flagged down the bartender. "Can I get a Diet Coke? No, wait, on second thought, can I get the IPA on tap?"

"Drinking in the middle of the day? Looks like my sister is a bad influence on you."

Adam opened his mouth to say something and then appeared to think better of it. He shrugged and said, "At least I'm not drinking alone in the middle of the day."

"Touché. But I didn't start alone. Ellen got called away by her husband. What's your excuse?"

"Strangely enough, also Ellen," Adam said with a small chuckle. "I had lunch down the street with a client, and saw Ellen on the way back to my car. I wasn't in the mood for one of your cousin's famous lectures, so I ducked in here to hide."

"Fate," I said drily.

"I don't believe in fate," he said, taking a sip of his beer.

"Me neither."

We both had, though, once. We had taken the similarities in our schedules as an omen, we had marveled at the way our hands seemed to fit perfectly together, and we had proclaimed each other soul mates. In the aftermath of my father's death and my mother's complete breakdown, I had so desperately wanted to believe in *something*, some grand design, that I had clung to Adam as proof that the universe was something other than cruel and random. That, of course, had been a mistake.

"How you holding up, Josie? Honestly?"

"Well, I'm drinking in the middle of the day."

"We've established that." He tipped his beer in my direction. "But at least you're not doing it alone anymore."

"Your wife threw a casserole dish at my head," I added, my voice catching on the word *wife*.

Adam looked startled. "What? When?"

"About thirty minutes ago."

"What happened?"

I looked into Adam's expectant face, at its familiar lines, the way he always tugged his right eyebrow up higher than the other when he was concerned, and reminded myself that he was no longer my confidant. I couldn't tell him about the questions the podcast had raised for me.

"Sister stuff." I shrugged.

He sighed into his beer. "I'm sorry."

I shrugged again. "Little-known fact, but you're not personally responsible when your spouse assaults someone."

"No, I mean I'm really sorry," he said, his voice cracking.

I looked down into my drink to avoid his eyes. I had heard this all before. My old email account contained a trove of rambling, overwrought emails from Adam, a combined hundreds of pages of apologies and excuses. I used to spend hours reading and rereading them, nearly enjoying the sick feeling they elicited, like pushing on a bruise. But it had been years since I had opened them, and I wasn't interested in falling down that particular hole again, in allowing Adam to pick open old wounds.

"I don't know what happened, but I can only guess it had something to do with me, and I'm sorry," Adam continued, closing a hand over mine. "I never meant to come between you two."

The heat of his skin on mine generated a confusing combination of revulsion and excitement, and I yanked my hand away, tucking it safely between my thigh and the barstool. "It wasn't about you, Adam."

He frowned, his disbelief obvious. "It wasn't?"

"Nope," I said, forcing a nonchalance I didn't feel. "Not today, at least. Today it was the podcast."

"That thing," Adam groaned, rubbing his face. "I should've known. Ever since it started, Lanie's been acting really out of character."

A small pinprick of hurt stabbed my heart to see how easily Adam transitioned from apologizing to me to worrying about my sister. I shook my head to clear the disloyal thoughts, and overcompensated by being purposefully glib. "Seemed like the same old sister to me, throwing things and everything."

"It's been a long time since you've seen her, Josie. She's really pulled herself together. She's still . . . well, she's still Lanie, if you know what I mean, but you would have been proud of her." He shook his head. "But then that podcast started, and it was suddenly like she regressed ten years. She stopped sleeping, stopped eating, started acting really weird. A few days ago, she forgot to pick our daughter up from school. She wasn't answering the phone, and I couldn't find her anywhere. When she finally showed up, she had hay in her hair and no explanation."

I flinched. That behavior sounded like our mother, and no matter how mad I might be with Lanie, I didn't like to think of her going down that road. I finished my drink and waited for the whiskey to harden me. The bartender set a new one in front of me; I nodded in thanks and lifted it to my lips.

"And one day," Adam continued, "she didn't get out of bed at all, and then she spent the entire next day baking cupcakes. The *entire* day, Josie. We had cupcakes coming out of our ears. I thought maybe there was some sort of party at the elementary school, but there wasn't. She just felt like baking cupcakes. Said something about using your mom's recipe."

The image of Lanie surrounded by cupcakes made me strangely queasy. A memory of our mother tickled at the back of my mind, but I refused to acknowledge it. There had been too much reminiscing today already.

I downed my drink and stood up.

"I should go."

Adam's forehead creased in disappointment, and his mouth formed the first syllable of my name before falling silent. He nodded.

"I should probably go, too." He reached for his wallet. "Let me get your drinks."

I mumbled my thanks and hurried out before Adam could offer me a ride. Squinting into the late-afternoon sun, I began walking home. I inhaled the crisp air greedily, hoping it would clear my head. I wanted to forget about death, and my sister, and the podcast for just a moment.

Suddenly I heard the sharp click of heels coming up behind me.

"Josie!"

I froze.

It was Poppy Parnell.

Discussion thread on www.reddit.com/r/ reconsideredpodcast, posted September 24, 2015

⬆ Chuck's daughters and their tangled love life (self. ⬇ reconsideredpodcast)

submitted 8 hours ago by elmparkuser1

I went to high school with the Buhrman twins. I was two years behind them in school (I graduated in 2007) so I didn't know them personally, but I certainly knew ~of~ them. Josie (aka the "good twin") dated this guy—I don't know if I can post his name, anyone know if that's kosher?—all through high school, but guess who's married to him now? LANIE (aka the "bad twin"). I don't know if it means anything within the context of the case, but it either shows that something was screwy with that family or that Lanie is not to be trusted.

> ⬆ **byenow** 7 points 8 hours ago ⬇
> of course they are all messed up, the mom joined a cult ffs

> > ⬆ **jennyfromtheblock** 18 points 7 hours ago ⬇
> > Or maybe the mom joined a cult and the kids are messed up because of that super-messed up thing that happened to them (i.e., that time Warren Cave killed their dad)?

> ⬆ **dancedancedance** 5 points 7 hours ago ⬇
> I don't know, wouldn't you be all fucked up if your dad got murdered?

> ⬆ **straightouttaptown** 1 point 5 hours ago ⬇
> wut

gingerftw 11 points 5 hours ago

Lanie Buhrman is not to be trusted, and her marriage to Adam is just further proof of that.

Source: Elm Park born and bred

> **miranda_309** 1 point 1 hour ago
>
> Are we allowed to use his real name? Can we get a mod in here for a ruling?

armchairdetective38 9 points 5 hours ago

This subreddit is for people to discuss the case, not spread gossip. This isn't some local board. Take it somewhere else.

chapter 11

Josie, wait a minute."

The audacity of Poppy's assumption that we were on a first-name basis appalled me. She might spend her time researching my family, but she knew nothing about me. Training my eyes on the sidewalk in front of me, I powered forward, moving as briskly as I could without running, refusing to wait even a single second for her.

But Poppy Parnell was faster than I would have assumed, given her slight stature and bulky shoulder bag, and she caught up with me quickly.

"Josie, hold up," she tried again, catching me above my elbow.

I yanked my arm out of her grasp with such force that I came close to dislocating it. Wincing in pain, I whirled around to face her. "Do *not* touch me."

She held her small hands up in a surrendering posture. "Understood. And I apologize. I just wanted to ask you a few questions."

"I have nothing to say to you."

She leaned forward eagerly like a terrier on the hunt. "But if you'll just—"

I should have walked away. The only way to avoid escalating the situation was to avoid it altogether, but I had been unsettled by the fight with my sister and then lubricated by the midday alcohol, and so I cut her off.

"Shut up. Don't you listen? I have nothing to say to you. You are a *parasite*. This is some sort of game for you, but this is *my life*. My father was murdered. *Murdered*. And it *destroyed* my family. Completely, utterly, irreparably. And now, thirteen years later, you've arrived to dredge everything up all over again? What could I possibly want to say to you other than *go fuck yourself*?"

Undeterred, Poppy took a step toward me, those huge eyes of hers even wider. "Aren't you interested in the truth?"

I shivered, remembering how I had said nearly that same thing to Lanie that very afternoon. Unwilling to let Poppy see the chink she had made in my armor, I crossed my arms over my chest and infused my voice with steel. "Warren Cave had his day in court. He was found guilty."

"Primarily because your sister claimed she saw him do it. But what if she wasn't telling the truth? I understand she may not be a paragon of virtue."

The instinct to protect my sister—something I thought I had outgrown long ago—flared, and before I was aware of what I was doing, I thrust my finger in Poppy's weasel-like face and snarled, "Shut your mouth, you gossip-mongering bitch."

Poppy Parnell did not recoil; instead, she seemed oddly thrilled. "That's a pretty strong reaction you're having there."

I retracted my finger and choked back a couple of profanity-laced retorts. With as much serenity and conviction as I could muster, I said, "My sister ruins everything. If you are even half the investigative journalist you claim to be, you should know that Lanie has betrayed me time and time again. But she is *my sister*, and I will not let you drag her name through the mud."

"Can I quote you on that?" Poppy asked, pulling some equipment from her bag.

"Go fuck yourself," I said, and turned away.

The ceiling of my old bedroom housed a constellation of glow-in-the-dark stars that Adam and I had attached one long-ago afternoon. Adam advocated for realistic placement, constructing Orion and the Big Dipper, while I bounced on the bed and attached them at random. When the last star had been hung, Adam shut the door and pulled the curtains, simulating dark as best he could to allow us to admire our handiwork. "I'll think of you every night when I see them," I had promised. Now as I stared at them, all I could think of was whether everything I had believed over the last thirteen years was wrong. What if my father's murderer was walking free? What if my sister was more of a liar than I had ever imagined?

Downstairs, the front doorbell rang. I reluctantly dragged myself off the bed, already exhausted at the effort required to politely converse with yet another well-meaning neighbor bearing a casserole or ham or Harry & David basket of cheeses.

Just as I opened the bedroom door, I heard an unambiguously Kiwi "G'day."

"Hello," Aunt A said pleasantly, unsuspecting.

Upstairs, my body had turned to stone. I held my breath, waiting for the caller to speak again. I must have misheard.

But then I heard Caleb—unmistakably Caleb—say, "I'm looking for Jo, please."

"And whom shall I say is looking for her?"

"You can tell her it's Caleb, ma'am."

"Please, come in," Aunt A said, her voice frothing with enthusiasm. "I've heard so much about you. It's such a pleasure to finally meet you. I'm her Aunt Amelia."

There was silence before Caleb cleared his throat and said, "Oh, ah, I see."

Oblivious, Aunt A continued. "It's so good of you to come. Please make yourself right at home. I'll run upstairs and fetch Josie. That little rascal didn't tell me you were coming."

"It was, ah, a surprise."

I stood motionless in my bedroom doorway, torn between the desire to hide and the desire to run. Neither was a viable option. In moments, I would be forced to admit that I had lied to Caleb—lied to him over and over again, about everything.

When Aunt A's footsteps sounded at the turn of the staircase, I ducked through the open door of her craft room. Before Aunt A had filled it with yarn and scrapbooking materials, it had been the spare bedroom that, for a matter of months in 2002 and 2003, housed my mother. I gently pulled the door closed behind me, nausea settling over me as I remembered hearing the muffled sounds of my mother talking to herself through this same door.

"Josie?" I heard Aunt A say.

In desperation, I glanced toward the open window. It was just over the roof of the front porch; I could slide out onto it and—My fevered thoughts were interrupted by the sound of heels clicking up the porch steps, and then I heard a voice that made everything eminently worse.

"Well, well, well. What have we here?"

"Ah . . . hello," Caleb said suspiciously.

"Oh! *Caleb*. I had no idea you were coming," Lanie said, affecting a breathless voice that I supposed must be her imitation of me.

Aunt A called my name again, her voice sounding closer.

I looked back at the window. The only certain way to avoid the disaster waiting downstairs was to disappear again, but I couldn't stomach the thought of running. I was almost thirty years old; it was time for me to face my reality, no matter how unpalatable it might be. With a breath of firm resolve, I abandoned the safety of the craft room and began descending the stairs. At the curve of the staircase, I paused to gather myself and took the opportunity to look around the corner at my sister and my boyfriend. Lanie turned in flirtatious circles in front of Caleb, diamond earrings sparkling. Jealousy and a dull sense of déjà vu combined into a hard, cold lump in my stomach, tinged with unease. The behavior was odd even for my unpredictable sister. What was she hoping to accomplish? Adam's concerns about Lanie's stability rattled around in my head.

"How do you like my new sweater?" Lanie trilled.

Caleb cocked his head and ran a hand through his loose hair, still in desperate need of a haircut, his expression one of complete befuddlement. "Uh . . . do we know each other?"

"It's me!" she said, barely able to contain her smirk.

"I'm not . . . Jo?" he asked unsurely, his brow deeply furrowed.

Lanie laughed triumphantly. It was time for me to put a stop to this bizarre charade.

"Josie!" Aunt A exclaimed, appearing at the top of the stairs. "There you are! Caleb is here. You should've told me he was coming! I would have had the cleaners come. Or at least picked up the place a little."

"Sorry," I murmured, beginning my unavoidable descent to the ground floor. At the base of the stairs, I cleared my throat and said, "Lanie, that's enough."

She inclined her head toward me, blue eyes dancing, and smiled innocently. "This one's a keeper."

"If you don't mind," I said stonily.

"Nice to meet you," Lanie said to Caleb, her voice sugar-coated. Then she stepped into the living room, shouting, "Aunt A? Did I leave my wallet here earlier?"

Caleb turned to me warily, as if I might not be myself, either. "Jo, what the hell is going on?"

I intended to meet his eyes but ended up looking at his right earlobe instead. "That was my sister."

Caleb made a noise that was part laugh, part incredulous exhalation. "What do you mean, 'That was my sister'? *What* sister? And perhaps you'd like to explain just how the bloody hell the door was answered by the aunt whose death you're supposed to be mourning?"

I opened my mouth, even though I had yet to formulate an explanation. Lanie giggled in the next room, and Aunt A's

174

hovering presence was audible from the staircase. Whatever I was going to say to Caleb, I needed to say it without an audience.

"Let's go upstairs."

Caleb looked over at the staircase and clenched his jaw. His hesitation was a punch in the stomach.

"Please," I said, my voice wavering.

After another agonizing moment, Caleb nodded silently and followed me upstairs.

I shut the door and gestured for Caleb to take a seat on the bed. The expression on his face indicated he thought the bed might be a lie, too, but he conceded to sit tersely on the blue-and-white quilt.

"I thought we agreed that you weren't going to come to Illinois. How did you even know how to get here?"

I instantly regretted starting on the offensive. Caleb stared at me as though he could not believe that I was going to try to make this into his fault, and then his expression hardened.

"Your aunt's return address was on an envelope on the desk. After I got over the jet lag and cleared my head, I realized I should've never let you come to the funeral—or," he said, hooking his fingers into air quotes, "the 'funeral'—alone. Your aunt raised you and you think of her as a mother. If that's even true."

"The truth is complicated."

"That's where you're wrong, Jo. The truth is never complicated. It's just the truth. Circumstances may be complicated, but the truth is always black and white." Caleb looked at me sternly. "Now, I need some answers. What the hell is going on?"

My throat was clogged with a lump so large I doubted words would fit around it. I swallowed hard, and my saliva was bitter and metallic. It seemed like an unpromising start, but I forged ahead. The only thing that could salvage our relationship was the truth.

"I haven't been entirely honest with you about my family."

Caleb snorted to signal that was an understatement.

I nodded miserably, uncertain what to say next. *My father is dead, my sister is crazy, my mother is both dead and crazy?* Nothing sounded right. Caleb was watching me expectantly, and I could feel the air between us cool with each moment I hesitated. In desperation, I reached for a literary trope, something I had often heard extolled in the bookstore: *Show, don't tell.* I stuck my hand in the top drawer of my bedside table and dug past decade-old notes, tangles of costume jewelry, sticky tubes of lip gloss, and a dog-eared romance novel until I found it. My fingers trembled as they closed around the edge of the frame and pulled it from the drawer.

I was almost too heartsick to look at it. The photograph had been in the drawer ever since Aunt A had received the letter from our mother, the one that informed us she had chosen the Life Force Collective over us, the one that did not contain a single line for Lanie or myself. Reading that letter, my blood had gone fiery with unfamiliar rage. I had wanted to destroy everything that reminded me of her, tear it into tiny, unrecognizable bits, set it aflame and curse the ashes, but my sentimentality had ultimately prevailed. Instead, I had buried the photograph beneath teenaged flotsam and done my best to forget about it.

The photograph had been taken Christmas 2001, the last Christmas that the Buhrman family numbered four. Using the camera's timer function had resulted in an off-center and slightly out-of-focus image, but it was nonetheless our last remaining family portrait. In it, Lanie and I sit in front of the Christmas tree in matching plaid pajamas, our father behind us, a pipe clenched between his teeth and his great arms encircling us and pulling in my mother, a reluctant figure in a cranberry-colored sweater offering a shy smile, diamond earrings twinkling in her ears. My father had not been a religious man—I couldn't recall a single instance of him attending church—but he had always loved Christmas, its emphasis on family and demonstrative affection.

I set the cheap, gold-edged frame in Caleb's hands and pointed at the faces as I identified them.

"This is me," I said, laying my finger on the head of a dark-haired girl with rosy cheeks and a gleeful grin. I could barely remember being that person. "And this is my twin sister, Lanie. We were fourteen here. And this is my father. Ten months after this picture was taken, my father was killed.

"And this," I said, placing my finger on my mother's soft expression without waiting for Caleb to absorb the information about my father, "is my mother. My father's death was hard on all of us, but it was hardest on her. My mother had always been delicate, but she fell completely apart after Dad died." Memories of my mother sitting in the courtroom, her face pale and utterly slack, or of pacing in the bedroom across the hall, making endless circles on the worn floor, flooded my mind, and I had to shake my head to clear them. "We essentially lost both parents the same night. Our mother shut down completely. She stopped speaking to us, she'd barely even look at us. Aunt A took care of us from then on. That part has always been true."

I hazarded a glance at Caleb. His brows were knit together and his mouth was tight, but I couldn't tell if it was an expression of sorrow or pity or anger.

"And then, a year after Dad was killed, when Lanie and I were sixteen, our mother ran away to join a cult. We hadn't heard from or about her until the other day, when Aunt A got a call. Our mother is dead. It was her visitation I went to yesterday, and it's her funeral you'll be attending tomorrow." I swallowed hard. "That is, if you stay."

Caleb frowned. "Why did you tell me that your aunt died?"

"Because I'd told you years ago that my mother was dead. How could I explain that no, actually, *this time* she was *really* dead?"

"But why did you lie in the first place? Why did you tell me that your mother was dead when she wasn't?"

"Because, Caleb, she joined a *cult*. She abandoned us. By the time I met you, I hadn't heard from her in seven years. For all I knew, she *was* dead. But it wasn't just about her. It was about me, too. I'd devoted a lot of time and effort to distancing my old life from my new one. I tried to forget about my family."

"Jo, I'm not trying to minimize anything that happened

to you in your childhood, but I don't understand what you were thinking. Didn't you think that someday I'd find out the truth?"

"Honestly, I wasn't thinking that far ahead. When I first told you about my family that night in Zanzibar, I didn't know we had a future together. I thought I was just something to keep you entertained while you were in Africa."

"Something to keep me 'entertained'?" Caleb repeated, his mouth twisted in horrified surprise. "Is that really what you think of me?"

"Caleb, that was years ago. It's not a reflection on you; it's a reflection of how jaded and cynical I was back then. I'm not that person anymore, and I have you to thank. You're the best thing that's ever happened to me, and I am not exaggerating in the slightest when I say that. I love you, Caleb."

"I don't know, Jo. Even if I could understand you lying about your parents—and I'm not saying that I do, but just for argument's sake—even if I could, why didn't you tell me about your sister?"

"Lanie is a self-centered, backstabbing drug addict. I try to forget she exists."

Caleb, who worshipped his own sister, looked pained to hear me speak about my own flesh and blood in such a manner.

"Trust me, Caleb. Lanie is a story for another day."

"What if I hadn't found out? Were you going to hide this from me forever?"

"I never meant for it to get this far. In the beginning, even while I was falling in love with you, I thought this was temporary." I put up a hand to stave off his outraged protest. "I know, I was wrong. But you can't imagine what I'd been through. By the time I met you, I had been completely lost for five years. I couldn't imagine anyone being permanent in my life ever again. And then you left, and I felt justified for thinking that."

"Jo, my contract ended," he objected. "I had to go back to New Zealand. I didn't *leave* you."

"I know. But you don't understand what a mess I was back then. I didn't trust *anyone*; I didn't know how. And then you wrote a few months later and asked me to visit you, and I started to think that maybe I could trust you. Maybe you were different, maybe this was something real. I was happier than I'd been in years, and I was too afraid of wrecking things to tell you the truth. I promised myself I'd do it when the time was right, but the time just never seemed right, and then we were moving to New York together and I couldn't tell you because I'd been lying to you for so long." I reached for Caleb's hands, but he pulled them out of my grasp. Choking back tears, I continued. "I'm sorry, Caleb. I'm so sorry. I know that an apology is probably too little and much too late, but I don't know what else I can do. *I'm sorry.* I should never have lied to you. You are the only thing that means anything to me in this entire world, and I would die if I lost you."

For one long, awful moment, Caleb stared at me with eyes as blank and cool as steel. It was a look I had not even imagined his empathetic face capable of making, and it made me sick. I had always known Caleb would someday realize

I wasn't as good a person as he, certainly not as good a person as he deserved, and that day had arrived.

But then Caleb wavered. His spine remained rigid and his jaw clenched, but there was a minute softening of his eyes. "Don't say that."

"I would," I insisted, my voice shaking with emotion. "I would *die* without you."

Caleb grimaced and lifted his shoulders in a half-shrug. "I don't quite know what you expect from me, Jo. If what you've told me about your life is true, it's horrible, but—"

"It's true," I promised. "And, Caleb, there's more."

"What else? A brother you keep chained in the basement?"

"A podcast. Have you heard of *Reconsidered*?"

He nodded slowly. "I haven't listened to it myself, but I've heard of it. True crime?"

"Yeah. And the murder at its center—the one being 're-considered'—is my father's."

Caleb frowned down at the frame still in his hands, at my father's jovial face staring up at him. "That can't be. Someone would've told me if it was about your family."

"My last name isn't really Borden," I admitted. "I mean, it is now. I went to the San Francisco County Court and filled out the appropriate paperwork and everything. But I was born a Buhrman. As in Chuck Buhrman."

"Fuck, Jo," he said, flinging the frame onto the bed. He ran his hands through his hair, hurt glistening in his eyes. "You never even told me your real name?"

"I'm not that person anymore," I insisted, gesturing to

the teenager in the picture. "Caleb, you have to believe me. Please—"

"Stop it," he said, standing up and backing away. "I don't know you at all. You've lied to me about everything. *Everything*."

"I love you," I said, my voice strangled. "That's not a lie."

"Don't," he said, his words loaded with disgust. "That's not fair. You can't expect me to just shrug and be okay with this."

"Please—" I started, but Caleb turned on his heel and stalked out of the bedroom. The door slammed, and everything inside me shattered.

From Twitter, posted September 24, 2015

Poppy Parnell ✓
@poppy_parnell

Josie Buhrman still refusing to speak with me. Why? What is she hiding? #Reconsidered #ChuckBuhrman

♺ ♥ ↩   50m

Samantha R.
@therealmissus1

@poppy_parnell She is definitely hiding something! Don't give up! The #truth **will set you free** #JosieBuhrman! #Reconsidered #ChuckBuhrman

♺ ♥ ↩   47m

Eric Qualls
@ercq54

Unpopular opinion: Maybe Josie just wants @poppy_parnell to leave her alone. #Reconsidered #ChuckBuhrman

♺ ♥ ↩   45m

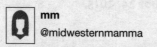

mm
@midwesternmamma

@ercq54 @poppy_parnell SHUT UP. DON'T STOP TRYING. GET THAT BITCH TO TALK. #JUSTICEFORWARRENCAVE

30m

chapter 12

The morning we buried what was left of my mother, the sky was clear and the air was crisp. It was the kind of early autumn day that made you feel good to be alive, if you were the type of person who believed the weather could reinforce your soul, or if you were doing something other than attending a funeral.

I made my way across the cemetery lawn, the ground unsteady beneath my feet. Grief tilted my vision, and the sight of the tent erected over the open grave, the chairs neatly lined up beside the earth's gaping maw, stopped me in my tracks. How could we commit my mother's ashes to the earth and then walk away? How could we have buried my father and left him here? I bit my lip to keep from crying out, and blood filled my mouth.

Sophie, Peter's youngest daughter, patted my arm gently. "Are you okay, Josie? Do you need a minute?"

A large, warm hand landed on the small of my back, and Caleb said, "I've got her."

Sagging with relief, I turned gratefully into his embrace, resting my forehead against his sternum.

"You came," I said against the smooth fabric of his dark suit.

Caleb kissed my head tenderly. "Of course I came."

The burial was harder than I had anticipated. Watching the remains of my mother and all our lost chances being lowered into the ground was gut-wrenching, but in the end it was Aunt A who nearly undid me. Aunt A, the bravest, most resilient woman I knew, was weeping openly, a spluttering sob occasionally tearing through the quiet, making the rest of us look away. She clutched Ellen with one hand and clawed helplessly at her own chest with the other. I wanted to comfort her, but I did not, part of me fearing that her complete and total grief was contagious.

If things had been different, my twin sister and I might have supported each other during this difficult time. We might have comforted each other with childhood memories and heartwarming anecdotes about our mother. We alone would understand our shared grief, and we could have found solace in each other. We would have known that, no matter how much worse things got, we would always have each other.

But as Reverend Glover spoke in uneasy generalities about my pagan mother's prospects for the afterlife, Lanie and I sat on opposite ends of the small row of chairs. She looked pale and exhausted, her under-eyes hollow and bruised. As she shook, her daughter, who looked so much like a miniature version of my sister that I startled, wrapped her arms around Lanie's waist, steadying her. Lanie clasped her daughter against her, closed eyes leaking tears, mouth moving in a silent whisper I could not decipher.

I wondered if Lanie remembered the last thing she had said to our mother, the violence she had inflicted on her. I wondered if that was on her mind as she stared down into the grave, wondered if Lanie worried that she had been the one to drive our mother away.

* * *

The night before our mother left us was a warm Saturday in early June. Lanie and I had just finished our sophomore years, and Warren Cave had been sentenced to life in prison a month earlier. We had expected the conclusion of the trial would lift our mother's spirits, but she only retreated further into herself. The trial had given her a reason to get out of bed each day, to shower and put on clothes; without that motivation, she had stopped bathing regularly and rarely left her bedroom. We saw her only on her occasional trips to the kitchen, where she would pour scant bowls of cereal that she would then ferry back upstairs to consume behind closed doors. If we pressed our ears to her bedroom door, she could alternately be heard pacing and muttering to herself or tapping away on an old laptop. After her nightly bowl of Kix, she would swallow a tranquilizer large enough to put down a horse and sleep for twelve hours. It was barely a life, but we told ourselves it couldn't last forever. We thought that if we just gave her time she would come back to us.

Adam and I made plans to meet our friends at the movies to see some psychological thriller everyone was excited about. The theater was starting to darken as Adam and I made our way inside, looking around for our friends. Just as I caught sight of Ellen's shiny blond hair, a familiar voice echoed from the front of the theater.

"Gimme the gummy worms, asshole."

I exchanged a worried glance with Adam. "That sounds like Lanie."

"At the movies? Shouldn't she be out vandalizing property or getting high?"

Lanie's voice reverberated again in the cavernous theater, an octave higher than usual. "I said, I want the motherfucking gummy worms."

"Sounds like she might already be high." I frowned. "Save me a seat. I'm going to go down and check on her."

"Josie, don't. She's just going to upset you. You aren't Lanie's keeper."

"Aren't I?" I asked, raising an eyebrow. "It's a twin thing. Don't worry; this will only take a minute. It's not like I'm going to stay down there and get caught up in her gummy worm dispute."

Adam registered his disapproval with a shake of his head, but slid into the row with our friends. My palms began to sweat as I hurried toward the front of the theater. Confrontations with Lanie were still a new and uncomfortable experience for me, and I dreaded arguing with her in front of an audience. The stench of liquor and weed reached me while I was still yards away, and my stomach tightened. By the time I reached my sister, slouching in the front row with Ryder and four scruffy guys I didn't recognize, I felt ill.

"What the fuck?" Lanie objected when she saw me. "Why are you following me?"

"Whoa, that chick looks just like you."

"Except," Ryder interjected, cackling like a hyena, "Lanie isn't a stuck-up bitch."

Ignoring Ryder, I addressed my sister. "Are you aware that everyone in this theater can hear you?"

She smirked and exchanged a high five with the guy on her left.

"What are you even doing here anyway?" I asked.

"Watching a movie, sis. It's a free fucking country."

"Now get lost, bitch," one of the boys growled, giving me the middle finger with both hands. "You're blocking our view."

"Are you going to let him talk to me like that?" I demanded of my sister.

"You heard him," Lanie said, stretching a gummy worm between her teeth and fingers. "Get lost."

At that point, it was still surprising to me how much of a stranger my sister had become, and for a moment, I could do nothing other than gape at her.

"Get lost, Josie," she repeated.

"Fine." I sighed. "Just keep your voice down, all right? You're embarrassing me."

Lanie's high-pitched laughter trailed me all the way back to my seat.

"I understand the vulgar screeching up front can be attributed to my least favorite cousin," Ellen said as I lowered myself into the seat between her and Adam.

"I don't want to talk about it," I muttered. I was grateful when the movie started and I could hide in the darkness and forget my own problems by focusing on those on the screen.

The movie was just as I feared it would be: tense and violent, and I had to watch a portion of it through my fingers. There was a particularly bloody skirmish near the end of the movie in which the villain attempted to kill his wife, but she wrestled the gun away from him and shot him instead, taking off a chunk of his head. The theater let out a collective gasp, and one single, piercing shriek arose.

Lanie.

By the time the second shriek pierced the air, I had already leapt to my feet. I vaulted over Adam and raced to the front of the theater.

Lanie had settled into a low, constant wail, and her supposed friends were staring at her as though she were a deranged stranger. Her arms felt surprisingly frail in my hands as I tugged on them, ordering her to stand up.

"Come on, Lanie. Let's get you out of here."

Hooking an arm under my sister's armpit, I was able to get enough leverage to drag her to her feet just as a flashlight shone in the back of the theater. While the beam bobbed down one aisle toward the front, I hurried up another aisle with my whimpering sister.

Adam was waiting for us just outside the theater. I tried to pass Lanie to him, but she slipped through his arms like a wet noodle and crumpled onto the carpet.

"What's the matter with her?"

"I don't know," I said, kneeling down to remove popcorn from her hair and examine her for obvious signs of trauma. "I think she's just freaking out because . . . you know. Guns. I want to get her home. Can I borrow your car?"

"Yeah, but Josie, do you think that you can handle her on your own? Should I come with you?"

"I don't want to get you involved in this."

"It's a little late for that," he grunted, lifting Lanie into a standing position.

"The keys, Adam, please. I'd like to get her out of here without getting arrested."

"Getting arrested might be good for her," he said, pulling the keys from his pocket.

"Don't start," I warned him.

In the parking lot, I propped my sister against the side of Adam's car while I unlocked it. With an elastic groan, she slid down the car's side and collapsed onto the filthy concrete, her hair landing in a damp oil stain.

"Goddammit, Lanie, *get up.*"

The sound she made in response was small and pitiful, and my frustration slipped into fear. Under the too-bright lights of the parking lot, her face was ashen and waxy, her mouth a twisted red slash. Was this what an overdose looked like?

"Hey," I said, crouching down beside her. "Do I need to call 911?"

Her eyelids fluttered and she shook her head.

"Come on, then. Let's go home."

She twitched. "No."

"Yes," I countered, dragging her to her feet. "We're going home. Now."

She slumped, deadweight in my arms, and I staggered to catch her, hitting one of my knees painfully against the ground in the process. In a sudden burst of anger, I slapped my sister across the face. It was the first time since we'd been out of diapers that I had hit her, and her eyes snapped open like a doll's.

"Stop it!" I screamed. "Just stop it! This needs to end. *Now.*"

She nodded, her head bobbing like a marionette's. "You're right."

Taken aback at the sudden change in temperament, I hesitated. "Really?"

Lanie nodded and let herself into the passenger seat of Adam's car. She spent the ride home staring straight ahead with wide, unblinking eyes. She kept muttering something to herself under her breath, something that sounded like "hurt the girl," but every time I asked her what she was saying, she would clam up.

When I pulled up to the curb in front of Aunt A's house, Lanie didn't even wait for me to kill the engine before she bolted from the car. Cursing her, I yanked the keys from the ignition and went after her. She tore through the foyer, almost tripping on the Oriental rug, and bounded up the steps, taking them two at a time, scrambling up the last few on her hands and knees when she lost her footing.

Aunt A emerged from the kitchen, wiping soapy hands on her apron, looking alarmed. "What's going on?"

Halfway up the stairs, I paused, but before I could say anything a muffled scream sounded from my mother's bedroom. The blood drained from Aunt A's face and she barreled up the stairs, reaching the door at the same time as me.

I flipped on the light, and we both gasped.

Lanie knelt on the bed, her dirty jeans smudging traces of parking lot grit on the pale yellow comforter as she straddled our mother, holding a pillow down over her face. I watched in horror as our mother, who had already taken her post-dinner tranquilizer, flailed her pale arms uselessly while Lanie, face twisted into a grotesque snarl and muttering unintelligibly, smothered her.

"Lanie!" I screamed. *"Stop!"*

Aunt A wasted no energy on words. Running to her sister's aid, she grabbed Lanie by the shoulders and flung her across the room with what had to be adrenaline-driven superhuman strength. Lanie hit the floor like a rag doll, arms and legs splayed, but she barely blinked before scrambling to her feet and rushing back to the bed.

Instinctively, I hurled myself into her path. "Stop!"

She skidded to a halt in front of me, her face just inches from mine. I shrank from her in fear. In the darkness of the movie theater and the parking lot, she had looked relatively normal. A little unwell, perhaps, but not markedly different from usual. But under the 75-watt lighting of our mother's bedroom, I saw just how unhinged she really looked: blood-shot eyes bulging, teeth bared, debris-filled hair wild, pupils totally blown. I was half afraid she would take a bite out of my cheek, but I grabbed her arms anyway, her skin hot and damp beneath my touch.

"Stop," I begged. "What are you doing?"

She said something under her breath, but her voice was rough, as if her throat was scratched, and her cadence sounded off. I couldn't tell what she said, but it sounded like the same phrase she had been repeating in the car.

"What did you say?"

"First the pearls," she said—or I thought she said. Her voice still sounded distorted, and the phrase made no sense.

"What? What does that even mean?"

Lanie began to laugh, a high-pitched, manic giggle that was so deeply unsettling I released her. She hesitated only a second before launching herself back onto the bed, slamming the pillow over our mother's face once more.

"This is your fault!" she screamed down at the pillow, veins popping and saliva flying.

"Stop!" Aunt A shouted, grabbing at Lanie to pull her off. This time, Lanie was ready for the attack and lashed out, her jagged nails catching Aunt A in the face, sending a bloody rivulet streaming down her cheek. Aunt A gasped and staggered back, touching her wound.

"What are you doing?" I shouted, shoving Lanie as hard as I could. I didn't succeed in throwing her off our mother, but I did knock her off balance, and Aunt A seized the opportunity to grab Lanie's leg and drag her off the bed and onto the floor.

I rushed to remove the pillow from my mother's face and help her sit up. Mom was wearing just her nightgown, and I was shocked to see how thin her shoulders and chest had become, how translucent her skin looked.

"Are you okay?" I asked her.

She looked at me without speaking and then turned her gaze to the floor, where Aunt A was using both arms and both legs to pin Lanie down. My stomach dropped as I looked from the ghost-like shell of my mother to my wild, thrashing sister. What had happened to these two women who I loved so much?

"Lanie, *stop it*," Aunt A ordered while my sister gnashed her teeth and twisted beneath her. "Tell me what's going on."

"Stop it," she repeated, her words thin and high. "Somebody's got to stop it. She said," she said, jerking her head as if to indicate me. Before I could respond, she jerked her head in the other way, possibly indicating our mother. "And she said."

"What?" Aunt A asked, her face wrinkling in confusion. "Who said what?"

"The pearls," she muttered, then snapped her head in my direction, her eyes suddenly wide. "This is your fault."

"Josie, what's she talking about?" Aunt A asked. "What's going on?"

"Stop it," Lanie snapped.

"I don't know," I said desperately, on the verge of frustrated tears. "I found her like this. Well, not quite like this, but . . . We were at the movies. Not together, but both of us at the same movie. And she just flipped out."

"What pearls?"

"I have no idea."

Aunt A nodded grimly and stared down at Lanie. "Lanie, I need you to tell me the truth. Are you on drugs?"

Lanie spit in her face.

"That's it," Aunt A growled. "Josie, call the police."

I looked at my flailing sister, her face twisted in an almost unrecognizable mask of madness. Aunt A was right. Adam was right. Lanie was out of control, and we should turn her over to the police. But she was my sister. My twin sister. How could I call the police on my twin sister?

"Josie," Aunt A barked. "Now."

"Call them!" Lanie taunted. "Do it! Call them, for God's sake! What are you, some sort of fucking chicken?"

195

I snapped.

I fell on my sister, screaming insults and scratching at her face, grabbing fistfuls of her ink-black hair. Aunt A separated us quickly, grabbing my shoulders and roughly pulling me off her. Brushing herself off, Lanie sat up on her knees.

Aunt A hurried to the bed, readying herself for Lanie's next move. But Lanie drew a rattling breath and looked from Aunt A to me to Mom. "This is your fault," she spit, then stood and walked away.

Breathing a sigh of relief, Aunt A went to her sister's side. She had already fallen back asleep, her face relaxed and serene. Aunt A tenderly brushed a stray hair off her cheek and kissed her on the forehead.

Outside, an engine started, and then we heard the crunch of gravel as Lanie pulled our shared car out of the driveway.

Aunt A glanced up at me. "Should she be driving?"

"No," I said. "But I don't know how to stop her."

By the time Lanie returned home the next morning, freshly stoned but blessedly calm, our mother was gone.

Arriving for the burial was hard, but leaving the cemetery was nearly impossible. There was nothing to do once the urn containing my mother's ashes had been lowered into the ground—nothing could undo the years of estrangement, the times that I had cursed her name because she had abandoned us—but just the thought of walking away and leaving her there in the ground made me shake with guilt.

"We're going to Mom's house, hon," Ellen said softly, squeezing my shoulder. "Did you want to come with us?"

"I—" I started, but couldn't finish, unable to articulate that I couldn't leave, not just yet.

"I'll stay with her," Caleb said to Ellen. He sat beside me and took my hand. "Take as much time as you need."

And so I sat in a chair, watching as the others dispersed. When Lanie walked away, she didn't look back once, and I had to wonder what she was feeling. Lanie had always been our mother's favorite—something I had rationalized away as a child, thinking that our father liked me best. Lanie was the one who volunteered to help our mother in the garden, the one who read *Wuthering Heights* with her; I was the one who listened to our father's mini-lectures on American presidents and spent weekends with him scouring yard sales for discarded reference books. On the family trivia nights my father regularly instigated, I teamed with him, combining his knowledge of history with my self-studied geography, and we battled Mom and Lanie, who together dominated the arts. Now it was just the two of us left, me and Lanie, virtual strangers where we had once formed the two halves of one magnificent whole.

From Twitter, posted September 25, 2015

Poppy Parnell ✓
@poppy_parnell

RIP, Erin Buhrman. Your story will soon be told!
#Reconsidered #ErinBuhrman #ChuckBuhrman

15m

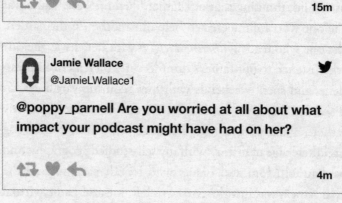

Jamie Wallace
@JamieLWallace1

@poppy_parnell Are you worried at all about what impact your podcast might have had on her?

4m

chapter 13

Caleb and I returned to find Aunt A's house full of her friends, who had arrived with store-bought appetizers and bottles of wine. I couldn't tell which friends I recognized and which ones I had never met, so I kept my conversations light and impersonal. At one point, I was certain I saw Poppy Parnell, but when I charged over to order her to leave, I realized it was just one of Aunt A's colleagues, and so I thanked her for coming and refilled her wineglass.

In the kitchen, I found Ellen arranging carrots on plastic crudités trays and opening containers of dip.

"There you are," she said, shoving a tub of something purporting to be French vegetable dip into my hands. "I need help. Open this."

Grateful for the distraction of minor manual labor, I began wrestling with the pull tab as I wondered aloud, "What about this dip is French?"

"Name alone. I guarantee that the French don't eat this crap. This is wholly American."

"Ze Americans have ze lard ass," I said, putting on my most comical French accent. "Although, I have to tell you, I have met some French people who were really into eating processed junk."

"Well, of course you did, darling. You were socializing exclusively with dirty backpackers."

"Hey, *I* was a dirty backpacker," I protested, setting the now-open dip down onto the table.

"And yet I love you anyway. Speaking of dirty backpackers and assorted foreign characters, do you want to tell me what's going on with Caleb?"

"No," I said, plucking a carrot from the tray and shoving it in my mouth.

"Tell me anyway," she said, spreading crackers out into a fan shape on a plate. "He's here. Did you call him after I left the bar yesterday?"

"No, that would have shown some maturity." I crunched through another carrot and admitted, "Caleb surprised me."

Ellen set down the cracker box and gaped at me. "You didn't know he was coming? I can't believe I let Peter talk me into staying at a hotel last night! I miss all the good stuff."

I nodded grimly. "It was quite the surprise. For both of us. First he met your mother, who I'd said was dead. And then he met my sister, who I'd never mentioned."

"I can see how that would be a surprise."

"Yeah. Oh, and Lanie pretended to be me."

"As she does."

A vision of my sister at that long-ago party flashed through my mind, her wearing my pink sweater, her hair rumpled and cheeks flushed. A spark of fury ignited beneath my breast-bone, and I snapped, "Well, she must be out of practice because she didn't fool Caleb."

"Of course she didn't," Ellen scoffed.

"It's not that crazy," I said, put off by Ellen's dismissive tone. "We're identical twins. And it's not like she's never fooled anyone before."

Even as the words left my lips, though, I remembered the puzzled expression on Caleb's face, the disbelief evident in his voice even as he said "Jo?" It was clear he hadn't believed she was me. Caleb could tell the difference between us and he didn't even know there was a difference to tell. How was that possible? Unless . . .

"Oh," I said suddenly, the realization a swift kick in the gut. "Adam knew."

I looked to Ellen for confirmation, but it was no longer a question in my mind. Adam had known that it was my sister he took by the hand at Benny's party, my sister who he locked himself inside an upstairs bedroom with, my sister who he had sex with that night. He had always known.

"Oh, honey," Ellen said, laying a sympathetic hand on my arm. "Yes. I thought you knew that."

In the aftermath, Adam had sent a deluge of emails, proclaiming over and over again and in all-caps, *I THOUGHT SHE WAS YOU*. Had I ever truly believed that? I had certainly *wanted* to believe it. It was easier to believe Adam thought she was me; it was easier to find only one villain in the situation instead of two. Lanie had been disappointing me for years, whereas Adam had been my lifeline, my rock. Knowing both of them had deliberately betrayed me would have completely destroyed me. Believing he had been fooled by my untrustworthy sister had been an act of self-preservation.

"But why?" I sputtered. "Why would he . . . with Lanie?"

"Why do eighteen-year-old boys do anything, Josie? Hormones. Beer. Idiocy. They're simple, base creatures."

At that moment, Lanie pushed open the kitchen door. *Speak of the devil,* I thought unkindly. She looked glamorous in a tailored black wool dress and understated pumps. I was wearing a black H&M sweater on loan from Isabelle and a pair of old black pants I found in my closet, neither of which fit me very well. It seemed grossly unfair that she could remain so composed given the havoc she had wreaked on so many lives.

Ellen clocked my discontent from underneath her eyelashes and shoved the platter of crudités in Lanie's direction. "Here, take these into the other room."

"No," Lanie said, staring at the platter while making no moves to accept it. "I'm not a servant."

"I'm just asking you to *help*," Ellen insisted, pushing the platter at her again. Lanie stepped to the side, and the platter sailed out of Ellen's hands. It clattered noisily to the floor, and carrots rolled in every direction.

"Thanks a bunch," Ellen snapped as she stomped out of the room, leaving my sister and me alone with the spilled vegetables.

"Josie," she started.

I stared at her, searching her face, hoping for clues that would unravel the mystery of her: how she ended up with Adam, why she turned on me, what she really saw that night.

She frowned. "Why are you looking at me like that?"

I sighed. "What do you want, Lanie?"

"I want to talk. About us," she hastened to add, "not that podcast."

"Not now, Lanie. We just buried our mother."

"Making it even more important for us to clear the air," she said, lifting her chin determinedly.

"I said, *not now.*"

Adam pushed open the kitchen door, an empty wine bottle in his hands, and paused, looking from Lanie to me, clearly trying to decide whether getting a fresh bottle was important. "Everything okay in here?"

"Yes," Lanie said sweetly at the same moment that I said, "No."

Adam's eyes locked on me, and my guts churned. Whereas I had once given him credit for apologizing while my sister remained silent and unrepentant, I now was certain that those apologies had been riddled with lies. If I had only been a bit more skeptical, had held his untruths up to the light . . . then what? I wouldn't have left? If I hadn't left, I never would have met Caleb, and I couldn't imagine my life without him.

"Josie, can we—?" he started.

As little as I wanted to speak to my sister, I wanted to talk to Adam even less in the moment. I turned sharply to Lanie and said, "Fifteen minutes. You and me."

Lanie paused in the entrance to our old bedroom, her manicured fingertips tracing the stained wood of the doorframe. If it had been another day, I might have made a joke about emotional vampires not being able to cross thresholds any better than their mythological counterparts. Instead, I took a seat in the desk chair and watched as Lanie looked around the room.

"Wow," she said quietly. "It's just the same."

I nodded stiffly. "You haven't been here lately?"

"Not to this room." She shook her head. "Not since I moved out."

"You're not close with Aunt A? Even though you live in town?"

"Come on, Josie," Lanie said scornfully. "What do you think? I'm the one who drives everyone away: our mother, you. Aunt A wants nothing to do with me."

"She said that? That doesn't sound like her."

"Of course she's never said those exact words. But I know. I know the only reason she tolerates me at all is because of my daughter."

"That's not true, I'm sure," I murmured, looking down.

I picked up the model Washington Monument and turned it over in my hands, clasping my fingers around it so that the jagged edge where the tip had once been bit into my palm. I waited while Lanie looked at the pictures on the wall, and then finally sat on her old bed. She stared at her feet for a minute, and when she finally spoke, it was not what I expected to hear. I had expected an excuse, a reason why the things that had transpired were beyond her control. If I was honest, I had hoped for an apology.

Instead, Lanie said, "I named her Ann. After Mom. Her middle name, you know."

I wanted to hiss that *of course* I knew our mother's middle name was Ann, that Ann was the name I had selected for my own hypothetical future children with Adam, and that Adam knew that. But there was nothing to be gained from saying these things, or even thinking them, so I kept my mouth shut and pushed the monument deeper into my palm. My eyes watered.

"I've been dreaming about her," Lanie said quietly.

I looked up. "Your daughter?"

"Mom. I've been dreaming about Mom."

"Oh." I turned the monument over in my hands, unwilling to admit that I had not been dreaming about our mother, afraid that it showed Lanie was a better daughter than I.

"The dreams, though . . ." Lanie trailed off. "Sometimes they feel like more than dreams. Sometimes I feel like she's trying to tell me something. Do you ever have those?"

"Yes," I lied.

"And if I'm not dreaming about her, I'm not sleeping. Honestly, I don't think I've gotten more than a collective ten hours of sleep since she died."

"Lanie," I interrupted. "What is this? You dragged me up here to talk about your insomnia?"

"I just thought you might understand," she said, looking chastened.

"There are so many things we need to talk about. We can't just skip all that and go directly to lamenting our sleep schedules. If we're going to do this, we're going to start with all the havoc you've wreaked on my life."

"Fuck that," she said, eyes darkening. With a curse on her lips and a scowl on her face, she looked more like the sister

205

I remembered from high school than the chic Stepford wife that had inhabited her body. Part of me felt relieved to see her calm veneer cracking once more; there was a certain comfortable predictability to her temper.

"Every time I see Aunt A, she's always telling me how *perfect* your life is." Lanie's scowl deepened and she affected a shrill voice that I assumed was supposed to be Aunt A's. *"Did you know that Josie's boyfriend is a humanitarian? Did you know that Josie and her boyfriend own a one-bedroom apartment in New York City? Did you know that Josie sold a book to that funny lady comedian from* Saturday Night Live?"

"Kristen Wiig? Yeah, I did," I said automatically. I caught myself and returned her scowl.

Lanie was wrong. My life wasn't perfect. It was good more often than it was bad, and some days it was close to great, but it wasn't perfect. I had Caleb, who was a decent, honorable man, and a place to call home and enough money to feel secure, but I also had a lifetime of pain and regret. I knew not all of that was Lanie's fault—no matter what I said, some of the blame fell on the shoulders of my father's killer, whoever that might be, and another portion rested on those of my late mother. Still, I held Lanie accountable for most of the lingering hurt.

There were so many things I could have said to Lanie, so many examples of how she had failed me, but, regrettably, when I opened my mouth, what came out was: "You married *Adam*."

"Yes," she said, nodding readily. "I did."

"You . . . How . . ." I stuttered, unable to find the words to express how I felt. "You shouldn't have done that."

She frowned a little. "I was just trying to do the right thing."

"How was that the right thing?" I demanded, a suppressed sob threatening to break my chest in two. I would not cry in front of her; I would not show her how much her betrayal still hurt me. "I just don't understand what happened."

"Do you really want to know?" she asked quietly.

No, I thought, as my mouth whispered, "Yes."

Lanie's finger danced across the quilt, tracing what looked like a heart. She cleared her throat and, in a tiny voice, said, "When Adam and I slept together—"

"When you *took advantage of* him," I corrected automatically, even though an electric jolt ran through my body, reminding me that Adam's account was untrue.

Her eyes flashed with sudden anger, and she sent her fist flying into the bed with a small *thwump*.

"That's bullshit," she spit. "Is that what he told you? That's not what happened."

"What happened, then?"

"Adam came on to me."

Unbidden, Ellen's voice came into my head, a line from the past: *Adam looks pretty wrecked.* Cursed with the last scheduled final, I had been driving home for summer break days after everyone else. I had planned on leaving first thing the following morning, but the campus was deserted and so I decided to leave that evening instead. I called Adam as I neared town, eager to see him. Because he had gone to school out of state and our spring break plans had fallen through, I hadn't seen him since the holidays. I was disappointed when he didn't answer his phone. I called Ellen next, who shouted into the phone over the din of music and laughter that Benny Weston's parents were out of town and he had a couple of kegs.

"Come straight here," she commanded. "Everyone's here."

"Is Adam there? He didn't answer when I called."

"Probably because he's too busy drinking his face off. Want me to tell him you're on the way so that he has a chance to sober up?"

"No, let's keep it a surprise," I said, imagining the delight on Adam's face when he saw I was home early.

It was a devastating mistake, but I hadn't known it then: I simply had never known Adam to be much of a drinker, and I didn't assume that one year of college could have changed him that much. I thought Ellen was just being Ellen—that is to say, overly judgmental.

"You might want to drive fast, then. Adam looks pretty wrecked."

"Adam was drunk," I said to Lanie, my voice wavering.

"And you think I was sober? Honestly, Josie, why do you think I was even at that party? Ryder had heard that Benny's mom had a decent stash of painkillers, and we raided the medicine cabinet. I was so high I didn't even know my own name."

I nearly snapped that it must have made it easier to pretend to be me, but I swallowed the response. *Adam had known.* Lanie didn't need to impersonate me. I closed my eyes, recalling how I had made my way into the sweaty mass of people in Benny's living room just in time to see Adam descending the stairs, Lanie at his side. Adam's cheeks were flushed, his golden hair tousled, his smile dopey. His T-shirt was on inside out. His glazed eyes landed on me, and his color drained. He ran a hand over his face, a gesture that I interpreted at the time as astonishment, but in retrospect was clearly guilt. How could I have missed it?

Adam had known. It was a punch in the gut, realizing that the anger I had clung to for so many years—the notion that my sister had purposefully imitated me in order to steal my boyfriend away—was misplaced. Adam was no innocent in this . . . but that didn't absolve Lanie. She owed me a duty of blood. Adam might have betrayed me, but Lanie was the one who broke my heart.

"You're my sister," I said, my voice nothing more than a whisper. "How could you do that to me?"

"I did a lot of things then that I'm not proud of," Lanie said, her voice hardening. "But what about you?"

"What about me?" I demanded, surprised. "I didn't do anything wrong."

"You *left*," she spit. "Without so much as 'goodbye' or 'have a nice life' or 'fuck you.' You just left. You were all I had, and you *left*."

"If I meant that much to you, maybe you should've thought about what you were doing," I snapped, "instead of just doing whatever your id demanded."

But Lanie was beyond listening to me, her face crumpled in anger and indignant tears streaming down her cheeks. "You didn't even tell me where you were going. You told *Ellen. Ellen.* She's not your sister. *I am.*"

"Ellen isn't the one who slept with my boyfriend!"

Lanie snatched a pillow off the bed and pressed her face into it, screaming. When she tossed it aside, her cheeks were mottled red and stained with mascara, but her temper seemed calm. "I needed you," she said. "Dammit, Josie, I really *needed* you."

"I needed *you*," I argued. "I didn't want to go through all that stuff with Mom and Dad alone. But you wouldn't have anything to do with me. You were too busy getting high with Ryder and God knows what else."

"I was a mess," she said quietly. "But you were supposed to understand. You, my sister. But then you left, and I was an even bigger mess, and the only person around to help me pick up the pieces was Adam. He was the only one who understood."

"What do you mean Adam understood?"

"You left him, too. You were the most important person in both of our lives. And, yeah, maybe we fucked everything up, but if you loved us half as much as we loved you, you would have forgiven us. Or at least stuck around to listen to the apology. But you were just gone, and neither of us knew what to do. We missed you, and no one else understood how gutted we felt to have lost you. No one understood us except each other."

"And . . . what? Missing me was foreplay?"

Lanie shook her head in disgust. "Don't make a joke about this. I know it's hard to understand, but we fell in love. Not at first, you know. At first it was . . ." She trailed off and waved her hand, a dismissive gesture that turned my stomach. "But I got pregnant. It was an accident. I was going to have an abortion; I had the appointment scheduled and everything. But then I started thinking about you, and about what you would do if you were in my situation. You wouldn't have the abortion. You'd keep the baby and dedicate yourself to being a good mother. So I called Adam and told him I was pregnant. And . . . And Adam said that he would, you know, do the right thing and marry me." Lanie paused to purse her lips wryly. "He also offered to support us financially, without any other commitment. I think he nearly had a heart attack when I said I accepted his proposal of marriage."

"And now? Are you . . . happy?"

"That's a simple question with a complicated answer," she said, her face twisted in an unreadable expression. She left the bed, dropping to her knees on the ground in front of me. "I know I don't deserve your forgiveness."

Embarrassed, I looked away. "Lanie, get up."

"I know I don't deserve it," she repeated, grabbing my hands earnestly. "But I'm asking for it anyway."

My instinct, honed after ten long years during which I was furious with her, was to snap that she had always taken things she didn't deserve, that maybe if she hadn't always been so goddamn *entitled* we wouldn't be in this mess. But one look at her wet eyes stopped me. It wasn't true, after all; Lanie hadn't always been like that. Once she had been my favorite person in the world, the one I trusted more than anyone else. She had changed once before; it was possible she had changed again. I might not be ready to forgive and forget, but maybe I was finally ready to talk.

"You really hurt me," I said.

One fat tear dripped cinematically down her cheek. "I know."

"You were supposed to be the one person who never betrayed me."

"I know. Jesus, Josie, I know. I've spent the last ten years telling myself that. I made a huge mistake, a huge mess of everything. There's nothing that I can do that will make it better."

She rocked back on her heels, more tears quivering in her eyes. I wished I could say something. I wished I could forgive her, or tell her that I would forgive her someday. But I couldn't make myself say the words, not yet.

"I know I can never take back what I did, but do you think we'll ever be okay again?"

I shrugged. "You're my sister."

It wasn't really an answer, but Lanie smiled anyway.

chapter 14

Later that night, long after Aunt A's friends and colleagues had gone home, after Aunt A had sent herself to bed, and after Ellen and her family had helped me clean up and then left for the hotel, I found myself alone in the living room with Caleb. I sat on the couch, staring at him while he hovered in the doorway, the few yards between us feeling ten times their size. We hadn't been alone since he'd driven me home from the funeral, and we hadn't had a conversation of more than twenty words since the previous night.

He picked up his suit jacket from the back of a nearby armchair and looked at me. "Jo—"

"How did you know?" I asked abruptly. I hated myself immediately for the question. I needed to mend my relationship with Caleb, soothe the hurt my lies had caused, not drag my sister into things.

He tilted his head at me, confusion flickering in his gray eyes. "What do you mean?"

"Yesterday, when Lanie pretended to be me. How did you know that she wasn't?"

"Dunno." He shrugged. "I just did."

"But you didn't even know she existed."

"Yeah, but I know you." He caught himself and looked away. "I thought I did, at least."

His words stole my breath, painfully reminding me of how much I had hurt the man I loved.

"Caleb—" I started, but my throat felt suddenly parched and I grasped at a half-empty glass of water on the coffee table, chugging the contents.

Caleb frowned slightly. "I think that was left over from the reception."

Grimacing, I set down the glass and crossed the room to stand before him. I had to tell him the whole, messy truth while I still had the courage. I knew how easy it would be for me to omit my history with Adam, to slip back into familiar patterns of lying, but I also knew how much our relationship now depended on honesty. If I wanted to make things right with Caleb—and I did, oh, I did—I needed to start being more truthful.

I took a deep breath and said, "Caleb, I have to tell you something."

His face hardened, and he backed away slightly.

"It's not . . ." I started before trailing off lamely. Better to just get it over with. "Before Adam was Lanie's husband, he was my boyfriend."

Caleb lifted his dark brows in surprise, and I wished I knew what he was thinking. I doubted that was the revelation he had been expecting.

"Adam and I had been dating for three years when Lanie slept with him," I continued. "Or he slept with her. Or they slept with each other. I don't know anymore. One of them was drunk, one of them was high, I don't know who was more culpable. I don't know that it matters. But Adam's defense has always been that he thought Lanie was me."

"Bullshit."

I cracked a smile. "That's the most succinct description of the situation I've heard yet."

Caleb reached out and gently tucked my short hair behind my ear. "Adam's clearly a bloody idiot."

"He is," I agreed quietly, holding myself very still in case Caleb wanted to lean in and kiss me.

He didn't. Instead, he pulled his hand away from my hair and replaced it at his side, falling silent. I felt on the verge of tears, but I hadn't earned the right to cry over the circumstances—they were, after all, of my own making.

"That's why I never told you about Lanie. She hurt me so much that I couldn't even stand to think about her. I just wanted to forget she existed. I didn't know how to explain any of that to you."

Caleb sighed heavily. "I wish you'd tried."

Swallowing back tears, I nodded.

Caleb looked down at the jacket in his hands and glanced toward the door.

"Well," I said, my heart feeling like lead. "I guess you're heading back to the hotel."

Then he lunged forward and kissed me, an abrupt, forceful kiss, the kind that left a person winded. When he pulled away, my lips felt bruised.

Reaching behind Caleb, I locked the front door, and he took my hand to lead me up the staircase. In the velvet darkness of my old bedroom, he lowered me down onto the twin bed and arranged his body over mine. I closed my eyes to blot out the subtle glow of the plastic stars; I wanted to focus on nothing other than Caleb, on the familiar scratch of his stubble against my face and the heaviness of his warm, callused hands on my rib cage.

"Are we okay?" I whispered.

Caleb's hand paused, and he pulled back slightly. "Let's not ask the big questions tonight. I don't know where we go from here. I just know that I've missed you, and I think you've missed me. It's been a hard twenty-four hours, and I just want you in my arms. Is that okay?"

I nodded fiercely and wrapped my arms around his neck, pulling him closer. As his mouth, lips soft and tasting of coffee, closed over mine, I willingly shuttered my mind and surrendered my body.

I woke up alone. I felt a crushing desolation, certain of the inevitability that Caleb had come to his senses and left me. Our ending had been in view since the moment we met. I had prepared myself for the end a hundred times before, but as the years wore on, I had gotten comfortable, fallen more in love, hadn't been able to believe that he would actually, truly leave me. I thought of all the things I should have done to be a better girlfriend, a better human being. I would call him, I would find him, I would make him love me again. Feeling resolved, I swung my feet over the edge of the bed and drew back in surprise.

Caleb's shoes were by the nightstand.

Gravity suddenly had nothing on me; I was weightless,

buoyed by sheer relief. He hadn't left me; he hadn't even left the house.

Opening the bedroom door, I heard strains of Pearl Jam and could smell coffee and the rich, golden scent of buttery pancakes, all of which served as further confirmation that Caleb was still there and hinted optimistically at his mood.

As I descended the front stairs, the doorbell rang. I tightened my robe and opened the door, expecting to find a contrite neighbor apologizing for skipping the funeral in the universal mourning language of casseroles. Instead, there sat a large cardboard box, taped up tightly and dented at the corners, and, beyond it, the retreating figure of a delivery person.

"Who was it?" Aunt A asked, coming down the stairs as I tugged the box, which wasn't so much heavy as it was large and awkward, into the living room.

"UPS. They left this."

"What is it?"

"I'm not sure. It's addressed to you, and the return address is some post office box in California." I froze as I said the word *California*. I glanced quickly at Aunt A, who looked stricken as well. "You don't know anyone in California, do you?"

"Open the box," she said dully. "Let me get you some scissors."

I ripped the tape from the box with my bare hands and flung open the lid. Together, Aunt A and I peered into the box, which was crowded with a jumble of incense-scented, light-colored cloth; strings of beads; and assorted knick-knacks. Her voice trembled when she spoke. "They've sent us your mother's things."

I reached into the box and delicately fingered a strand of beads, as though they might shatter at my touch, barely resisting the urge to wind the long ropes of color around me, to wrap myself in my mother's essence and try to breathe her in one last time. Did these things help her find peace? Did they fill her with love and purpose, like we once had?

Why did you go, Mom? And why didn't you say goodbye?

Aunt A and I got no further than the beads before Caleb announced breakfast was on the table, and we agreed it would be a shame to allow such delicious-smelling pancakes to get cold. Aunt A went upstairs to fetch Ellen (who I was fairly certain hadn't eaten a pancake since the early 2000s), and I folded the box's flaps closed. There was a certain sense of relief at being forced to abandon the project, albeit temporarily. It had been a brutal and emotionally devastating week, and I wasn't certain I could withstand the added trauma of confronting my late mother's personal effects.

But after breakfast had been consumed and the kitchen had been cleaned, Aunt A returned to the box and I felt compelled to follow her. I had to imagine that Aunt A was feeling some of the same dread at the thought of opening it, and I couldn't allow her to suffer alone.

"I wish this hadn't come today," she said, staring down at it.

"Me too," I agreed, my voice catching. "After everything . . . You know, we don't have to open it right now."

"It's not going to get any easier."

"No." I sighed. "It's not."

"Come on," she said, kneeling beside the box and patting the ground beside her. "Let's do this together."

I nodded and sank to a seat. She was right: sorting through my mother's belongings would never be anything less than heartbreaking, and I knew that we could each use the moral support. As Aunt A pulled open the box, I took a deep breath, futilely hoping to catch a whiff of my mother's unique scent, vanilla and lilac and something green. But all I smelled was cardboard, and the musty scent of stale objects. My heart nearly cracked open.

Aunt A extracted a long, beaded necklace and dangled it before her, the glass beads twirling and catching the light. "This would've looked pretty on her," she said quietly.

I nodded in agreement, not daring myself to speak, feeling the lump of tears working its way up my throat. I plunged a hand inside and extracted a sky-blue scarf. I rubbed the gauzy fabric between my thumbs and against my face, hoping to feel some kind of connection. I felt nothing. Nothing about that piece of cloth reminded me of my mother. For all I knew, it wasn't even hers. We could have been mailed items belonging to someone else's dead mother. How would we ever know?

Unsettled, I reached into the box once more. There had to be something that would stir me, something that felt un-equivocally hers. My fingers hit something papery but soft, something that felt like a well-worn piece of stock paper, and I carefully pulled it free. I caught my breath when I recognized it as the cover to our mother's treasured copy of *Anna Karenina*. The book had been one of her favorites, one that Lanie and I had tried—and failed—to read on many occasions. One cold winter, stuck in Berlin while I raised money to keep traveling, I found a copy in the hostel's library and finally made my way through the tome. None of it stuck with me so much as its famous opening line: "Happy families are all alike; every unhappy family is unhappy in its own way."

As Aunt A and I sifted through the modest, sad artifacts of my mother's existence, fruitlessly searching for the rest of the book, I realized that this was the uniqueness of this unhappy family: a mother who had left behind nothing but broken incense burners and threadbare scarves that reeked of patchouli.

My fingers hit something else that felt book-like, and I pulled it out, hoping for more of *Anna Karenina*, or perhaps one of her journals. Our mother had been an inveterate journal-keeper, and, for as long as I could remember, she had chronicled her life in a series of notebooks. She guarded both their contents and location with extreme secrecy; I would only spot a journal in the wild when she had it in her hands, curled up in a chair by the window, lounging on the front porch swing, or, sometimes, holed up in the playhouse behind our house. Lanie would sometimes uncover them, but she never told me where. In the dark months after she had left for California, I had torn apart her bedroom looking for them, hoping they might contain some explanation of why she left or where she had gone. I never found them.

Instead, I extracted a thick pamphlet, its bright yellow cover torn and stained, its pages dog-eared. This book, whatever it was, had been well-loved. My stomach soured as I read the title: *The Official Handbook of the Life Force Collective:*

Ideals and Practices for All Members. I almost threw the book down, but curiosity overtook me. This might be the best chance I had to learn more about the cult that had consumed my mother, to understand why she had left us for them and never once looked back.

Gritting my teeth, I opened the book. After the title page, the first full page was dominated by a glamour shot of LFC founder Rhetta Quinn. From the gloss on her hair and the smoky eye makeup, I suspected it was one of her former head-shots. I resisted the urge to curse at her image and turned the page.

What We Believe, it said in bold-faced letters at the top of the page.

We believe in the restorative power of the sun. We believe in the energy it instills in us, and we believe that we are vessels of that energy. We believe that it is our duty as human beings to cultivate the energy bestowed upon us by the sun, the giver of energy and thus the giver of life.

I didn't have the patience to read any more of the hippy-dippy manifesto, not when I had lost my mother to its inane worship, and I flipped the page. *A Brief Biography of Our Founder, Rhetta Quinn*, accompanied by another glamour shot. This time, I couldn't help but spit some choice words.

"Josie?" Aunt A asked, looking up from some photographs. "What do you have there?"

"This," I said, handing it to her. "*The Official Handbook of the Life Force Collective.* Check out the two huge pictures of Rhetta Quinn before you're even five pages deep. What an egomaniac."

Aunt A frowned as she began flipping through the book. A few pages in she stopped, spots of angry color rising in her cheeks.

"I can't do this," she announced, dropping the handbook as though it had burned her. "I'm sorry. I know I said . . . but I need a break. I'm sorry."

"Don't apologize," I said, feeling guilty for handing her the book that had so upset her. "Are you okay?"

She nodded brusquely and headed for the stairs. Her abrupt departure was so unlike my normally calm aunt that I wondered what it was that she had found so objectionable. Was she as frustrated with Rhetta Quinn as I was, angry that this woman was tearing apart families for what seemed like an ego trip?

But when I picked up the book from where it had fallen, splayed open to Chapter 1, I saw that wasn't the source of her displeasure. Chapter 1 was (rather clumsily) titled *We Are Your Family Now. Plus, Helpful Hints for Disassociating with Non-Member Persons (Including Blood)*.

But even worse, the word *best* had been written in the margin in my mother's distinctive handwriting. I had no idea what she meant by that, but I could only imagine, and, given the context, it made me feel slightly sick.

I shoved the things back inside the box and decided to take a run to clear my head. But because I am nothing if not a glutton for punishment, I scrolled through the #Reconsidered hashtag as I climbed the stairs to change. According to Twitter, a special episode of the podcast had been uploaded that morning. Against my better judgment, I downloaded it and queued it up for my run.

Excerpt from transcript of *Reconsidered: The Chuck Buhrman Murder,* Episode 4: "All About Erin," September 25, 2015

Who was Erin Buhrman? That's the question on everyone's mind, so I decided to devote a special episode to her. We'll be back on Monday to our regularly scheduled programming.

Erin Buhrman was born Erin Ann Blake in Elm Park, Illinois, in 1966, the daughter of a farmer and a first-generation American of Irish heritage, the second of three children. As far as I can tell, Erin had a generally happy childhood . . . until January 1978. That was when eleven-year-old Erin was playing with her eight-year-old brother Dennis near a frozen pond on the family farm. Somehow, Dennis fell through the ice and drowned. According to local legend, Erin went in after him and nearly died of hypothermia.

Sarah Spicer, a former classmate of Erin's, spoke with me about how Dennis's death affected Erin.

SARAH: Erin used to be my best friend. I was a farm kid, too, so we had that in common. She was so sweet and silly, always ready to tell a joke or play a prank. But everything was different after Dennis died. It was like the life had just been sucked out of her. I don't think I ever saw her smile again. I know that sounds like an exaggeration, but it's not. She became a completely different person.

Erin may never have wholly recovered from losing her brother, but she did smile again. After graduating from high school, Erin enrolled in Elm Park College. It was there, of course, that she met her future husband, Chuck Buhrman. While some may have disapproved of the relationship—Chuck was, after all, her professor—those close to Erin saw it as a positive. Jason Kelly, Erin's former brother-in-law, remembers being pleased at the impact Chuck was having on Erin's life.

JASON: Chuck was the best thing that ever happened to Erin. By the time she met him, I'd been dating Amelia for three years or so, and I don't think I saw Erin smile, really smile, once during all that time. Then she started dating Chuck, and all of a sudden she was smiling and laughing and telling jokes. Terrible jokes—she had no sense of comedic timing, but she was trying.

She started baking again, too. A always talked about how much her sister loved to bake when they were kids, and then she stopped when their brother died. Shortly after she and Chuck started dating, we had them both over for A's birthday. Erin brought over this cake she'd made. It was a horrible cake, just awful. She'd made some sort of serious error in the measurements, but she was so damn pleased with herself for baking again that we all raved about how great it was. Then she took a bite herself and realized it was practically inedible, and we all kind of held our breath, wondering how she was going to react. She just laughed until she cried. I remember how happy A was that night, thinking Erin was returning to her old self.

Erin and Chuck were married two years after meeting,

and their twin daughters were born the following year. Jason hinted at some dark periods for Erin in the intervening years, saying that he knew sometimes his wife would be worried about her sister's mental state, but in general, he reported that life in the Buhrman household was happy and uneventful.

Then, in 2000, Erin and Amelia's beloved parents were killed by a drunk driver. I was told that this event plunged Erin into a depression. She became withdrawn and her mood swings became sharper and more prevalent.

JASON: A and I were splitting up back then, so I wasn't really around. But a mutual friend told me Erin took the accident really hard. For example, some people had organized meal deliveries for both A and Erin, but Erin refused to accept it. I guess she just left the baskets on the front porch. Sometimes the girls would come outside and collect them, sometimes Chuck would bring them in when he got home—and he was getting home really late, I guess, like nine, ten o'clock. It didn't sound like a good situation.

It seems cruel and unimaginably unfair for a woman whose brother died before her eyes and who lost both parents in one night to then have her husband snatched away from her as well, but that is, as we know, exactly what happened.

And that's when things really went sideways.

Already depressed and prone to bouts of reclusiveness, Erin became despondent after her husband's death. She and her daughters moved across town into her sister Amelia's house. She refused to leave the house other than to attend

Warren Cave's trial, and while there she didn't engage with anyone, declining to even give reporters the courtesy of a "no comment." Once the trial had concluded, Erin retreated to her sister's house, and no one outside her immediate family saw her in Elm Park again.

Even friends were shunned. Beverly Dodds White, the high school friend Erin was visiting while her husband was being murdered blocks away, explained to me just how much Erin had changed.

BEVERLY: Erin and I were close in high school, but we fell out of touch after she got married. We reconnected when I moved back to Elm Park after my divorce. It was October 2002, and, before I'd even finished moving in, I learned I needed emergency oral surgery to remove my wisdom teeth. They said I should have a friend come, and I didn't know anyone in town besides Erin. I took a chance and gave her a call. I was so grateful she agreed to come with me.

POPPY: Did you find her as you remembered her?

BEVERLY: She hadn't changed a bit. Still very quiet. Of course, that didn't matter because I couldn't talk. Still such a kind woman. I was a real wreck post-surgery, zonked on pain medication, slipping in and out of consciousness, but Erin took such good care of me, fetching me ice chips and whatnot.

POPPY: Did Erin say anything that made you think she or her husband felt threatened? By Warren Cave, or anyone else?

BEVERLY: I don't remember her saying anything like that, but I'm afraid that doesn't mean much. That entire day is a blur for me. Like I said, I was on a lot of pain medication. The only clear memory I have is waking up to the sound of someone pounding on the door, and that was when the police arrived to tell Erin her husband was dead.

POPPY: What about afterward? Did you and Erin ever discuss Chuck's murder? Maybe she mentioned something about Melanie or Warren Cave?

BEVERLY: I only spoke to Erin once after that. A few days later, after I'd recovered, I called to see if there was anything I could do for her. She was completely beside herself. Sobbing, saying it was all her fault, just heartbreaking.

POPPY: She said it was all her fault?

BEVERLY: She blamed herself, you know. If she hadn't been at my house that night, her husband wouldn't have been alone and he might not have been killed. That was the last time I talked to her. She wouldn't return any of my other calls. Her husband's death really just destroyed her.

Beverly's experience isn't unique. Erin wouldn't return anyone's calls. She stopped leaving the house. It was like she'd disappeared.

And then, one day, she really did.

Pamela Boland, a fellow teacher at the middle school where Amelia teaches, remembers how she learned that Erin was gone.

PAMELA: It was June. School was out for the summer, but that
was the summer they renovated the classrooms in the
north wing and expected all the teachers to pitch in.
Amelia didn't show up one morning, which was completely unlike her. She didn't even call anyone to say she
wasn't coming, and that had me worried. Amelia Kelly
has always been one of the most responsible people
I know. I figured she must be really ill, and so I swung
by her house that afternoon to check on her. Erin was
gone. Amelia was completely distraught, saying she was
certain her sister had harmed herself. I did my best to
console her, but what could I really say? Everyone knew
her sister was a few crayons short of a box. Then, a few
weeks later, Amelia told me she'd received a letter from
Erin saying she had joined something called the Life
Force Collective. We looked that up on the internet, and,
well, you know what *that* is.

The infamous Life Force Collective, a cult located in Northern California, promotes a simpler, sun-drenched lifestyle.
Little is known about the life that Erin Buhrman—or Sister
Anahata, as she was known within the LFC—lived for the last
decade. Amelia Kelly never heard from her sister again. Indi-
vidual LFC members eschew the outside world, and Sister
Anahata was no different.

And then, as we all now know, earlier this week, Erin Buhrman's tragic life came to a tragic end. Her body was found
hanging from a tree, an apparent suicide. As far as I am aware,
hers is the first instance of an LFC member taking his or her
own life. Suicide goes against everything the LFC stands

for, and its public relations officer is running himself ragged attempting to dispel any rumors of generalized unrest and depression within the ranks. This man, who calls himself Brother Earnest—that's Earnest as in the virtue, not as in Hemingway—agreed to join me on a call to discuss Erin Buhrman's mental state in the days and weeks leading up to her untimely demise. He would not, I was advised, comment on LFC practices, authentic or rumored.

POPPY: Do you know how Erin Buhrman learned about the Life Force Collective?

EARNEST: Like many of our brothers and sisters, Sister Anahata was guided to us during a difficult period in her life. She decided to reject the conventional Western lifestyle and embrace a more enlightened approach.

POPPY: So you don't know how she found you? Like, on the web or something?

EARNEST: The Life Force Collective does maintain an internet presence.

POPPY: Were you around when Erin—excuse me, Sister Anahata—first arrived at the Life Force Collective?

EARNEST: Yes, I remember her arrival well. Many new members experience a feeling of liberation once they've committed to our way of life, but Sister Anahata's sheer *relief* was notable. She was one of the most sensitive individuals I have ever met, and the outside world had fractured her spirit. Upon arrival, she was in a dire state.

POPPY: Did she mention her husband, Chuck Buhrman?

EARNEST: Not by name, but it was obvious that she'd suffered a great loss. An aura as scattered as hers is nearly unheard of without intense trauma. But with the love and care of our brothers and sisters, Sister Anahata left the burdens of the modern world behind. Within a year's time, she had made remarkable progress and was an integral part of our community, caring for children, taking lovers, and gracing us all with her unique blend of kindness and light. We are all devastated by her death, and we will miss her terribly.

POPPY: Do you know if Sister Anahata had access to the internet?

EARNEST: As I mentioned, we maintain an internet presence. This is managed by our Outreach Team, which is a small, carefully selected group staffed only with members who are unwaveringly devoted to our way of life. Members of the Outreach Team are the only ones who have official access to the internet, a policy that is designed to shield our more sensitive members from the pervasive temptation of the modern world. Sister Anahata was one such sensitive member, and she therefore would not have been accessing the internet in any sanctioned way. That said, our community is hardly a prison and she could have gotten online if she chose.

POPPY: Do you think Sister Anahata was aware of this podcast and the renewed interest in her husband's murder?

I am well aware some corners of the internet blame me for Erin Buhrman's suicide. Since her tragic death five days ago, the possibility that I somehow played a role in it has haunted me.

EARNEST: I am certain that she was. Not long before Sister
Anahata took leave of us, our community was infiltrated
by a group armed with cameras and recording devices.
They ambushed Sister Anahata as she left morning
meditation. Morning meditation is designed to help our
members open themselves spiritually, and, following
it, she would've been particularly vulnerable to abuse.
After this encounter, Sister Anahata fell into long-forgotten patterns of self-destruction.

While she might have recovered with the love and
support of her brothers and sisters, the following day,
a gang of teenagers interrupted a ceremony and began
spewing antagonistic venom at Sister Anahata and
other members of our collective in attendance. We were
all traumatized by the experience, Sister Anahata especially. We here at the Life Force Collective did our best to
help her through that darkened period, but ultimately I
regret to say that we could not save her.

I have to be honest, Brother Earnest's words disturbed me.
But after many, many hours of reflection, I have come to the
conclusion that I don't think this podcast is to blame. At all.

"But Poppy," you say, "what about the groups of strangers
breaking onto LFC grounds to torment her? Weren't they fans
of your show?"

It seems that way—and let me state for the record that
while I am infinitely grateful for the incredible audience participation this podcast has inspired, I never, *never* want any of
my listeners to invade the privacy of anyone connected to this
case. Please remember they are not characters—this is real

life, and they are real people. Please treat them with respect.

Perhaps if this podcast didn't exist, no one would have sought out Erin Buhrman at the LFC compound. Then again, they might have. I'm not the only one interested in the Chuck Buhrman murder; I just happen to have the biggest platform. I know of at least twenty different websites—regularly updated websites, I might add—that are dedicated to the case, and conspiracy theories often pop up on the CrimeJunkie.net boards.

And let's not forget what really killed Erin Buhrman. It wasn't a group of strangers. It was the ghosts of her own past. She might have found solace from her painful memories in the LFC—or she might have just hidden them deep inside herself—but those memories were still a part of her. Everyone who knew Erin Buhrman knew she was a troubled woman. Even Brother Earnest, whose interactions with Erin were limited to the time she spent with a cult premised on sunshine worship, stated there was a darkness inside her.

And so, while I am sorry if my podcast played any role in the harassment of a vulnerable woman, I can confidently say that it was not to blame for anyone's death.

chapter 15

I stumbled at the first mention of my late uncle Dennis, and I tripped over a crack in the sidewalk when I heard Uncle Jason's voice. By the time Poppy Parnell began interviewing Beverly Dodds White, I was so disoriented by hearing that fame-chasing impostor narrate my mother's life that I had to take a seat on the curb. That was where I remained for the next thirty minutes, listening in horrified curiosity. Every few minutes I would stop the podcast, certain that I'd had enough, that I couldn't take any more, but I listened until its conclusion.

Even then, I remained seated, stunned. Poppy Parnell might not blame herself for my mother's death, but she should. Even if her theory was right, even if Warren Cave was spending his life in prison for a crime he didn't commit and my father's murderer was walking free . . . well, that would be a tragedy, but there were other ways to remedy that. There were legal channels to follow; there was nothing that forced her to turn my father's untimely death into a commodity. I might have sat there all afternoon, thinking black thoughts about Poppy, but the man whose home I was sitting outside of came out to the curb with a bottle of water and asked me if I was feeling all right. I decided it was time to return to Aunt A's.

"That was a long run," Caleb commented amiably as I walked through the front door.

I nodded blankly, still processing what I had heard.

"You okay, love?" he asked, squinting at me while he placed the back of his hand against my forehead. "You look pale."

My instinct was to tell Caleb I was fine, but I remembered my new resolution to be completely honest with him. Just as I opened my mouth to tell him about the podcast, Aunt A stepped into the foyer. I quickly censored myself. I didn't know whether Aunt A knew an unscheduled episode had been devoted to my mother, and I didn't want to be the one to break that news.

"I'm fine," I said, the lie tasting bitter on my tongue. "I think I just pushed myself too hard. I'm a little light-headed. Nothing a warm shower can't fix."

"This is why I don't believe in running," Aunt A said, patting her soft midsection.

"You'll outlast us all, Aunt A," I said with false brightness. "Caleb, come upstairs and give me a hand?"

Upstairs, I shut the door and collapsed onto the bed, fighting back tears. Caleb took a seat beside me, the mattress sinking slightly with his weight. My hip collided softly with his, and I instinctively rested my head on his firm shoulder. He hesitated for a moment longer than I would have liked, but then he caught my head in his hand, holding it in place and gently twisting my hair.

"I want to be honest with you," I said, my voice muffled by his shoulder. "But I'm worried how you'll react."

His body stiffened; his hand stilled. "React to what?"

With an inhalation of firm resolve, I sat up to look him in the eye. I hated the misgivings I saw there, hated that I had given him reason to doubt me. I tamped down the fiery pain in my heart and began to speak. "Poppy Parnell released a special episode this morning. None of the episodes have been easy to listen to, as you can probably guess—she's taken the single most horrible thing that's ever happened to me and repackaged it as entertainment—but this episode was the hardest by far."

Caleb reached out and squeezed my hand. Heartened by his support, I continued.

"It was all about my mom: her childhood, her mental health, that cult she joined. There were so many things she could have said about my mother, and she focused entirely on making her look insane. It was such a transparent attempt at dodging responsibility for her role in Mom's suicide. Poppy thinks she can get herself off the hook if she can prove Mom was crazy all along."

Caleb winced. "Oh, Jo. I'm sorry you had to hear that."

"But that's not what made it so hard. The hard part is that she's right. Kind of, at least. Mom . . . had troubles. It's one of the reasons I never told you about her. Talking about it was too painful."

Caleb rubbed slow, encouraging circles on my hand with his thumb. "Do you want to talk about it now?"

I gulped and nodded. "I do. If you want to listen."

"Of course I want to listen," he said quietly.

So I told Caleb everything I could think of about my mother, from the fantastical games she would play with us on her good days and about her ethereal, woodland-nymph brand of beauty, to her dark moods, the times she would lock herself in her bedroom or our playhouse out back. I told him about our thirteenth birthday party, when Mom baked a perfect three-tiered cake and decorated it with small marzipan characters; I told him about the time Mom smashed all the drinking glasses in the cabinet.

I concluded with a ragged breath. "What if it's hereditary?"

"You're not going to turn into your mother, love," Caleb said gently.

"But what if I do? Will you leave me?"

"Of course not," he said, taken aback.

"You can't promise that," I said, shaking my head.

"Listen, love, I'm not laboring under the belief you're perfect. You're not. You kick me in your sleep, kill all my houseplants, and are a shit housekeeper."

"And you're a slob, selfish with the remote control, and have embarrassing taste in reading material," I countered quickly. "Oh, and I know about the cigarettes you hide in your sock drawer."

"You do, eh?" He frowned. "The point I was winding toward before you interrupted me was that I love you, flaws and all. Sane, not sane, it doesn't matter to me because I'll love you always, no matter what." He paused to smile crookedly. "And I hope that you can still love me, even though I've been outed as a slovenly, selfish, illiterate smoker."

"Of course I do," I said, tears starting to drip down my cheeks. "But those minor shortcomings you listed just proves you have no idea what I'm talking about. I'm talking about real darkness, Caleb. You can't promise that you'll still love me. You have no idea."

"In case you've forgotten, I just learned that you lied to me for years. And I'm still here professing my love. I think it's safe to say that I'm in this for the long haul. No matter what. Anything that happens, we'll face it together. I love you heaps, Jo."

Something cracked open inside, and I flung my arms around his neck, sobbing. "I love you, too. I don't know what I ever did to deserve you, but I promise I'm going to spend the rest of my life making this up to you."

"You don't owe me anything," he said quietly into my neck. "Just be honest with me from now on. That's all I ask."

By that afternoon, I had yet to hear from my sister, and I was beginning to wonder if our tentative reconciliation had been nothing more than a by-product of grief. Perhaps nothing had changed. The latest *Reconsidered* episode had me longing to talk about my mother with someone who remembered her, but I was reluctant to call my sister, afraid not only of her legendary temper but of the questions the podcast had raised. I had nearly convinced myself that our entire reconciliation was a fluke when Lanie called to invite Caleb and me over for dinner.

I was glad to have Caleb by my side; it was one thing to hug my sister in the room we had once shared, but it was another to eat an entire meal in her home with her family. It would be the longest I had been in the same room as Lanie since before she moved out of Aunt A's house at seventeen. Caleb took my hand as we mounted the pristine steps to Lanie and Adam's mini-mansion by the country club, and I squeezed it gratefully.

My sister answered the door wearing an apron ordering me to "Kiss the Cook," and I couldn't help but stare. Even stranger than the notion of Lanie living in this home with its picture windows and manicured lawn was the sight of her wearing a kitschy apron with a fleck of chopped garlic clinging to her cheek. This person standing in front of me, smiling a pleasant, lipsticked smile, was not the same sister who had locked me out of our bedroom so she could get high or who had stumbled down Benny Weston's stairs; I wasn't even certain she was the same sister I had grown up with, the one to whom I had once whispered all my secrets in the dark.

"Thanks for coming," Lanie said, embracing each of us in turn.

"Thanks for having us," I said, holding out a bottle of red wine.

"Thanks," she said, glancing quickly at it. "Come in. I'm finishing up dinner, and Adam ran to the store—we forgot the tomatoes for the salad."

Stepping inside the living room, I noticed the decor was a near-complete rip-off of Adam's parents' house. Either the original Mrs. Ives had done most of the decorating, or the new Mrs. Ives had taken her cues literally from Adam's mother. The walls were a muted taupe, the furniture matched, and accent pillows were carefully placed around the room. Ann sat in the middle of the floor, the carpet littered with small, colorful plastic blocks. She looked up as we entered and announced, "I helped Mom with the crescent rolls."

"That's great," I said, nodding enthusiastically, unsure how to speak to an eight-year-old girl. "I'm sure you were a big help."

Caleb, who had no such hang-ups about speaking with children, glanced down at her. "Quite a Lego collection you've got yourself there."

"I'm working on a city," she said. Pointing to a few small amalgamations of blocks, she narrated, "This is the town hall. This is the school. And this is going to be the skyscraper."

"Ambitious," Caleb said, folding his long legs beneath him on the ground. "I like it. Mind if I help?"

She nodded and pushed some blocks in his direction.

"Be nice to Uncle Caleb," Lanie said to Ann, as she led me into the kitchen. To me, she said, "She must like him. She won't even let me or Adam play with those blocks."

I looked over my shoulder to see Caleb earnestly discussing building plans with Ann and smiled. "Caleb works with children a lot. They tend to gravitate to him."

"He's a natural," she said, setting the wine down on the counter and reaching for a pitcher of iced tea. As she poured me a glass, she continued, "He'll make a good father."

"Mm," I murmured noncommittally. I had never allowed myself to consider children—or marriage, or any other trappings of the future—because I had always believed Caleb was one breath away from leaving me. Now that he not only knew the truth about my past, but also had reaffirmed his love, I didn't have anything standing in the way, but I didn't yet feel comfortable enough with my sister to reveal any of my insecurities to her.

Lanie, misunderstanding my hesitation, reached over and touched my hand. "And you'll make a good mother."

My skin warmed under her touch, reminding me of a time

that Lanie's body had once felt like an extension of my own. My heart twisted, tugged in opposite directions by the pain of past betrayals and the hope of a reunited future.

But I couldn't find the words to say those things, and so instead I laughed and told her about the time that I had somehow been roped into presiding over a children's story hour at the bookstore, and how the children had smelled my fear and run roughshod over me, how the entire situation had devolved into thrown cookies and armpit noises.

Just as I reached the conclusion, Ann came running into the kitchen, holding some sort of Lego construction in her hands. After Lanie had praised her and held the object (an ambulance, I was told) out for me to similarly laud, Ann retreated to the living room.

I noticed the tender smile on Lanie's face as she watched her go. It was an expression unlike any I had seen on my sister before.

"She's a great kid," I said.

"Thanks." Lanie smiled. "But you know who she reminds me of? You."

"Me? No. She looks just like you."

Lanie laughed and swatted at me. "And you know who else looks just like me. But I mean her personality. Take those Legos, for example. Do you remember when Grammy and Pops gave us that Lego set for Christmas? I was completely uninterested in it, but you constructed all these amazing structures."

"Yeah, and *then* you wanted to play with it." I smiled.

"And do you know what I caught her watching on TV

yesterday? Some sort of documentary about Magellan on the History channel. You *know* she didn't get that from me."

"Or Adam," I couldn't help but add. "History always bored him."

"Yeah." Lanie nodded, quiet. "It's nice, though, you know? Having her take after you so much. It made missing you hurt a little less."

"Lanie—" I started, unsure what I wanted to say.

"But," she continued quickly, determinedly upbeat, "it also makes me happy for her. Because I think it means that she's going to turn out okay."

"Of course she's going to turn out okay," I said, surprised. "Why would you even think that she wouldn't?"

"Because of me." She shrugged. "Because half the time I send her to school without any lunch money, I regularly forget to sign permission slips, and with the frequency with which I do laundry, I'm surprised she has anything to wear at all."

"I don't think you're giving yourself enough credit. Being a parent is hard work."

"It's worth it, though," she said, looking up suddenly, her eyes wide and shiny. "I didn't really understand what I was getting myself into when I decided to keep her. And there was a point where I thought maybe I was making a terrible mistake. It was going to be so much responsibility, completely change my life, and then, to top it all off, she was going to be completely dependent on me for years. But then she was born, and all of a sudden it all made sense. I didn't know that I could ever feel this strongly about anything; I didn't even know love like this *existed*. She's my whole world, Josie."

"I'm glad," I said, reaching out to squeeze her hand. "You've really changed, Lanie. I'm proud of you."

She turned her hand over in mine and hooked her ring finger around mine, the way we had when we were kids. She smiled ruefully. "I haven't changed, though, not really. I'm still the same mess I've always been. I've just learned how to hide it better. I have to, otherwise Adam will leave me and take Ann, and she's all I have."

"Adam wouldn't—" I started to say, then realized I had no idea what Adam would or would not do.

"Yes he would. Not to be spiteful, but because he worries I'm going to turn out like Mom. Or worse."

I looked at her sharply, suddenly wary. "What does that mean?"

Before Lanie could respond, the back door swung open and Adam entered, carrying a grocery bag. He glanced at me, and a strange expression passed over his face—something between concern and relief.

"Josie, hi," he said, his smile not quite reaching his eyes. "Good to see you."

I returned a distracted hello, wondering what exactly Lanie had meant by *or worse*. Was there something specific she was worried about?

"Got those tomatoes," Adam said to Lanie as he pulled a box of grape tomatoes from the grocery bag and rinsed them in the sink.

"Thanks," Lanie said, fishing out a handful and dropping

them on a cutting board. As she selected a knife, she asked me, "You like tomatoes, right, Josie?"

I nodded, vaguely troubled that my own twin sister couldn't remember whether I liked tomatoes. It might have been nearly a decade since we had shared a meal, but we had lived together for more than half our lives.

"I ran into Ted Leland at the grocery store," Adam said. "My dad's friend, remember? We went to a Christmas party at his house a couple of years ago."

Lanie frowned, her hand hesitating above a tomato. I gave her a sharp look, but Adam, oblivious, continued.

"Anyway, he's got a son who's a couple of years older than us and is moving back to town. The Lelands are throwing a welcome party in a couple weeks and invited us."

"Ted's wife," Lanie said tightly, her fingers curling and uncurling around the handle of the knife. "She teaches at the college, right?"

Adam nodded. "Yeah, I think that's right."

"And she's pretty?"

"She's nice-looking, I guess," Adam said, tossing me a confused look. He didn't know what Lanie was getting at, but I did. Professor Leland had been a colleague of our father's, and she was quite pretty—I remembered meeting her on campus several times. Poppy Parnell had reported a rumor that our father was involved with students . . . or possibly other professors. I had dismissed it as just gossip, but, from the expression on Lanie's face, I could tell she felt differently. The only question was whether she had a specific reason for suspecting Professor Leland. I waited to see if she would tip her hand.

"Her name's Pearl, right?" Lanie asked, her voice soft.

"Yeah," Adam said. "Good memory."

"I wish," Lanie said quietly, bringing the knife down through the tomato with a sharp *thwack*.

Lanie sent me into the dining room to collect the salad bowl, and as I stood in front of the china hutch, surveying the matching cups and saucers and cut crystal glasses, Adam entered the room.

"Come to help me find the bowl?" I asked lightly.

Adam glanced over his shoulder, and stepped so close to me that I drew back. "Lanie hasn't slept in two days," he hissed.

My skin prickled a warning, and I glanced toward the kitchen, mentally running through the checklist I had developed when we were teenagers. Pupils? Normal. Breath? Neutral. Demeanor? Unremarkable, even pleasant, with the brief exception of her fixation on Professor Leland, but that could easily be explained. The podcast was making us all crazy.

"Are you sure? She seemed okay enough to me."

"I guess I'm not sure she hasn't slept at all," Adam amended. "But she hasn't come up to bed in two days. And when I've gotten up to check on her, I found her down in her study, painting."

Despite Adam's obvious anxiety, I smiled. "She was always a good artist."

Adam nodded shortly. "I know. I've tried to convince her to teach some classes at the community center. But that's not the point, Josie. The point is that she's not sleeping, and I'm worried."

I bit my lip, remembering my father saying nearly those exact words to me about my mother. The first time I could recall him saying them, I had been about the age that Ann was now. Our mother had begun vacuuming the upstairs hallway at six in the morning, rousing Lanie and me, and we had complained to our father.

"Be kind to your mother," he had advised. "She's going through a bit of a phase. She hasn't been sleeping, and I'm a little worried about her. But I'm sure if we all just work on being extra-nice to her, she'll be able to sleep again."

Over the years, she had suffered from frequent bouts of insomnia, although it was a kind of insomnia where she would never even try to sleep. We would come down for breakfast and find her just where we left her, wearing yesterday's clothing, scribbling in her journal or reading a book. It was how she had gotten through *Anna Karenina* so many times.

"What do you want me to do, Adam?"

"I don't know. I just hoped you might have some insight. She does this sometimes, you know—just goes a little off for a few days—but she's been on edge for weeks, ever since that podcast started." He shifted and cast another nervous glance toward the kitchen. "From some of the things Lanie's said, it sounds like your mom might've had some similar patterns. I was wondering—"

"She's not our mother," I cut him off. "Has she been to see someone?"

"Multiple someones. I'm starting to get desperate."

The anguish in Adam's eyes was evident, and, despite the circumstances, a small part of my heart warmed. I was glad Lanie had someone who loved her and looked after her, even if that someone was Adam.

"I don't know what to do," he continued. "She won't talk to me. She says there's nothing to talk about. But Josie, the longer the podcast goes on, the more erratic her behavior becomes."

"It has to end soon," I rationalized. "The podcast can't keep going forever."

"I don't know how much longer we can wait. We've got to protect your sister. She's *unraveling*, Josie."

The niggling doubt that had formed when I listened to the podcast throbbed in my mind. *Reconsidered* had been hard on all of us, but if it was really affecting Lanie as severely as Adam claimed . . . was Lanie worried? Did she know that Poppy Parnell was onto something?

"Adam," I said carefully, "when Lanie and I got in a fight the other day, it was about the podcast."

"What do you mean?" he asked, his voice tense.

"I'm starting to think there might be some truth to Poppy's theory," I said, dropping my voice to just above a whisper. "Do you think Lanie might be wrong about Warren?"

Guilt flashed through Adam's eyes, and I realized I wasn't the only one influenced by the podcast.

"Adam?" I prodded.

"Don't," he said quietly. "Not you, too. It'll kill her."

"Just between us—"

"There is no 'between us,' Josie. Not anymore."

"What's going on here?" Lanie suddenly demanded.

Color rose in my cheeks as I turned to face my sister, half-formed excuses coagulating in my head.

"Nothing," Adam said, lying with an ease that surprised me. "I was just helping Josie find the salad bowl."

Lanie's eyes narrowed suspiciously, darting from me to Adam. "She couldn't find it on her own?"

"Nope, this sister of yours is blind as a bat."

Lanie stared at me.

That was when I realized the soft underbelly of Lanie's left forearm had a gash, a thin trickle of dark blood sliding down her pale skin.

"Oh my God," I exclaimed. "Lanie, what happened to your arm?"

She looked down at the wound, her face unreadable. "The knife must have slipped."

"Jesus, Lanie, that looks bad," Adam said. "Come on, let's get a bandage on that right away."

She nodded and allowed him to lead her out of the room. I took the salad bowl from the shelf and followed them, my limbs prickling with unease.

We dined on the back porch, as Lanie had hoped, eating salad and green beans and roast chicken, watching the sun dip behind the other houses. I watched my sister closely, uncomfortable with the way she pressed an index finger against her bandage and smiled when she thought no one was looking. What had happened in that kitchen? Had the knife slipped, as she had said? Or had she done that to herself on purpose?

Was the incident evidence of the unraveling Adam had described?

Despite its inauspicious beginning, dinner ambled along pleasantly. Ann entertained us all by reciting a poem she had written for class, and Lanie was, for the most part, a charming hostess. Adam began explaining the Elm Park housing market to Caleb, who gamely nodded along and asked relevant questions even though I knew he cared nothing for real estate. Somewhere in the middle of all this, Lanie reached for the open bottle of wine. Without so much as missing a beat, Adam casually moved it out of her reach. His movement was so deft that I don't think Caleb even noticed, but I did. I glanced at my sister and realized that her wineglass was not only empty, it was clean—she hadn't had any wine all night. I struggled to remember if I had seen her drinking at Aunt A's house after the funeral.

"More chicken?" Lanie turned to me and asked brightly, no resentment that Adam was monitoring her alcohol intake evident on her features.

I accepted and complimented her on the food, and she told me she had learned the secret to a perfect roasted chicken from some new cooking show. My head spun as though I had stepped into some alternate dimension. I couldn't decide what I found more disturbing: the bandage on her arm or the earnest sheen in her eyes as she expounded on oven temperatures.

And then Caleb mentioned the podcast.

In his defense, he knew I had wanted to ask Lanie how she felt about the most recent episode, and he hadn't been privy to Adam's concerns about my sister's mental state. I should have warned him. But I had been so busy keeping my eye on Lanie, waiting for her to do anything that felt off-kilter, that I forgot to tell him I had decided *not* to bring up the podcast.

And so, as he reached for a second helping of green beans, he casually asked, "Lanie, what do you think about this 'special episode' of *Reconsidered*? Were you just as upset at her portrayal of your mother as Jo was?"

Adam choked on a mouthful of chicken; Lanie's face froze. I could see the storm clouds brewing in her eyes, the familiar click of her jaw, and sensed her calm about to shatter. In desperation, I did the only thing I could think to do: I knocked over my iced tea.

Everyone jumped to their feet, throwing napkins at the mess. I thought that the ruse had worked until Lanie excused herself to refill the iced tea pitcher and never returned. After five minutes, the memory of her bloody forearm compelled me to rise.

"I'm going to see if Lanie needs any help," I said casually, trying to contain the panic welling up inside me so as not to alarm Ann.

"Thank you," Adam mouthed.

The kitchen was empty; the iced tea pitcher sat unfilled on the counter. My stomach somersaulted, and I froze, straining to hear any sound of my sister. I told myself that I was being ridiculous—perhaps Lanie had just used the opportunity to take a bathroom break—but between Adam's concerns, the "accident" with the knife, and the torment that had flashed across her face when Caleb mentioned the podcast, I was certain something was wrong.

There was a rustle of paper in the living room, and I hurried in to find Lanie sitting cross-legged on the floor in front of a bookcase, a large book open in front of her.

"Hey," I said tentatively. "What are you looking at?"

"Adam's college yearbook," she said, not looking up. "He transferred from the University of Michigan to Elm Park College after we got engaged, you know."

"I didn't know that," I said, sitting beside her. "That was good of him."

She shook her head. "I think he resents me for it. I think he thinks I ruined his life."

"Lanie, that's not true. And, anyway, Adam's life isn't ruined. It seems like you guys are doing pretty well for yourselves."

She smiled without warmth and looked down at the open yearbook. I followed her gaze, bracing myself to see a picture of young Adam, that carefree smile I remembered so well.

But Lanie wasn't looking at the student photographs. She had the book open to the professor headshots. From the center of the page, Professor Leland smiled up at us.

Lanie's strange reaction to Adam's mention of the Lelands replayed itself in my mind. Carefully, I asked, "What's on this page?"

She slammed the yearbook shut. "Nothing."

"Are you okay?" I asked tentatively.

"Of course," she said, her tone free of inflection. "Why wouldn't I be?"

I wanted to tell her that I was worried about her, but I didn't want to reveal that Adam had told me she wasn't sleeping. Instead, I said, "You seemed upset that Caleb mentioned the podcast. He feels badly."

She looked away. "You know that saying that we marry our fathers?"

"You think Caleb is like our father?" I asked in surprise.

"I think Adam is."

I glanced down at the closed yearbook, her fixation on our father's possible lovers starting to take shape. "Do you think Adam's cheating on you?"

She leveled her eyes at me. "He doesn't exactly have a good track record for fidelity."

I swallowed the bitterness that rose in my throat and said, "Adam loves you."

"Dad loved Mom," she responded stubbornly. I was just glad that she hadn't said *Adam loved you.*

Before I could respond, Ann stepped into the living room. "Mom?"

"Yes, sweetheart?" Lanie said, her voice suddenly sugared. The darkness cleared from her face as she smiled at her daughter. *Adam is wrong,* I thought decisively. *Lanie is nothing like our mother.* Our mother had never shielded us from her black moods.

"Daddy and Uncle Caleb are looking for you and Aunt Josie."

We followed Ann back to the porch, where the rest of the meal passed without incident. Soon we were nibbling on cookies and a small posse of neighborhood children was collecting Ann for a game of Ghost in the Graveyard.

"Don't forget your coat!" Lanie called after her as she ran down the steps.

"That was wonderful," I said, standing up to help Lanie clear the plates. "Thank you so much."

"Sit down, Josie," Adam insisted. "We can get this."

Adam and Lanie disappeared into the house, each carrying a plate in both hands, leaving Caleb and me alone on the porch. Caleb inhaled deeply and surveyed the trees separating the backyard from the golf course, their leaves just starting to tinge golden.

"Who knew Illinois was so lovely?" he said.

"I did," I admitted. "But I'd forgotten. It's been ten years since I've been here."

"A fella could get used to this." He smiled.

The evening calm was shattered by the sound of breaking ceramic. Heart pounding, I jumped to my feet and rushed through the back door. Lanie was standing in the center of the kitchen, fragments of plates still vibrating around her feet, the discarded remains of someone's dinner splattered on her bare feet. Her fists were clenched at her sides, and even from behind I could tell she was shaking with rage.

"Goddammit, Adam," she shrieked.

Adam touched his wife on the arm, saying something soft and quiet to her. That was a mistake. Lanie snatched up the pitcher of iced tea from the counter and flung it at him. He ducked, and the heavy glass vessel hit the wall behind him with a dull thump, and then fell to the ground, cracking.

"Lanie!" I shouted. "Stop!"

She whirled to face me, her eyes the familiar manic I remembered from her teenaged years, and my blood went cold.

From Twitter, posted September 26, 2015

 Amy Thomas
@amytee71

Hey @poppy_parnell serious Q: If Melanie did it why did she call you? #Reconsidered

 27m

 Poppy Parnell
@poppy_parnell

@amytee71 I've never said Melanie did it. I'm just presenting all perspectives.

 25m

 Poppy Parnell
@poppy_parnell

@amytee71 But to play devils advocate, maybe she thought it'd keep suspicion off her while potentially freeing her son. 2 birds, 1 stone.

 24m

mm
@midwesternmamma

**@poppy_parnell @amytee71 MELANIE CAVE JUST
WANTS #JUSTICEFORWARRENCAVE**

 19m

 mm
@midwesternmamma

**@poppy_parnell @amytee71 SHE'S A LOVING
MOTHER SHUT IT WITH YOUR LIES**
#JUSTICEFORWARRENCAVE

 18m

 Carolyn S.
@carrieofthecity

**@poppy_parnell @amytee71 Is anyone else starting
to think that @midwesternmamma is actually
Melanie Cave?**

15m

chapter 16

I struggled to sleep that night, guilt and worry coursing through my veins. After Lanie had thrown the pitcher, I'd offered for Ann to spend the night with us so that Lanie and Adam could work out whatever was obviously brewing between them, but Lanie declined, insisting things were fine even as her face softened back into its Stepford Wife–esque mask. Should I have done something when I saw Lanie throw that pitcher? Years ago, I had learned the best way to handle my sister's moods while keeping my own sanity intact was to ignore them, but now there was a child in the mix. How much did I really trust my sister? I would never forgive myself if something happened to Ann. I shook Caleb awake at two, and insisted we drive to Lanie's house and make sure that everything was okay.

He blinked blearily at me. "Are you mad, Jo? It's the middle of the night."

"I'm worried. The way she threw that pitcher at Adam . . ."

"Calm down, love," he said, stroking my cheek. "Your family is under an unimaginable amount of stress right now, your sister included. So she's got a bit of a short fuse. I'm sure everything's fine by now. You can call her first thing in the morning."

He rolled over and fell almost immediately back asleep, leaving me alone to turn over each part of the night, looking for clues. *We've got to protect your sister*, Adam had said. What exactly had he meant by that? It almost sounded as though he knew—or at least suspected—that Lanie had done something wrong.

Lanie's own words came back to me suddenly: *How could I ever admit that now?*

I was becoming more and more convinced that my sister was hiding something.

Caleb's alarm serenaded us awake to "Come as You Are" at seven o'clock. Five months ago, Caleb had discovered he could set his alarm to music, and we had been rising to the same song ever since. (Incidentally, this was one of the few aspects of Caleb's presence that I emphatically did not miss while he was in Africa. I liked Nirvana as much as the next person, but not first thing in the morning.)

I had only managed to fall asleep three hours before, and was therefore not in the mood for an early alarm. Pulling the pillow over my head, I complained, "Too early, babe."

"Sorry, love," he murmured, his voice thick with sleep, wrapping warm arms around my waist and tugging my body against his. "I've got a conference call in a half hour."

"Who schedules conference calls on a Sunday?"

"My boss. And since I haven't been in the office in weeks, I don't feel as though I have much standing to argue." He pressed himself against my back. "But I don't have to really get up for another fifteen minutes."

"Wait, honey," I said as he slipped a hand between my thighs. "Not with Aunt A in the next room."

"I can be quiet," he said in my ear, his hand starting to move beneath mine.

"I can't. You're just going to have to contain yourself."

Caleb let out a comical groan. "What I'm going to have to do is take a cold shower."

"Maybe if you're lucky, I'll take that cold shower with you."

"You're killing me, love," he said, shaking his head in jest as he climbed out of bed.

Just a couple more minutes, I thought to myself as I rolled back over to sleep.

When I next awoke, it was ten thirty and I was alone. I shuffled downstairs in search of coffee and found Aunt A seated at the kitchen table, working a crossword puzzle while wearing a floral dress, her graying hair carefully pinned up.

"Good morning, dear," she greeted me. "Must have been a fun night with your sister for you to sleep so late!"

"Oh," I said, freezing. From the cheerful, optimistic expression on Aunt A's face, I could tell she wanted details about the dinner at Lanie's, but the kind of details I knew she wanted—the hugging, the forgiving of past sins—had been overshadowed by the more ominous aspects that had kept me awake all night. Rather than tell the truth and crush her hope, I hedged. "It was nice of Lanie and Adam to have us over. Ann's sure a doll, huh?"

Aunt A's face lit up at the mention of her grandniece, and she began telling me about a dance recital last spring in which Ann—according to Aunt A, at least, hardly an unbiased party—had been the star of the show.

"Caleb seemed pretty taken with her, too," I said. "Hey, where is Caleb?"

"He's set up an office in the craft room," she said, gesturing upstairs. "Poor man, it sounded as though he had a bunch of work to take care of."

"Yeah, he's always really busy when he gets back from abroad." I nodded. "Is Ellen around? When was that Pilates class she was mentioning?"

Aunt A frowned. "Your cousin is off ruining the good looks God gave her."

"Oh," I said, suppressing a smile as I remembered Ellen's morning plans. "The Botox."

The previous afternoon, Ellen had informed me she had arranged to have Trina Thompson highlight her hair and treat her wrinkles. I had been horrified she was letting Trina—who had been legendary in high school for freaking out during dissection day in Biology—go anywhere near her face with a needle.

"She's a *trained aesthetician*," Ellen had informed me rather huffily. "Besides, Gabby Aldridge got Botox from her, and you saw Gabby the other day. She looks just like she did in high school, if not better. You might want to consider making an appointment yourself."

I had changed the subject just as her probing fingers reached for my forehead.

"Do you want to come to church with me?" Aunt A asked. "I'm leaving in a few minutes, but I'll wait for you to shower if you want to come."

"Oh, you go ahead," I said, dropping a piece of bread

into the toaster. "I need breakfast and coffee before I can even think about going anywhere. Anyway, I need to look for flights back to New York."

"You're leaving already?" Aunt A asked softly.

"Unfortunately, Caleb and I both have to get back to work. He can't operate out of the craft room indefinitely. But last-minute airfare is out of our price range, so I'm sure we won't be leaving for a few days yet." I avoided looking at Aunt A's face as I spoke, already knowing without seeing her that her ever-present smile would have drooped slightly, the prominent worry lines around her eyes deepening as she ingested my impending departure. I couldn't bear to disappoint her again, like I must have when I left the first time. But we needed to go. I needed to know that the new me still existed somewhere, safe and happy and blissfully separate from her trainwreck of a past.

After Aunt A left, I carried my toast and coffee into the living room. The old house settled audibly, its walls shifting and groaning, and the floorboards directly above my head creaked. I instinctively shivered, then reminded myself it was just Caleb. The room above me was Aunt A's craft room, where he was currently working . . . and my mother's old bedroom. I remembered sitting on this very same couch, listening to her pace around the room. Then she stopped pacing. And then she was gone.

I turned on the television, cranking the volume up to drown out the house's ghosts. I smiled when I saw Aunt A's favorite soap opera, *The Bold and the Beautiful*, in her DVR queue. I had not seen the show in nearly a decade, but I found comfort in the familiar characters. Aunt A had recorded the show religiously, and many evenings had been spent beside her on the couch, drinking mugs of hot chocolate or sipping sweetened iced tea, depending on the season, engrossed in the tangled affairs of the characters.

As I pressed *Play*, I heard gravel crunching in the driveway and footsteps on the front porch. I set down my coffee in preparation for answering the door, but it swung open without a knock. I glanced up and saw my sister's image reflected in the hall mirror. I studied her face: she didn't look like a woman who could knowingly send an innocent man to jail. But then again, I knew all too well that Lanie only looked out for herself.

"Josie?" she called.

"In here," I said, reaching out to pause the show.

She stepped into the living room, a smile flickering across her face, the equivalent of emotional static. "Hey. What are you up to?"

I waved a hand in the direction of the television. "Watching my stories."

A mirthful grin erupted on Lanie's face; she looked nothing like the unhinged woman I had seen last night, nor the woman on the verge Adam had described.

"No way. You watch this one, too?"

"First time in years. Brooke and Ridge are still together, it seems."

"*Back* together," Lanie corrected, joining me on the couch. "There have been plenty of intervening love affairs. She married his brother at one point, if you can believe it."

I looked sideways at my sister, uncertain whether she was being purposefully ironic.

"Listen, Josie," she said. "I'm really sorry about last night. It's been a rough couple of weeks. Poppy Parnell has been hounding me incessantly, and then Mom . . . I guess I'm just a little more on edge than normal."

I forced myself to nod while I scrutinized my sister, wondering if she was being entirely honest or if there was something more sinister lurking behind her big, sad eyes.

"What's that?" Lanie asked suddenly, pointing at the UPS box still sitting in the corner.

"Mom's stuff from the LFC. They sent it to us yesterday."

Lanie rose silently and crossed to the box, kneeling almost reverentially before it. Carefully, she pulled open the flaps and dipped a hand inside.

"Look!" she exclaimed, lifting a pile of photographs. There had to be thirty or forty of them, neatly stacked and bound with green ribbon. The gummy infant smiles of my twin and me beamed up from the top photograph, and my heart swelled. She *did* think about us when she left. I moved to Lanie's side, and we began peeling the photographs from the stack, one by one. I was in tears by the time we reached the last one, a snapshot of us as toddlers "helping" our mother bake cookies. Her arms were around both of us, beaming proudly, and there was pink frosting in our hair and on our noses.

Lanie traced the curls of our mother's hair lightly with a fingertip. "I didn't know she took these with her."

"Me either. I thought she was trying to forget us."

"Oh, Josie," Lanie said, looking up with a pained expression. "You didn't really think that."

I briefly described my meeting with Sister Amamus in California, when I was told in no uncertain terms that our mother did not want to see me.

"We don't know what her reasons were," Lanie said. "But she always loved us."

"Sometimes that's hard to remember."

"Here," Lanie said, snatching one of the photographs and pushing it into my hands. Lanie and I were six years old, with gap-toothed smiles and sunburned cheeks, squinting at the camera, while our mother knelt in the middle, one arm around each of us, her dark hair caught in the wind, Mount Rushmore looming large and out of focus in the background. "Do you remember this road trip?"

I struggled to remember the trip as I studied the laughing, seemingly carefree face of our mother. Was she happy then? Or did she hide her sadness well?

"Was this the vacation where they sent us down to the pool on our own, and we got in trouble with the management?"

"No, you're thinking of when we went to Yellowstone and stopped at that motel in Kansas. That was a few years later. The trip to Mount Rushmore was the one where Dad got lost, and we couldn't find anywhere to eat. Remember? And they let us eat bags of potato chips in the backseat until we found that all-night diner? And then we had scrambled eggs and milkshakes at, like, ten o'clock?"

I smiled, the long-ago memory suddenly fresh: tired, smelly, barefoot, sitting in a shiny red vinyl booth, swapping sips of my strawberry milkshake with Lanie's chocolate one, while Mom and Dad hunched over the counter, pointing at a map and talking with the smoky-voiced waitress, trying to figure out where we had gone wrong.

I picked up the pile of photographs again, hoping to recover more memories. As I flipped through the stack a second time, a vague sense of unease settled over me. I closely examined my mother's face in a photograph of her in the garden with the two of us, trying to remember the exact tilt of her lips when she smiled, the pitch of her laughter. My eyes landed on a blurry figure over my mother's shoulder in the photograph, and I squinted. I could make out the blond hair, the pink sundress. Melanie Cave.

Placing my thumb over Melanie's unfocused face, I swallowed hard and asked Lanie, "Did you know about Melanie Cave?"

"What do you mean?" Lanie asked, her voice sounding strangled.

My stomach flipped at the tone of her voice. She knew Melanie had been having an affair with our father, I was certain of it. She knew Melanie Cave had reason to kill our father. But why would she have said that Warren did it?

Before I could answer, a sharp knock sounded on the front door.

I opened it to find Poppy Parnell, her right fist raised, about to knock again. Her frog-like eyes were wide behind a pair of glasses with thick black rims, and they jumped eagerly from me to Lanie.

"Oh, good," she said by way of greeting, practically salivating. "You're both here."

"Go away," I said, starting to shut the door.

Poppy jammed out her arm to hold the door open. To Lanie, she said, "I came by your house this morning."

"I know," Lanie said, joining me in the entryway. "I didn't open the door because I didn't want to talk to you."

Poppy wagged a finger at Lanie, a gesture that seemed infuriatingly familiar, and stepped into our foyer without waiting for an invitation. "When you do things like that, it makes me wonder what you're hiding."

"This is a private home," I said. "You can't just come in without an invitation."

Ignoring me, Poppy said, "I know you've both declined participating in my podcast, but I wanted to make one last plea."

"We're not interested," I said. I was surprised to realize I was holding Lanie's hand, and I was unsure whether I had grabbed hers or vice versa.

"I can understand your hesitation, but I wish you would reconsider," Poppy said earnestly, apparently oblivious to her ironic usage of the word. "Right now, the only story I can tell is the one I'm getting from people who knew your father casually. The narrative could really benefit from the perspective of those who knew him intimately."

"Fuck your narrative," Lanie said, tightening her grip on my fingers.

"I think there's been a misunderstanding. I know my podcast has been cast as a campaign to free Warren Cave, but that's not my objective. My goal is to review the case as a disinterested outsider. Your father's murder was shocking, and it's possible emotions interfered with accurate processing of the case. All I want is for the truth to be known, and for your father to be properly avenged."

"Bullshit," I said. "That's a nice line, but I don't believe it for a second. All you want is to make money off rumors."

"I'm a journalist, Josie. I don't trade in rumors. Unless they're confirmed, that is."

Lanie twitched beside me. "What does that mean?"

Poppy's smile turned menacingly saccharine. "It means that I've heard some very interesting things about you, Lanie. For example, I heard that your husband was your sister's high school sweetheart."

"Leave Adam out of this," Lanie hissed. "It doesn't have anything to do with him."

"Maybe not," Poppy said, lifting her thin shoulders in an irritatingly innocent shrug. "But when the paramount piece of evidence damning a man to life behind bars is the word of one woman, that woman's reputation had better be pretty darn impeccable, don't you think? If, instead, she's the kind of woman who would steal her twin sister's boyfriend . . . well, I think that's the kind of character flaw that could call certain other things into question."

"That's ridiculous. Besides, Lanie didn't steal my boyfriend," I said, surprised to hear how fluidly the lie rolled off my tongue. "I decided to do some traveling. Lanie and Adam got together after I left."

"That's not what I heard," Poppy said, her tone revealing she didn't believe my fib.

"So now you're accusing us *both* of lying? Come on, you can do better than that."

"I certainly can," Poppy said, her eyes glittering behind her glasses. "You might want to tune into my podcast tomorrow. It's a bombshell."

The hair on my arms rose. I glanced at my sister, but her expression gave nothing away.

"More rumors?" Lanie asked coldly.

"You'll have to listen to find out," Poppy said, twitching a finger at us. "I don't give previews. Unless, of course, I can record your reaction for the show."

"Not a chance," Lanie scoffed.

"Think about it," Poppy prodded.

She might have said more, but that was the moment Ellen strolled through the open front door, looking exceedingly blond and swollen, and a little crabby. Putting her hands on her hips, she demanded of Poppy, "What are you doing here?"

"Telling your cousins that my podcast would benefit from interviews with people who actually knew their father." Poppy inclined her head toward us and offered Ellen a slight smile. "I haven't been having much luck. Perhaps you could help them see the benefit of participation—or maybe you'd be interested?"

"You're kidding, right?" Ellen said, deadpan. "Get out of my mother's house, you hack."

"I'm finishing up tomorrow's episode tonight," Poppy said,

turning back to us, unperturbed. "This is your last chance to listen to the interview before it goes live, and to tell your side of that night."

Lanie's palm felt slick in mine, but when I glanced at her, her face was blank.

"You need to leave," Ellen said. "My husband is a lawyer. Don't make me call him."

"There's no need to be so adversarial," Poppy said, her thin eyebrows jumping behind her glasses as she seemed to consider whether to heed our demands or whether anything could be gained from sticking around. Finally, she nodded. "All right, I'm going. But I'm leaving my card—please, please think about speaking with me." Her cold, impartial gaze zeroed in on me. "Together we can make sure that your father has justice."

From Twitter, posted September 27, 2015

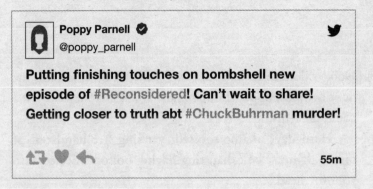

Poppy Parnell ✔
@poppy_parnell

Putting finishing touches on bombshell new episode of #Reconsidered! Can't wait to share! Getting closer to truth abt #ChuckBuhrman murder!

♻ ♥ ↩   55m

Samantha R.
@therealmissus1

@poppy_parnell Yesss! The #truth must come out! #Reconsidered #ChuckBuhrman

♻ ♥ ↩   21m

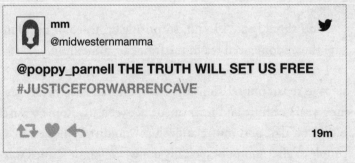

mm
@midwesternmamma

@poppy_parnell THE TRUTH WILL SET US FREE #JUSTICEFORWARRENCAVE

♻ ♥ ↩   19m

269

chapter 17

Good riddance to bad rubbish," Ellen said, slamming the door behind Poppy. "I don't know about anyone else, but I could use a drink."

"Hard day?" Lanie sneered, yanking her hand out of mine. "It must be exhausting having poison injected into your forehead."

"Lucky for you, I don't need forehead muscles to do this," Ellen said pleasantly as she flipped her middle finger. "Join us for a drink or don't."

"I don't drink," Lanie said stonily.

"Oh, right," Ellen said, snapping her fingers in mock remembrance. "You're a dry drunk."

Lanie's eyes flashed, and she opened her mouth to say something, but glanced at me and shut it. "I was just leaving anyway."

"You should stay," I said, surprising all three of us. "I'm sure there's some iced tea in the fridge or something."

I trailed off. Lanie and I might have been making some steps to repair our relationship, but there had been nearly ten long years of hurt and resentment between us. Rome wasn't built in a day, and our relationship wouldn't be healed in a couple of afternoons—especially not when Poppy Parnell was raising questions about our father's death.

"I would, but I'd rather have hot pokers stuck through my

eyes than have to listen to our vapid cousin talk about the latest advances in plastic surgery."

"Sick burn," Ellen said sarcastically.

Lanie gave me an annoyed look that I supposed was intended to reprimand me for choosing Ellen over her yet again. I looked away. Ellen had been the one there for me when things had really gotten bad, the one who had held my hand while I wept for my family; Lanie hadn't been around.

So as my sister walked down the front porch, I followed Ellen into the kitchen. She retrieved a bottle of fizzy Moscato from the refrigerator and poured the sweet wine into a pair of stemmed glasses.

"Do tell," she said. "What was everyone's least favorite podcast host doing here?"

"Just what she said. Trying to get Lanie and me to talk. She claims to have some sort of bombshell for the next episode, and said she would only tell us what it was if we promised to comment."

"She's fishing," Ellen said dismissively. "Everything she's put out thus far has been nothing more than rehashed gossip."

I swirled the wine in my glass. "Did you listen to the third episode? She actually made a really solid case for Melanie Cave being the one to kill Dad, not Warren. Especially after that scene at the funeral home."

"Is that what you think? That Melanie Cave let her son go to prison for something she did?"

"If she's a murderer, why shouldn't I believe that she'd let someone else take the rap?"

"The *rap*?" Ellen repeated with an amused smirk. "When did you become a television cop?"

"It makes *sense*, Ellen," I insisted. "She had motive. She had opportunity. And there was this voicemail . . . The only thing that doesn't fit is Lanie saying she saw Warren." I sagged against the counter. "I can't believe I'm letting this get in my head so much. It has to be Warren Cave. If Warren didn't kill Dad, then why would Lanie say he did?"

"Don't hate me for saying this," Ellen said carefully, pouring more wine into our glasses, "but have you ever considered that maybe your sister lied?"

"But *why*? Why would she lie to protect Melanie Cave?"

Ellen held my eyes, uncharacteristically at a loss for words. She lifted the wineglass to her mouth, and into the globe, said, "Maybe that's not who she was protecting."

My blood froze in my veins. "What are you saying?"

After her morning at the salon, Ellen's face was impressively blank. "Have you ever wondered if Lanie killed your father?"

My extremities went numb; the wineglass slipped from my hand and shattered on the kitchen floor.

"*No*," I said emphatically. "Jesus, Ellen, no. He was our *father*."

"You're right," Ellen said, her voice sounding far from convinced. "Forget I said anything."

Such an accusation was, of course, impossible to forget.

Ellen knelt down to collect the shards of glass, deftly changing the subject to harmless gossip overheard at the salon. I nodded numbly and laughed at the appropriate intervals, drinking wine from the sturdy mug Ellen had handed me in lieu of another glass, but I wasn't listening. Ellen's words throbbed obtrusively in my head, calling to mind images of my sister smothering our mother, upending all the furniture in our room in an apoplectic frenzy, using a lit cigarette to burn her own face from a family photo. I shivered.

"Afternoon, ladies," Caleb said, descending the back staircase, interrupting my dark thoughts and whatever gleeful story Ellen was telling.

"How's the work going?" I asked, eager for the distraction.

"Eh, it's going," he said with a mild shrug. He yelped suddenly, and looked accusingly at the ground. He bent down and produced a chunk of glass, which he held up in confusion. "What's this?"

"Josie broke a wineglass," Ellen said.

Caleb frowned slightly, glancing from Ellen to me to the bottle on the counter. He flickered on a lopsided grin and said, "Little early in the day to be shit-faced, huh, gals?"

"It's five o'clock somewhere," I offered.

"Not on this continent."

"That's my cue," Ellen announced, giggling into her hand as she swept out of the room.

Caleb stood and squinted after my cousin. "Does Ellen look a little odd to you this afternoon?"

"She says it'll settle."

"Did something happen down here? I heard some people come over."

Ellen's egregious accusation raced around my brain, but

I couldn't bring myself to give voice to it. The very idea was insane. Lanie might be a lot of things, but a killer wasn't one of them.

"Poppy Parnell came by," I finally said.

Caleb looked disgusted. "Bloody piranha."

"Yeah." I nodded, wracking my brain for an alternate topic. I didn't want to talk about Poppy's big bombshell, didn't want to have to consider what it might be, didn't want to have to worry that Ellen might be right. "Hey, do you have a minute to look at flights?"

Caleb nodded. "Are you sure you're ready to go home? You don't think you need to stick around for your aunt? Help her probate the estate and all that?"

"My mother spent the last decade living on a commune where they shared chickens and sexual partners. All of her belongings are sitting in the living room in a UPS box. She doesn't have any *estate* to probate."

"Ah," Caleb said, flashing a quick, humorless smile. "Of course. Let me grab a snack, and then we'll get right to it, okay?"

I nodded. "I'll go upstairs and get my laptop."

But as I passed through the living room, I saw the stack of Mom's pictures, and I grabbed them without thinking. Sitting on my bed, I pored over them, blinking through tears at the smiling faces of Mom, Lanie, and myself. Looking at Lanie's cheery smile—a genuine smile I hadn't seen in years—Ellen's accusations seemed even more insane. Lanie had loved our father. I flipped through the stack, looking for evidence of that, but couldn't seem to find any pictures of him. A feeling of disquiet washed over me. I flipped through the stack again, more quickly this time. Perhaps she kept the photos of Dad somewhere else? Maybe they were still in the box?

Dropping the photos on my bed, I moved to the framed picture I had shown Caleb, the one that I had since propped up beside the bed. There, our father had one of his big hands resting on Lanie's shoulder, and she was grinning, cheeks flushed with excitement, leaning into him adoringly. Ellen was insane. There was no way my sister killed our father.

The following morning, I sat cross-legged on my bed, emailing my boss to inform her I was returning to New York the next evening and could be back at work on Wednesday. As I waited for a response, I navigated to Facebook and scrolled idly through my feed. My stomach flipped when I saw an acquaintance—a girl who had lived on my floor during my one semester at college, and whom I had never thought about again until that instant—had shared a link to the Reconsidered website. *New episode!!!* she had written. *Nobody bug me for the next 60 minutes!*

It's a bombshell, Poppy had said.

I didn't want to listen, but I felt compelled to do so. The notion that this girl, this girl who used three exclamation points and misused an *o* as a zero, would soon know something about our family that I did not yet know made me feel a little crazy. My return to New York forgotten, I clicked over to Poppy's website and began downloading the episode.

"What are you up to?" Caleb asked casually, yawning as he wandered in from his own makeshift office across the hall.

He froze when he saw the look of grim determination on my face. "Seriously, Jo, what are you up to?"

"Poppy Parnell posted a new episode."

"Are you sure you want to listen to that rubbish?" Caleb asked, frowning in concern. "Remember how stressed it's made you?"

"Of course I don't want to listen," I snapped. Caleb's soft eyes widened in surprise, and I was immediately contrite. "God, Caleb, I'm sorry. I didn't mean to yell at you. I'm just . . ." The end of my sentence was lost in exhausted, defeated tears.

"Hey now," he said, sinking onto the bed beside me and wrapping an arm around my shoulders. "It's okay. Things will look different tomorrow when we're home."

I wanted to believe him. As I rested my head against his chest, listening to the reassuring drumbeat of his heart, I commanded myself to believe him. The following night, I would be climbing into our own bed back home in Brooklyn, not tossing and turning in this old twin bed, knowing that my sister was just across town.

But it didn't matter that the view was different from New York: things would still be the same. My parents would still be dead, my sister would still be unraveling, and the podcast would still be making headlines.

With black resolve, I pushed away from Caleb's comforting embrace and reached for my earbuds.

Excerpt from transcript of *Reconsidered: The Chuck Buhrman Murder*, Episode 5: "A Question of Character," September 28, 2015

Personal reputation plays a huge role in the case against Warren Cave. It was easy for police—and later, a jury—to trust Lanie Buhrman, a sad-eyed, conventionally attractive teenaged girl, the progeny of a well-liked college professor and a local daughter. And it was similarly easy for them to be suspicious of Warren Cave, who was purposefully subversive in his appearance, an admitted drug user, and newer in town.

But these last couple of weeks I've spent in Elm Park have made me wonder if these reputations aren't little more than tropes and prejudice; I think the truth surrounding some of the major players is more complicated than we know.

I'll start with Lanie Buhrman. Before I do, I want to say that I know some of you have accused me of "victim-blaming" every time I dare to question Lanie Buhrman's character. First, allow me to remind you who the real victims in this case are: Chuck Buhrman, whose life was tragically cut short, and possibly Warren Cave, who I am growing more and more convinced is innocent. Lanie Buhrman is not a victim, and I'm certainly not blaming her for anything. I'm not accusing her of any wrongdoing or any misconduct. I'm simply directing sunlight onto her character so that her statements can be properly evaluated.

Unfortunately, finding anyone who knew Lanie in the time period immediately preceding her father's death is easier said than done. Chuck and Erin home-schooled their children, so there are no teachers or classmates to talk to. Chuck, Erin, and all four grandparents are dead. The rest of her family has declined to participate in this podcast.

In fact, the only person I found who would speak to me about Lanie Buhrman's teenaged years was Jason Kelly, Amelia's ex-husband. He remembers Lanie as a happy, playful child. However, his recollections are limited, as he and Amelia divorced two years before Chuck's death, and he admits that he didn't see the Buhrman family after the divorce. A teenager's mood can change drastically in two years.

What is certain is that, at some point, Lanie Buhrman stopped being happy and playful and became a delinquent. Police records indicate she was ticketed a handful of times for minor offenses such as curfew violation, loitering, and possession of alcohol. She was arrested once for vandalism and once for possession of a small quantity of marijuana; she wasn't charged either time. I spoke with Harold Greenway, the principal of Elm Park High School during the Buhrman twins' tenure, and he remembered Lanie as a troublemaker.

GREENWAY: We tried to be accommodating, of course. The Buhrman girls came from a homeschooled environment, and they'd tragically lost their parents. We expected there to be something of a learning curve with them, but Lanie pushed us to our limits. She regularly skipped school, failed to complete assignments, and ignored rules such as dress codes and a prohibition on tobacco products. We attempted to intervene—we assigned counselors to her, we talked to her guardian—but nothing seemed to get through to her.

Lanie's former classmates echoed the sentiments of the principal: people wanted to help her, but she rebuffed all advances. I spoke with Trina Thompson, a former classmate of the Buhrman twins, and she described Lanie's behavior to me.

POPPY: When did you meet the twins?

TRINA: In January 2003, when they transferred to public school. Everybody was talking about them when they arrived, of course. Their father's murder was the most scandalous thing to happen in this town since that time someone set fire to the Family Tree restaurant. Everybody had been reading the newspapers, plus it was interesting to have two homeschooled students arrive, especially when they're twins.

POPPY: Were you friends with either of them?

TRINA: I wouldn't say I was friends with either of them, but I was friendly with Josie. She started dating a friend of mine, and we ran in the same social circles. She was nice enough, but difficult to get to know.

POPPY: And Lanie?

TRINA: Definitely not. Lanie Buhrman had absolutely no interest in anyone other than the school's most burned-out losers. Everyone was super-friendly to her at the start, but she was just plain nasty to all of us. And then she got really deep into drugs and whatever. I heard she used to steal money from people's lockers during gym class. Oh, and she was part of the group that vandalized the football field the night before the Homecoming game senior year.

Every person I talked to had the same sorts of stories to tell about Lanie Buhrman. One girl claimed that Lanie had spit on her in the hallway, one boy told me that Lanie had stolen his mother's prescription drugs during a party at his house. It's safe to say that Lanie Buhrman did not have the best reputation.

But back in 2002, Lanie Buhrman was just a wide-eyed girl, and Warren Cave was the one with a bad reputation. Based on appearance alone, it was easy to think that he was a bad guy. I thought the same thing when I saw pictures of Warren from the early 2000s. When I first began speaking with his mother, I assumed fond remembrances of her son were outdated or wishful thinking. Then I met Warren and found him to be polite and articulate. I initially assumed that he was just putting on a good face to meet me, but I learned from prison guards that Warren is generally regarded as one of the best-behaved prisoners on the block.

Since arriving in Elm Park, I have encountered more people who are willing to vouch for Warren Cave's personality than Lanie's—even from the 2000s. Earlier this week, for example, I was getting coffee at the local coffee shop when a woman approached me and identified herself as Jeanette Ragnorak, Warren Cave's high school math teacher. She told me she was glad I'm on the case because she's certain that Warren isn't guilty.

JEANETTE: You'll never convince me that Warren Cave killed
anyone. He was in my Algebra II class the year before all
this happened, and he was much more of a softie than
he wanted anyone to believe. Sure, he dressed like the

Grim Reaper, but he was as tough as a gerbil. One afternoon, I noticed he wasn't paying attention in class—he
was nudging a piece of paper along the back of the chair
in front of him. I was about to reprimand him, but then
I realized he was trying to catch a spider. So many other
students—particularly the boys—would've smashed the
spider, but Warren coaxed it into his hands and gently
released it on the window ledge. I recall that so clearly
because it was so unexpected. He didn't look like the
gentle soul who would do that. But appearances can be
deceiving. And it was the first thing I thought of when I
later heard they'd arrested him for murder. He couldn't
even hurt a spider, I thought—there's no way he murdered a man in cold blood.

Warren's former math teacher wasn't the only person who
reached out to me to defend Warren. A woman who described
herself as a high school friend of Melanie's told me how Warren
used to babysit her child.

MONICA WOOLEY: Sure, Warren could look a little off-putting
with that hair and those clothes and, well, that sneer,
but he was the only one my Danny tolerated. Warren's
biggest secret was that he had a heart of gold.

I heard from several other Elm Park citizens who had re-
deeming things to say about Warren, but who didn't want to end
up on the podcast. But you know what they say: the plural of
anecdote is not data. That's all that these stories are: anecdotes.
Yet, it's important to note that, while people have approached me to relate nice things about Warren, I've heard

only the opposite about Lanie Buhrman. Jeanette Ragnorak, for one, also had some choice things to say about Lanie:

JEANETTE: I had Lanie Buhrman in class two years after I had Warren. I'm a math teacher, so I'm used to children hating my class, but Lanie was something else altogether. If I wasn't directly interacting with her, she'd put her head down on her desk. On multiple occasions, she just got up and left. And, in all my years of teaching, I have never had to charge a student for a textbook, but Lanie Buhrman used a marker to black out entire pages.

I heard from many other people who had stories of Lanie cutting class, smoking in the bathroom, and stealing from the cafeteria.

Again, though: anecdotes. Still, all these anecdotes are interesting because together they provide some context for the mind-sets of the major players. But without a doubt, the *most* interesting interview I had this week was about more than context—it was about fact.

As you undoubtedly recall, Warren Cave had no alibi for the night Chuck Buhrman was killed. His story has always been that he was getting high off cough syrup in the local cemetery, and that he then got in a fight with some kids in the park. These unidentified kids are the only ones who could verify that Warren was somewhere else at the exact moment that Chuck Buhrman was getting killed, and they have, for the last thirteen years, remained unidentified. Even though Warren's attorney put out a call for these individuals to come forward, no one did.

Until last week.

I received a call from a woman named Maggie Kallas. In October 2002, Maggie was a senior honors student at Elm Park High School, and she claims that she was at the park the same night Chuck Buhrman was murdered—and that she saw Warren there.

MAGGIE: Warren Cave was telling the truth about getting thrown in the lake that night. I was there.

POPPY: Tell me what happened.

MAGGIE: Some of us were drinking at the park. It wasn't the kind of thing we normally did, you have to understand, but it was the fall of our senior year, and we were feeling invincible. There were five of us, I think. Maybe six. Me and Keith and . . . Oh, never mind that. It's hard to remember at this point. We were all pretty drunk, and Warren Cave came riding his bicycle through the park. And he just looked ridiculous. I mean, he was this goth kid, all gangly with this bad dye job, riding a bicycle, for heaven's sake, and he was weaving all over the place. And the guys . . . well, they were wasted and started throwing things at him. And that made him mad, and they got to pushing and shoving, and next thing you know, Warren was in the water.

POPPY: Warren has said that he was held underwater until he passed out.

MAGGIE: Well, I don't know about that. Like I said, we were all drinking, and we girls stayed back. I just know that at

283

some point the boys came running back from the lake, and we all ran away.

POPPY: Were you aware that a request had been issued for information about Warren Cave's whereabouts that evening?

MAGGIE: Yeah.

POPPY: Why didn't you come forward?

MAGGIE: We were scared. You're not supposed to be in the park after dark, you know, and you're definitely not supposed to be drinking there. We knew that we'd be in trouble if we admitted anything. We were all, for lack of a better description, good kids. We were on the student council and sports teams, and we were scared that something like that would ruin our futures. We thought we'd never get into college. And so we decided to stick together and stay quiet. You have to believe me, though: we didn't think it would have any impact. We assumed that if Warren was innocent, that would be evident in court no matter what we said. We were so stupid. I'm so ashamed. I was worried about ruining my life, but instead I helped ruin someone else's.

POPPY: Why are you coming forward now? Warren has been in prison for more than twelve years.

MAGGIE: Like I said, I hadn't thought that our testimony would've made a difference. I didn't know when Mr. Buhrman was killed exactly, and I figured that Warren could've been in both places. That girl saw him pull the trigger, right? And his fingerprints? If he was found guilty in a court of law, there had to have been a reason. But then I started listening to your podcast, and I realized that it was important to have all the facts.

Maggie played coy when I asked her for the names of the other people she had been with. She said that she wanted to let them decide whether to come forward on their own, but she did slip at one point and mention someone named Keith. I looked at yearbooks from that time period and figured she was referring to Keith Baron, a student council member and varsity athlete. Keith now works in tech and lives in Silicon Valley, but he speaks fondly about his time in Illinois, and he agreed to speak with me on the phone. Our conversation began amiably enough, chatting about Elm Park and how it's changed over the years. But when I mentioned my recent conversation with Maggie, things took a turn.

POPPY: Maggie Kallas told me she was with you and some others in Lincoln Park on the night of October 19, 2002, and that you saw Warren Cave there.

KEITH: No, that's not right.

POPPY: Are you sure? Why don't you just think about it a little bit more?

KEITH: I don't need to think about it. I'm positive. I wasn't at the park that night, and I never saw Warren Cave outside of school.

POPPY: Why do you think Maggie would tell me you threw Warren Cave in the lake, then?

KEITH: She said that?

POPPY: She said that you and some others got in a fight with him in the park, and that it ended with Warren in the lake.

KEITH: I . . . I'm done with this.

POPPY: This is your chance to come clean, Keith. Tell me what happened in the park that night.

KEITH: Go to hell.

At that point, Keith hung up and refused to return any of my attempts at communication. Maggie declined to name any other friends who had been in the park, and cold-calling likely suspects from the yearbook didn't lead to anything. I'm therefore issuing a request: if you have any information about what happened in Lincoln Park that night, please, please let me know. You can remain anonymous if you want, but please. The truth wants to be set free.

chapter 18

I lay back on the bed and stared blankly at the ceiling, unable to stop hearing Maggie Kallas's throaty voice, saying to Poppy Parnell and anyone else who would listen, *Warren Cave was telling the truth about getting thrown in the lake that night.* The conclusion was impossible to escape: if Warren was telling the truth, Lanie was not.

I shuddered as a sudden memory flashed through my mind, the two of us pressed together in the pitch-dark of the bedroom closet, squeezing hands so tightly I thought our bones would break, Lanie hotly whispering, *It's my fault.*

"I'm thinking manicures," Ellen announced, pushing open the door. "We need to cram in as much cousin-bonding as we can before we both go home tomorrow."

I sat up slowly, Lanie's damning words screaming through my mind.

"Oh." Ellen startled when she saw my face. "Josie, what's wrong?"

I shook my head to clear it, forced myself to tell Ellen about the podcast. "Poppy Parnell was right. She had a bombshell."

"What was it?"

"She interviewed this woman named Maggie Kallas—"

"Maggie Kallas?" Ellen interrupted. "I know her. She was a senior when we were sophomores. What does she have to do with anything?"

"She's substantiating Warren's claim that he was in Lincoln Park that night. She says she saw him. She says her friends were the ones to push him in the lake."

"So what?" Ellen shrugged. "Unless she's claiming that she saw him at the exact moment that your dad was killed, I don't see the bombshell. I mean, we knew he was in the park. He couldn't have ended up in the lake otherwise."

"Right," I said, my voice shaking. "But the theory that he went into the lake on purpose to destroy evidence doesn't hold if someone threw him in."

"Maybe—"

"Ellen, no. That would have to be an incredible coincidence." I took a deep rattling breath. "Besides, listening to Maggie talk about that night reminded me more about it. I fell asleep early that night. I have no idea whether Lanie was in bed or not. And she was so shaky when she came back upstairs. And sweaty."

"Breathe, Josie," Ellen commanded. "Listen to yourself. Your sister had just seen your father murdered. Of course she was distraught. I would be more worried if she *hadn't* been shaky and sweaty."

"But yesterday you said . . ." I trailed off, unable to vocalize the worst part, the thing that Lanie had said in the dark.

"Oh, please," Ellen said, waving her hand as though she could erase the suspicions she had voiced. "I was buzzed and talking out of my ass."

"So you think Lanie saw Warren shoot our father, and then he went to the park where Maggie saw him."

"I don't know," Ellen said, her voice softer. "Look, you

know there's no love lost between me and your sister. She's a real asshole, and the ingratitude she's shown my mother is disgusting. I'll never forgive her for what she did to you. But I don't think she's actively evil, and she certainly wasn't back then. If Lanie said she saw Warren, I believe her."

I nodded, but my chest was still tight with doubt. Before our father died, Lanie had not been the delinquent she would later become, but neither had she been infallibly truthful: she snuck readings of our mother's diary, hid books, and stole candy. None of those minor offenses rose to the level of perjury, and certainly none of them came close to patricide, but they nevertheless contributed to my profound distrust of my sister.

A scene from that last afternoon flashed through my mind with sudden clarity: we had just finished the first set of tennis, and Lanie and I sat panting on the side of the court while our father ran around the fence to collect a stray ball. His cell phone rang in his gym bag, and Lanie reached for it, suggesting it might be our mother. When she looked at the caller ID, her face changed.

"Who is it?" I asked.

"No one," she said, powering down the phone and burying it at the bottom of the bag.

When our father had come jogging up to us with the errant tennis ball, the smile that Lanie had given him had been cold and mean. She hadn't mentioned his ringing phone, and I understood from her demeanor that I was not to bring it up, either.

Could the caller have been Melanie? Could Lanie have

known about our father's affair? Could she have decided to take matters into her own hands?

The thought that Lanie might have killed our father was too horrible for me to entertain, and so I raced to a more comfortable conclusion: Maggie Kallas was lying. I didn't know why—could someone be paying her?—but I didn't care. If Maggie was lying, that meant my sister wasn't. I almost regretted not agreeing to give Poppy Parnell a quote; maybe she would have let me talk directly to Maggie.

An online search turned up women named Margaret Kallas living in Omaha, Portland, Charleston, Phoenix, and somewhere called Telephone, Texas. Uncertain which (if any) she was, I snagged Ellen's phone and combed through her Facebook friends. Sure enough, Maggie Kallas was listed, and, in an unexpected boon, Maggie's number was listed on her profile. I jotted down the number and replaced Ellen's phone where I found it.

Later, I hid in the garage and dialed Maggie's number. I held my breath as the phone rang, nearly choking when she answered.

"Is this Maggie Kallas?" I asked, even though I recognized her voice from the podcast.

"It is. Who's this, please?"

"This is Josie Buhrman," I began.

"How did you get this number?" she demanded, her cordial demeanor vanishing.

Panicked that she would hang up before I had a chance to learn anything, I blurted, "Are you lying about seeing Warren Cave?"

All I heard was the subtle click of the call disconnecting. When I tried to call back, the phone rang once and then diverted to voicemail. As I called again and again without success, I wondered what it meant: Was she avoiding me because she was lying? Or just avoiding me because she worried I would accuse her of such? How would I know if she wouldn't talk to me?

For our last night in Elm Park, Caleb suggested taking Aunt A (and, by default, Ellen) out to dinner. We skipped Ray's Bistro in favor of one of the self-consciously hip restaurants that recently popped up near campus. These new additions made me smile, remembering how my father used to theatrically moan there was nowhere to get a decent meal on campus. The particular restaurant we visited was a farm-to-table outfit that called itself The Three Sisters and featured murals of the three sisters themselves (squash, corn, and bean) created by local artists. With its herb-heavy cocktail list and water glasses made from repurposed bottles, it would blend seamlessly into our block back in Brooklyn. When I mentioned that, Aunt A surprised me by saying she would love to visit us. She had never expressed interest in New York before—which was just as well, considering the lies I had told Caleb about her—and I was pleased to see Caleb encourage her visit, taking a pen to a paper cocktail napkin and beginning a list of sights she might be interested in.

The four of us had such a nice dinner that by the time our waiter, a college-aged kid with the beard of a lumberjack, set the letterpress dessert menu on the table, I had almost forgotten that I had ever heard of Poppy Parnell.

"What do you think, ladies?" Caleb asked with a grin. "Dessert?"

"None for me," Ellen said, smiling daintily as she pushed the menu away.

"Well, I for one could use some indulgence," Aunt A said.

"What do you recommend?" I asked the waiter as I glanced down at the selections.

I froze.

"My personal favorite is the brown-butter blondie served with vanilla bean ice cream and a cinnamon-chocolate drizzle," the waiter was saying, but all I could see was the first item on the menu, something called "Ma's Chocolate Cupcake." My stomach soured; an unexplainable sense of déjà vu disoriented me.

"Jo?" Caleb asked. "Are you okay?"

Ma's Chocolate Cupcake.

Why was that dessert so unnerving?

Ma's Chocolate Cupcake. Ma's Chocolate Cupcake.

A fragment of something flashed across my mind, the same memory that had nagged at me when Adam had mentioned Lanie baking all of those cupcakes. Only suddenly it crystallized and became clear. My stomach flipped, and I pressed a hand to my mouth.

"The cupcake," our waiter continued, oblivious, "is also very special."

That cupcake was special.

Abruptly, I pushed myself away from the table, rattling the funky water glasses and startling not only my family and our waiter, but also the other tables surrounding us. I rushed to the dimly lit restroom, thanked my lucky stars that it was a single stall and that it was unoccupied, and proceeded to gag up my $30 piece of fish.

I remembered the day of the cupcakes.

The summer I was fifteen, I had a nasty case of the stomach flu. After three straight days of vomiting, I awoke from an afternoon nap feeling slightly better and also ravenous, having eaten nothing for the last fifty hours. I pushed myself out of bed and weakly made my way downstairs.

There were cupcakes on the table: three of them decorated with small pink flowers on one plate, a larger cupcake with red rosettes resting apart on a blue china plate. The chocolate frosting glistened, tempting me. Too hungry to resist, I grabbed the largest cupcake and took a huge bite.

As I chewed, I heard the back door open and my mother and Lanie enter the house. I froze. My desperate hunger subsiding, guilt surfaced. Our mother was a frequent baker, but she had little patience for decorating cupcakes unless there was a specific reason. More likely than not, the cupcakes had been destined for an event at my father's school, or some celebration my mother had been planning. At that point, however, there was no way for me to disguise my bite marks, and so I settled for destroying the evidence and crammed another huge bite in my mouth.

My mother entered the dining room with a vase full of freshly cut flowers and stopped in her tracks when she saw me.

"Josie! You're up!"

I nodded, chewing furiously while I hid the remainder of the cupcake behind my back.

She blinked. Her eyes jumped to the empty plate and then back to me.

"Did you take that cupcake?" she asked, her voice high and thin, a telltale sign that she was irritable.

Ashamed, I produced the rest of the cupcake. Still chewing, I mumbled, "I'm sorry."

She dropped the vase on the ground and flew at me, one hand yanking open my jaw and the fingers from her other hand digging in my mouth, pulling masticated bits of cupcake out and flinging them on the ground.

"That cupcake was special!" she barked. "It was for your father for our anniversary. Can't you see that? You stupid, selfish girl!"

"You're hurting me!" I cried, trying to twist out of her grasp. "I'm sorry. Please stop!"

"You've ruined everything," she insisted, readjusting so that my neck was lodged in the crook of her elbow, her fingers still in my mouth, choking me. Tears streamed down my face as she continued. "This was supposed to be special, and you *ruined* it. *Everything* is ruined."

"Mom!" Lanie screamed from the doorway. "Stop!"

My sister's voice seemed to bring our mother back to reality, and she immediately loosened her grasp on me. I fell to the ground, choking and gasping. Lanie ran to fetch me a glass of water, but our mother simply began picking up the flowers that had scattered when the vase had dropped. In the end, I learned my lesson: I should have eased my way back into solid foods, and by the time I had returned to my room,

I felt ill once more. It was two more days before I could consume anything other than clear liquids.

Wiping my mouth in the Three Sisters restroom, I stared hard into the mirror. My mother's dark hair and pale blue eyes stared back at me. The physical resemblance to our mother was uncanny; what else might we have inherited from her? I thought of Lanie throwing the pitcher, her eyes wild and unfocused. Was there something more sinister lurking beneath the surface?

Later that night, I was startled awake by my buzzing phone. 2:32 glowed on the clock radio; Caleb groaned in his sleep. I had cleaned myself up at the restaurant and, after telling everyone I was fine despite the memory now pulsing insistently in my brain, we'd driven home and fallen right into bed.

"Hello?" I whispered into the phone.

"Josie?" Lanie's voice sounded muted and far away. "Are you sleeping?"

I had forgotten how vulnerable my sister could sound in the predawn hours. Two o'clock had always been her witching hour, when she would whisper across the gap between our beds how much she missed our father, our mother, our bond, our life. The first few such confessionals had left me hopeful, thinking she was returning to the sister I had once known and loved. But then, as always, morning came and she once again armored herself with black clothing, blacker eyeliner, and bad attitude.

"Lanie? What is it?"

"First the pearls. Does that mean anything to you?"

The disjointed phrase and the faint hint of a slur harkened back to those earlier calls and suggested she was not entirely sober. "Have you been drinking?"

"I can't sleep. That phrase is stuck in my head, and I can't remember where it came from. *First the pearls.* I'm associating it with Mom, but I can't remember when or where she might've said it."

"If she said it at all."

"Right. If she said it at all." Lanie sighed in frustration. "I feel like it's right there, just out of reach. Every time I'm about to get my hands on it, it fades away. I hate how jumbled my memories of Mom have become."

My heart beating in my mouth, I asked, "What about your other memories? Are they jumbled, too?"

"What do you mean?"

She sounded genuinely befuddled, but I pressed forward anyway. "How certain are you about anything? About any of the things that you think you remember?"

My sister was quiet, and I thought for a moment that she had hung up.

"Lanie?"

"Do you remember the time that Mom gave us that English test?" she asked. "The one where we had to diagram sentences? And you cheated off my paper?"

"Huh? No. Lanie, I never cheated."

"You must have. I was always better at English than you, how else do you explain your perfect score?"

"Okay, fine. I cheated on an English test administered by

our mother fifteen years ago. It was the only time I ever did it, and I felt terrible. So what?"

"So I gave you the benefit of the doubt. Even when I was sure that you'd cheated, I didn't contradict you when you said you hadn't. And when Mom accused you of cheating, I stood up for you."

"That doesn't—"

"You have to take care of the people you love," she hissed. "Or you lose them."

"What is that supposed—?" I started, but she had already disconnected the call.

I immediately called her back, but the call went straight to voicemail. Dread collecting in my chest, I almost called Adam, but then I reminded myself that inciting a reaction was Lanie's raison d'être. I was simply out of practice in knowing how to respond.

⬆ **Episode 5—Lanie credibility (self.reconsideredpodcast)**
⬇
submitted 4 hours ago by jennyfromtheblock

I just listened to episode 5 and I think I have some concerns about the way that Poppy is using Lanie's high school years to evaluate her credibility. These people are all saying that she had an attitude problem after her father was shot. Wouldn't you feel the same way?

> ⬆ **elmparkuser1** 10 points 3 hours ago
> ⬇
> But Josie didn't react that way. She was on the soccer team and student council and ran around with the popular kids.
>
> > ⬆ **jennyfromtheblock** 3 points 3 hours ago
> > ⬇
> > So people react differently. I still think that Lanie's reaction was totally within the realm of reason.

chapter 19

Caleb and I bought tickets for an 8:30 p.m. flight out of O'Hare, and we planned to leave Elm Park around four, allowing us plenty of time to drive to Chicago, return the rental car, and make our way through the TSA line. By three thirty, our bags were packed, Ellen had laden my arms with a stack of fashion magazines (the pages with haircuts she liked for me helpfully flagged), and I had promised Aunt A we would come back for Christmas. The one thing I had not been able to do was connect with Lanie. I had been calling all day without getting a response, and I was growing increasingly anxious. Her post-midnight phone call seemed like a portend. *Something bad has happened.*

The tenth time I mentioned Lanie within a span of so many minutes, Caleb handed me the keys to the rental car. "Why don't you go on over there?"

"Thanks," I said, kissing him on the cheek. "That's a good idea. I'd rather say goodbye to her in person anyway."

I opened the front door, so focused on my sister that I nearly plowed over her daughter, who was reaching for the doorbell.

"Ann!" I said, surprised. "What are you doing here?"

"Mom said I should come here and see you," she said with a bright smile.

Unease rumbling in my stomach, I glanced up and down the street for evidence of Lanie. "Where is your mother?"

With her mother's superlative talent for avoiding a question, Ann handed me a sticky envelope. "Mom asked me to give you this."

My name was scrawled on one side of the envelope in smeared pencil, and the flap was sealed shut with jagged lengths of tape. An indistinct buzz of worry sounded in my ears, and my hands shook as I ripped open the envelope and extracted a sheet of notebook paper. The paper was dotted with coffee rings, the green-inked words scrawled in painfully familiar handwriting.

Josie-Posie,
it began, employing the nickname Lanie had used for me when we were kids.

I shouldn't have called in the middle of the night. I'm sorry. I forget other people sleep. I don't anymore. No rest for the wicked, and all that.

The benefit, though, of not sleeping is that you have plenty of time to think. The world is awfully quiet at three a.m., and that makes it easier to hear yourself. And this is what I've realized: I ruin everything. Do you remember King Midas, that mythical ruler whose touch could turn anything to gold? I'm like him, but in reverse. Everything I touch turns to garbage and spoils.

The one thing that I haven't managed to wreck yet is my daughter, but I know that, given enough time, I'll ruin her, too. It's inevitable. She deserves better than me. Adam deserves better than me. You deserve better than me. You've always been right about me: I'm untrustworthy, I'm a traitor, I'm a horrible human being. My hope is that, when I'm gone, you, Adam, Ann—all of you—can move past the mess that I've made of everything and just remember this: I always loved you. I know it doesn't make anything any better, and it doesn't absolve me, but it's the truth. I love all three of you, just like I loved Mom and Dad, and love and loyalty—along with a hearty dose of bad judgment—are my downfalls.

God, Josie, I'm just so tired.

Always,
Your Sister

"Oh, bloody hell."

Caleb, reading the letter over my shoulder, summed up my feelings perfectly. Turning to him in bewilderment, all I could say was, "I never called her a horrible human being."

He rubbed my shoulder quickly, and then knelt down to Ann's level and affected a friendly smile. "G'day, little lady. Did your mum bring you here?"

"I got a ride with the mailman." She frowned slightly. "He wouldn't let me deliver any mail."

"The mailman, eh?" Caleb inquired, shooting me a worried look. "How'd that happen?"

Ann grinned, oblivious to our concern. "Mom and I are having an adventure. She didn't make me go to school today, and instead we went to the movies and the roller-skating rink and the park! Then we got doughnuts, and then she said she needed to go off-grid and that I should find someone to bring me here." She pointed to the envelope in my hands. "She wrote the address on there."

"She wanted you to find anyone to drive you?" I asked, my voice thin with panic. "Anyone at all?"

Ann nodded.

"Is everything all right out here?" Aunt A asked, stepping into the foyer. "Oh! Ann! Shouldn't you still be at school?"

"Mom said I didn't have to go today."

Grimly, I passed Aunt A Lanie's note. She cried out as she read it, her hands flying to her heart.

Ann's expression clouded. "Granny?"

"What has she done?" Aunt A squeaked.

"We're having an *adventure*," Ann insisted stubbornly, but I could see she was starting to absorb our sense of doom.

I bobbed my head like a marionette, my heart not in the motion. "Right. Hey, you want Uncle Caleb to get you a glass of orange juice?"

"Sounds like a brilliant idea, Jo," Caleb said, taking her hand without waiting for an answer and leading her to the kitchen.

"Where do you think she is?" Aunt A asked, her expression still bewildered.

"I don't know," I said grimly. "I'm going to go talk to Adam. Call me if you hear from Lanie. Call me if you have any idea where she might be."

"Good afternoon," the receptionist greeted me cheerily as I banged my way through the door, either oblivious to my agitation or too well trained to acknowledge it. "Welcome

302

to Ives Real Estate and Dream Homes. How may I help you today?"

I barreled past her and threw open a closed door marked ADAM IVES, JR. to find Adam leaning back in his padded desk chair, chewing thoughtfully on a pencil as he worked a crossword puzzle.

"Josie?" he said, setting down the pencil. "What are you doing here?"

I slammed the door before the approaching receptionist reached it, and shoved Lanie's note in his face. "Your daughter just gave me this."

"What is it?" he asked, taking it from me.

"Why don't you read it and tell me."

Adam's face dropped as he skimmed the note. "Fuck."

I exhaled, deflating completely. I had wanted Adam to laugh, to tell me that the note meant nothing, that Lanie was just messing around. I had wanted him to say that she was safely at home, that she was sleeping off a bender. I had wanted Adam to have an explanation.

I sank down into the chair opposite his desk. "Is it . . . Do you think it's a suicide note?"

"It could be," he said quietly.

"Goddammit, Adam," I said, pounding my fist on his desk. "You're the one who's spent the last week telling me how worried you are about her. How could you let something like this happen?"

"I didn't know . . ."

"So she seemed fine this morning?"

He lifted his shoulders slightly.

"This is important, Adam," I insisted. "How did she seem this morning?"

"I didn't see her this morning. I spent the night here." Adam inclined his head to indicate the couch, the misshapen pillow resting on it, the afghan sloppily folded over its side. It was only then that I noticed the faint stubble on his chin, the wrinkles in his shirt. "Lanie and I got in a fight."

"What were you fighting about?"

He shook his head. "You're just going to get mad at me, too."

"Adam, I swear to God, if something happens to her while you're wasting my time, they'll be finding your body for weeks."

"The new episode of *Reconsidered*," he said, frowning. "Did you listen to it?"

My stomach sank; I remembered my own reaction to hearing that same podcast. "Let me guess: you accused her of perjuring herself."

He shifted and looked down. "I might have gone a little further."

Don't, Adam had said when I had suggested Lanie might have been mistaken about Warren. *It'll kill her.*

"What did you do?" I whispered, almost afraid to hear.

"Do you think . . . ?" Adam trailed off. He looked up at me, his light-brown eyes wide and wet. "Be honest, Josie. Do you think Lanie might have pulled that trigger?"

Hearing Adam vocalize the same inconceivable, disloyal thoughts didn't reinforce them in my head; if anything, it turned my stomach and made me realize that we were wrong, we were all wrong. We *had* to be. Lanie could be violent and irrational, but the only person she had ever done true, honest harm to was herself.

"Tell me you didn't say that to her."

"You've never thought it?" Adam pressed, the edge of his voice slipping into desperation. "Honestly? If Warren Cave didn't shoot him, what other reason would she have for saying he did?"

"Adam, this is your *wife* we're talking about. The mother of your child. Do you honestly think she's capable of murder?"

He chewed the inside of his cheek before answering. "I never know what to expect with Lanie."

"It doesn't matter," I said, standing up. "Our priority right now is finding her. Can you take the rest of the day off?"

Adam nodded, one of the tears making its way down his cheek. "Let's go."

I felt slightly sick as I followed Adam to his house, remembering too many dates that had been ruined by Lanie, too many times Adam had driven me home in tears because someone told me they had just seen my sister and, boy, was she wasted. The worst, of course, had been that other early fall night, back in 2003, just a few months after our mother had left.

I had known something was wrong the moment Adam pulled up to the curb. It was one minute to midnight and Aunt A's house was lit up like a Christmas tree, lights shining on every floor and the unmistakable flicker of the television through the living room window, while the front door stood ajar. Bubbles perched on the front porch swing, carefully licking a paw.

Dread heavy in my chest, I brushed off Adam's attempt at a good-night kiss and vaulted from the car. I raced up the porch steps, my pounding heart nearly shattering my rib cage with its wild rhythm. I scooped up Bubbles, who meowed loudly in protest and slashed at me with his claws, and carried the cat through the house as I called out for my family. There was no answer. I was throwing open the cellar door in complete and utter desperation when I heard them mount the porch steps. Dropping Bubbles, I raced into the living room to meet them.

There were only two of them.

"What's going on?" I demanded. "I came home and the house was wide open. I was really scared."

Aunt A dropped her keys on the foyer table and exhaled a rattling sigh. "Your sister tried to kill herself."

I think my heart stopped beating. I know I stopped breathing. My entire existence hinged on the word *tried*.

"Tried?"

"She swallowed half a bottle each of vodka and what was left of your mother's Valium before she came into my room and told me that she had changed her mind. She didn't want to die after all." Aunt A sniffled and shook her head, a failed attempt at concealing her tears. "We got her there in time, honey. She's going to be all right."

A sob ripped its way from my throat. "Why didn't you call me?"

"I'm sorry, Josie. She told us not to."

"What? Why?"

"Because your sister is a crazy bitch," Ellen muttered before stalking up the stairs.

Aunt A frowned after Ellen. "I'm sorry," she said to me before climbing the stairs herself, leaving me to wonder exactly what she was apologizing for.

I spent that night tangled in a series of increasingly bloody dreams. My relief at waking lasted only until my eyes landed on Lanie's empty bed, and reality washed over me. I had to see her. I stomped down to the kitchen and voiced my demand.

The coffee cup wavered in Aunt A's hand. "I'm not sure that's such a good idea."

"She's my *twin sister*," I insisted, tears forming in the corners of my eyes. "She tried to kill herself. I have to see her."

"Josie—"

"She's all I have left. Please, Aunt A. I have to see her."

"All right," Aunt A said, nodding grimly. "I understand. I'd feel the same way if I were in your position. But honey, I have to warn you: she might not be too happy to see you."

Once the elevator had deposited me on the third floor—the pediatric ward—I almost lost my nerve. The hospital smelled like rubbing alcohol and sickness, and the third floor was haunted by pale, whisper-like children. I hated to think of my sister in a place like that because she had thought that being dead was better than being alive. I couldn't understand what she had been thinking. We might not have perfect lives, but we had each other. That had to count for something.

"Hi," I said, stepping into her room.

Lanie was propped against a pillow, staring out the window, her reflection uncharacteristically bleak. I shivered.

"Lanie," I tried again. "How are you doing?"

Lanie whipped her head around to face me so quickly that

her hair, clumpy with grease, spun around her like a carnival ride. She glared through raw, red eyes and hissed in a hoarse voice, "How do you *think* I'm doing?"

I shifted my weight uncomfortably and wished that I'd taken Aunt A's advice, or at least asked her to come with me.

"Cat got your tongue?" she sneered. "Or are you just at a loss for words when the topic isn't super-fun pep rallies and super-important schoolwork and your super-special goody-two-shoes boyfriend?"

Blood rushed to my cheeks and hot tears burned a path down my face. "Lanie, what's going on?"

"I tried to kill myself last night," Lanie said, narrowing her eyes and keeping her voice absurdly calm. "I took a lethal combination of prescription drugs and alcohol. While you were on your sweet little date, probably knitting sweaters for homeless kittens and saving the goddamn whales with your virgin boyfriend, I was trying to sedate myself out of existence. *That* is what's going on."

I sucked in my breath. "Does this have something to do with me?"

She laughed shortly, a harsh laugh that ended in a choking cough that caused her to clutch at her throat and wince in pain. Blinking watery eyes, she arranged her features in an expression of disdain and said, "Of course you'd think that. Try to be less self-involved, Josie. The only person this has anything to do with is *me*. I'm just illustrating the difference between our evenings." She swallowed and grimaced. "But you know what? Turns out we have more in common than I thought. It's true: you and me, sister, we're nothing but mice. I thought being timid was your jam, but I found out that when it counts, I'm just as scared as you. I couldn't go through with it. Now get out."

Discussion thread on www.reddit.com/r/
reconsideredpodcast, posted September 29, 2015

⬆ **more Lanie B gossip (self.reconsideredpodcast)**
⬇
submitted 1 hour ago by elmparkuser1

I know some people in this sub think that we spend too much time on Lanie's obvious issues, but something I think Poppy missed that's important is this: in October 2003 (or thereabouts) Lanie Buhrman intentionally overdosed. I've always wondered if she tried to kill herself because she felt guilty about railroading Warren. Or . . . because she killed her father herself.

⬆ **toopunkrockforthis -3 points 1 hour ago**
⬇
You're disgusting. Take your baseless accusations somewhere else.

⬆ **caffeinecold 18 points 1 hour ago**
⬇
Hi, Lanie!

chapter 20

You have to take care of the people you love, she had said. *Or you lose them.*

I hadn't taken care of my sister. That morning's phone call had been a cry for help, and I had ignored it. I had done nothing for *thirteen hours* while my sister fell even further to pieces. Adam had warned me she was fragile, and I had let decade-old hurt feelings stop me from helping her.

"Are you okay?" Adam asked, glancing over at me while he unlocked the front door. "You look kind of white."

I shook my head, sinking to a seat on the porch steps. "I don't think I can go in there, Adam. What if she's . . . ?" I blanched, squeezing my eyes shut to block out terrible images of my sister's lifeless body that suddenly materialized.

Adam sighed and sat down beside me. "You've been gone a long time, Josie. I think you've forgotten what it's like to live with Lanie."

"You're saying you think this is just a stunt?"

"No, of course not. But disappearing isn't entirely out of character. A couple of months ago, I came home from work to find the house locked and Ann sitting on the porch. Lanie hadn't picked her up from school, and she'd walked the whole way home. Lanie wouldn't answer the phone, and no one knew where she was. Lanie finally showed up at eight that night, eyes all glazed, and do you know where she was? At the library. I'd been panicked for hours, calling the hospitals, certain something horrible had happened to her, and she'd just been downtown reading *Gone with the* fucking *Wind* all day." He shook his head a little. "I know this is different. She's been agitated for weeks about the podcast, and there's that note. I'm just saying that I don't think we should immediately jump to the worst conclusion."

"God, I hope you're right."

"Listen," Adam said, standing up. "I'll check the house, okay? You call your aunt to see if Ann's said anything else, and then we'll regroup."

I nodded, biting back hot tears. I hadn't taken care of her, and I could only hope that it wasn't too late.

Adam and I spent hours combing the town for evidence of my sister. We talked to the doughnut shop employees (who remembered Ann but not Lanie). We checked the park, the gym, and the public library. Adam checked Lanie's credit card usage, and we drove to a gas station where it had been used and showed Lanie's picture around, hoping someone would remember her, that she might have given some hint of her destination to the cashier. No one remembered anything. Adam called everyone he could think of who might have crossed Lanie's path while I searched the #Reconsidered hashtag on Twitter. Nothing.

It was nearly nine o'clock by the time we returned to Adam's house, numb and exhausted. We plodded up the front steps, and I paused with my hand on the doorknob, a sudden memory of Lanie opening the door wearing that ridiculous apron stealing my breath. It had just been days since she had stood there, smiling and hugging me. Where had she gone?

"I really thought we'd find her," Adam said hollowly.

"We will," I said without conviction.

"Maybe she'll come home."

It pained me to hear the hope in his voice; I had spent the last twelve years nurturing the same kind of hope, thinking that someday my mother might come home. I couldn't bear to remind Adam of the similarities, though, and instead I pushed open the front door.

Inside, we found Ellen seated cross-legged on his living room floor, paging through a phone book.

"Ellen, hi. What are you doing here?"

"Going through the phone book to see if Lanie circled any numbers." She frowned at my surprise. "Don't give me that look. I might not get along with Lanie, but that doesn't mean I want her to die. God."

"You're back," Caleb said, entering the living room. "Any news?"

I shook my head in defeat. "No. Anything over here?"

"Sorry, love," Caleb said. To Adam, he said, "Amelia's helping Ann get ready for bed."

"Great, thanks." Adam nodded. "Does she seem upset?"

"Not yet. She still thinks it's all part of some adventure."

"Poor dear," Ellen said, putting a hand over her heart.

"We've looked everywhere for Lanie," I lamented. "No one has seen her. I don't get it. How could she just disappear?"

"Your mom did," Adam said. "You didn't know where she was for weeks."

"Oh," I said, an idea forming suddenly in my head. "You're right. I didn't think of that. Maybe Lanie's in California."

Ellen wrinkled her nose. "You mean the LFC? I can no more imagine Lanie joining that sunny commune than I can imagine her enlisting in the armed forces."

"Not to join," I said impatiently. "But what if she went there to connect with Mom's memory? She's been thinking about her a lot. And we've looked everywhere else. It's the only thing that makes sense."

"But she hasn't bought any plane tickets," Adam protested. "Remember? I checked her credit card statements. She hasn't charged anything other than that gas."

"So maybe she's driving there."

"On one tank of gas?"

"So she hasn't needed to refill yet," I argued desperately. "Come on, guys. It's the last possible place she might be. You know I'm right. I'll get a flight in the morning. I'll beat her to California."

"Jo, even if that's where she is, you'd never find her," Caleb said gently. "It would be like looking for a needle in a haystack. Worse—a needle in a barnful of hay. We don't even know where the Life Force Collective compound is located."

"No," I agreed slowly. "But I might know someone who could tell me. Five years ago, I met an LFC member named Sister Amamus in San Francisco. I bet I still have her information. She told me never to contact her again, but she might at least tell us if any of them have heard from Lanie. Or maybe she could give her a message."

I scrolled through my archived correspondence for Sister

Amamus's phone number, and quickly dialed. The call was immediately answered by a mechanical voice informing me that the number was out of service. Frowning, I composed an email to the author who had provided me with Amamus's contact information, sketching out the dire situation and begging for an alternate lead. Almost instantly, I received an automated message stating the email address was no longer valid.

I flung my phone to the ground, cursing loudly. As I bent to retrieve it, my eyes caught sight of a composition book resting on an end table.

"What's that?" I asked, pointing.

"Baseball stats," Adam said. "I like to keep score while I watch the games."

"Lanie used to journal in a notebook just like that one when we were kids. Does she still keep a journal?"

Adam shrugged. "Not that I've seen. Where do you think she'd keep it?"

"She used to hide it under her mattress," I remembered.

"Come on. Let's go look."

I followed Adam upstairs to the bedroom, pausing outside a closed door to listen to Aunt A's calm, quiet voice reading aloud to Ann. I distinctly remembered the tenderness in Lanie's expression when she had been discussing her daughter on Saturday night, and it was hard to reconcile that with the fact that Lanie was now gone. Surely she couldn't believe that her daughter was better off without her.

In the bedroom, I was surprised by how my chest tightened at the sight of their shared bed, but I forced any lingering feelings of betrayal from my mind and focused on the task at hand. Pushing aside the creamy sheets, I felt around underneath the mattress, disappointed when my searching hands found nothing. I turned to the nightstand, pulling open the drawer and rifling through its contents. I extracted romance novels, night creams, and a handful of pill bottles, but no journal.

I held an empty pill bottle up accusingly at Adam. "She's taking Valium?"

Adam shrugged. "She has a prescription."

"You remember she tried to kill herself with this once, right?" I asked, my voice shaking.

Adam blanched. "That was a long time ago, Josie," he said unconvincingly.

"Goddammit, Adam, if she . . ." I trailed off, unwilling to complete the sentence. I rummaged through her closet and chest of drawers without finding anything of interest and then turned to Adam. "Where else can we look?"

Adam guided us into a downstairs room he referred to as "Lanie's study." It turned out to be the only space in that handsome house that looked like my sister. A large library table was being used as a desk, and it was heaped with magazines—all kinds, glossy fashion magazines, *National Geographic*, cooking magazines—and bits of paper and scraps of fabric, ribbons, and something fluffy that looked like the innards of a stuffed animal. An open MacBook rested in the middle of the floor, next to an empty coffee mug and a plate with a half-eaten cinnamon roll, stale with indeterminate age. A half-painted canvas rested against the far wall, a farm scene gradually taking shape, while a discarded palette dabbed with crusted paint lay before it. A finished painting, this one of a crumbling farmhouse that resembled Grammy and Pops's old home, was propped up on a chair. I was surprised by the skill demonstrated on that finished piece, and a lump developed in my throat.

"Sorry about the mess," Adam said. "She won't let the cleaning lady in here. She barely lets me in here."

I nudged aside a puddled sweater with my foot, revealing an open photo album, and found myself staring down at the same photo of our family that I kept in the bedside drawer. My heartstrings tugged. I picked up the album and flipped a couple of pages, stopping when my hands landed on a familiar picture that looked a bit off. I squinted at it until I realized what the problem was: it was a family picture from the farm, the four of us sitting on bales of hay . . . but, in Lanie's copy, my father had been snipped off the end.

"Is that her phone?" Caleb said, interrupting my thoughts.

I followed his eyes to the ground. Panic fluttered in my throat. Why would she leave her phone behind? Unless . . . I thought of the pills upstairs, and shot a concerned look at Adam, whose complexion had turned gray.

Caleb picked up the phone and tapped its screen. "It's passcode protected," he said, holding it out to Adam.

Adam shook his head in defeat. "I don't know her passcode."

I reached for the phone, and punched in the date of our birthday—the same insecure passcode for my own phone. The phone unlocked, revealing a snapshot of Ann as the background on the home screen. Adam pressed his knuckles to his mouth and looked away. Quickly, I navigated to her contacts and scrolled through the short list: Adam, Ann's babysitter, Ann's doctor, Ann's school, Aunt A, Ellen, a Pilates studio—and Ryder Strong.

"Bingo," I said. "Ryder Strong."

"Lanie isn't friends with Ryder anymore," Adam said. "That number must be years old."

"She was at the funeral," I reminded him, dialing the number. Either it wasn't as old as Adam thought or Ryder hadn't changed her number in years because after three rings, Ryder answered, her gravelly voice rushed and hopeful.

"Lanie? Jesus, you scared me."

"No, Ryder, it's her sister, Josie."

"Oh," Ryder said, her voice cold. "I'm on my way out the door."

"Wait, please," I begged. "I'm looking for Lanie."

The only thing I heard was the soft click of Ryder disconnecting the call. I immediately redialed. This time there was no answer. I cursed loudly, tears springing into my eyes.

"What's happening?" Ellen asked, reaching for my arm.

"She hung up on me," I grumbled. Tapping out a text message that I hoped Ryder would not be able to ignore, I wrote: "Lanie disappeared and left a strange note. I think she might hurt herself. Please tell me if you know anything. Life or death."

And then I waited, too tense to breathe.

Within seconds, Lanie's phone vibrated.

"Josie?" Ryder said hesitantly.

"Thank you," I breathed. "What do you know?"

"First tell me what the note said."

"It reads like a suicide note, Ryder. And I just found an empty bottle of Valium in her bedroom, so stop wasting my time and tell me what you know."

I saw Ellen's eyes go wide at the mention of the Valium; she remembered that awful night.

"Shit," Ryder said quietly. "Look, I didn't know."

"I don't care. Have you seen her?"

"Yeah, I saw her."

I exhaled in half-relief. "Where? When?"

"Here. She showed up this afternoon, saying she hadn't slept in days and wanting to know if she could sleep here. I told her sure, and she fell asleep on the couch. I thought she might want some coffee when she got up, so I ran out to grab some milk. By the time I got back, she was gone."

"Where did she go?"

"I don't know. She didn't say."

"Think, Ryder," I pressed, unwilling to believe we were so close and yet still knew nothing. "Please. This is really important. Think hard. Did she say anything else?"

"Nothing you want to hear. I asked her why she came to me, seeing as how she hadn't seen fit to call me in months. She said she didn't have anywhere else to go, that she couldn't be with Adam anymore and that she couldn't go over to your aunt's place because you were there and you didn't want to see her."

I bit my lip, remembering how harsh I had been on the phone that morning. "Did she say anything else?"

"Not really. She said she was tired, and she said some nonsense about wanting to sleep so she could stop being herself." Ryder sighed. "I don't know, Josie. To be honest, it sounded like she was on something."

My spine prickled as I recalled the faint slur to her words during her early phone call. "Do you know what she took?"

"I didn't see her take anything," Ryder clarified. "But I mean, I've been around Lanie enough times when she's messed up to recognize it."

"Yeah," I acknowledged grimly. "Can you tell us anything else? Anything at all?"

"Not really. All she said was that she was tired and wanted to sleep. Oh, wait. She said something about wanting to turn back time to where she was brave. To end this, I think she said."

"What?" I gasped in horror.

"Yeah, but like I said, I think she was stoned. I don't think that actually means anything."

"Jesus, Ryder," I breathed. "I sure hope it doesn't."

I hung up and sank into Lanie's desk chair, body trembling with unshed tears.

"Calm down, Josie," Ellen said soothingly, putting a hand on my shaking shoulder. "What did Ryder say?"

"That Lanie was there this afternoon. She said she hadn't slept in days. She also said that Lanie said something about going back to where she was brave. Does that mean anything to you?"

Adam furrowed his brow. "Not specifically. Anything else?"

To end this. I swallowed and looked away. "That was it."

"So we still don't know anything." Adam sighed, his shoulders slumping.

"We know she was at Ryder's this afternoon," I said. "She had quite a pill collection up there, and Ryder said she seemed out of it. Maybe we should call the hospitals again. Caleb, can you do that? And I suppose there's a chance she got picked up for DUI, so maybe Ellen could call the police station. Adam, call anyone and everyone you can think of who might have some connection to Lanie. And I . . . I'll do something."

As I hung up the phone, Aunt A came into the room. "Josie, Adam, you're back. Did you find any leads?"

A pit forming in my stomach, I brought Aunt A up to speed on what I had learned from Ryder.

"Oh, *no*," Aunt A said, her eyes starting to water. "Oh, honey. I can only imagine what you're thinking. I still remember the worry that your mother gave me, and it was nearly unbearable."

Of course, I thought. Our mother.

The dashboard clock read 11:00 p.m. when I pulled up to the cemetery gates. They were locked, with a sign informing me the cemetery closed at dusk. I knew posted hours would not deter my sister, and so I parked the rental car down the street and scrambled over the fence. I immediately tripped over a low tombstone, and reached for my phone to illuminate the path but found I had left it in the car. Involuntarily, I shivered, suddenly realizing I was locked in a cemetery in the middle of the night. A breeze shook the leaves of a nearby tree, producing an ominous rattle.

I swallowed my sense of unease and picked my way through the dark, stricken with the irrational fear of falling into an open grave. At one point, I thought I heard someone moving across the dry grass, an eerie shuffling sound. I froze. It could be the caretaker, come to place me under citizen's arrest for trespassing, or it could be some degenerate skulking around the cemetery, like Warren Cave claimed he used to like to do.

Or it could be my sister.

"Lanie?" I called, my voice coming out a tiny croak. "Lanie, is that you?"

There was no response.

I held my breath and waited, but I could no longer hear the noise. The cemetery was completely still.

Unsettled, I continued my path to my parents' final resting places. My mother's grave was easy to find, the only plot topped with fresh earth. My chest tightened as I drew nearer and saw no sign of Lanie. No flowers or trinkets had been left adorning the graves, no mascara-stained tissues hid in the grass. She hadn't been here—or, if she had, she was gone. I turned to leave, eager to get out of the creepy cemetery, but something held me back. I knelt before the headstones marking my parents' side-by-side graves and stretched out a hand to touch their names.

I don't know what I had hoped for, but I felt nothing. Disappointed, I sat back on my heels. Somewhere in the distance, the shuffling sound started up again, and I jumped to my feet and ran the entire way back to the car.

From Twitter, posted September 29, 2015

Poppy Parnell ✓
@poppy_parnell

Can't sleep. Have a hunch that something is going down. @ me with leads. #Reconsidered #ChuckBuhrman

50m

John Underwood
@johnmunderwood8

@poppy_parnell Haunted by the ghost of Erin Buhrman? #Reconsidered #ReconsideredKills

49m

Carolyn S.
@carrieofthecity

@poppy_parnell I heard #LanieBuhrman **is missing. . . ?** #Reconsidered #ChuckBuhrman

48m

Wendy Gillespie
@wendyg_109

@carrieofthecity @poppy_parnell My son is in school with L's daughter. Daughter not in school today. Not sure if it means anything.

↻ ♥ ↩

47m

 Carolyn S.
@carrieofthecity

@wendyg_109 @poppy_parnell
It definitely means something.

↻ ♥ ↩

45m

 mm
@midwesternmamma

@poppy_parnell #JUSTICEFORWARRENCAVE #Reconsidered #ChuckBuhrman

↻ ♥ ↩

30m

 John Underwood
@johnmunderwood8

@midwesternmamma Way to stay on message, lady.

↻ ♥ ↩

10m

chapter 21

Once I was safely back in the car, I began to cry tears of frustration. My mind raced in aimless circles, replaying the previous day's events over and over on an endless loop. I had the nagging sensation that I knew something—or should know something—but it felt just out of my field of vision.

I replayed our last conversation in my head, concentrating on every word I could remember, turning each inside out to look for clues. I came up empty. She had mentioned our mother a couple of times, but if she wasn't at the cemetery and she wasn't in California . . .

Was I sure she *wasn't* in California? Adam said she hadn't used her credit cards to buy a flight, but what if she had a secret credit card? Or what if she had paid cash? Hands shaking with desperate energy, I pulled up an airline's phone number, the first step in an impractical plan to call every potential air carrier and describe my sister. As I listened to the automated message, I remembered Caleb saying it would be difficult to find the LFC, even if we got to California.

It would be like looking for a needle in a haystack. Worse—a needle in a barnful of hay.

I hung up the phone.

Lanie's paintings. The hay Adam had seen in her hair.

I knew where my sister was.

* * *

A neon-lettered No Trespassing sign was affixed to the rusted gate, but the gate itself hung open. My heart leapt; *someone* was here. Even though the early-morning sky was still inky dark, I turned off the car's headlights as I pulled through the gate, allowing me to creep undetected along the rutted dirt road. I could hear the feathery tops of weeds brushing against the car's undercarriage as I slowly inched forward in the darkness, squinting to make out the confines of the over-grown road. There was a time I could have found my way to the farmhouse in my sleep, but now I worried about missing a subtle curve and finding myself mired in the marshy grass surrounding the pond or driving out into the fields. I consid-ered switching the headlights back on, but I was too close to finding my sister to allow some farmer with a gun and strong sense of personal property to keep me from her.

And then, under a moonless sky, the farmhouse took shape. My heart caught in my throat; I let the car idle as I stared up at what was once a home so picturesque it could have been a Grant Wood painting. Now the paint was peeling from the house in chunks; what remained had faded from bright white to a dingy gray. The wooden railing surrounding the porch was missing spindles, and the steps leading up to it had rotted and fallen away. It looked more like something from a horror flick than the site of rose-tinted family memories.

The farmhouse was empty, and clearly had been for some time. Frankly, I was surprised the house remained at all. Fam-ily farms had long gone out of fashion, and I assumed the farm's new owners would have razed the building to make way for more money-making fields. But, for whatever reason, they hadn't, and the house stood before me, neglected and ominous.

I turned off the car and stepped outside. I heard nothing other than the frenzied chirping of crickets and the occasional eerie call of an owl. I crossed to what was left of the porch and hoisted myself up on the rotted beams beside where the stairs once stood. The wood was soft and damp, and I could feel my feet sinking slightly with each step. I held my breath as I carefully neared the front door. I took the knob in my hands and twisted, almost expecting the door to spring open as it had in my youth, unleashing the scents of freshly baked bread and Grammy's cinnamon-scented candles. The knob rattled uselessly in my hands, unyielding.

I took a step back, surveying the house. One of the front windows had been smashed in, and I eased through the gap, stepping around shards of broken glass.

Then I was in the carcass of my grandparents' living room. Their things—the patriotic plaid couch, the circular rag rug, the framed family photos assembled on the plain Shaker furniture—were long gone, the furniture carted off and sold at auction, the family photos and memorabilia tucked safely away in cardboard boxes in Aunt A's attic. Without their belongings, the room felt naked. The bold floral wallpaper still clung to the walls, and even in the dark I could see the ghostly imprint where an oil-painted pastoral scene once hung above the fireplace. Now, instead of tiny farmers plowing fields while tiny cattle grazed nearby, someone had spray-painted a tag in yellow characters.

I held my breath and listened for sounds of life. Nothing.

"Lanie?"

No answer, not even a creaking of floorboards.

"Lanie?" I tried once more.

Despite the complete silence, I refused to give up. There was a pulsing beneath my breastbone, a familiar urgency that was telling me my sister needed me. I moved from the living room into the dining room, the striped wallpaper there covered in graffiti and the moldering carpet littered with crushed beer cans. Without the large dining table, the one that Pops had assembled by hand and that had since taken up residence in Aunt A's dining room, the room seemed much smaller than I remembered. I moved into the kitchen, pausing to yank open the door to the pantry. But there was nothing other than empty shelves and the furtive sound of mice feet. Standing on the peeling linoleum, I closed my eyes and remembered helping Grammy stir fresh blueberries into pancake batter and slicing lemons for lemonade with my sister. I could almost smell the sugar, the fresh fruit—but it was just a mirage. I was about to start up the back stairs to the second floor when I paused to look out the window.

The moon had emerged from behind a cloud, illuminating the stretch between the farmhouse and the barn. And glimmering in its light I saw the shiny black of my sister's SUV. The vehicle was parked haphazardly in front of the barn, the door of which was yawning open like a sleepy beast. The lock on the house's back door stuck, and I nearly broke it in my hurry to get outside. I rushed toward the barn, the loud drumbeat of my heart sounding my arrival.

The vast, absolute darkness of the barn stopped me at its

threshold, and I stood there, blinking without seeing. I activated the flashlight function on my iPhone and swept the barn with the feeble beam, revealing little more than blurry columns of dust and the vague outlines of discarded farming equipment.

"Lanie?" I called. "Are you in here?"

There was no response, but the sensation that my sister was here was too strong to ignore. I stood stock-still, straining to hear something, anything.

And then I did. A small, shuffling noise, so soft I nearly missed it.

Stepping into the barn, I called my sister's name again. "Lanie. I know you're in here."

The silence that responded was so deafening, I almost wondered if I'd imagined hearing something.

"I'm not leaving until you come out," I said.

Something creaked above me, and I snapped my head upward, squinting into the darkness. My eyes were slowly adjusting to the lack of light, and I could see just enough to catch a subtle flutter of movement near the ceiling. The loft. I pointed my iPhone skyward, but the weak beam petered out long before it reached the loft. In the dark, I heard a faint humming noise—with a start, I recognized it as the "Brother John" nursery rhyme.

"Lanie," I pleaded. "Come on. I know you're in here."

A streak of light erupted from above. My sister stepped to the edge of the loft, holding a flashlight under her chin. The light cast long shadows on her pale face, transforming her into a ghoulish impersonation of my sister.

"I'm here."

"What are you doing up there?" I called, even though I wasn't certain I wanted to know.

"Do you remember that time you and I were playing up here, and a bat swooped down at us?"

I nodded. Lanie and I were eight, that in-between age when we still wanted to play make-believe but were getting too adventurous for our own good. We had loaded knapsacks with dolls and pink plastic teacups and had scaled the steep ladder to the barn loft, intent on hosting a tea party on the bales of hay. Never comfortable with heights, I had always been afraid of the loft—even before the bat descended upon us. It had grazed my head, its leathery wings stirring the air and raising goosebumps on the back of my neck. I shrieked in terror and ducked, my arms clutched over my head. I didn't recall my sister screaming. Lanie had remembered it right— she really had always been the brave one.

"Yeah," I said. "Dad said it wanted to join the tea party."

"Remember how Pops climbed up here with a broom to save us? And how he was swinging the thing around? And Grammy was standing there on the barn floor, hollering to Pops to be careful, that he was going to fall and break his neck?"

"I do."

"Do you ever think it's funny how concerned humans are with their own mortality? Pops didn't fall and break his neck. He didn't die that afternoon, but he did die five years later. And do you think that those five years really made a difference, in the scheme of things? A few more harvests, a few more

Christmases. A heart attack. And then, bam! Some drunk kid takes you right out of existence."

"Five years is a long time, Lanie. And life is a precious thing."

"But is it really? What if you don't do anything worthwhile with your life? What if, instead of making the world a better place or doing anything even remotely redeemable, you're actually responsible for destroying the happiness of others?"

"Lanie, why don't you come down? I'd feel a lot more comfortable getting existential if you were on solid ground."

She dropped the flashlight to her side, plunging her face back into darkness. "Sorry, sister. I'm not coming down. Not that way."

"Then I'm coming up," I said, my pulse thundering in my ears. "Okay?"

"Suit yourself."

The ladder felt more insubstantial than I had remembered, and I struggled to quell a wave of fear. I allowed myself small comfort in the fact that the wood felt solid, unlike the soft, rotting planks of the front porch. I was grateful for the darkness as I ascended the ladder; it kept me from seeing the ground. I was only minimally more comfortable once I had pulled myself up onto the loft, the forgotten remnants of ancient hay whispering under my feet. I couldn't bring myself to approach the edge where Lanie stood. As children, she loved to stand at the edge and stare down at the busy barn below, like a queen surveying her kingdom. I could never stand beside her; I was too scared. It always struck me as unfair. We were twins. How did the ability to withstand heights fail to imbed itself in my genes? In time, I would come to realize that it wasn't just heights; my sister wasn't afraid of anything.

"What are you doing here?" I asked.

"What are *you* doing here?" she echoed back.

"Looking for you," I said, wanting to take a step toward her but finding my feet unwilling to move.

"You weren't supposed to," she said, lifting one foot and dangling it over the void. My heart leapt into my throat. "Didn't Ann give you my letter?"

"She did. Can you please stop doing that with your foot?"

Lanie met my eyes and leaned forward slightly, daringly. Even though she said she didn't want me to find her, part of me wondered if she had been waiting for me. She knew I'd look for her. Maybe she wanted me to save her. Maybe, after all those times when I had done exactly that, she expected it.

"Lanie," I begged. "Don't."

She sighed and put her foot back where it belonged. "I don't know what to do, Josie. I've made such a mess of everything."

At one point in the not-too-distant past, I would have agreed with her. Lanie was the emotional equivalent of a bulldozer: nothing—and no one—was safe. She had consistently abused our long-suffering aunt, driven our delicate, tormented mother into the arms of a cult, and destroyed my relationship with Adam, robbing me of any sense of stability in the process. For nearly a third of my life, I had blamed my sister for everything—but I was starting to realize just how unfair I had been. Adam had played more than a passing role in his betrayal, our mother had emotionally abandoned us long before Lanie put that pillow over her face, and my time abroad had, in the end, probably been good for me. The only thing that Lanie was responsible for making a mess of was herself.

And so I extended a hand to my sister and said, "That's not true. Come on. Let's go home."

"I can't go home." She aimed her flashlight over the edge of the loft, to the hard ground that I knew existed beneath the cover of darkness. "I'm sorry."

"Think of your daughter, Lanie. She needs her mother."

Lanie's face twitched. "She'll be better off without me."

"That is absolutely not true," I said, summoning all my courage and taking a reckless step toward her with an out-stretched arm.

Lanie whirled toward me, moving so fast that she wobbled. I stopped short, choking on fear while my sister regained her balance.

"It *is* true. A girl needs a mother she can look up to, some-one she can emulate. She needs a role model. That's not me. I can't be that person. I've tried—oh my God, have I tried—but I can't do it. I'm a bitter, unhappy mess, and all I can give is pain and suffering."

"Lanie, no. You might be unhappy right now, but you won't always be. Trust me. You have people who love and care about you, people who will help you. You have me."

I reached for my sister's hand, and this time she didn't jerk away.

"I'm sorry I ruined your life," she said softly.

"My life is just fine," I said, squeezing her hand tightly. "You didn't ruin anything."

"I ruin everything."

"Stop it. That isn't true."

She tugged her hand away from me and switched off her flashlight, receding into the shadows. "You don't know everything I've done."

Do you think Lanie might have pulled that trigger? Adam's words materialized in my head, pulsating and bloodred. *If Warren Cave didn't shoot him, what other reason would she have for saying he did?*

Swallowing my fear, I said, "Then tell me."

There was no answer, and I swept a hand in front of me, looking for my sister in the pitch-black. The small flame of a lighter flared suddenly, and I startled backward.

"Cut that out. Think of the hay. It's a fire trap in here."

She ignored my warning, inhaling audibly and making the tip of a cigarette glow cherry-red in the darkness.

"Lanie," I insisted. "Please. Let's get out of this barn."

She said nothing, the up-and-down movements of the cigarette the only evidence I had she was there. Then, on an exhalation, so quiet that I almost missed it, she said, "I don't think it was Warren Cave."

"What?" I demanded, sure that I had misheard her mangled words. "What did you just say?"

"I don't think it was Warren Cave," she repeated more clearly. "I don't think he killed our father."

My blood went cold in my veins. *If Warren Cave didn't shoot him—*

"Wait," I said, interrupting my own thought process. "You don't *think*? You mean you don't *know*?"

"No," she whispered. "I don't know. I used to be certain. But now every thing's all mixed up. I don't think it was him."

"Who was it?" I asked, barely daring to breathe.

She shrugged slightly.

I exhaled; my blood thawed and began to travel sluggishly through my body once more. This wasn't going to be a confession; this was confusion.

"Lanie," I said carefully, "tell me the truth. Have you taken something?"

She sniffled and dropped the cigarette, its glowing tip disappearing under the blackness of her foot. "That's not what this is, Josie."

"When was the last time you slept?"

"You don't believe me," she said, her voice incredulous in the dark. "I'm finally telling the truth, and you don't believe me."

"I believe you," I said, worried that I was about to lose her again. "I believe you when you say you're not certain anymore. But I also believe that you're extremely tired and possibly not entirely sober right now. Let's just go home, and we can talk again after you've had some sleep. I promise."

"I can't sleep yet, don't you understand? Everything is a mess." She grit her teeth audibly. "On the one hand, I have this really clear memory of seeing Warren Cave walk through the back door. I remember his big black coat, his dyed black hair. I remember seeing him put a gun to the back of Dad's head, and I remember hearing him say, 'This is all your fault.' And then I remember him pulling the trigger."

Something sparked in a recess of my brain. I opened my

mouth to ask Lanie to repeat herself, but she'd already moved on.

"But then sometimes that memory isn't quite as clear. Sometimes I think he said something else, something . . . something about a pearl. Sometimes I can see his hair, but not his face. And then sometimes it's more clear, but clear in a way that I know can't be right. Like, sometimes I can see his hand on the gun so clearly that it's like a photograph. But I can also see this flash of gold on his hand."

"Warren could have been wearing a ring," I said. "That doesn't necessarily mean anything."

"Except," Lanie said slowly, scratching at her chest with her nails, leaving angry little welts down her skin, "I can see the ring because it was facing me. I was standing to his left. The ring was on his left hand. It was a wedding ring."

I blinked. "A wedding ring? You mean like what Melanie might wear?"

"Was Melanie left-handed?" she asked. "The hand with the ring was the hand holding the gun." She paused to gulp. "And Warren was right-handed."

"How can you know that?"

"Remember how he spent most of the trial with his head bent over his notepad, scribbling? I stared at him so much during that trial that I'm certain. He was writing with his right hand."

This is all your fault.

"You know—" Lanie started.

This is all your fault, and you will answer for it.

"This is all your fault," I interrupted. "That's what you heard? Are you sure?"

"As sure as I am about anything."

"But it's not new, right? That you think that?"

Confused, Lanie shook her head. "No, I've always thought that was what I heard."

"Melanie Cave," I said confidently. "She left a voicemail for Dad the day he was killed. She said, 'This is all your fault.'"

"Are you sure?" she asked, something akin to hope flickering through her eyes.

I nodded. "Yeah, I'm sure. Poppy played it during one of the podcasts."

"Melanie Cave," she said quietly. She exhaled a sigh that sounded like relief and switched on her flashlight, blinding me suddenly. "It was Melanie Cave all along."

⬆ The Melanie Voicemails (self.reconsideredpodcast)
⬇

submitted 8 hours ago by jennyfromtheblock

Can we talk about those voicemails Melanie Cave left for
Chuck Buhrman? "You will answer for it"? That seems incredibly damning right? Why didn't anyone bring that up
at trial?

> ⬆ miranda_309 72 points 7 hours ago
> ⬇
> Because Melanie was the one paying the defense attorney.

>> ⬆ attractivenuisance 30 points 6 hours ago
>> ⬇
>> But zealous advocacy!
>>
>> Source: second-year law student

>>> ⬆ miranda_309 49 points 6 hours ago
>>> ⬇
>>> You're cute.
>>>
>>> Source: practicing attorney

>>>> ⬆ attractivenuisance 12 points 6 hours ago
>>>> ⬇
>>>> Are you suggesting that Warren's attorney was
>>>> violating ethics rules? And that she was doing so
>>>> on purpose?

>> ⬆ jennyfromtheblock 81 points 4 hours ago
>> ⬇
>> MELANIE CAVE, GUYS. Come on, stay on topic.

chapter 22

I coaxed Lanie into the passenger seat of the rental car, promising we could return for her vehicle later. On the ride back to town, she sat so silently I thought she might have fallen asleep, but when I glanced over at her, I saw she was staring out the window at the moonlight streaming across the flat, empty fields. Her face was like a mask, betraying no emotion. I wondered what she was thinking, if she was replaying that horrible night in her mind's eye and now recognizing the perpetrator as Melanie Cave.

"I don't want to go home just yet," Lanie said as we crossed the city limits. "Take me to Aunt A's."

"Are you sure? Adam is really worried about you."

"I'll call him and let him know I'm all right."

"Lanie—"

"It's two o'clock in the morning, Josie. Coming home at this hour would upset Ann. Besides, I don't want her to see me like this. Not until I've had some sleep, or at least a shower."

"You're her mother, Lanie," I reminded her softly. "She loves you just as you are."

"I know," she said, still gazing out the window. "All the same. I don't want her to worry about me the same way we worried about Mom."

* * *

Aunt A's house was dark and quiet, the sole sound the steady ticking of the hallway clock. Bubbles was the only inhabitant who was awake, and he greeted us by weaving circles around our ankles, rubbing himself insistently against our shins until Lanie scooped him up.

"Do you want me to make up the daybed in the craft room for you?" I offered.

Lanie shook her head. "I'm not tired."

I regarded her suspiciously, cataloguing the dark circles under her eyes and the tension in her jaw. "When was the last time you slept?"

"Fine," she conceded. "I'll try to sleep, but I'm not promising anything. Don't bother with the daybed. I'll just stretch out on the couch."

"I can stay down here with you," I offered, uneasy with the thought of leaving Lanie alone in such close proximity to the door.

"I'm not a flight risk, Josie," she said softly. "I'm going to be all right. Go upstairs and sleep in your own bed. You look like you could use the rest, and I'm probably just going to end up watching TV."

"Are you sure?"

"I'm sure," she said, kissing my cheek. "Now go to bed."

Upstairs, I crawled into bed beside Caleb. Still mostly asleep, he murmured something indistinct and threw an arm over me, pulling my body snugly against his. With Caleb's heart beating against my back and the comforting knowledge that Lanie was safely in the house, my body finally began to relax, and I fell headlong into the deepest sleep I had gotten in weeks.

* * *

"Josie."

I blinked into the darkness, unsure whether hearing my name had been a dream, unsure whether I was even actually awake.

"Josie," my sister's voice hissed. "Are you sleeping?"

"Mm," I murmured, coming awake. "Lanie?"

"Get up," she whispered, clutching at my hand. "I need to show you something."

The urgency in her voice tripped an alarm inside me. I eased out of Caleb's embrace and followed Lanie down the front stairs. The hallway clock chimed four just as Lanie led me into the living room, where the UPS box of our mother's things sat open on its side. Beads, scarves, photographs, and other objects had all been removed and heaped into small piles arranged in a circle on the floor.

"You were supposed to be sleeping," I reminded my sister.

"I told you I wasn't tired," she said. "So I started going through Mom's things."

"Obviously."

"Have you seen this?" Lanie asked, snatching something bright yellow up from the floor. She held it out to me. *The Official Handbook of the Life Force Collective*.

"Yeah." I frowned, remembering our mother's notation. *Best.* What had she meant by that? Getting away from us was the best part? Or leaving us was for the best?

"You've read it?" she asked, her voice turning shrill. "And no one bothered to tell me? You didn't think I'd want to know?"

"Whoa, calm down. I didn't know that you cared about the handbook. I'm sorry."

Lanie paused, peering at me curiously. "How far did you read?"

I shrugged. "Only up to the first chapter. Aunt A got pretty upset, so we stopped."

"There's something I think you should see," she said somberly. "Start at the back."

My skin prickled as I took the handbook from her and flipped to the end. I was so surprised by what I saw that I cried out. The last pages of the handbook were blank pages titled *Space for Notes*—and they were covered in our mother's handwriting. It was cramped, shaky, and upside-down, but I could recognize her distinctive scrawl, the little flags she put on her *k*s and *h*s.

"What is this?"

"I think it's her journal from when she was with the LFC. Or something like that."

With trembling hands, I flipped the book over and squinted at the words. Mostly written in blue ballpoint pen, some of the words were smudged beyond recognition and others were written in such tiny handwriting that I couldn't make them out. But even the words that I could read were difficult to understand. It might have been a journal, but it might have also been her LFC notes. It was hard to tell.

You are here, the first line read. *End of the rainbow. Gold is sun. Sun is life. shiny sun safety serenity sanity.*

My stomach twisted. I had spent so many years longing to know more about our enigmatic mother, but now that a glimpse into the life she spent with the cult might literally be beneath my fingertips, I wasn't sure I had the guts. I wanted to remember my mother as the gentle, caring woman she had been, not the incoherent person who had scribbled these notes. I didn't think she would want me to remember her like that, either.

"I don't think we should read this," I said, closing the handbook. "You remember how secretive she was about her journals. She wouldn't want us to read her private thoughts."

"She's not going to mind," Lanie said softly.

I shook my head, unable to explain the truth to Lanie: *I didn't want to know.*

"Josie, this is our only chance to know what she was like after she left us. We have to read it. We owe it to her." She took the handbook from me and began reading aloud. "Get it out. Start at the beginning. Start here. You are here. You are here. Here. Everywhere you go, there you are."

"This isn't going to tell us anything," I protested. "Listen to her."

"Come on," Lanie urged, pulling me down into a seat beside her and spreading the book open on our combined knees. "Let's just keep with it. Maybe some of it will make sense."

Lanie's instincts proved correct: as we flipped the pages, each of us reading silently, our mother's cursive became less shaky, her sentences more complete. As it became easier to follow her thoughts, I realized it wasn't a journal in the sense that she was recording present-day events. Rather, she seemed to be documenting major events from her life, both good and bad, and not necessarily in chronological order: there was her marriage to our father (*happiest girl in the world*) and there was Uncle Dennis's death (*all my fault all my fault all my fault*).

Then I came across a sentence that said, *And there were the cupcakes. Shocked myself. If J hadn't . . . Didn't sleep for a week after. Stupid, careless. But lesson learned: no sense in doing a job halfway.*

My stomach dropped. What about the cupcakes? I quickly scanned the page but saw no other references to them. Had she done something to them? But what? And why? Had she . . . had she tried to *poison* me? With a start, I remembered: that cupcake hadn't been for me.

It had been for our father.

I turned to Lanie, unsure how to put the wild theories flying around in my head into words, unable to believe it myself, and saw her face completely devoid of color. Was she remembering the cupcake incident as well?

"Lanie? What's wrong?"

"This," she said quietly, laying her finger down on another portion of the page.

And I saw her wearing pearls. Pearls. It was a sign. It all comes back to pearls, from the first. That horrid Pearl Leland was only the first.

"Pearl Leland," I read aloud. "What is . . . Is she saying that Dad had an affair with Professor Leland?"

Lanie nodded, squeezing her eyes shut. "I think so."

As I watched my sister rock back and forth, arms wrapped tightly around her and eyes shut, I realized there was something more upsetting to her than learning that our father had carried on more than one affair.

"There's something else, isn't there?" I asked, touching her lightly on the shoulder.

"Yes," she whispered. "The night Dad was killed . . ."

"Are you saying Pearl Leland killed our father?" I gasped.

Lanie shook her head. "I think . . . I think Mom did."

Cymbals crashed in my head; my mouth went metallic. A hundred tiny explosions went off in my mind, the shrapnel falling together into something that looked like order. Still, I resisted.

"No," I said firmly, ignoring the fact that I had been about to voice a similar concern.

"Listen," Lanie said, speaking quickly, her voice thin. "The night Dad was killed, I heard someone before I reached the kitchen. They said something that sounded like, 'First Pearl, and now . . .'"

"Are you sure?" I demanded. "Why is this the first time you've mentioned it?"

"Because I wasn't certain what I heard. It wasn't clear, and I couldn't make out what it meant. Honestly, sometimes I thought it was all in my head. I mean, it didn't make sense for Warren to say that, right? And I was certain it was Warren."

"Then how can you be certain now?"

Lanie swallowed. "Because I'm starting to remember. Not just that. Other things. Like what I saw."

"Melanie Cave," I said weakly. "You saw Melanie Cave, remember?"

"I'm sorry, Josie," she said, her eyes wide and wet. "But it was Mom. And I think I can prove it with the gun."

I shook my head stubbornly. "They never found the gun."

"No," she allowed. "But I'm certain the shooter held it in a left hand. *Mom* was left-handed."

"Lanie—"

"And I think I know where it is."

I looked from Lanie's grim face down to the words scribbled in the back of the handbook: *And there were the cupcakes.* Even if Lanie's memory couldn't be trusted, *something* had been wrong with those cupcakes. If she was admitting to poisoning them . . . I thought of the stack of photos she had brought with her to the LFC, my father's clear absence in them. Had she really been angry enough to attempt murder?

And, if she had tried it once, would she have been determined enough to try again?

chapter 23

It was half past five when Lanie and I arrived on Cyan Court. It was, as ever, a calm little loop of road in a tidy subdivision. I had not seen my childhood home in more than ten years, and the sight of it took my breath away. Part of me had always assumed that the house would forever carry the indelible mark of the tragedy that happened inside it. I expected to find it encased in a perpetual cloud of gloom or fallen into disrepair, my father's murder permanently visible to passersby.

And yet, there it was, looking perfectly unremarkable. The house stood just as we had left it: a white Dutch colonial with jaunty blue trim and window boxes crowded with the remains of colorful petunias. The porch had been repainted and the swing straightened, but the big elm tree in the front yard remained the same.

Standing on that sidewalk, where the initials we had traced into wet cement so many years ago were still visible, our suspicions seemed absurd. If our mother had killed our father, we would see the evidence of it. The trim little community could not have concealed such a ground-shaking secret; it would have withered under its weight.

Hand in hand, Lanie and I crept toward our old backyard. The unfamiliar landscaping was difficult to navigate in the predawn darkness, and I tripped over an unfurled garden hose and stumbled through rosebushes, their tiny thorns tearing at my ankles. I froze at the door of our old playhouse, nostalgia and a sense of dark foreboding preventing me from going farther. Lanie barreled past me, yanking open the small door with determination and stepping inside.

Tentatively, I followed her, my sense of dread so strong I nearly expected to see the walls smeared with blood. Instead, the interior of the playhouse looked bright and cheerful. The walls, which had originally been painted the same moss green as our dining room, had been repainted a sunny yellow, and pink flowered curtains had been hung over the miniature windows. A pink plastic table stood in the corner, and a one-eyed doll and a stuffed panda were seated at it, small pink plastic teacups in front of them. A box of Fig Newtons was on the table between the toys.

Lanie looked around briefly and then headed straight for the sink.

A cheap plastic frame holding a picture of Prince William and Princess Kate had been propped up over it, and Lanie tossed it onto the table. She struggled to dig her fingertips between the edge of the sink and the wall, groaning with effort.

"Help me," she hissed. "They've caulked it or something."

"What are you even doing?"

"Remember the hiding place behind the sink?" she asked grimly.

Numbly, I stepped to her side, trying hard not to think about what we were doing. This little playhouse held so many happy memories; I couldn't imagine it concealing such a horrific secret. I dug my nails into the rubbery caulking, my fingertips scratching against the wall until they finally closed around the edge of the sink.

Lanie let out a triumphant yelp. She counted to three, and together we tugged with all our might. The sink resisted at first, but finally pulled away from the wall with a shudder. We stumbled backward, surprised by our effort, and dropped the sink on the ground. Where it had once been, there was nothing but a small, dark hole. Limbs heavy with dread, I pulled out my phone and switched on its flashlight. I aimed the small beam inside the hole, illuminating a stack of books, a pile of shiny candy wrappers, and something dark with a dull, menacing gleam. My stomach dropped so fast I nearly fainted.

Lanie was right. She knew where the gun was. That meant . . .

I regained my senses just in time to stop Lanie as she reached for it. "Don't touch it."

"Freeze!" someone shouted behind us.

We turned in unison to find a man in running shorts and a Chicago Bears sweatshirt outside the playhouse door, brandishing a baseball bat and glaring at us.

"I've called the police," he announced. "So I think you better scram."

"Actually," Lanie said, casting a sad smile toward the hidden gun, "I think we'll stick around. I have something I'd like to tell them."

We spent the day in stunned silence. I repeatedly chastised myself for permitting Lanie to leave with the unsmiling police officers who had met us on Cyan Court. They were young, squarely in Poppy Parnell's target demographic, and the smirk they exchanged upon hearing Lanie's name made my stomach turn. It was obvious they didn't believe Lanie had simply found the gun. They thought she put it there.

When they suggested—their tone indicating it was less of a suggestion and more of a command—Lanie accompany them to the station to make a statement, I should have insisted on driving her myself. I never should have let her climb in the backseat of their car, or, at the very least, I should have insisted on riding back there with her. I should have demanded she call an attorney.

But I was too stunned by the discovery that my father had been murdered by my *mother* to behave rationally, and I drove back to Aunt A's house alone. After haltingly explaining to the others what Lanie had remembered (a report that was greeted with shocked silence), I spent the day repeatedly calling the police station, alternating between politely inquiring after my sister and sarcastically asking just how long it took them to take a statement. I was finally told to stop making a nuisance of myself and it was hinted that any further calls might be considered harassment, and so I took to pacing the floor. I ignored the calls from my boss, who was following up on my vague voicemail stating I wouldn't be back in New York that day after all, and the calls from Clara, obviously dispatched by my boss. The only thing I could think about was my sister.

As upset as I was, I couldn't blame the officers for suspecting Lanie had hidden the gun. After all, she had been the one to finally find it. And it hadn't been that long since I had entertained similar thoughts myself, and she was my own sister.

Like this was my own mother.

Bile surged into my mouth, and I swallowed it, cringing as the acid burned my throat. I reached for a glass of water on the coffee table and spotted the LFC handbook resting harmlessly beside it. Slowly, I picked it up and flipped to my mother's words, half hoping that I would find them different, that lack of sleep had made the two of us paranoid and delusional. But there they were: the reference to Pearl Leland, the mention of the cupcakes.

I flung the journal across the room, where it hit the wall with an unsatisfying clunk and fell to the floor. Rage fluttered in my limbs; I wanted more destruction. Her belongings couldn't just sit there intact, as though she had been a normal woman. She hadn't been—she had been a murderer. My own mother. Emitting an anguished shriek that sent Bubbles scurrying from the room, I turned to the rest of my mother's belongings, still heaped on the floor where Lanie had left them. I snapped strands of beads and tore at scarves, smashing an incense burner under my foot and throwing the shards at the wall. I didn't stop my rampage until Caleb rushed into the room and physically pinned my arms to my sides, whispering soothing words in my ear until I sagged against him, nothing left but tears and an unbearable sadness that threatened to eat me alive if I let it.

"Don't you think we should have heard something by now?" Aunt A worried, using a chopstick to push a breaded piece of chicken around a paper plate, leaving behind a bright smear of technicolor sauce. She had ordered in enough Chinese

351

food to feed a small army: boxes of sweet-and-sour chicken, beef with broccoli, sesame pork, General Tso's chicken, and vegetable lo mein, along with multiple tubs of soup and piles of egg rolls, fried wontons, and crab-less crab rangoon. None of us felt like eating, but we had nonetheless assembled glumly around the table, piling food onto our plates that we knew we wouldn't eat. Only Ann, oblivious to the seriousness of the situation, ate more than a mouthful. Bubbles made off with a crab rangoon and scarfed it greedily in the corner.

"These things can take time," Ellen said. "But she's in good hands. Alec Greene is one of the best criminal defense lawyers in the whole state."

I disassembled a fortune cookie, methodically breaking it into small shards. I did not share Ellen's optimism. It had been twelve hours since Lanie had gone to the police station, six since Adam had called bullshit on Lanie being there voluntarily, and one since Alec Greene, the attorney Peter had recommended, had arrived in Elm Park to confer with Adam in his home. As far as I knew, neither Adam nor Alec had yet made it to the police station. There was no news, but that definitely did not make it good news.

"Should she even have a criminal defense attorney?" Aunt A asked, forehead creases deepening. "Doesn't that imply she's done something wrong?"

"No one should submit to police interrogation without an attorney," Ellen said authoritatively. "*Especially* if they've just pointed to a murder weapon that's been missing for thirteen years."

I unfolded the slip of paper hiding inside the cookie: *The truth will set you free.* I resented maxims masquerading as fortunes, and, given the circumstances, it seemed particularly obnoxious. I shredded it and buried it in my untouched pile of white rice. Caleb squeezed my knee under the table.

"This is a nightmare," Aunt A murmured, her chin trembling. "Just when I think we've hit rock bottom, that things can't possibly get any worse, we get knocked to our knees again by something even more awful. The things Lanie is saying Erin did . . ."

Aunt A trailed off in a ragged choke, and I reached out to touch her soft shoulder. More than anything, I wanted to tell her that things were going to be okay, to reassure her the way she had done for me so many times when I was young. But I couldn't say with any certainty that things *were* going to be okay; I could barely even conceive of a scenario in which that would be a possibility. All I could do—all any of us could do—was hope.

"How can that be true?" Aunt A asked, her voice thick with suppressed tears as she clutched desperately at my hand. "I used to worry your mother was a danger to herself, but I never imagined she could hurt someone else, especially your father. She loved him so much."

"Obviously not that much," Ellen said darkly. "Shooting someone in the back of the head isn't usually how you demonstrate your affection."

"Ellen Maureen," Aunt A snapped. "For God's sake, show some respect."

Ellen looked away, chastened.

353

"And on that note," Caleb said, abruptly pushing his chair back from the table, "I'm going to start clearing the table."

I stood to help him, but he gently pushed me back into my chair and began stacking our hardly touched paper plates. As he ferried them out to the kitchen and began making return trips to collect the still-full takeout boxes, Ellen murmured an apology to her mother and Ann passed Bubbles another crab rangoon. On a different day, Aunt A might have reprimanded her grandniece for feeding fried food to the aged cat, but on that evening, when Lanie sat at the police station, her future unknown, the shadow of her accusation hanging over us, Aunt A merely winced.

"When's Mom coming home?" Ann asked suddenly.

"Soon," Aunt A said, her voice cracking on the lie.

Ellen's face was pained as she watched Aunt A swallow back tears, struggling to maintain an unconcerned façade for Ann. She squeezed her mother's hand and then turned to Ann with false brightness and suggested a game of "beauty parlor" upstairs. I remembered how dismissive my sister had always been of Ellen's attempted makeovers, and I had to wonder what she would think of Ellen turning the nail polish brushes and mascara wands on her eight-year-old daughter, but Ann eagerly agreed. As Ann raced for the stairs, Aunt A nodded a silent thanks to Ellen, who kissed the crown of her mother's head in return.

As Ellen and Ann mounted the stairs, Aunt A turned to me, her eyes dripping with new abandon, and asked, "It's possible Lanie's wrong, isn't it? More than possible, actually. It's *likely*—don't you think? She was so certain it was Warren

Cave. If she was confused once before, doesn't it make sense that she would be confused again?"

"I don't know," I murmured, offering a noncommittal shrug. I wanted to tell her that she was right, of course, that Lanie was obviously just confused, that all those years of drug abuse had eaten holes in her brain and made her memory unreliable. Of course our mother—her sister—hadn't committed the horrific crime Lanie had accused her of. *Of course* Lanie was wrong. But I had read the words our mother had written in the back of the handbook, and I had seen the look in my sister's eyes. There had been no confusion there, only horrified realization. Lanie wasn't wrong, not anymore.

"This can't be true," Aunt A moaned stubbornly, more to herself than to me.

"Listen," I said, taking her warm hand between both of mine and squeezing tightly. "It's been a rough couple of days. No, screw that, it's been a rough couple of *weeks*. We're all exhausted and our emotions are raw. None of us are thinking clearly right now. Let's just try to put this out of our heads for a bit, okay? Soon Lanie will be home and we'll have a chance to talk to her ourselves."

"You're right." Aunt A sniffled, returning the squeeze. "My nerves are completely frayed. I'm going to go upstairs and lie down. Please get me if you hear from Lanie."

I nodded.

She paused with her hand on the doorframe and looked back at me. "You're a strong woman, Josie. I'm proud of you."

I hung my head as she walked away. I wasn't proud of myself. I was ashamed of my childhood obliviousness to the tension that must have existed in our home, and I regretted the years I had spent at war with my sister. What if I had come home earlier? Might we have put our heads together and figured out the truth? If we had done that, maybe we could have found a way to find our mother and gently approach her, and maybe she wouldn't have felt compelled to hang herself. Maybe we could have saved an innocent man years in prison. I shuddered to think of Lanie in custody, and I once again reproached myself for allowing her to go unaccompanied with the police. I shouldn't have let her out of my sight, and I shouldn't have sat still for so many hours, trusting first the police department and then Adam and the attorney. Where *were* Adam and the attorney? Shouldn't they have some news by now? I fired a text message to Adam, a demand for an update phrased as a request.

There was a sudden knock on the front door. My heart leapt.

Lanie.

In retrospect, I should have known that it couldn't be her. Lanie never knocked. But I was too anxious to think clearly, and I raced through the living room, picking my way through the aftermath of my earlier rampage, and yanked open the door.

Poppy Parnell stood on the front porch, her strawberry blond hair professionally blown out, her glasses nowhere to be seen. She smiled a predatory, lipsticked smile, and my stomach sank even before I saw the cameraman behind her.

"Josie," she said, her voice frothing with enthusiasm.

"Go away," I barked, trying to shut the door in her face.

"Not so fast," she said, wedging herself in the door. "I have something I think you'll want to see."

"You're a little late," I said bitterly. "Didn't you see our white flag waving? You were right. Warren Cave didn't kill our father."

She glanced over her shoulder at the cameraman. "Did you catch that?"

"What is all this?" I demanded. "Adding videos to your website? What's the point? You've gotten what you wanted. Don't you think enough is enough?"

"Not hardly," she said, laughing a little. "And, trust me, you want to see this."

Barely able to contain her triumphant grin, she held up a thick book. It was missing a cover and held together with duct tape, but I recognized it immediately: my mother's copy of *Anna Karenina*.

"Where did you get this?" I asked, my voice trembling.

"I have a friend in the LFC." Poppy smirked. "She found this in your mother's room and thought you and your sister should have it."

"The LFC sent us our mother's things," I said, confused.

"What can I say? She wanted to make sure it reached you. She sent it to me, hoping I could personally deliver it." Poppy smiled magnanimously and held the book out to me. "And here it is."

Sensing a trap but unable to keep myself from falling into it, I snatched the book from her hands.

"I hope you don't mind, but I couldn't help flipping through it. *Anna Karenina* is one of my favorites." She paused to nod to her cameraman, and then turned to me, her cheeks nearly trembling with excitement. "Look at page 880."

"No," I said, my heart beating so fast I felt dizzy. I didn't know what Poppy was up to, but I would be damned before I was her puppet.

Poppy's expression flickered, and she yanked the book out of my hands. She flipped the pages roughly, ripping some of them in her haste, and then shoved the open book at me. Cheeks pink with excitement, she stabbed at the page with a finger.

"Look."

I resisted for as long as I could, stubbornly glaring at her rather than following her orders, but finally a sick sort of curiosity overtook me and I looked down. My heart skipped a beat. The margins of the page were filled with scribbled words, the handwriting undeniably my mother's.

Darling girls,

Those two words alone were nearly enough to undo me. The edges of my world went black, and I nearly dropped the book. Leaning against the doorframe for support, I took a deep breath and read on.

I write this knowing I will never see you again. There are so many things I want to say to you, but I don't have the words to say them all, and so this will have to do: I love you. More than I had ever loved anything, and that was why I had to leave you. I loved your father, too, and that killed us both. I beg you

not to think poorly of either of us. Your father made mistakes,
but they weren't fatal mistakes, and I shouldn't have treated
them as such. I thought my unhappiness was all his fault, but
that was only partially true. Am I being oblique? I'm sorry.
I killed your father. I was out of my head. You might think
I'm the same way now, but I promise you, I've never been so
sure of something in my life. You were better off without me,
and you'll be better off with me dead. Take care of each other.
Love, Mom

By the time I finished, my legs were trembling so badly
I could barely stand. We had thought she hadn't left us a
goodbye note, but she had. More than that, she had left us
a confession. I pictured my thin mother, sitting in a dark
room at the commune, hunched over the worn book, pouring her guilty heart out into the margins, and I had to gulp
back a hot wave of tears. I ached for the power to turn back
time to when things had gone wrong for us, to stop my
father from straying or at least to force my parents to confront
each other, air their grievances before they mutated into lethal
jealousy.

"Tell us how you're feeling, Josie," Poppy said, her smile
almost leering.

"You disgusting vulture," I whispered. "Get out of here."

The cameraman stepped from behind Poppy to zoom in
on my face.

"Get out of here!" I screamed, lunging forward, covering
his camera lens with one hand and shoving it downward.

"Jo?" Caleb asked, jogging into the entryway just as I

slammed the door on Poppy and her one-man entourage. "What's going on out here?"

I broke down in sobs, and collapsed on his shoulder.

After holding my sister without charging her for more than twelve hours, it took only fifteen minutes for the police to release her once they had seen the copy of *Anna Karenina*. Even I, who had stormed into the police station nearly incoherent with rage—at Poppy Parnell, at my mother, at my sister, at everyone—was surprised by the relatively quick turnaround. After I had slammed the book into the hands of a poker-faced police officer and explained what it was and how it had come to be in my possession, I had been directed to a small, windowless room. I wasn't sure if it was an interrogation room or a waiting room, and the officer who showed me inside slipped away before I had the presence of mind to ask him. I sat on a molded plastic chair under buzzing fluorescent lights, aggressively picking at my cuticles and ignoring calls from Aunt A and Caleb, both of whom thought I shouldn't have gone to the police station alone. I expected to sit there for an hour or more and halfway wished I hadn't relinquished the book so I would have something to help pass the time, but it wasn't long before a different officer escorted my sister into the room.

I couldn't help but gasp at her appearance: under the harsh lights, she looked like death barely warmed over. Her hair clung greasily to her scalp, her complexion was sallow, and her under-eyes were a sunken, bruised purple. A capillary had broken in her left eye, leaving her iris swimming in a sea of bright-red blood.

"I wouldn't leave town until that handwriting can be authenticated," the officer gruffly warned Lanie. He cast a hard look at me. "You, either."

"Wouldn't dream of it," Lanie sneered as he walked away, handcuffs jangling from his belt.

"You look terrible," I said.

"Trust me, I feel even worse." She grimaced. "Let's get out of here."

I followed Lanie through the station's narrow halls and out the front door. She walked briskly, with purpose, and I couldn't blame her for wanting to make a quick escape. Outside, the sun was completing its final dip below the horizon, throwing long shadows across the nearly empty parking lot. I glanced around quickly, certain that Poppy Parnell and her new cameraman had been lying in wait to ambush us, but they were nowhere to be seen. I exhaled a sigh of relief, thankful for small mercies.

In Caleb's rental car, I placed the key in the ignition but then hesitated. I turned to look at my sister, small and disheveled in the passenger seat. Lanie was staring straight ahead, her blood-streaked eyes desperate, her jaw tense.

"Are you okay?"

She laughed a short bark, a sound that was anything but amused. "I've never felt so fucked in my life. And that's saying something."

I swallowed. "But they didn't arrest you, right?"

"Right. You can't arrest a person for a crime someone else has been convicted of." She paused to sniff disdainfully. "Or so I'm told."

"They can't think that you had anything to do with Dad's murder. Especially not now, not after they got Mom's note."

"Thanks for bringing that. And for coming to get me." She paused, gnawing on her chapped lower lip. "I imagine Adam's not here because he's mad at me?"

"Adam's not here because I didn't tell him I was coming," I admitted. "I wasn't thinking too clearly when I left the house. He was at your place, meeting with your lawyer."

"I have a lawyer?"

"One of the best, according to Ellen."

Lanie sighed and looked out the window. "I suppose I need one."

"Maybe not. Adam called him before Poppy showed up with Mom's note. That changes everything, right?"

She shrugged. "Maybe they no longer think I murdered my own father, which seemed to be their working theory for most of the day. But I think it will take more than that to convince them that I didn't purposefully lie about Warren."

It was my turn to shrug, and she looked at me sharply.

"You know I didn't intentionally lie about that, right?"

"Right," I said without conviction.

Lanie heard the uncertainty in my voice, and her mouth twisted, her expression hurt. "I can't believe you think I would do that."

Old resentment swelled inside me, a familiar acrimony born of my sister once again claiming victimhood based on my perfectly reasonable reaction to her pattern of bad behavior, and I snapped, "Come on, Lanie. Don't act like it's completely out of character for you to lie."

"I don't lie to *you*," she said, her eyes going wide and shimmery. "I never lie to you."

"But you don't always tell me the truth, do you? All these years and you never told me that it was *Mom*?"

"Because I didn't know!" she shouted, her sudden outburst seeming to startle both of us. She took a deep breath and looked at her hands, tugging at a broken nail. "I know that sounds crazy, Josie, but I swear it's the truth. I saw her—I'm sure now that I saw her—but I couldn't understand, couldn't process it. Somehow I convinced myself that it had been Warren Cave."

"I don't know, Lanie." I sighed. "I want to believe you. I do. But I just don't see how that's possible. You must have known, even if you didn't want to accept it."

"I didn't," she said resolutely. "I swear. Sometimes I would have these weird flashes about that night, times when I thought that it might not have been Warren, but honestly, Josie, I never thought they meant anything. I thought they were just nightmares. One shrink I saw thought it was PTSD, another thought it was anxiety. I've seen plenty of people and been put on plenty of medication, and no one—*no one*—ever suggested that my memory might be faulty."

"Forget the doctors, though. What about *you*? You never thought you might be wrong? Never? Not even that summer you tried to smother Mom with a pillow? Can you really look me in the eye and say that had nothing to do with what you're claiming not to know?"

Lanie shuddered and looked away. "I don't know, okay? Maybe it did, maybe it didn't. I don't really remember; I was tweaking pretty bad. Anything I thought that night is just as likely to have been drug-induced paranoia as it is to have been an actual memory." She dug her dirty fingernails into the soft flesh of her palms and winced in pain. "Do you think that's why she left? Because she thought I knew?"

"I don't think so," I said gently, seemingly biologically programmed to soften when faced with my sister's anguish, no matter how skeptical of her I felt. "That's not what it sounded like in the note, anyway. Did you ever raise it with her another time?"

"No," she said, shaking her head fiercely. "I couldn't have. I didn't know! Besides, Josie, you remember what she was like then. Even if I had remembered something, do you honestly think I could have talked to her about it?"

An image of my mother's blank face, her eyes pale and vacant, filled my mind, and my stomach tightened. Lanie might have been the twin unfortunate enough to witness the murder, but should I have known, too? Were there clues that I had missed, telling behavior on my mother's part that I had overlooked? I thought back to that awful night in October, remembering the sound of the slamming door, the way color drained from Lanie's face when she looked out the window, the urgency in how she had pulled me into the closet.

"Lanie," I said suddenly. "Do you remember what you told me the night Dad died? When we were in the closet, in the dark? You said, 'It's my fault.' What did you mean by that?"

Her eyes darkened. "I knew Dad was sleeping with Melanie."

"You did?"

"Yeah. I snuck a peek at Mom's journal. She wrote about it." Lanie dragged her nails up the inside of her arm, squirming. "But I didn't understand the significance of any of it until it was too late. I should have said something, done something . . . If I had, then maybe things would have been different. We could have stopped it. *I* could have stopped it. And when I saw Warren—or who I *thought* was Warren—come through the back door, I knew it was because I hadn't spoken up, hadn't saved our families. And then I froze. I couldn't stop it, even then. It was my fault."

She clenched her jaw so tightly her teeth ground audibly, and I realized for the first time the true extent of the pain and guilt my sister had carried since the night our father was murdered. It went beyond witnessing his death, it even went beyond seeing our mother be the one to pull the trigger—it was the unrelenting torment of unconsciously believing she could have done something to stop it, that she was responsible for the loss of our parents. I reached across the center console for her hand. Understanding the depth of her misery didn't excuse all that she had done over the years, but it did begin to explain it.

"It wasn't your fault."

"I know that now," she said, squeezing my hand so tightly the bones overlapped and throbbed with pain.

"A lot of things *were* your fault," I couldn't help but add, "but that wasn't one of them."

She smiled ruefully and loosened her grip on my hand. "Do you think we can ever start over?"

"You and me?"

"All of us. You, me, Adam, Aunt A, Ellen. My daughter. Warren Cave. Do you think we can just put this awful past behind us and start over?"

"I'm not sure it works like that. We might be able to move on, but I don't think we can ever start over."

She swallowed and tentatively shifted her hand so that her fourth finger was hooked around mine. "But you think we can move on?"

I looked down at our hands, joined together in that long-ago sign. So much had changed since we had invented it, so much death, betrayal, and estrangement. I didn't know if it was possible for us to find our way back to being the kind of sisters who had a private handshake, the kind who whispered secrets to each other in the dark.

But I didn't know that it wasn't.

"Well," I said, entwining our fingers more firmly, "we can try."

Excerpt from transcript of *Reconsidered: The Chuck Buhrman Murder*, Episode 6: "The Finale," October 5, 2015

Welcome to the final installment of *Reconsidered: The Chuck Buhrman Murder.* I want to take a moment to thank everyone who made this project possible. From the good folks at Werner Entertainment Company to my assistant, I'm grateful for the support. Most importantly, though, I want to thank you, my audience. During this program's short life span, I've been repeatedly humbled by the insightful responses received from listeners like you. I appreciated every tweet, email, and phone call sent my way, and trust me when I say that this program could not have happened without you.

When I began looking into the circumstances surrounding Chuck Buhrman's death, I didn't know what to expect. I couldn't begin to guess whether there was any truth to Melanie Cave's claim that her son had been convicted of a crime he didn't commit, or whether she was just a heartsick mother who refused to accept an ugly truth about her child. I wasn't sure what—if anything—I could contribute. The wildest I allowed myself to dream was that I might uncover evidence that would force a new trial.

Instead, we now know exactly what happened to Chuck Buhrman—and that Warren had nothing to do with it.

Here with me is Stephen Goldberg, who currently owns the former Buhrman home on Cyan Court. Stephen, can you please tell my listeners what happened on Wednesday morning?

STEPHEN: Around 5:30 a.m., I was leaving my house for my usual run when I heard strange noises coming from the playhouse.

POPPY: Let me interrupt you here and describe the playhouse. It's a single room about one hundred square feet, but the exterior is crafted to look like a miniature version of the family home. The small interior includes a play kitchen, with a fake refrigerator, stove, and sink. I understand that it was built for Chuck Buhrman's daughters by his father-in-law.

STEPHEN: Our daughters love that playhouse. Anyway, I heard these noises, and thought it must be an animal or a homeless person. But it turned out to be those Buhrman girls. One of them had ripped the sink away completely from the wall. It had always been a little loose, so I'd caulked it up when we moved in. I'd done it in a hurry, and I hadn't really taken the time to do the job right . . . If I had, maybe I would've found that gun sooner.

That's right. Chuck's missing weapon was found in the wall of the backyard playhouse, along with a bloodstained plastic poncho.

Even more shockingly, after the discovery of the gun, Lanie recanted her testimony against Warren Cave. She now says that she did *not* see Warren shoot her father.

Incredibly, there's more: Lanie told the police that it was actually her mother, Erin Buhrman, who pulled the trigger. Chuck Buhrman was killed by his wife.

"But Poppy," you say, "you've just spent four weeks arguing

that we shouldn't believe a word that Lanie says. And now you want us to believe that Erin killed her husband on Lanie's word alone?"

No, of course not. I know that you're all smarter than that. But here are the reasons that I'm convinced Erin Buhrman is the culprit: Ballistics proved that Chuck's gun was the murder weapon, and police found exactly two sets of fingerprints on that gun—one belonging to Chuck, the other to Erin. Erin claimed she'd never handled, or even seen, that gun—so what were her fingerprints doing on it?

Most importantly, however, a shocking suicide note was found written in the margins of one of Erin's books. One of my sources inside the LFC sent the book to me, completely unaware of its importance, and I discovered the note . . . in which Erin confesses to killing her husband. Officially, the Elm Park Police Department is still awaiting authentication of the note, but I have some experience in handwriting analysis, and I am convinced the note is bona fide.

Unfortunately, it doesn't answer all the questions we might have. It hints that Erin killed her husband because she was jealous of his affair with Melanie, but it doesn't say it outright. Was that the true motive? Was the murder premeditated? Did she join the Life Force Collective to repent for what she'd done, or to hide from the law? With Erin Buhrman dead, we may never know the answers to some of these questions.

I had hoped Lanie would grant me an interview to discuss this surprising turn of events. No such luck. I was, however, able to get my hands on a copy of her official statement to the police. According to her new statement, on that fateful night in

October 2002, she went downstairs to get a drink of water. As she approached the kitchen, a dark-haired, black-clad figure entered through the back door and shot her father. She claims to have believed this figure to be Warren Cave.

Could Lanie have legitimately mistaken Erin for Warren? Or did she purposefully lie to protect her mother?

I sat down with a psychologist, Dr. Eileen Whitehall-Lynch, to discuss what might be at work here. Please note Dr. Whitehall-Lynch has *not* spoken directly to Lanie Ives; she is merely postulating about what a likely scenario might be.

POPPY: Thanks for your time, Dr. Whitehall-Lynch. In your opinion, could Lanie have mistaken her mother—her own mother—for the seventeen-year-old neighbor boy?

DR. WHITEHALL-LYNCH: The human brain is a funny thing. It does what it can to protect us. Lanie had just witnessed her father's brutal murder at the hands of her mother. It's almost too horrible to imagine. Her traumatized brain was struggling to process what she had just seen. Skinny, black-haired perpetrator who looks like your mother, but logically cannot be your mother? Must be the skinny, black-haired neighbor. Once Lanie's brain made that connection, I suspect she used existing information to validate her belief. Statements Lanie made to the police in 2002 indicate that she had been uneasy around Warren since his family had moved in next door. Her brain was simply unable to process the truth, and so it substituted an image that made more sense.

Now, the question I'm sure most of you are wondering: What about Warren? Is he on his way home?

Almost. The wheels of justice are turning, albeit slowly, and I have it on good authority that Warren will soon be free. You may recall that in an early episode of this podcast, Melanie Cave stated neither she nor Warren intends to pursue civil penalties against Lanie. Both of them are holding to that earlier statement. Warren lost twelve years of his life, but he's told me that God would want him to forgive.

WARREN: "For if you forgive men when they sin against you, your heavenly Father will also forgive you. But if you do not forgive men their sins, your Father will not forgive your sins." Matthew 6:14–15.

Melanie tells me that she is following her son's lead.

MELANIE: There has never been any doubt in my mind that Lanie lied about what she saw that night. I'm so relieved that she has finally admitted it, and that this long nightmare of ours is coming to an end. While the petty, vindictive part of me wants to see Lanie Buhrman pay for robbing my son of more than a decade of his life, Warren and I are choosing to take the high road. Instead, we're focusing on the excitement of his upcoming release. I've already started planning his welcome-home dinner.

My work here is done. Thanks for listening, and, above all, thanks for being a part of this. If you loved this program, please make sure to let my bosses at Werner Entertainment know that you'd like to hear from me again.

This is Poppy Parnell, signing off. Thanks again for listening to *Reconsidered*. It's been a hell of a ride . . . but it's not over yet! Join me next spring on the ID network for *Reconsidered with Poppy Parnell* as I dig into more cases that are cold but not forgotten!

acknowledgments

A million thanks to all the people who have devoted their time and energy to make this book a reality: my superlative agent, Lisa Grubka, who has provided invaluable assistance at every step of this process; my brilliant editor, Lauren McKenna, who understood these characters from the very beginning and whose insightful comments and suggestions helped me give them the story they deserved; everyone at Fletcher & Company who has advocated for this book (Gráinne Fox, Melissa Chinchillo, and Erin McFadden); everyone at Gallery Books who has played a role in the editing and publishing process (Louise Burke, Jennifer Bergstrom, Elana Cohen, Marla Daniels, Chelsea Cohen, Akasha Archer, Liz Psaltis, Diana Velasquez, Melanie Mitzman, Mackenzie Hickey, and Kristin Dwyer); Catherine Richards at Pan Macmillan, whose thoughtful comments and enthusiasm were incredibly helpful; and Michelle Weiner, Michelle Kroes, and Olivia Blaustein at CAA. I also owe a debt of gratitude to Mollie Glick, who was an early supporter of this project, and who introduced me to Lisa. I am truly humbled to have worked with such talented people, and I appreciate everything each of you has done more than I can say.

I am also deeply grateful to my friends, family, and assorted loved ones who have supported and encouraged me along the way: my husband, Marc Hedrich, who gave me the courage to follow my dreams and who has been a pillar of strength during the emotionally tumultuous writing process; my mother, Mary Barber, who has always been one of my biggest cheerleaders and believes in me (even when I don't); my brother, David Barber, who patiently and thoughtfully answered all my questions about Illinois criminal law and who introduced me to *Serial*, the podcast that sparked the inspiration for this book; my late father, Richard Barber, who nurtured my creativity from a young age and from whom I inherited the storytelling gene; and all my friends who didn't say I was crazy for quitting law to write (or who at least had the decency not to say it to my face). I love you all.

Finally, a special shout-out to the staff at V-Bar on Sullivan Street in New York; Starbucks on Piedmont and 41st in Oakland; Philz Coffee in Washington, DC; and the lounge at the Warsaw Marriott, all of whom kept me in coffee and/or wine while I wrote, cursed, and rewrote huge sections of this book. Thanks for not kicking me out.